P9-EMM-987

IMPULSE

Tor Books by Steven Gould

Jumper
Wildside
Helm
Blind Waves
Reflex
Jumper: Griffin's Story
Impulse

Steven Gould

IMPULSE

TOR®

A TOM DOHERTY ASSOCIATES BOOK

NEW YORK

IMPULSE

Copyright © 2012 by Steven Gould

Edited by Beth Meacham

A Tor Book
Published by Tom Doherty Associates, LLC
175 Fifth Avenue
New York, NY 10010

www.tor-forge.com

Tor® is a registered trademark of Tom Doherty Associates, LLC.

Library of Congress Cataloging-in-Publication Data

Gould, Steven.
        Impulse / Steven Gould.—1st ed.
            p. cm.
        "A Tom Doherty Associates book."
        ISBN 978-0-7653-2757-4 (hardcover)
        ISBN 978-1-4299-8754-7 (e-book)
        1. Teenage girls—Canadian Rockies (B.C. and Alta.)—Fiction.
2. Teleportation—Fiction.   3. Isolation (Philosophy)—Fiction.   I. Title.
    PS3557.O8947147 2013
    813'.54—dc23

                                                        2012026478

First Edition: January 2013

Printed in the United States of America

0 9 8 7 6 5 4 3 2 1

For my sisters,
Christy and Terry

IMPULSE

ONE

Millie: The Underlying Problem

It was more of a lodge than a cabin but "cabin" is what they called it. The walls were made of heavy, thick logs, after all. The main living area was a broad space leaking from kitchen to dining area to a two-story-high lounge arranged around a tall, fieldstone fireplace.

Millie sat on one of the couches, staring out the windows, and frowned. It was snowing outside—big, fat, fluffy flakes—but she really wasn't noticing.

She was alone in the room and then she wasn't.

Davy was wearing a tropical-weight suit with the sleeves of the jacket rolled up on his forearms. He unrolled them as he asked, "What's wrong?"

Millie sighed, her eyes tracking up to the ceiling before returning to Davy's face.

Davy glanced up to the second-floor landing. "The usual?"

Millie jerked her thumb up. "Go look at her door."

He sighed. "She is an irritation of the spirit . . . ."

Millie completed the phrase, ". . . and a great deal of trouble."

Davy vanished. After a brief pause Millie heard laughter drift down the staircase. Millie stood and jumped, appearing beside Davy in the upstairs hallway.

A sign, scrawled on butcher paper, was tacked to a closed bedroom door. It said:

HELP!
BEING HELD PRISONER BY TELEPORTING ALIENS!
KEPT FROM NORMAL LIFE.
SEND FRIENDS.
ALSO ICE CREAM.

Davy was shaking his head and still laughing.

"Stop it!" Millie said. "You're not helping!"

"You gotta admit, she *is* funny," Davy said. "Takes after me that way."

Millie snapped. "What—you think *you're* funny?" She pulled at Davy's arm, leading him back toward the landing.

Davy raised his eyebrows at Millie and grinned.

"Okay, she *is* funny, but the underlying problem is no less a problem."

Davy's smile faded and he jerked his chin down toward the kitchen, and vanished.

Millie followed to see him putting the kettle on.

"What choice do we have?" Davy said. "I mean, really?"

Millie shook her head. She felt like she *should* have an answer but she didn't.

Davy hugged her and that was good . . . but the underlying problem was still no less a problem.

And it could only get worse.

TWO

Cent: "But it will kill you dead,
just the same."

I don't really exist, you know.

We live in the Canadian Rockies, sixty miles south of the Arctic Circle. I was born here, in this house. Mom and Dad paid a nurse midwife to live with us for the last month of the pregnancy. Dad was prepared to transfer Mom to a hospital if things went wrong, but things "worked out" as did I, apparently. Mom said it was definitely "work."

But there's no birth record. No birth certificate. No Social Security number.

We're in the middle of nowhere. The second largest city in the province is a hundred miles to the southeast, but I've never been there. Next nearest town is 140 miles north: Old Crow. No roads to Old Crow, it just has an airstrip and the river.

No roads to our house, either. It was built by a billionaire as a hunting lodge at the head of a mountain valley using helicoptered labor. We get moose, caribou, deer, wolves, lynx, and rabbits. Starbucks? Not so much.

The walls are heavy logs, two feet thick. The roof is steeply pitched anodized steel to keep the snow from piling up. It sloughs off the snow in the winter until the bottom floor windows and doors are buried. One year the snow rose high enough to cover the second floor, but Dad melted it away, making sure that the chimney, ventilation stacks, upper doors, and triple-glazed windows remained clear.

There's a log-surfaced helicopter pad, but Dad does nothing to keep it clear, no matter what the season. Moss, brush, and small trees are taking it over.

Dad doesn't care. That's not how he rolls.

He does spend a lot of the summers fixing up the lodge itself—that and the springhouse out back.

The springs are the reason the billionaire built the lodge here: one hot, one cold. One tasting of sulfur and one tasting like a deep breath of winter. We don't need a hot-water heater—the hot spring provides bath, washing, and soaking water—though it leaves mineral stains in the tub. We drink from the cold spring and use it to make showers less scalding. For two thirds of the year we run hot spring water through radiators to heat the house, and all year round we use the temperature difference between the two springs to generate electricity.

That was Dad's doing. I think back when it was a hunting lodge, they had a diesel generator. But it was rusted solid when Dad bought the place. The billionaire had become a mere millionaire during the economic meltdown and a vacation home that required two-hundred-mile round-trips by helicopter became something he couldn't afford.

Dad's not a billionaire, but then he doesn't need a helicopter to get here, either.

The electrical generator came from an Icelandic power company that built it as a proof-of-concept device at one of their geothermal wells. When they upgraded that installation to the megawatt commercial version, Dad bought the prototype for mere thousands of dollars.

When I was little, I named it Buzz since that's what it does, sits in the basement and buzzes. To be fair, it also gurgles, hisses, and thumps, but for a four-year-old, buzz is as entertaining a word as ever there was, especially if you add extra "zzzzzzzzzzz" at the end.

And then one day, when I was fifteen, it stopped buzzing.

I was watching an old anime on my desktop, but the screen blipped out along with the lights and then I was sitting in the dark, listening to the DVD drive spin to a halt.

I heard Mom yell from her office across the hall. "Davy!"

Dad's voice answered from downstairs, "Yeah, yeah. I'm on it!"

I felt my way over to the door and opened it. The battery-powered emergency light in the stairwell had come on. The windows were dark—it was late afternoon and October, and what little dusk light was on the southern horizon was blocked by the ridge on the far side of the valley.

Dad had just come out of the library when I tripped down the stairs. He smiled briefly at me. "Hey, Cent. Pretty dark up there, I bet."

"You think?" I said. "What's wrong with Buzz?"

He shook his head. "Not sure. Let's go see." He reached out to ruffle my hair.

I was styling it these days with a lot of gel and I slapped his arm away. "Rule one, Daddy! How many times do I gotta tell you?"

He laughed again. "Don't touch the hair. Right. Sorry."

I swear he does it just to mess with me.

When he opened the door at the top of the basement stairs, I heard a high-pitched beeping noise, one I'd never heard before. I started to take a step down and Dad grabbed me by my collar and pulled me back.

"Damn!" Dad said. "Well, at least we know what's wrong with Buzz. Don't go down there."

"What's that alarm?"

"Halogen detector. There's a leak in the system. The Freon is leaking out." He was no longer smiling.

I knew about the Freon. The hot water from the spring boils it to vapor, which expands through the turbine generator. The cold spring water condenses it again. I'm homeschooled, so the generator has been the source of many science lessons: state changes of matter, Boyle's law, electromagnetism.

"Freon isn't poisonous, Dad."

"No. But it will kill you dead, just the same." The serious look on his face eased at my expression. "Definitely not poisonous. We're okay up here. Let me give you a clue: Freon is heavier than air."

I thought about it for a moment. "Ah. Like water?"

"Like water you can't see or feel or smell, yes. Which means?"

"The air is on top. The Freon fills up the basement and pushes the air out."

He grinned, big. "On the nosey, little posy."

"You'd pass out, eh?"

"Before you died. Heard about a shrimp boat with a refrigeration leak down in the hull. Different members of the crew kept going down into the hold to see what happened to the previous guy. The coast guard found the vessel going in circles, everybody suffocated."

I eyed the stairs dubiously. "You sure we're okay?"

He got that look on his face and smiled.

"No!" I said. "I don't need another real-life math problem!"

He led me back upstairs where we found Mom typing at her computer. *She* had a laptop with a battery. *She* didn't have to stop what she was doing because Buzz was busted.

"What's wrong with Buzz?" she asked.

"Leaking Freon," Dad said calmly.

"And displacing all the air in the house!" I said.

Mom's eyes widened and she looked at Dad. Dad shrugged. "Not very likely, but Millicent is going to calculate the answer to that."

Mom raised her eyebrows and pushed a pad of paper and a pen toward me across her desk.

Dad said, "Assume an eight-foot-high ceiling. The generator room is twelve by ten feet. It's about a quarter of the entire basement."

I did that part in my head. "Nine-hundred-sixty cubic feet. How much Freon?"

Dad jumped and I don't mean he bounced in place. He disappeared, vanished. I said something under my breath, which caused Mom to sit up straight and give me "the look."

"Sorry. I was watching my show. I already *did* homework today." I sounded whiny. I *hate* sounding whiny. I tried again, with a more reasonable voice. "I work hard, don't I?"

"The look" faded and Mom said, "Yes, honey, you do. But you know your father. He never finished school. He's one of the smartest men I know but he has this thing about education."

"Tell me about it. If I hear the phrase 'teachable moment' one more time, I'm gonna barf."

Dad reappeared at my elbow, a manual and a sheet of paper in his hand. "Had to go to the library for the Material Safety Data sheet. Didn't know the density."

I looked at Mom and sighed heavily. Dad put the books on the desk by the notepad and slid a chair over for me to sit.

It was dark, but when he pulled the bedroom door all the way open, the emergency light from the hall shone across half the desk.

"Dad! This is Buzz's manual—you went into the basement!"

He shrugged. "As you said, it's not poisonous. I held my breath. Wasn't in there more than five seconds." Mom and I both gave him "the look" but after so many years, he's impervious. He reached down and tapped the notepad.

I sighed and sat down. The manual specs said the generator was charged with 175 pounds of Freon, the ozone-safe R-22 version. The Material Data Sheet told me the density, and when I converted, I got .225 pounds per cubic foot. That seemed pretty heavy but I double-checked it. "Must be a big molecule." I grabbed Mom's laptop and called up a calculator. "Seven hundred and eighty cubic feet. Uh, in the generator room that would displace the air up to, uh, six and a half feet off the floor."

Dad held his hand over his head. "Worse than that, I think. You didn't account for altitude."

"Oh." I blushed. As I'd said, we'd already done Boyle's law but I'd forgotten. I knew the conversion factor for our forty-five hundred feet of altitude by heart. "Okay." I multiplied the figure by 1.18. "Call it 920 cubic feet." I tapped away. "It would fill the room to seven and two-thirds feet."

Mom spoke. "I guess we *don't* have to worry about the whole house."

I felt the need to make up for my earlier slip. "Really, not even the basement. When we open the door to the generator room it will flow out into the other rooms and be less than two feet high. Not a problem if we don't lie on the floor."

Mom turned to Dad. "You won't leave it there, will you?"

Dad shook his head. "I'll twin to a higher altitude and suck it out. But before it all leaks out, I want to find out where it's leaking, so we can fix it. Hopefully without hauling the thing back to Reykjavik."

"We can put the stuff from the freezer on the porch," Mom said, glancing at the window. It was eighteen degrees Fahrenheit outside and would probably drop another ten degrees before morning. "But the stuff in the refrigerator needs not to freeze. Ice chest?"

Dad shook his head. "I'll go get a backup generator. I've been meaning to for some time, but Buzz has been so reliable and I've been worried about carbon monoxide."

"Well," Mom said. "Since it looks like we'll be without power for a while—" She looked at me. "—Let's go shopping."

"Clothes?" I asked, hopefully.

"You've got plenty of clothes," Mom said. "I'm thinking lentils . . . about nine tons."

Yes, I have enough clothes. I know that, but it's not the clothes I'm interested in. It's the people—the clerks, the other customers, the people walking by on the streets. Mom and Dad never let me spend significant time with other people.

It's like being in a cult.

Mom said summer so that meant Southern Hemisphere. I

changed out of my sweater into a T-shirt and put on running shoes. When I came out onto the landing Mom was waiting, jeans and a T-shirt like me, plus a cotton work shirt and a broad-brimmed hat.

"Africa?" I asked.

"Australia."

"Let me grab my shades." I had to fumble in the dark but I found my snowboarding shades and grabbed a Yomiuri Giants baseball cap.

When I came out again, Mom opened her arms and I walked into her embrace. When she let me go my ears popped, the sun was blazing down, and I could smell a feedlot. I put on my glasses and hat. It's warm enough at home, with the hot spring radiators, but in the depth of winter you're always aware of the cold at the edges, in the corners, near the windows.

At least for the moment, the sun felt as good as Mom's embrace.

It was a small town, I could tell. There was a train yard with large grain silos, a passenger station, and a railroad museum. An old-fashioned railway water tank sat among eucalyptus trees. Old-fashioned letters spelled *Kalgoorlie Bitter* across one square face, with a small image of a foaming beer stein. A street sign below said *Allenby Street*. Across the road was a Chinese restaurant, and my stomach rumbled.

I pointed at it and Mom shrugged. "Perhaps. Business first."

Her business was near the grain silos at the office of the *Co-operative Bulk Handling Group*. A passenger train pulled in while Mom was inside and I watched people get off. Many of them went into the train museum or headed into the restaurant.

I overheard enough to determine that the train had come from Perth and would continue on to Kalgoorlie, and that a few of the passengers were doing the entire run across the continent to Sydney.

Mom came back outside with a man who said, "Down this way. We loaded 'er up yesterday arvo."

The accent was broader than I was used to. We'd been to Perth and Sydney and Melbourne but this was more like Crocodile Dundee.

He led us around the corner to where a medium-sized dump truck stood outside warehouse doors. He stood up on the step and stuck his his head in the open window. "Yair. Keys are in 'er."

"Great," Mom said. "I'll have it back in four hours?"

"Tomorrow morning be all right," he said, grinning broadly. "This your daughter?"

Mom nodded. I stood up and nodded politely. His face was like an old piece of leather, lined and tan. I tried not to stare. I don't get to see people much, not up close.

I started to get in on the right-hand side of the truck and froze in the doorway when I realized it was right-hand drive. I knew there was something odd about the traffic I'd been watching. I got into the seat and slid under the wheel to the passenger side, banging my knee on the stick shift.

Mom followed me in, started it up, and pulled out into the wrong-side-of-the-road traffic like she drove here every day. She took a piece of paper out of her shirt pocket and handed it to me.

"You're the navigator."

We left the town of Merredin, Western Australia, on 94, the Great Eastern Highway, but only as far as the first exit. Mom drove south a mile, and turned off onto a weed-filled dirt road lined with high brush on both sides. It curved away from the paved road and Mom pulled off as soon as it was out of sight of the highway.

"Watch out for snakes," she said.

"Great," I said. "Visit exotic Australia. Get bitten by an exotic snake. Die exotically."

Mom jumped away, vanishing like a lightbulb turning off.

I climbed out the window and up onto the roof of the cab. After what she'd said about snakes, I wasn't going anywhere near the bushes.

Mom was in the back of the truck, intermittently. That is, she was picking up burlap sacks one at a time and disappearing, reappearing, grabbing another sack and repeating.

They were stenciled *CBHG Yellow Lentils fifteen kilos.* I did the math while I watched Mom empty the truck. Nine tons of lentils, presuming she meant English tons, would be about 545 bags. Mom was doing one every five seconds, though she took an occasional break. Straight through, it would have taken about forty-five minutes, but she slowed down near the end. The truck was empty in an hour and ten minutes.

She was sweaty and dusty, too.

"Back to the warehouse?" I said.

She shook her head, vanished, and reappeared, a bottle of cold water in each hand. She handed me one and guzzled the other, sprinkling some of it over her hair.

Before driving back into Merredin, she drove a half hour further out of town and the half hour back. "Mileage," explained Mom. "Don't want them to think I'm too local if we buy more."

We listened to a call-in show on the radio, entertained by the accents. "Why do they pitch their sentences up at the end, like every line is a question?" I asked.

Mom shook her head. "Don't know. I've heard the same thing in parts of the UK. It's just a variant. I'm sure we sound odd to them, too."

We gave the truck back to the man at the co-op and he returned a fat envelope. "Darn. Halfway hoping I'd get to keep your deposit."

Mom smiled and thanked him, and said, "I may need another nine tons next month. Will they still be in season?"

"You like your lentils, I guess. There'll be some in our warehouse for at least a month after the last harvest, too."

We went to the Chinese restaurant then, but I was yawning like a fiend by the time we'd eaten. It was early afternoon here, but well after midnight at home. After Mom paid, we went to the restroom and she jumped us home from there.

I barely remember falling into bed. I don't remember taking off my shoes, but they were in the closet when I woke up which means, of course, that Mom pulled them off. I would've kicked them into the corner.

It was gray outside. The sun was up as high as it was going to get and it still hadn't cleared the far ridge. The sky was clear, though, and you could see the whole valley, trimmed with evergreens and draped with heavy white snow, except where our local elk herd had used their hooves to cut through to the grass on the flat.

It wouldn't be long before the elk moved down the mountain to the river valley for the winter.

This time of year the light never wakes me. Instead it was a grinding noise, like a snowmobile or an off-road motorbike, that brought me out of sleep, and I realized Dad must've made good on his promise to bring in a backup generator. As I moved downstairs the sound got louder, but it was still a background noise, not overwhelming.

Dad had spread newspaper on the dining room table and was fiddling with some mechanical parts. He smiled at me. "Sleep okay? You guys were back late."

I made my noncommittal noise: half grunt, half hum. "Where's Mom?"

He looked around, then said, "Oh, that's right. She's organizing the warehouse."

The warehouse was on the outskirts of a small town in Michigan, a steel building thrown up by one of GM's vendors right before the local plant was shut down. Dad bought it cheap, and never used.

I gestured at the parts. "Too noisy downstairs?"

He shook his head. "It's not the noise in the basement. It's the noise outside, where the exhaust pipe pokes though the wall. Need to get a longer pipe. Run it above the roof, perhaps."

"Wouldn't that just make it louder up by our bedrooms?" Dad got that look in his eye, and I said quickly, "Just yes or no. I don't want another physics lecture!"

Dad grinned. "Okay. No. It wouldn't make it louder, not if the mounting brackets were dampened."

"Fine."

I made it all the way through cooking pancakes, buttering them, and pouring the syrup before I asked, "Okay. *Why* would an exhaust pipe sticking up above the roof be quieter?"

Dad grinned. "Up there the noise doesn't have anything to reflect off of. The sound waves exit the pipe in a hemispheric pattern mostly up. Down where it's coming out now, it echoes off the ground and the snow and the trees and even the springhouse. So we're hearing it pretty loud."

"Buzz was never that loud," I said.

Dad pointed at the pipe before him. "And as soon as I get this piece welded we can get back to Buzz. Well, welded and reinstalled, and the Freon charged back into the system."

"And you'll get rid of the noisy generator?"

"Oh no. We'll keep it for backup. Hopefully we won't have to run it much."

Mom showed up shortly after that. She was wearing shorts, a tank top, boots, and work gloves, and she was sweaty.

Dad brushed the damp bangs back from her forehead. "You done already? I said I'd help."

Mom kissed him. "You load sixteen tons, whaddya get?" She flexed a bicep. "It's better than a gym, any day."

I said, "I thought it was nine tons?"

"Cultural reference," Mom said. "Mid-twentieth century. Tennessee Ernie Ford." I must've looked even more puzzled because she clarified. "He was a singer. 'Sixteen Tons' was a song."

"Oh," I said. "Old stuff. Like Green Day?"

Dad choked.

"Or Beethoven?"

Mom said, "Somewhere in between. When you've eaten, we need to distribute some lentils."

"What climate?"

"Pakistan. The mountains. Pretty cold. Also," she gestured toward her head.

I grimaced. *"Hijab."*

She nodded and looked at Dad. "I'll want your help transporting, okay?"

"Where are you working?"

"The IRC refugee camp on the border, west of Peshawar."

"The one Patel works at?" Dad said.

Mom nodded. "The UN supplies have not been getting through. In the south, the Pashtun militias are diverting them for profit, and on the Afghan side, it's a tossup between the Taliban and the poppy growers."

"Pretty dangerous area." Dad's voice was mild, but he was frowning.

"We're distributing from the women's clinic compound. No men allowed. The main problems are outside camp, as usual. Safe enough inside."

"Okay. While you change, I'll get this to the welder. Be back in a bit."

I dressed warmly—long underwear, my snowboarding pants, a fleece pullover. Over these I put on the traditional pants, tight at the ankle, baggy at the hips, and the knee length tunic, then the headscarf. I'd gone with Mom several times into areas where women wore the full burka, veil and all, but I wouldn't have to today.

Mom jumped me to the interior of a canvas tent, a large ten-by-ten structure over a dirt and gravel floor. It was cold, and the only light was a Coleman lantern Mom brought with her. My ears popped, but not as badly as they had in Australia, which meant the altitude was more like the mountains, where our house was. There were plastic drums and collapsed cardboard boxes stacked across the back, but the tent was mostly empty.

Mom pointed at a tied-shut door flap. "It won't be dawn for another two hours. We'll be distributing through that door."

Dad showed up after that, with a folding screen, six feet high, eight feet long. He set it up close to the door so they could jump discretely from behind it, if necessary, after the distribution started.

Working together, they took a half hour to bring all the

lentils from the warehouse. Dad was bringing two bags at a time and he jumped much faster than Mom, flicking in and out without pausing. Of course, he's been doing it far longer. I dragged the sacks within reach of the door and began stacking them. Our breath was still steaming but I wasn't cold anymore.

Dad left after all the lentils had been brought in and stacked. Mom jumped out and came back with cartons of plastic bags and big measuring scoops. "Two liters each, right?"

We'd filled about fifty of the transparent bags, ready to hand out, when there was a scratching at the flap.

Mom tensed and then said, "*As-salaam alaikum.*"

The voice on the other side was a woman's. "*Bonjour, c'est moi*, Magrit."

Mom relaxed and untied the tent flaps. The sun was hitting the surrounding peaks and the air that flowed through the door was markedly colder, not warmed by all our activity. Magrit was a tall woman wearing khakis and a white medical clinician's coat buttoned all the way up to the neck. She had a wool scarf wrapped up over her chin and ears, and her arms were crossed, her hands tucked up into her armpits. A stethoscope stuck out of one pocket.

"Good morning, Doctor," Mom said.

Magrit took a step back. She wasn't looking at us, but at the stacks of burlap bags visible past the screen. "*Sacredieu!* They told me, but . . . I saw this place last night, late, before I came to bed—empty! How?"

Mom did that thing she does, that *therapist* thing. She nodded her head and said, "That must be very disturbing."

"How did you get this into the camp? *Les soldats* are checking all vehicles."

Mom said, "I would think that whoever moved it here would want to keep their methods a secret, so *les soldats* could not stop the food."

Magrit opened and shut her mouth a few moments, then exhaled heavily. "There are women waiting for clinic hours. I will send them over, yes?"

"Yes," Mom said. "*Merci beaucoup.*"

The women spoke Pashto and mostly it was *"ma-nana"* which I figured out pretty quick means, "Thanks." Some of them asked *"Ta la cherta rahg-ley?"* Mom answered, *"Ze la Canada."*

Mostly, though, I tied a loose knot in the tops of the bags and passed them over, smiled, and bobbed my head. The word spread and by midmorning the line snaked around the compound formed by the clinic's tents, and out into to the camp proper.

I wasn't the only one handing out the lentils. Five other women, recruited by Magrit, were filling bags and handing them out. The line was moving at a slow walk, but there was no end in sight.

After a consultation with Magrit, a covey of young girls my age began carrying plastic bags outside the clinic to where a line started for men—orphaned boys, bachelors, or widowers— who couldn't come into the compound. This line was small, though, because the camp was largely filled with women whose men had died in the fighting, or who had fled from their own husbands and fathers and the Taliban's strict application of religious rule. "And also," Magrit said, "they're men. Some of them would rather be hungry than collect the food. Women's work."

At one point Mom disappeared behind the screen and came back with a mug of hot tea, heavily sugared. She took over my job while I drank it behind the screen, grateful for the hot drink, and at the same time, ashamed. The women helping us wore extra clothes, shawls, men's shirts, but they were still woefully underdressed for the temperature.

"Let me bring some hot tea to *them*," I said, pointing at our helpers.

Mom reached out and tugged my *chador* forward, over my bangs. "Okay. There are Styrofoam cups over the sink. Oh, and while you're there? Use the bathroom. I just saw the latrine and you don't want to go anywhere near it."

Mom jumped me home from behind the screen. I put the

large kettle on and, while it heated, used the bathroom and washed my hands multiple times. Mom got me inoculated for *everything* but as she'd pointed out, I'd brushed hands with hundreds of people just this morning.

I brewed the tea in a plastic pitcher and sweetened it almost syrup thick. When I came out from behind the screen and began handing out cups, I think they thought I was bringing water, but when I tipped the pitcher steam rose in the air. They cradled the cups and breathed in the steam and smell. When one of them tasted it her cry of surprise started the others sipping.

The line ran out before we ran out of lentils and Mom sighed in relief. She did a quick inventory and told Dr. Magrit, "Almost five hundred kilos left. For the next emergency."

Dr. Magrit nodded. "There is always another. But the army *says* they're coming to deal with this latest problem with the militias. The UN has a large convoy waiting for their escort."

We tidied the tent, stacking the bags neatly, and when Magrit went to do rounds, Mom jumped us away.

Dad came into the kitchen swearing. "The weld is still leaking. I have to get the part machined from scratch."

Mom and I were in our bathrobes. We'd used the hot tub on the upper deck to cook the chill from our bones. There's something decadent about sitting in 110-degree water while fluffy, fat snowflakes are falling all around you. But this time it hadn't been as good because of the noise and smell of the generator exhaust, which was way worse than the slight smell of sulfur that comes from the hot spring.

When I thought about the girls and women in the refugee camp I felt really petty complaining, but I still said, "Can't we go stay someplace else while that thing is running? It's smelly and loud."

Dad and Mom looked at each other, then back at me. Mom looked sad and Dad looked grim. I knew his answer before he spoke.

"No. We can turn off the generator at night, though. The fridge will be okay for seven hours."

Right. As if I cared about the refrigerator.

We never slept anyplace else. We'd go places but we'd always come back quickly. I was trying to remember if there was ever a time that I'd spent the night away from home, even when Dad taught me survival camping. Sure we gathered and cooked our own food, but how real is it if you get tucked into your own bed every night?

The next morning Dad went off to get his part made and Mom said, "Your room . . . clean it."

"Mom!"

"It looks like a laundry and a library exploded. You have shelves, use them. Put up your clean laundry and start washing the dirty stuff, *if* you can tell which is which. They're all jumbled together."

I opened my mouth to protest but she raised her hand. "Seriously. Do it. I've got some meetings so I won't be back until this afternoon, but you should be done by then."

"I need more shelves."

"You *need* to cull your collection. If you're not going to read it again, put it in a box. We'll donate it to a reading program."

"*Dad* said I could have another shelf." Dad has books all over the house. You don't see *him* culling his collection.

Mom sighed. "One more shelf isn't going to do it. Okay— one more shelf unit, but you'll have to move your boy-toy posters."

"No!"

"It's the only wall space left."

"We could put the shelf in front of one of the windows."

"Absolutely not!"

"I don't see why—"

Mom jumped away.

It's not fair.

Oh, yeah, I can see that we really shouldn't put bookshelves in front of the windows. There's a great view down the valley, and in the summer I would want it open. But jumping away in the middle of an argument really isn't fair.

Dad does it, too.

If I could jump, it might be different. I'd fantasized about disappearing in the middle of one of *their* lectures often enough.

When I was a little girl, maybe four years old, I would stand in front of my mother and say, "Mommy, I'm going to jump!"

Mom would cover her eyes with both hands and I would quietly walk to another part of the room or into another room entirely and say, "Boom! I jumped!" And she would drop her hands, gasp in amazement, and say, "Wow, you jumped!" If I was in the room with her still, she would say. "There you are!" And if I'd left the room, she'd say, "Where did she go?"

I wasn't going anywhere. At this rate I would never go anywhere.

I stomped up the stairs to my room. I was still in my pajamas: sweatpants and a T-shirt. I tried to slam the door but it caught on a pile of clothes, books, and DVD cases. I groaned. Bad enough that she left in the middle of the argument, but the fact that she was right about the room only made it worse.

I kicked at the pile, trying to shove it aside, and jammed my toe on a book wedged up against the shelf by the door.

"Shit!" I yelled, hopping around on the other foot. I didn't care that I wasn't supposed to say that. At that moment I wouldn't have cared if Mom and Dad were standing there listening. It would be hard for them to bug out in the middle of that one emphatic word.

The posters were old, dating back to when my idea of what a girl's room should look like was based on girls' rooms in movies and television shows. I don't think I'd ever been inside an actual girl's room. Mom's mother lives in an apartment in one of those retirement communities now and though Mom once showed me the house she grew up in, we never saw inside. Even if we had, the room she'd had as a girl would've been different.

Mom told me, though, that when she was my age, she had pictures of Rick Springfield, Andrew McCarthy, and Tom Cruise. "Yeah, I know," she said. "But this was pre-Scientology, *Risky Business* Tom Cruise."

I had three posters: the Jonas Brothers, Zac Efron, and Rupert Grint. Rupert's too old but that smile and those shoulders and that hair! I didn't really care about the Jonas Brothers or Zac, not anymore, but when I was balancing on my desk chair to take Rupert down, the chair rolled sideways while one of the pushpins was still in. The poster ripped diagonally down through his face *and* I banged the jammed toe when I landed.

"Fuck!" I yelled. It was so loud I *imagined* it echoing through the mountain valley, the elk lifting their heads to listen. I ripped the rest of the glossy paper down and crumpled it into a ball. Then I did the same thing with the other two posters and slung the damn chair across the room where it knocked a lower shelf out of one of my bookcases and spilled more books across the floor.

I started crying and this made me mad. Mom's a family therapist by training. There is no stigma attached to crying in our house, though it makes Dad uncomfortable, but I hated how it made my eyes puffy. Also, the thought of Mom comforting me or asking me those open-ended therapy questions while I was still mad at her really pissed me off.

My bed is chest high with a reading nook underneath, with cushions and a light. It's been my hiding place, my crying place, my safe place since I was little. I hadn't used it in months but I wanted to crawl into it and bury myself in the cushions. I even crouched to do so but then I saw my snowboarding pants lying across the entrance, where I'd kicked them off the day before.

"To hell with this," I said, and got dressed instead.

There's a covered walkway at the back of the house that becomes more of a tunnel in the winter. It's mostly used to reach the springhouse but it continues up the mountain from there, a steep stairway, steps of squared timbers set into the ground. I use it for exercise, when the house gets to be too much, pushing the snow off to the sides until it's banked high enough to keep even the blizzard-driven snow out. The stairway leads to a pavilion fifteen feet square, a hundred yards up the slope, where the mountain shelves a bit and the black spruces and sub-Alpine fir thin out. It's glorious there in the long summer days, if there's a breeze to keep the mosquitoes away. In the dead of winter it's lethal, especially when the wind blows. But now, in the fall, the temperatures were still above zero, though the snow was piling deep.

The pavilion marks the top of my snowboard run, which curves north, down a gully, through a birch grove, and down a natural half-pipe that's a series of short waterfalls in the summer. At the bottom it winds down one more steep slope before curving around to the valley floor, a hundred yards below the house.

I'm not supposed to snowboard unless Dad has checked the run, making sure all the rocky areas are deep under snow and there's nothing dangerous around. All of the Yukon is grizzly territory and they like to hibernate near the tree line. Despite the snow, this was early enough in the year for grizzlies to still be active.

So, too early, and you can run into grizzlies. Too late, and the temperatures get to forty below zero. Fahrenheit *or* centigrade. Doesn't matter. That's the place where it means the same thing on both scales. Do the math—Dad made me do it.

I hauled my board up the stairs, kicking through some of the newer drifts, my coat open and my hat off. I knew I'd be sweating by the time I reached the top. The snow was even deeper than I'd expected, since the freak storm we'd had back in September dumped three feet and the temperature had never risen high enough for it to melt.

I took the first run slowly. I was breaking *so* many rules. Dad hadn't checked the run. I was supposed to be cleaning my room. And I wasn't wearing a helmet.

Dad would have a stroke if he saw me.

I only had one biff, not really a boomph, when I buttslid out of a carved turn, cutting up short to avoid a rock sticking out of the snow. The rest of the run was clean, and now that I'd marked the rock in my head I could shred the whole thing at speed. There was even a cornice to the left after I exited the pipe that would let me bust huge air above the last steep pitch down into the valley.

I didn't even look in the windows as I climbed up past the house. Dad might think I was with Mom and vice versa, but if either of them saw me or realized my board was gone from the back hall, I was busted anyway.

I was gasping by the time I reached the top again and I sat until my breathing slowed and I was feeling the chill. I buttoned up and snapped my bindings over my boots and started down the slope, aggressive, keeping closer to the fall line. I hit air twice in the pipe and remembered to cut hard at the bottom so I could catch the cornice. To hit the right part of the slope below I had to cut hard, right before the lip, and under the pressure of the turn I felt something shift below my board. I was airborne when I heard a deep thudding sound overlaid with a sharp crack.

I hit the steep slope below, my knees bending to absorb the landing shock, and risked a glance upslope.

The entire cornice, fifty yards across, had let go. As avalanches went it was small, but it filled the last slope, funneled even tighter by the near-vertical cliffs on each side. I couldn't cut sideways out of its path.

My only hope was to get down before it caught me. I steered straight down the fall line and leaned forward, putting my arms behind, slipstreaming.

I might have made it, but a slight bump in the slope concealed a loop of willow branch. It wasn't thick but it was ropy tough, and even though it broke, it took me down, tumbling, to fetch up against another drift just in time to watch tons of snow bear down on me.

"Sorry, Dad," was all I had time to say.

It's the air in front that hits you first, driven by the snow. The blast popped me into the air and then the snow was all around and pushing me down, down, down . . . and then I hit something and everything was dark.

I wasn't unconscious so the darkness surprised me a little.

I'd fallen in deep powder and the snow conducts the light surprisingly well, but not this time. I thought there must be tons of snow above me, but I didn't feel any pressure. I'd wrapped my arms around my face, to keep an air pocket, which is one of the things they say you should do. Now I thrust forward, hard, trying to make the air space bigger while the snow was still soft. But the snow gave way and my hand hit something hard and smooth. I kept thrusting, pushing the snow . . . and then there was light coming in from where the snow had cascaded away from me, and I saw a stretch of carpet, a stack of underwear, and six paperback books.

I was in the reading nook under my bed with about two cubic yards of snow.

I'd jumped.

THREE

Davy: Wet Dream

Davy had the dream, again, the one where the scars on his chest were fresh, and if he tapped just below his right collarbone, there was a solid disk-shaped lump under the skin. In the dream he felt the tingle in his throat, the coughing, followed almost immediately by the nausea—the titanic heaving of his stomach muscles as he vomited—and he woke up on a steeply pitched roof on the south shore of Martha's Vineyard in ice-cold, driving rain.

The vomit, at least *this* time, was only in the dream and once fully awake, he flinched back to their bathroom, swearing loudly. Despite being awake now, he couldn't stop his fingers from probing the old scar below his right collarbone, but the old device had not magically reappeared below the skin.

Millie sat up in bed, abruptly, a sharp intake of breath. "Davy?"

In the dim illumination that leaked from the bathroom nightlight, Davy saw her patting the bed beside her, searching for him.

"Here," he said. "It's all right. Had the dream again."

"Oh," she said. "*Just* the dream?"

"No, dammit." He took off his wet pajamas and groped for a towel. "They're having a northeaster on the Vineyard."

"You haven't done that in a while." Millie sank back against her pillow. "So, on the rooftop in the rain? That's good."

He snarled at her through the towel.

She laughed. "Sorry. I mean that if it's unpleasant enough, we stand a chance of getting rid of the compulsion. They spent so much time making it unpleasant everywhere else. It's good to counter that."

Davy picked up the wet pajamas and threw them violently into the laundry bin. "Too bad they replaced the building, then. Falling to the foundations from three stories up would be really unpleasant."

"At least they didn't rebuild it exactly. You wouldn't want to reappear in someone's bedroom." Millie said reasonably.

The current owners of the property had torn down the flood-damaged old mansion sixteen years before and replaced it with a two-story beach house.

"I'm going to soak in the springhouse," he said. "Chilled." *Come with me?* He didn't voice the thought. It wasn't fair to wake her up in the middle of the night as it was.

"Come back to bed soon," she said. Her voice trailed to a whisper by the last and she smacked her lips and closed her eyes.

She was breathing deeply, sound asleep, when he came back. He was thoroughly warmed by the hot spring, overheated in fact. He toweled dry, put on dry pajamas, then slipped between the sheets carefully. She made an "mm" sound and resumed her deep breathing.

He stared at the ceiling until dawn.

FOUR

Cent: "I thought Dad was the ruthless one."

The second time was like this:

"Why is there a water stain on the library ceiling?" Dad asked.

Shit. I had an answer ready but I hadn't expected that *particular* question.

"I was cleaning my room and I took some water in to scrub out a stain in the carpet. I'm sorry, I tipped over the bucket."

The question I'd *been* expecting was "Why is your carpet wet?"

I'd disposed of the snow in the bathtub, running the shower hot to melt it. My room never looked better. I'd gotten to the books soon enough to keep them from getting soaked but, as noted, a substantial amount of snow melted into the rug—more than I'd realized.

I'd run three loads through the laundry. Mom was right. The dirty clothes were mixed up with the clean and all of it was wet. Also the cushions in the reading nook. Between loads, I'd also culled three cartons of books that I would never read again.

I am *so* over vampires.

Mom looked surprised, pleased, and finally suspicious when she saw my room. On the grounds that the best defense is a good offense, I said, "See? Boy-toy posters gone. I get that new bookshelf, right?"

She pulled open a drawer at random. It was full of clean, *mostly* folded T-shirts—shirts that had been on the floor that very morning.

"A new bookshelf. Right."

Dad jumped to IKEA Funabashi in Japan, since that was the time zone that still had a store open, and purchased a matching shelving unit. I told him that I wanted to put it together so he left the unopened flat pack in my room. But instead of leaving, he leaned against the doorframe.

"Dad."

"Yes?"

"I don't need, or want, an audience."

He looked mildly offended. "Oh. Okay."

I felt guilty but I really didn't want him to discover just how wet the carpet really was.

Yes, I would tell them eventually. Well, maybe not about the avalanche. But about the jumping, certainly. I finished assembling the shelf and putting the rest of the books up. That lousy generator was still chugging away in the basement so I turned up the living room stereo to drown it out. After an hour of this, Dad, shouting to be heard over the music, said, "Okay! We can go someplace."

You'd almost think he preferred the grind of the generator to Electroclash.

I turned the music down. "Where?"

Mom stuck her head over the railing of the upstairs landing, a surprised look on her face.

"Someplace quiet," Dad said.

"Someplace with people?" I said.

"Someplace warm?" Mom suggested, walking down the stairs.

"Mall of America," I said.

Dad said, "No."

"Why not?"

"Surveillance cameras. Thousands."

"Wear a disguise," I said. He has disguises. So does Mom. Dad got a stubborn look on his face. "No."

"Well, where do *you* want to go?" I said belligerently.

He frowned at me. "Queensland."

"It's night there," said Mom. "And you *both* need to calm down. You don't mean overnight, do you? One of the islands on the Great Barrier Reef?"

Dad backtracked. "Uh, not overnight."

"That sounds wonderful," I said. "We could go snorkeling in the morning. And I could do some marine science units."

Mom bit her lower lip. I could see she liked the idea.

Dad got that wild, desperate look in his eyes. He lifted his hand to his collar and I winced. He wasn't going to pull out the big gun, was he?

He did.

"You see these?" Dad pulled his shirt collar to one side, exposing two parallel scars, three-inches long, just below his right collarbone.

"Yes, Dad. I see them. I've seen them. I've *heard* the story."

Mom stepped closer. "Davy, your concerns are real but you need to stop doing that."

Dad's voice rose, "She's *got* to realize how dangerous it is out there!"

I didn't think we'd be going to Queensland.

Dad was captured once by some nasty supersecret multinational corporate group. They put a device in him to try and condition him, to control him. It was nasty and it went on for *months*. Eventually Mom got him out, but he's been super paranoid ever since.

"I *do* know, but it's not dangerous *everywhere*," I said. "I was in Pakistan two days ago and Australia the day before that. Do you expect me to live in this house the rest of my life? I *need* to make friends."

"You have friends!" he said.

"*What* friends?"

"What about Awrala and Xareed?"

"Awrala has two babies and a husband who is afraid of us.

Xareed is married with sons. He's almost twice my age." I
like them both. They live in Somalia and I've known them
since I was little, but they're more my parents' friends. "I
need to go to school. I need to know girls *my* age." I pulled out
my big gun. "I'm an overbright, undersocialized, discipline-
challenged teenager who is going to grow up to be a malad-
justed sociopath at this rate."

Mom's eyes went wide and her hand went to her mouth. I
guess she hadn't realized I was listening when she'd said that
to Dad.

"You *aren't* going to school. It would be like staking you
out for the bastards!" Dad's eyes were wide, the whites showing all around, as bad as I'd ever seen him.

"You can't follow me around all my life to protect me!" I
said.

"Wanna bet?" he yelled.

"Stalker, *much?*" I yelled back.

Mom started crying and I flinched.

I mean, I flinched so good, I was upstairs in my reading
cubby.

That was the second time.

I heard Mom scream, then Dad—a startled, hoarse yell.

I almost screamed myself.

Now they know how it feels.

They started calling my name. Mom even said the old line,
"Where did she go?" but there was nothing playful about it. I
almost stayed there, under the bed, but the note of desperation
in their voices was too much.

I walked out onto the landing and said, "Boom. I jumped."

Mom's mouth twitched, not quite a smile, but she remembered. She got it.

Dad's knees buckled and he sat down hard on the floor.
Relief, I guess.

Before they said anything, I said, "Unless you're willing to
chain me up or cut me open and put one of those things inside
me, I'm *going* to school.

"Now, do you want to be a part of that or do I have to do it alone?"

Mom sent Dad away, to keep him from hovering. "Go work on the generator. Or relieve a drought. Wait a minute." She ducked into their bedroom and reemerged with a book in her hand. "Go read this."

Dad looked at the book. "I read this. When she was little."

"She's not little any more. Time to *reread* it."

"Is it still current?"

"Sadly."

Dad tucked it into his coat pocket and then, almost shyly, hugged me. I squeezed him back and kissed his cheek.

Mom made shooing motions with her hands and he almost smiled, then he vanished.

The memory of his almost smile was so vivid that for a moment I felt it was hanging in the air, like the Cheshire Cat's.

Mom shook her head. "Poor boy."

"Daddy's hardly a boy."

Mom smiled. "Sure he is. In his head. He's the same young man I met in New York City. Or, sometimes, the frightened kid who flinched at every sound from his father's end of the house." She looked at me. "And you frighten him so very much."

"Me?"

"Well, something happening to you. It's his biggest fear."

"What about you? Isn't he afraid something can happen to you, too?"

"Sure, it's only natural. But I'm afraid when he was captured that time—" Mom made an abbreviated gesture toward her right collarbone. "Well, lots of people have had PTSD from less. After that, he tried to control *everything,* especially while I was pregnant." She sighed. "At first it was nice. But my second trimester, when I felt great and could really do anything, he started hemming me in, trying to say what I could and couldn't do and where I could and couldn't go." She laughed softly. "I used to tell my clients that they needed to not run away from fights, to stick it out . . . but it was only my ability to jump away that made him ameliorate his behavior."

My mouth dropped open.

Mom nodded. "Right."

"He's seeing reason because I can jump now? Because he has no choice?"

Mom shrugged. "To be fair, there's more to it than that. Now he thinks you might have a chance out there. That he doesn't have to be there every second to jump you away from danger. You can do that yourself." She glanced at me. "Hopefully."

I stuck my jaw out. "Of course I can."

She said seriously, "Your father jumped *into* trouble often enough. It's not automatic."

"Well, so far it's been automatic," I muttered.

"Well, yes. About that—what happened?"

I knew what she meant. "Pardon?"

She raised her eyebrows and looked at me over her glasses. I hate it when she does that. Well, I hate it when she does that and I have something to hide. I blushed furiously.

She nodded to herself. "Like that, eh? Was it really stupid?"

"It wasn't stupid! It wasn't my fault!" I clamped my mouth shut. I'd broken several rules by going snowboarding. Perhaps it was my—no! Stupid avalanche!

"What wasn't your fault?" Mom asked.

"Uh. My jumping."

"I didn't say anything about fault, did I?"

I felt my mouth set stubbornly.

Mom left it alone. "How many times, then? How often have you jumped?"

If it had been Dad, I don't think I would have said, but I thought Mom was on my side in this. "Twice."

Mom nodded again. "Right. Thought it was recent. You can't actually jump, can you?"

"What!? You saw me, didn't you?"

"Well, yes. What I mean is, go ahead. Jump. Upstairs to your room, say."

I tried.

"Go on," she said mildly.

It didn't work.

If she nods her head again . . .

Mom nodded.

I screamed.

She nodded again.

I couldn't even scream. I just stood there with my mouth gaping.

"Calm down. Come with me."

Mom led me upstairs into their bedroom and then through the door to the upper deck with the outside hot tub. It was twenty degrees outside, but we hadn't had more snow so the deck was either clear where it had been swept or icy where the snow had packed down to a slippery crust. She went over to the railing and swung open the gate.

The gate's there for the dead of winter, when the accumulated snow has actually buried the bottom floor of the house. It happens most years, but right now, even though there was a good six-foot deep drift against the wall below, there was still a twelve-foot drop down to the snow's surface.

Mom pointed over the edge and said, "What do you see?" She stood aside to let me look. I stepped forward and looked down and she shoved me from behind. Hard.

I twisted, clawing for the railing but I was already out and falling, feeling the drop.

My own mother.

I didn't reach the snow.

I was under my bed, in my room, nestled in the cushions.

I heard Mom come in from the deck and shut the door behind her. She came into the room, looked around, and then crouched down, to look me in the face.

"So *that's* your safe place. Makes sense. It always was."

"Get *away* from me you evil woman."

Mom grinned. "The drift would've cushioned your fall."

"I thought *Dad* was the ruthless one."

"Your dad is a big softie." She held up three fingers. "So *that's* the third time."

Mom jumped us to New York City, an alley in the West Village. She was wearing a blonde wig and enormous sunglasses. I was wearing a wig, too, which itched like the dickens, but it was my idea, more for fun. She walked us east until we hit Washington Square, and we sat on a bench in the sun. It was thirty degrees warmer here, which meant forty-five or so, but the air was still and the sky was clear, which meant sitting in the sun felt lovely.

"I always liked this park. Your Dad and I visited it for the first time the day after I met him. There were jugglers and musicians and vendors and someone even had a monkey. Summer, of course. Two people tried to sell us drugs. We came back later that week. A bunch of NYU students did *A Midsummer Night's Dream.*"

I looked around and didn't see a stage.

"Where?"

"Everywhere. It ranged from the playground over there, across the dry fountain, up to the dog run. The audience had to follow them around. It was really cool."

Mom was really big on Shakespeare.

I said, "All the park's a stage, and all the men and women merely players."

Mom pointed at the walkway to the west side of the park. "They have their exits and their entrances; and one man in his time plays many parts, his acts being seven ages."

She can go on for hours so I butted in, "If you like it."

"What do you smell?" she asked.

I closed my eyes then wrinkled my nose. "Cigarette smoke."

"Yuck. You're right—guy on the next bench just lit up. Let's move."

We took the diagonal pathway toward the southeast corner

of the park, passing a fenced playground. The young mothers who clustered around the entrance while their kids played were not smokers.

We moved around the edge, close to the wrought iron fence but away from the entrance, to a grassy spot between two trees and a bush.

"This is better anyway," Mom said. "Screened from most sides. Try again."

I inhaled. "Grass. They mowed this morning. Car exhaust. Ugh. Some diesel. I hate diesel. Something tasty. One of those vendors. Grilled chicken? No. Falafel!" I opened my eyes. "Can we buy some falafel?"

Mom shrugged. "Perhaps." She stepped closer and jumped me back to our house.

I raised my eyebrows. Mom went into her room and came back with a five-dollar bill. "Here. Go buy us some falafel."

I blinked. My stomach rumbled. "We were *already* there," I said.

Mom smiled. "So we were."

I tried. Nothing happened. *Shit!* I took off the wig and threw it onto the kitchen table. "Do I gotta be starving or something?" I winced. My chances of going to school were dropping rapidly, especially if Mom told Dad I couldn't control it.

"Shhhh," Mom said. She stepped behind me and placed her palms on my shoulders. "Close your eyes. Remember the smells? Mowed grass? Car and truck fumes. And . . ."

"Falafel," I said. But she didn't hear me. I was back in the park, between the bush and the trees, a five-dollar bill clutched in my hand.

My knees buckled and I dropped, ending up crouched on the ground, one hand flat to the dirt.

I don't know why. I've been jumped by my parents thousands of times, but this was only the fourth time I'd jumped by myself. It was the first time I'd jumped without being upset or frightened. Or about to die.

And the other three times I'd ended up curled in the cushions under the bed. Not standing.

I bought two flatbread-wrapped falafel sandwiches with lettuce, tomatoes, and yoghurt dressing and returned to the little screened spot. I tried to think about what it smelled like in my room, or the kitchen, or even the bathroom, but all I could smell was the falafel. I held the bag behind my back and exhaled.

The one place at home that had an overwhelming distinctive smell was the springhouse. It was a thick mix of steam and sulphur and a touch of mildew from the wet corners, though Mom attacked it with a brush and chlorine bleach every month or so. When you stand in there, it's like standing in an equatorial rain forest, like the interior of Borneo or deep in the Amazon basin. But with sulphur.

There was more powdery snow in the covered walkway and the wind cut like a knife. I walked quickly to the house. Through the glass in the kitchen door I could see Mom seated at the table, her elbows resting on the surface, her hands clenched tightly together. When I started stamping my feet to knock off the worst of the snow, she jerked and looked around. Her hands went flat on the table and her shoulders dropped.

I came through, still stamping my feet, and put the falafel on the table.

"They might be cold."

And they were, a little. But delicious.

"Stop that!" Dad said, from where he was reading on the couch.

I was jumping from my room to the living room, back and forth. I froze, looking at him, surprised.

"I'm practicing."

"Do you have to do it in *here*?"

"I could jump to Washington Square Park instead."

He held up his hands. "Uh, no. Do it here. I'd rather you weren't jumping where people could see you."

I jumped back up to my room.

I was using smell, mostly. Sure I was picturing the places, but smell was really helping. I had a cinnamon-scented votive candle burning on my windowsill. I also had a small fire burning in the colossal living room fireplace. It was piñon wood that Dad brought all the way from the Southwest, so the smell downstairs was also distinctive.

Though my parents didn't know it, I'd also been back to Washington Square a few times. The falafel guy was gone so *that* smell wasn't there anymore, but it was still the *memory* of that smell that let me jump to the little nook by the playground, even when it was after dark there.

I snuffed the candle. If Dad was freaking out because I was jumping in the living room, maybe I should try someplace else. I jumped to the springhouse and back to my room a few times, but the steam-laden air began dampening my clothes and I could smell the sulphur even in my room.

I went back to jumping down to the fireplace and eventually Dad put his book aside and said, "Let's try something else."

"What—"

We were someplace else.

Dad's that quick. From the couch he'd jumped, snagged me, and jumped again before I could say "one thousand."

I blinked. It was late afternoon, wherever we were, but the sun was much higher in the sky than it was up by the Arctic Circle. It was desert, American Southwest I thought, or Northern Mexico—very rugged, not flat. There was mesquite and ocotillo and ground-hugging prickly pear cactus, too. Temperature was pleasantly warm, even on the hot side of comfortable, with a dusty wind blowing fine grit through the air.

"Where are we?"

"West Texas. We're near the Eyrie, on the eastern side of Big Bend Ranch State Park."

The Eyrie is Dad's old cliff house, a place up a box canyon several hundred feet from the canyon floor. Mom and Dad used to live there, but when they decided to have me, they moved to the house in Canada. Dad still has some books there, I think. I've been there a couple of times, as a toddler, but Dad wasn't comfortable with me being near the cliff's edge.

"Okay. Why?"

"It's pretty comfortable this time of year, especially compared to northern Canada. There are very few people out here. And, most important of all, it *isn't the living room.*"

"Oh."

He shrugged. "This was where I learned how to jump to places I could see, but that I hadn't been to yet." He turned and jumped to a spot a hundred feet away and called back, "Like this." He jumped again, another hundred feet. Then another hundred. "See?" he yelled. I barely heard him over the gusting wind.

He jumped back again. "It was after your grandmother was killed and I was out here walking. I couldn't stand to be around other people and I needed to be doing something, but I twisted my ankle and it hurt like the dickens to walk."

I stared at Dad. He hardly ever talked about his mother, especially about her death.

He continued. "Most of the things I've discovered about jumping have been like that. From necessity."

I nodded. "Like when you were prisoner on Martha's Vineyard?"

"Yes. Like that. Or figuring out that I could fall big distances and jump away without carrying the accumulated momentum with me. Like we just did, actually."

"We didn't fall, did we? My ears didn't pop. The altitude can't be *that* different."

"In Canada we're closer to the pole—to the earth's axis of rotation—so our rotational velocity was less than it is here. I don't know what it is exactly, but south of the house, at sixty degrees latitude, it's 233 meters per second. Here, we're below thirty degrees latitude where the rotation is 349 meters per second. If we'd retained that speed when we jumped, we would have arrived here with the ground speeding eastward under us at over 116 meters per second."

I did a rough conversion in my head. "That's over four hundred kilometers per hour."

"And if you jumped to the equator the difference would be twice that. Good thing we're *not* carrying the velocity difference. It would probably rip our limbs off."

I shuddered.

"Enough of that," Dad said. "I'm pretty sure you can jump home now. Do what you need to do to acquire a jump site here."

I closed my eyes and sniffed. The dust was overlaid with something that smelled like old railway ties or telephone poles. "What smells like roofing tar?" I asked.

Dad pointed to a low-lying shrub with small green leaves and yellow flowers, off to my right. "Creosote bush."

I jumped back to my room, then jumped right back again, the slight tarry smell locking it in easily.

Dad nodded, satisfied. "So, experiment. You see any people, stay away from them. They're probably just visiting the park but they could be drug traffickers or *coyotes*."

He opened his mouth to explain but I said, "People smugglers, I know."

"Yeah. But the regular folk are dangerous, too. They see you out here, they'll want to try and *rescue* you." He shook his head. "Don't let them see you jump, either. It's not just you I'm concerned about. Those who watch for us like to squeeze every drop of information out of witnesses. And when the lemon is squeezed, it's hard on the lemon." He waited until I nodded. "Right. Sunscreen and a hat and probably boots. I've been stabbed through athletic shoes by this damn prickly pear. Hell, the lechuguilla will get you through a leather boot."

He vanished.

I went and did as he said—sunscreen, hat, boots. He didn't mention the damn rattlesnakes.

I was just walking around. It was good to be out of the house and to feel the wind and sun on my skin. The gusty wind was shaking the brush and there were some tumbleweeds caught in the creosote that made a rattling sound, which is why I didn't hear the snake's rattle until I'd almost stepped on it.

It struck and I flinched away, to my room, and *it landed on the carpet.* In my room.

"Oh, shit!" I said and hopped up the rungs and onto my bed.

It was a little guy, with only a few rattles, but it had the triangular head. It was limestone gray with darker bands that had almost been invisible in the desert, but it stood out in stark contrast to my green carpet. It coiled up again and looked around. The room was colder than the southern hillside it had been on. It moved across the floor with that figure-S sideways motion, past one of my snowboarding boots and then went *into* the other boot, at the foot of the bed. I jumped down and stepped on the top of the boot, pinching it shut. There was a bumping, thrashing vibration which I could feel even through my hiking boot, but I kept my weight on it.

I bent down and kept the boot top closed with my hand while I took my foot off, then clamped it shut with both hands. My heart was still thudding but my breathing was slowing now. I was really glad it hadn't crawled into the cushions under my bed.

Back in the desert I tossed the boot away from me, about fifteen feet. It fell over and the snake spilled out rather agitated, shaking its rattle and moving its head around, looking for something to bite. I held my breath, ready to jump away if it came my direction, but it took off into the brush and I recovered my boot, putting it back in my room.

After that I saved the sightseeing for when I was standing still. While I moved, I kept my eyes on the ground.

I got pretty good at seeing a spot and jumping to it, even though I'd never been there. Three days later I could do it with binoculars, moving up to half a mile if I had good light. On the fourth day I found the pit.

I remembered splashing in the cold water there as a kid. I jumped back to the cabin and asked Mom if my memory was right, or was I imagining things. She said, "Jump there, to the rim above. I'll do the same."

When I arrived, Mom was there, a quarter of the way around the rim from me. I jumped to where she stood.

"Yes, this is the place." She scuffed the rock she stood on, right at the edge. "Your father used to drop terrorists off this point into the water. Well, about ten feet out, that is." She pointed down to the riot of green that covered the sandy island in the middle of the dark water. "Even when they couldn't swim they'd splash over to the island, but if you're not set right, dropping fifty feet into the water is rough."

"Have you ever done it?" I asked.

"No, when I took people here I just put them on the island." She looked at the expression on my face. "What's wrong?"

"I meant have you ever jumped into the water from up here?"

Mom laughed. "Oops. Uh, no. I tried several times but I always jumped away before I hit the surface. Scaredy cat, I guess. I tried breaking it down to smaller increments but I never managed higher than twenty feet."

I stepped up beside her to peek over the edge, then took an involuntary step backward and made a squeaking noise.

Mom looked concerned. "Huh. I didn't think you were scared of heights, Cent."

I glared at her. "I quite *like* heights. But I have this brand-new fear of being *pushed.*"

"Huh? Oh—" She started laughing, then tried to stop, but couldn't. I glared harder and she laughed more. I held up my finger and she covered her mouth, trying to stifle the laughter but it wasn't working.

She turned away to try and get control of her expression and I pushed *her* off the edge.

FIVE

Davy: Realty

Millie chose the town, doing her research from a Minneapolis Public Library computer. Davy activated their cover.

The cover identity was actually old. Davy and Millie had been "growing" it ever since Cent was born. The family "Ross" annually paid state and federal income tax, social security, and capital gains tax from very healthy investments, filed returns, and purchased items by check and bank card every so often in the city of Cleveland, Ohio.

Millie had wanted the identity and funds for Cent's college years. Davy wanted it as a form of life insurance, in case anything ever happened to Millie or Davy, so Cent would have something, someplace to go to, some*one* to be.

But Cleveland was not the place they decided on.

Millie showed him her choice on the map. "I like *this* town. Only one high school so there won't be a poor school and a rich school. Generally conservative but that's offset a bit by good cultural and ethnic diversity. They have a moderate tax base for the school. Some crime, but well below big-city rates and, best of all, the local police aren't jack-booted thugs—the entire department has only ten deputies."

Davy asked, "What other law enforcement?"

Millie said, "There's a highway patrol unit in the county

and, of course, on the rez there's the Navajo Nation Police. Also the Bureau of Indian Affairs Police, federal marshals, and some FBI, but the nearest FBI field office is two hundred miles away, in the state capital."

"Military?"

"There might be a DIA unit at one of the Air Force bases but that's halfway across the state."

"Okay," said Davy. "I'll go check it out."

His nearest jump site was in Albuquerque. He joined a gambling junket heading across to Las Vegas, and left the tour bus on the interstate as it cruised past the exit.

He walked up the state road until he was well past the ramps and held out an arm, three twenties in his hand. He offered the money to the first person who stopped, in exchange for driving him the last thirty miles into town.

The man was going farther than New Prospect, but it was only a matter of an extra ten minutes for him to divert through town instead of sticking to the bypass. He dropped Davy where the road crossed Main near the hospital, thanked him for the "gas money," and drove on.

Davy bought the local newspaper at an Allsup's convenience store and jumped back to the Yukon to read it.

The lead story was about a hoped-for improvement in the local economy based on higher natural gas prices and new wells in the area. The high school football team finished six and six for the season. A local man was arrested for termiting homes.

Davy imagined a man introducing pale heaps of multilegged insects into soft wood floors and walls, but further down the column, the reporter explained that termiting was the process of stealing fixtures, copper tubing, and copper wire from houses sitting empty.

For budget reasons, the town Christmas decorations were going up a week later than usual, and the school district was settling out of court in an ongoing lawsuit involving a false arrest.

Davy turned to the classifieds, which took up most of the

rest of the paper. There were a *lot* of homes for sale, also cars, tractors, mowers, bicycles, kitchen appliances, and services of all kinds. The "Wanted to Buy" section was much smaller.

The real estate agents' paid ads, with head shots of the agents, ran down the edge of the classifieds. Davy cringed when the first agent, a dark brunette with her hair pulled tightly back in a severe bun, reminded him of Hyacinth Pope, the woman instrumental in imprisoning him on Martha's Vineyard.

It wasn't her, of course. This woman's apparent age was what Hyacinth's had been sixteen years before, and Hyacinth had spent that period in prison. He was willing to bet that Hyacinth didn't look the same, now.

Nevertheless he moved his thumb down the page and picked another woman Realtor whose hair was, to put it kindly, as far from dark, tight, and severe as possible.

He jumped to New Prospect's Main Street and walked east until he came to the Dunbar, an old hotel, newly renovated to a bed and breakfast.

They had a vacancy and he registered using the new ID (David Ross) and called Ms. Meriwether from his room.

"It's 'Mrs.' Martha also works," she told him on the phone. "Are you trying to sell a house?" She sounded unenthusiastic.

"Buying. We're relocating here in early January."

Cent had wanted to start school immediately. Davy had suggested the following school year, in the fall, "moving" in the summer. Cent hadn't bought it, but Millie talked her into the two-month delay. Davy still felt like he had lost the fight.

Mrs. Meriwether sounded surprised. "Oh! Right." She paused for a second. Davy could swear she was holding the phone away from her and taking deep breaths. When she spoke again she sounded suspiciously casual.

"What are you looking for?"

"Something close to the high school. Walking distance."

"Bedrooms?"

"Yes. Uh, bathrooms, too."

She laughed. "You're a riot. How many of each?"

He blushed. "At least two of each." He didn't really care. He had no intention whatsoever of *sleeping* in that house. Why, people could probably drive *right up to it*!

"And if I had something with more rooms? Would you look at that?"

"Certainly." Davy remembered the guy who'd been arrested for selling off the fixtures in empty homes. "As long as they haven't been 'termited.' "

"Of course not, Mr. Ross. I don't handle those kind of homes. When will you be in town?"

He glanced out the window. The street was darkening. He was one time zone east of the cabin, which put local time just after four in the afternoon. "I'm here now, but I was thinking about tomorrow morning, if that works."

"Certainly! Where are you staying?"

"The Dunbar Bed and Breakfast."

"Isn't that the cutest place! I can pick you up there and show you a few places and start you on the paperwork."

Paperwork? "What time?"

"Any time after 8:30."

"That works for me."

He returned to New Prospect the next morning and met the Realtor in the Dunbar's breakfast parlor. Her hair was as blonde and bouffant as her picture had advertised, like Dolly Parton in the eighties.

The paperwork turned out to be a credit application. He pushed it back across the table to Mrs. Meriwether without touching pen to it.

"Did you already arrange financing? I'm not one to brag, but I've gotten some awfully good deals, requiring very little down payment."

"We'll be paying cash," Davy said.

Mrs. Meriwether tried to say, "Oh," but her mouth just made the shape, not the sound.

Davy gestured to the waitress, pointing at Mrs. Meriwether's cup. "More coffee, please?"

By the time the waitress had refilled their cups, Mrs. Meriwether had recovered. "So you must've had good equity in your previous home."

Davy made a neutral, "Um."

"I'm sure we can find you some excellent candidates! Where will you be working? Do we need to think about that for your location? Not that anything in town is more than fifteen minutes away."

"Just close to the school. We're self-employed."

She raised her eyebrows and he felt compelled to add, "Consultants. We work with NGOs dealing with emergency relief efforts around the world."

Mrs. Meriwether nodded. "My church does some stuff in Africa."

"Oh? Where?"

"Africa."

Davy winced. Second largest continent. Over a billion people. Fifty-six countries. You could overlay all of the U.S., China, India, and Europe on Africa's landmass.

"Oh—*Africa.*"

He'd promised Millie he wouldn't buy the first house he looked at or reject them *all* as unsuitable because of his "paranoid security concerns," so he stuck it out through six different showings, then asked to be taken back to the second one they'd seen, on Thunderbird Road, ten minutes' walk to the school, either through the woods, or along the road.

He picked that one because of its seclusion, because of its proximity to the high school, *and* because of his "paranoid security concerns."

While trees screened the house from the surrounding lots even in the winter, they weren't so close to the building that they would conceal anybody approaching.

He showed Millie the house in the early light the next morning, then met with the Realtor again.

"This is the most expensive home on my list," Mrs. Meriwether said. "But they took a job in the Bay Area and now they're paying two mortgages and have been for over a year and a half. I'm sure we can get them to drop the price by almost a quarter."

"That's okay. I'll pay the asking price."

"But the asking price was inflated. They *expected* to be lowballed! They've got some equity on their loan. It's not like they're upside down!"

Davy had to ask what that meant.

"When someone is upside down, or underwater, they owe more on their loan than the property is worth."

"Oh." He added these terms to "termiting." "So for over a year and a half, they've had to pay two mortgage payments?"

Mrs. Meriwether nodded her head. "Right. So they'll very likely take a substantial reduction in the asking price."

Desperate and running out of cash? At least they were employed, but that didn't mean they didn't need the money. "Are you afraid the deal won't go through if I offer to pay the asking price?"

"What? No. They'll probably break their necks getting back to us. But you shouldn't spend money you don't have to!"

"Uh, Mrs. Meriwether, don't you get a bigger commission if I pay the asking price?"

Mrs. Meriwether shut her mouth with a snap. She put her hands primly together and said, "So. Offer the asking price?"

Davy frowned. He didn't want all of Mrs. Meriwether's friends discussing the family that paid asking price in a buyer's market. "Offer them ninety percent."

They closed two weeks later.

SIX

"Or is it to be a food fight?"

New Prospect is in the American Southwest, about two hours' drive from Durango. If you do the maps thing you'll find that this circle could put New Prospect in Arizona, New Mexico, or Utah, as well as Colorado. And the map thing would show that there *isn't* a town called New Prospect in any of those states. An internet search shows towns of that name in North Carolina, Tennessee, and Texas, and a place called Nova Prospekt in Eastern Europe near the Black Sea.

That's because my New Prospect doesn't exist, not by *that* name. And if I'm lying about the name, keep in mind that I *might* be lying about other things, too.

But there *is* a town, somewhere, that we drove into, about lunchtime, in early January, in a large U-Haul truck, with Mom driving, Dad fidgeting on the passenger side, and me bouncing up and down between them.

The town was situated on an elevated bench, one side backed onto the mountainside, the other sloped down into the arid scrub of the lower foothills. Ten inches of snow had fallen the week before but the roads had been plowed. Though melted snow had refrozen into occasional patches of black ice, the asphalt on State Road 87 was mostly clear and dry.

"That's the municipal complex," Dad said, pointing.

"Courthouse, city hall, and police. The middle school is over there—see, between those two buildings?"

I knew all this. I'd been studying the town for a month, using online maps and satellite images, blogs, photo galleries, and official and unofficial websites. But Dad was nervous, so I let him rattle on.

"The middle school used to be the high school, but they built a new one when they decided it made more sense to bring kids from this side of the reservation here, rather than bus them forty-five miles to the on-reservation school."

We went a few more blocks and passed the County Medical Center, a three-story hospital with an attached building for medical professionals, and a helicopter pad near the ER driveway.

Mom turned onto Main Street, an old-fashioned avenue where the new buildings were built to blend with the late nineteenth-century architecture. The streets were concrete but with a surface molded like cobblestones. I'd walked on real cobblestones in Europe and nearly broken my ankle. I wondered what the local emergency room frequency for knee and ankle injuries was. Good thing it was only a few blocks away.

Though it was mostly cloudy, a patch of open sky was letting the sun hit the north side of the street. A bunch of teens were out in the sunshine on the corner outside a coffee shop. I stared at them as we went by.

Dad saw me looking and glanced over at the corner, reading the sign on the coffee shop. "*Java, East of Krakatoa*. Way, *way* east. I wonder if any of those kids have seen the movie?"

"What movie?"

"It was called, *Krakatoa, East of Java*. Krakatau, the volcano, is actually *west* of Java, but that's Hollywood for you. At least the store has it right."

"Indonesia," I said, half asking.

"Yeah. Biggest volcanic eruption in modern history. An explosion, really. Heard thousands of miles away."

I was only half listening, more intent on the kids—what they looked like, what they were wearing, but it was hard to tell since they were bundled up for the cold. At least my snow-boarding jacket would fit in.

"Did you hear it?" I asked, absently.

Mom laughed and Dad said, "I'm not *that* old. It was in the 1800s. I wasn't even born when the *movie* came out. I caught part of it on afternoon TV when I was a boy."

We left the downtown area behind and threaded toward the lower edge of town, passing the high school and then a set of four grain silos that reminded me of our trip to Merredin, Western Australia.

The property sloped deeply away from the road. A garage with a short drive was level with the road, but the house itself was down the hill. A gravel driveway ran all the way down to the house, but it was scary steep.

The snow was piled high to the sides and Dad and I got out to direct Mom before she backed down the hill.

"Who plowed the driveways?" I asked.

Dad said, "Mrs. Meriwether, the Realtor, got someone to do it."

My heart skipped a beat when the truck backed over the edge, the thing was still at an angle to the road and it lurched alarmingly to one side, but then it completed the turn and righted itself while still angled down the steep hill. It did slip backward once, when all four wheels were on the packed snow, but Mom got it down the driveway and stopped beside the house without further scares.

When she'd climbed down from the cab she said, "I'm afraid it won't make it up the hill with that snow there."

Dad looked around. The property was wooded, a mixture of cedar, piñon, and a bunch of bare deciduous trees I couldn't identify without their leaves. Despite the bare limbs, the combination was thick enough to hide the neighboring houses from view. "I'll take care of the snow before its time to get it back up the hill."

"Oh, look," Mom said.

There was a banner across the door saying "Welcome!"

"Mrs. Meriwether?" Mom said.

Dad shrugged. "Probably. Like I said, the local housing market is in the dumps. She was . . . *pleased* with the commission."

The house was built into the hillside, with the top floor exposed all around but the bottom floor exposed only on the downhill side, opening onto a large deck that stuck out over the rapidly steepening hillside. Down below, through the trees, I could see a glint of sunlight on water.

"What's that?" I asked.

"The creek at the rear property line." Dad thought for a moment. "They told me the name of it, but I don't remember. Some Indian name. Diné maybe, or Ute. It's on the plat I got at the closing."

I carried boxes into the house and we took a couple of disassembled bedsteads and leaned them against the porch, but Dad and Mom jumped the majority of stuff from inside the truck to inside the house. We could've done without the truck entirely but that would've looked odd, a house full of furniture and other belongings, showing up as if by magic. We could hear the occasional car going by on the road above, but we'd nearly emptied the truck before one slowed and turned into the upper driveway with a quick double tap of the horn. I looked up and saw a woman climb out of a large SUV.

Mom came to the door. "The Realtor, I'll bet."

Mrs. Meriwether was a middle-aged, big-haired blonde wearing a full-length down-filled coat. A boy in a sheepskin jacket walked behind her, dragging his feet. He was carrying a large wicker hamper.

"My goodness, girl, aren't you cold?" the woman said.

I was wearing a long-sleeved shirt but I'd been in and out of the house. If she wanted cold I could take her to our other place. The temperature in the Yukon had been twenty below zero Fahrenheit that morning. Here, with the sun shining, it was fifty degrees warmer. Which, admittedly, was right at freezing, but it felt like spring to me.

Mom spoke from the porch. "Hello. Mrs. Meriwether, I presume?"

"And you must be Mrs. Ross."

I tried to keep my face still. That was the name we were using. I even had a nondriving state ID and a Social Security card with that name on it, but I wasn't used to it. "Call me Millie, please," said Mom. First names were the same. We'd agreed that it would be too confusing otherwise.

In fact, Dad said, "Introduce yourselves with first names only. Someone asks who you are, again, just the first name. They push for your last name, you'll have time to remember what it is now."

He put it like that. Don't think about who you're pretending to be. Don't think of it as a lie. Instead, think of it as *who you are now.*

"I'm Martha. I'm so glad to meet you. Did you have any trouble with the roads? The snows last week were just awful, but I guess the interstate must've been cleared." Almost as an afterthought she said, "This is Grant, my youngest. He's a freshman at Beckwourth High School—your new school." She turned to me. "Aren't you the spitting image of your mother, uh—"

I stuck out my hand. "I'm Cent, ma'am. Like a penny." I added the obligatory, "It's short for Millicent." If I didn't explain, they always asked.

"What nice manners. Very nice to meet you, Cent. Oh," she said, gesturing at the basket Grant was carrying. "This is for y'all. You can't have your kitchen set up yet. I hope you like chicken."

Grant helped me carry in the two bedsteads we'd left outside while Mom set the food out. He was slightly taller than me, but younger, I thought.

We took my bed around the outside, tromping through the snow, to get to the lower level, via the deck. Mom and Dad had the master suite, which was upstairs, as was the kitchen, formal dining room, and a formal living room. Downstairs were two more bedrooms opening onto a large family room.

"The pool table came with the house," I said as we took off

our snow-packed boots just inside the sliding glass door to the deck.

"I know," said Grant.

Of course he knew. His mother was the Realtor after all. "You've been here?"

"Yeah. Naomi and I have been taking care of the grounds—sweeping the leaves off the deck and porch, keeping the weeds back from the house. It's been on the market for over two years." He looked toward the stairs. "If we finished early enough, we'd shoot some pool. Uh, I *think* Mom knew, but we didn't exactly discuss it."

"Got it. Who's Naomi?"

"Big sister. She's a senior at Beckwourth. Off to college next year."

"Only sister?"

"Yeah." We set the bedstead in my new bedroom, next to the box springs and mattress leaning against the wall.

"Are you a junior?" Grant asked.

"I don't know," I said.

"Huh?"

"I was homeschooled. We've been out of the country. I'll be taking placement tests before school starts up again."

Grant nodded. "Next Tuesday."

It was Thursday.

"The Gorgon," Grant added.

"Huh?"

"The guidance counselor. She'll be testing you. They call her Morgan the Gorgon."

"She turn somebody to stone?"

"Dr. Morgan *does* have this stare. But it's really the problem kids—the ones she sees for discipline problems. That's what *they* call her." He shrugged. "I got to test out of Algebra I so *I* like her."

Dr. Morgan had a sense of humor but it was very dry. My first hint was a brooch of Medusa's head dangling from Perseus' hand, like the famous statue in Florence.

The tests were computerized, given in the testing center, a small room lined with computers, connected to her office. She set me up for the science exam first, and twenty-eight minutes later I stuck my head back in her office.

"Did you have a question, Millicent? Sometimes those stupid computers act up—did it freeze?"

I shook my head. "No, ma'am. I'm finished."

"Dear, you have an hour and a half to take it. You don't need to give up so soon."

I raised my eyebrows. "Give up? I answered every question, then went back and double-checked my answers." Had I screwed up? Was I supposed to sit there for the whole time? I thought I was being careful as it was—I didn't want to make another stupid mistake like failing to take altitude into consideration.

Dr. Morgan rolled her chair over to her desk computer and moused through a couple of screens. "Oh."

"Did I do okay?"

Dr. Morgan cleared her throat. "Well enough. I'll set up the math assessment. Why don't you go get a drink of water and, if you need to, use the restroom?"

Mom had left me with the understanding that I'd be taking tests in the morning and afternoon, but when she showed up to take me to lunch, I was done.

I *did* have trouble with the history assessment. I was so worried about the math and science and language arts that I thought my general reading in history would be good enough.

We sat with Dr. Morgan and she analyzed my results. "I am not a fan of the state history requirement, but every state in the union does it and ours is no exception. You're very strong in science and math. I can put you in precalculus immediately and Biology II. We can definitely place you out of composition one and two. My thoughts are to bring you in as a junior. I could see an argument for bringing you in as a senior, but you're only just sixteen. . . . What do you think?"

She looked at me, not Mom.

Mom and I exchanged glances. We'd talked about this possibility. Softly, I said, "Sophomore, please."

Dr. Morgan's eyebrows lifted.

Mom spoke. "As you said, Dr. Morgan, Cent is only just sixteen. We've been out of the country most of her life but we've worked hard—*she's* worked hard—to make sure her academics are up to par. But she's . . ."

"Really unsocialized," I said.

Dr. Morgan laughed outright, then put her hand to her mouth. She said, "You seem quite mature, actually."

Mom smiled. "Well, yes—with adults. But she hasn't really had much interaction with teens or even children when she was younger. If we were just concerned about academics, we'd continue homeschooling."

I nodded firmly. "Right."

"Not my *usual* situation," said Dr. Morgan. "I'm usually fighting with parents who want their kids to skip a grade or, worse, to avoid repeating a grade they've failed. You could be in college in one or two years, easily."

Mom touched her tongue to her lips then looked at me. "Could you give me a moment with Dr. Morgan, Cent?"

I frowned. This wasn't like Mom. "Uh, okay. I'll go look around, right?"

"Right."

As the door shut I looked both ways down the hall. Though school proper wouldn't start for three more days, the teachers were back. But the only person in sight was at the far end of the hall walking in the other direction. I jumped back to the testing center, near the still-ajar connecting door to Dr. Morgan's office.

"—I'm no longer practicing," Mom was saying, "but I was a family therapist for ten years before we went abroad. Cent is going to have a big enough problem learning how to interact with her peer group when they're the same age. Put her in with kids one or two years older and it will make it harder."

Dr. Morgan was silent for a moment, then said, "I can see that but you *do* realize she's academically ahead of most of the *seniors* at this school, not to mention the sophomores. There's going to be friction there."

"Certainly. But look at it from the other side. If you had a classmate who was substantially brighter than you, wouldn't it be *more* annoying if she was substantially younger, too? It's Cent's curse to be profoundly gifted. She'll always have a good chance of being the smartest kid in the class."

"All the more reason to get her up to college where she can find that place where she *isn't* the smartest kid."

"That will help with intellectual challenges but socially, it will be a disaster. I don't want my daughter starting college as a lonely, estranged, unhappy young woman whose only point of esteem is her intellect."

"No," Dr. Morgan said dryly. "That's what high school's for."

Mom laughed. "Precisely."

I jerked my head at that and my shoulder brushed against the wall, making a slight noise. I jumped back to the hallway.

There was a gray-haired woman walking down the hall toward me, but luckily, her head was down, examining a clipboard she held in one hand. She nearly walked into me before noticing I was there.

"Oh!" She glanced at the closed door to Dr. Morgan's office. "What are you doing here?"

"My mother is talking with Dr. Morgan."

She looked at me directly. "I don't recognize you. Are you one of our students?"

"I hope to be. I've been testing this morning. We just moved to town." I held out my hand. "I'm Cent. Millicent Ross."

She stared at my hand, then shook it briefly, barely squeezing as if she was avoiding too much contact. "I'm Ms. Mc-Claren, the assistant principal."

"Nice to meet you," I said.

The door opened. Mom and Dr. Morgan were still talking as they came out. "I don't see any problem with that. I'll arrange with . . . ah, Janet. Have you met our newest student?"

"Yes. Where did she transfer from?"

"Abroad. Where did you come from last, Ms. Ross?"

"Most recently, Canada," Mom said truthfully. That very

morning, in fact. Dad was not letting us sleep in New Prospect, despite our supposed residency.

"This is our assistant principal, Janet McClaren. Cent here was homeschooled, so we've been doing placement tests."

"Oh," said Ms. McClaren. "Any, uh, deficits? Remedial requirements?" She looked at Mom. "We often have our work cut out for us, with homeschool transfers."

Mom raised her eyebrows.

Dr. Morgan said irritably, "No more so than some of the kids coming out of our own middle school."

Mom said mildly. "I think Dr. Morgan is satisfied with Millicent's test results."

Ms. McClaren raised her eyebrows and looked at Dr. Morgan. "No trouble entering as a freshman?"

"Sophomore," Dr. Morgan said firmly. "She'll need the state history, but that's it."

"She'll be able to catch up in math, science?"

"Advanced placement, Janet. You really need to trust me to do *my* job."

"We should go," Mom said. "I'll get the supply list off the school website and we'll come back on Monday to talk with Mr. Kinlichee about Cent's electives."

As we walked down the hall I heard Ms. McClaren say again, "Math *and* science?"

"Yes, Janet. Math *and* science."

I waited until we were outside before I said, "I don't think I like Ms. McClaren."

Mom made a noise in her throat. It wasn't a yes or a no but I don't think she liked Ms. McClaren, either.

I've been in crowds before, in all sorts of places: the Piazzo San Marco in Venice; Tokyo train stations where the attendants shove you through the doors to pack more in; and, once, Times Square, midnight, New Year's Eve.

But they were all strangers.

Well, the kids at James Beckwourth High School *were*

strangers but they were strangers that I had to get to know. I'd be seeing them every weekday for the rest of the school year.

It didn't help that I'd slept badly, waking several times from anxiety dreams where I was wearing just my underwear or said the wrong thing in front of large classrooms where the rows of desks went back and back and back until they disappeared into the distance. In that dream, guess where *my* seat was.

Before school started I was breathing rapidly and my heart was pounding. I nearly jumped away, several times, just walking down the long hall to my first class.

I felt like puking.

It was an obstacle course. There were kids standing around, talking in pairs or groups. You could usually go around these. There were kids walking without looking where they were going, and there were kids who made room for you by swerving to let you by. These were in the minority.

I did my eel thing, like when I was a child, chasing pigeons in the piazza, sliding sideways and turning my shoulders. My backpack was light—the school issued books for home and kept copies in the classroom, too. But things were so crowded that more than once I was clouted by someone's shoulder or backpack. Once, one of them said, "Excuse me," but mostly it was, "Hey!" and "Watch where you're going!"

By the time I'd dropped my coat in my locker and reached my first class, Mr. Hill's Biology II, I felt like a rabbit with dogs on my tail, and I ducked through the door like the classroom was my burrow. There were only two students in the room and Mr. Hill, a thin man with long, gray hair braided down his back, who sat hunched over a laptop connected to a projector at the front of the class.

I walked closer and he glanced up.

"Yes? Oh." He glanced down at a sheet of paper. "Millicent Ross, right?"

"Yes, sir," I said.

"Welcome to Beckwourth. What do you like to be called? Millie?"

"Cent, please. My mom is Millie. Her first name is Millicent, too."

"Cent, okay." He wrote that down on the page. "We do assigned seating. You don't have any vision or hearing issues, do you?"

"No, sir."

"Okay, then. I'm going to put you back here." He led me to a seat two thirds of the way to the rear, and at the wall farthest from the door. "Let me know if this causes any problems. Today we're doing a review of cellular microstructures—from chapter sixteen. We covered it in December but a review is always a good idea after the break." He pointed at a row of bookshelves between the two large windows. "You got your home copy already, right?"

I nodded.

"Great. Feel free to grab one for class but remember to put it back." He sighed, "They're not all so good about putting them back."

"Yes, sir."

I grabbed a book while a few more students filtered in, but the majority didn't come until after the bell rang.

Mr. Hill introduced me in class but, unlike every movie I'd seen about high school, he didn't make me stand and say a few words. As part of the review, he did ask questions and, once, called on me. "What's the purpose of the Golgi bodies?"

I licked my lips. One of the things reading and movies had shown me was that kids don't like a know-it-all. I tried to give a minimal answer. "It's like a post office for the cell. It modifies, packages, and distributes macromolecules to be excreted or used inside the cell."

Mr. Hill smiled. "Exactly. What kind of macromolecules?"

"Carbohydrates," I said. "And proteoglycans."

He stared at me blankly and I thought I wasn't being detailed enough. "And Golgi antiapoptotic protein."

He raised his eyebrows. "You had me at carbohydrates. What's an antiapoptotic protein? That's not in the textbook."

"It has some role in protecting the cell from apoptosis."

"Apoptosis is programmed cell death," Mr. Hill added to the classroom at large. "I wasn't aware of that protein. Where did you find that?"

"On the internet," I said.

He raised his eyebrows and I added, "Public Library of Science. I forget the author."

They were all staring at me now, like I was an alien. "I can look it up."

He shook his head. "I'll take a look for it." Louder he said, "Pop quiz, ladies and germs. Shouldn't be hard. We just went over the material."

I finished the sheet in three minutes but pretended to work at it until half the class had turned in theirs. When I went up to his desk to hand it in, Mr. Hill pointed to something on his screen. "Found it," he said quietly. "Gubser, et al, in 2007. You learn something every day."

I blushed. "Sorry."

"I'm happy to learn new things. I'm more of a physical chemist by training—not so much cell biology." He looked around and lowered his voice further, "Don't be afraid to know the answer. Don't be afraid to know *more* than the answer. Not in *my* class."

In between periods I hit the bathroom, but my heart sunk when I saw the crowd of girls entering ahead of me. I doubted I'd have time to use the toilet before the next bell, but inside, the majority of them went straight to the mirrors and began working on their makeup or hair. Most of them stopped talking when they saw me. I smiled briefly and locked myself in the nearest stall.

I couldn't pee.

It was weird. I knew they were out there and that they'd hear me and they'd laugh or look at me when I came out or *say* something. I needed to go. I just couldn't.

I gave up after a moment and flushed the toilet.

There were two other girls in precalculus and sixteen boys. The teacher, Ms. Hahn, moved one of the boys and put me in the front row, close to her desk.

"I don't mind sitting in the back," I said.

She pointed at the seat emphatically.

I sat.

Like Mr. Hill, she spent the class reviewing the preholiday material—in this case, logarithmic rules of exponents. During the review she asked me, "If I have the natural log of X over Y, how can I convert it to a nonfraction?"

I glanced around, remembering the looks on my classmates' faces in biology when I'd answered.

Ms. Hahn snapped. "I'm asking *you*, not him."

I reddened. "It's equivalent to the natural log of X minus the natural log of Y."

Ms. Hahn looked surprised. "Yes."

Later, after the bell rang, the older of the other two girls in class came up to me. "Hi. I'm Naomi—my mom was the Realtor on your house."

"Oh, you're Grant's sister." She looked a bit like him.

She grimaced. "Well, yeah."

We drifted into the hall. When we were away from the classroom door she said, "Ms. Hahn is, uh, complicated."

I raised my eyebrows.

"She keeps pushing for girls to take higher math but once we do, she seems to think we're only there for the boys. She's moved me four times because she thinks I'm cheating off the boys."

"Why does she think that?"

She laughed sourly. "Well, it couldn't possibly be because I was helping *them*, could it?" She jerked her head at another classroom door. "I'm here. You need any help in math, let me know, okay?"

"Thanks!" I felt ridiculously grateful. It wasn't about the math, of course. It was about the offer itself.

"Give me your cell number," she said.

"I don't have one."

She looked at me, perplexed, like I'd said, "I don't have a head."

Again I felt my ears go red. "Yet! We just moved here from out of the country and all."

"Oh. Okay. Write down mine, okay? And you can text yours to me when you get it."

Lunch was an education, which is good, I guess. I mean school is supposed to be about education, right? But I never knew you could do that to chicken. Mom had warned me of the evils of institutional food, but told me to try it anyway. "You never know. This may be *Le Cordon Bleu* of school cafeterias."

I was turning over the side vegetable with a plastic fork when someone said, "I think they're *supposed* to be Navy beans."

I jerked, surprised, and looked to my left.

The girl was not so much dressed as draped. She was hidden in baggy jeans and a hoodie sweatshirt so oversized it reached her knees. The sleeves were pushed up to free her hands, making the cloth bunch in thick folds from her wrists to her elbows. I could barely see her face. Most of her head was covered by the hood of the sweatshirt and the rest was obscured by dark bangs that dropped over her eyes.

Tentatively, I said, "I saw something like this once in a tidal pool. It was *moving*."

She was poised there, on her toes, not quite facing me, her body language saying "just passing, don't mind me."

I took a deep breath and said, "Sit down."

She turned a little more and let her heels touch the floor. "You don't mind someone else sitting here, too?" She gestured at the lunch line. "I sit with Jade."

"The more the merrier," I said.

She still hesitated. "We're not very popular," she said. "This is your first day, right? You don't want to get off on the wrong foot."

"Why aren't you popular?" I asked. "I mean, you're not

going to beat me up and take my lunch money, are you? Or is it to be a food fight? I've never been in a food fight," I said wistfully.

Her shoulder dropped slightly, relaxing. I hadn't been aware they were hunched until then.

She said, "You have discovered Our Evil Plan." I could hear the initial caps. She put her tray down and slung her backpack under the bench seat.

"It's not much of a plan," I said. "It'll need work. The 'evil' part's all right but the food fight bit really doesn't go with it. You're going to need something with neurotoxin darts or a bucket of pig blood, you know?" I tasted the beans. "Oh. Never mind. These beans are as good as a neurotoxin dart any day."

She snorted, jerking her head, and the hood slid back and dropped to her shoulder. She was Hispanic or Native American, with her hair cut short in back and long in front. "I'm Tara." She gestured back behind me. "This is Jade."

Jade was a Goth girl—black clothes and black lipstick, white eye shadow and mascara so thick, I marveled that she could keep her eyes open. The right side of her nose was pierced.

"I'm Cent," I said.

"Like a smell or like a penny?" said Jade. She spoke in a breathy monotone with hardly any inflection.

"Like a *bad* penny," I said.

"It's short for Millicent," Tara said. "But it's her mother's name, too, so she goes by Cent instead of Millie."

I stared at her.

"I'm in your biology class. I heard you tell Mr. Hill."

I blushed—maybe because of the overlong answer I'd given in class, or because she'd noticed me but I'd completely spaced her. There'd only been a few people in the room when I'd told him that. "For a second there I was afraid of your madd mind-reading skilz."

Jade breathed, "People say I'm psychic."

"No, they don't," said Tara. "People say you're psycho."

"Oh, yeah. I get those confused."

I laughed, which, apparently, was the right thing to do.

Tara was a sophomore and Jade was a junior. They weren't the least popular kids in school.

"That would be *you*, once you've had lunch with us."

But they certainly weren't the most popular.

"Goth is on its way out," said Tara, "As well as being alt. So, Jade is not only a freak, she doesn't even get credit for being trendy."

Jade stuck her tongue out at Tara before saying, "And Tara just doesn't belong. Nonwhite half-Hispanic, half-Diné, which wouldn't be so bad if she'd been raised on the rez but she wasn't, so she doesn't fit in anywhere."

They looked at me and Tara said, "So what's your damage?"

I raised my eyebrows. *Raised in paranoid isolation by super powered freaks?* "Homeschooling," I said. "Never been in a real school before."

"Harsh," said Tara.

"Lucky," said Jade.

Tara got a wary look on her face. "Uh, why'd you do homeschooling?"

Because we're hunted by governments and secret multinational organizations? "International travel."

"Oh," said Tara. "Not religious reasons?"

Religious about avoiding capture or death. "No, not really." I frowned. "Uh, why?"

She shrugged. "There's a bunch of fundamentalists in town. Some of *them* homeschool. Didn't know if you were of that stripe."

"We're not exactly churchgoers," I said. Dad was an outright atheist. Mom was an amateur student of comparative religions, but it was far more anthropological than spiritual. I'd been in mosques, synagogues, churches, and temples of every stripe and flavor from India to Japan. "What about you?"

"Christ, no!" said Jade.

Tara was less emphatic but she also shook her head. "That table over there is the evangelical bunch."

I glanced over at a table on one side of the lunchroom,

where some of the kids were reading, which I was pleased to notice earlier. Now I saw that there were white crosses on the covers of their books.

"Any other groups I should be aware of?"

Jade started gesturing around the room. "Football team. Basketball team. Pep squad. *Cholos*. Gangstas. Wangstas. Geeks. Nerds. Gradeworms. McClaren's Pets. Slackers. Skateboarders."

Tara said, "But it's more complicated than that, of course. Joe, there, gets straight A's and he's a skateboarder, and he's also a jock since he's on the school snowboard team. Perry is on the football team but is a wangsta. Felipe is on the basketball team but he's a gangsta—I mean the real deal. He runs with a gang that's associated with the *Sureños*." She tilted her head to the side. "A lot of the geeks get straight A's but they don't act like the gradeworms, like they're already doctors or lawyers. Some of the nerds are also potheads."

I'd been doing my research. "What about the economic stuff?"

Tara looked at Jade, puzzled. They looked back at me.

"Rich kids? Welfare kids?"

"Oh," said Tara. She colored slightly and I wondered if I'd struck a nerve. "Some. Colleen Crossman is one of McClaren's Pets. Her father owns the Crossman Oilfield Services which is all over the southwest. Another big employer is John Chanlee's dad, who owns the quarry. He wouldn't have made the team if his dad hadn't donated all this new equipment. Now he's the alternate quarterback."

Jade's face twisted. "He likes 'em young. *Don't ever* let him get you alone."

The bell rang. I slung my backpack and grabbed my tray.

Jade touched my wrist. "I mean it."

I nodded seriously. "And I heard it."

I should just pass over the horror that was PE class.

I'd thought PE would be fun. I mean, games and sports. I'm fairly athletic. I like to run and jump. What's not to like?

I'm not used to changing clothes in front of strangers. In front of anybody, really. Sure, we'll use the hot tub at home without a swimsuit, but otherwise Mom and Dad are careful to give me my privacy, knocking if my door is closed and all that.

The locker room . . . well . . . the collected mass of my classmates, smelled a bit, but I'd smelled worse. Once, on a bus trip between Kathmandu and Dhunche, on the Chinese border, I was on a bus with livestock and passengers who smelled bad *before* the first case of motion sickness. They tried for the windows and some didn't make it. Mom and I were on that bus for six hours—Dad bailed after the first upchuck.

"Flat-chested thing, aren't you?"

I was already hunched over as I dressed, facing the wall, trying to change from jeans to gym shorts as quickly as possible. I didn't turn until I'd pulled my T-shirt over my head.

The speaker wasn't flat chested at all. She was at least a C cup if not a D. She had green eyes and hair bleached almost white with a half-inch of pitch-black roots. She was a full head taller than I.

"I'm Cent," I said.

She turned away. "Who cares?"

Another girl, balanced on one foot as she pulled on one of her athletic shoes, was between the blonde and the door. The blonde shoved past her, causing her to fall forward against the locker, just barely getting her hand up in time to avoid banging her face. The taller girl didn't even look back.

"Not very nice," I commented, neutrally.

The girl who'd been shoved shrugged. "Caffeine. If my locker wasn't next to hers I'd stay as far away as I could." She looked around like she was afraid someone would hear her and didn't say anything else.

Caffeine? I wondered if that was the girl's name or the cause of her behavior?

Class activity was basketball but when Coach Taichert found out I'd never played, he had me do dribbling exercises up the side of the gym while the rest of the class split into teams and played a game. I had no trouble dribbling while I was standing still but when I tried to run I ended up booting the ball with my foot and having to run after it. Several of the girls laughed and my ears felt hot.

"Never mind, Cent," said Coach, taking the ball from me. "Work it out to the side, or if you're really running, you've got to bounce it forward so that you meet it when it comes up again."

Ten minutes later, I was doing well enough that he had me go shoot baskets from the free throw line on the unused court. There was more laughter as I missed or overshot but then I got the range and, by luck, made four baskets in a row.

"That's better," Coach said. He turned and called to the bench where the extra girls rotated out of the game were sitting. "Paula, and, uh Caffeine. Passing drills with Cent here. Paula and Cent, you're moving the ball up the court. Dribble up. Caffeine puts the pressure on, pass. Caffeine switches. Pass. When you pass the key, whoever's clear takes the shot. Then head back the other direction. Got it?"

I nodded.

Coach went back to refereeing the game.

I threw the ball to Paula, a short Native American girl with muscular legs and waist-length hair. She began dribbling up the court. I started moving up the other side but Caffeine, instead of pressing Paula, blocked me. I started to go around her and she shifted. I stopped.

"Aren't you supposed to be after the person with the ball?" I asked.

She slammed into my chest with her shoulder, knocking me back onto the floor.

It hurt.

Caffeine turned her back and ran lightly after Paula. Paula waited until Caffeine was almost to her and threw the ball back toward me. I scrambled to get it but I was still on the floor. The ball passed just beyond my fingertips.

More laughter from the girls on the bench. My ears burned. I chased the ball down and started dribbling up the court.

Caffeine came for me and I passed, but she kept coming. I feinted right and she threw herself forward, trying to knock me down again, but completely missed when I went left instead. She was ten feet behind me by the time she was able to stop. Paula, seeing me clear, passed. I dribbled some more and, hearing Caffeine's footsteps closing in, passed again.

Paula took the shot, made it.

Caffeine's footsteps kept coming and I stopped and dropped to one knee, bending over as if I were going to tie my shoe. Caffeine didn't quite fall, but she had to jump over me and then take several steps, flailing with her arms to keep upright.

Paula snorted and I looked over at her, but her face was expressionless, and I might have imagined it.

Someone on the bench giggled, but when Caffeine glared in that direction it stopped like it was cut off with a knife.

Paula threw the ball to me and then Coach blew his whistle and class was over.

Caffeine came at me in the shower.

I was nervous enough, bathing with strangers, but Coach had made it clear that everyone showered. Most of the girls were in and out in the time it took me to undress, wrap myself in the tiny school towel, and get over to the large communal shower.

"You little bitch!"

Caffeine was standing in the shower entranceway in her bra and panties. The two girls still showering scurried out past her, snatching their towels from the hooks by the door and leaving mine hanging all alone.

I stepped under the water and turned so my back was to the wall with the water spraying out between me and Caffeine.

"What's up?" I said, voice level. Worse came to worst, I could jump away, but I certainly didn't want to do that in front of anyone. The calm voice freaked her a little. She jerked her head back and even checked behind her. Coach Taichert wouldn't come into the girls locker room, but there was a female PE teacher I hadn't met yet who could wander through at any time. Caffeine looked back at me and glared. She started across the wet floor.

"Showering with your clothes on?" I said. I reached over and turned off the hot tap on the shower. I wasn't standing in the stream but the spray around the edges was icy.

"Turn off the shower," said Caffeine.

I opened the cold water tap more. With nobody else showering, the high water pressure splashed cold water onto Caffeine's lower legs. She flinched.

"Oops," I said.

"I'm going to pound you," Caffeine said. She stepped forward, raising her fists.

I reached up and flipped the shower head up, spraying her from head to foot.

She screamed and charged through the water at me. I jumped past her—and I don't mean "hopped"—to the doorway. Behind me I heard her slam into the wall, slip, and fall to the floor.

I didn't look back as I grabbed my towel, but listened carefully as I went to my locker, dressed quickly, and left.

SEVEN

Millie: Roadblock

Millie checked her e-mail every morning, but it wasn't as simple a matter as booting up her computer.

First of all, they didn't have network access in the Yukon. They could've done something with a satellite dish, but that could be tracked back to the general area of the cabin. They did have Internet access in New Prospect, but if their enemies ever connected Millie, the fugitive jumper, with one of her e-mail accounts, checking those accounts from that IP address could lead them directly to the new house.

Instead, each morning she used a program to randomly choose from a list of open WiFi access points across the world, then jumped her laptop within range, downloaded, and returned to the cabin. It usually took less than thirty seconds.

If she needed to answer an e-mail, she composed it offline, had the program spit out *another* access point, and jumped there to send. This morning, when she read her e-mail, she answered it in person.

Patel's office was in one of the few permanent structures in the camp, a brick building with a metal roof. She knocked and entered. It was a bit warmer inside, but not much.

Patel was sitting behind his "desk,"—two boards across

two cut-down oil barrels. His eyes widened when he saw her. "How did you get past the roadblock?"

Millie shrugged. She was wearing a *hijab* and a heavy wool coat over that. It was colder than her last visit, when she and Cent had dished lentils in the camp.

"I came a different way. Where is the roadblock?"

Patel stood and took some binocular hanging from a nail in the wall and said, "I will show you." He led the way back outside.

There had been some snow on the mountains the last time. Now the hills were solid white, and crusted snow crunched under her feet in the camp itself.

"They've been there all week. The refugees can just detour through the hills or along the river below, but the trucks can't. The militia won't let the aid convoy by unless they can divert *half* the supplies." He rounded one of the tents and pointed, then handed her the binoculars. "They don't have enough men to just *take* the supplies, but they can keep them from passing."

She focused the binoculars. The roadblock was where the road cut into a steep hillside. Above, the hillside rose steeply to the ridge top. Below, it dropped off cliff-like, fifty feet above a rocky, but mostly dry, riverbed. "What *is* that? A tank?"

"It's an old Soviet armored car. Amphibious. But that turret has a heavy machine gun for shooting armored targets—14.5 millimeters. If they have ammo, it could tear the convoy to pieces."

"Where did they get it?"

"Over the border, I'm sure. The Soviets abandoned hundreds when they left. The Afghan army still operates a lot of them, but I'm sure some ended up on the black market."

"How many men?"

"Eight."

"What does the Pakistani army say?"

Patel shook his head angrily. "I think they paid off the regional commander. His forces are 'otherwise' committed, and I should talk to the militia's commander! If something isn't done soon, we'll have to concede and give them a cut."

Millie handed back the binoculars.

Patel wrapped the neck strap around his hands. "I was hoping we might be able to get some supplies in *your* way, to hold us over. My people are working on the army from Islamabad."

Millie mentally reviewed the contents of the warehouse. They could help, but if there were rations just ten kilometers away, waiting . . . if something could be done about the roadblock . . . She thought about moving *those* supplies, instead, with Davy's help.

One way or the other.

"Let me see what I can do," she said.

"How about tear gas?" Millie suggested. "To flush them out?"

She couldn't see his face but she thought Davy sounded appalled. "How about *not*? With my luck, they'd have asthma, and I don't want to haul any of them to a doctor."

They were on the ridge crest above the roadblock. While it was early afternoon in New Prospect, it was black predawn here. Davy was studying the scene below. The armored car was idling, its headlights shining up the road away from the camp. Two sentries leaned against the armored car, and several men slept away from the headlights, nestled between the hillside and a fire.

"Uh, besides," Davy said, "I don't think there's anybody *in* the armored car. You said there were eight, right?"

"That's what Patel said. We can't be sure."

"Right." He vanished.

Millie swore and looked down at the campfire. Something flickered, and then Davy was back beside her, six rifles in his arms.

"They notice?" he asked.

She looked back down the hill. The two sentries continued looking up the road, away from the fire.

"No."

"Well, help me set these down without making a lot of noise. They're not as light as you'd think."

She helped set them down, barrels pointed away. "What are those, AK-47s?"

"Chinese version: the Type 56." Davy grinned. "They had them stacked, leaning against each other, just like in the movies."

They looked back down at the sleeping men.

"You're sure no one is in that thing?" Millie asked.

"Sure? No. But it's the first thing I'll be checking, right? *You* don't let them point their rifles at you, okay?"

"Right." Millie took off her coat and laid it on the ground. She was still wearing a *hijab,* and was grateful for the *chador* over her head.

She jumped down to the road, beyond the range of the headlights, and started walking. Her clothes were light colored and her scarf had silver thread worked into its trim, so the headlights soon lit her up. She saw the sentries straighten, but they left their rifles slung over their shoulders.

Behind them, she saw Davy appear on the roof of the armored car, by the open hatch over the driver's seat. But the guards still looked in her direction. Davy stuck his head down into the hatch and disappeared.

Millie held her breath.

Davy had spent some time the day before in Russia, at the Museum of Artillery in St. Petersburg. The museum had two different models of the BRDM-2 armored car. He'd told Millie, "It has a steering wheel, accelerator, and a brake pedal. If I can get it into gear, we'll be good to go."

There was a mechanical sound from the armored car and both sentries twisted around, then ran to the side of the road as the car lurched toward them. They began shouting and the men sleeping around the circle sat up.

Millie jumped back to the hilltop and looked down in time to see the armored car turn sharply to the right and off the cliff.

Davy appeared beside her in time to see the armored car crunch nose first into the rocks below, then fall over onto its turret in shallow water.

Millie said, "Ha. They'll never—"

"Cover your ears!" said Davy, following his own advice.

The explosion came in stages: a sharp, loud bang; a fireball as the fuel tank detonated; and then the ammo, en masse. A hunk of metal whizzed by and they both stepped back away from the edge of the ridge.

In the glow from the fireball, Millie saw Davy's teeth gleam. He said something, but Millie's ears were ringing. She cupped her ear.

He spoke louder. "They had eight of these on a bandolier behind the driver's seat." He reached into his pocket and took out a grenade.

"Why did you take *that*?"

He pointed at the six rifles lying on the ground. "Thought I'd just leave it with when we go. But take the pin."

Millie scooped up her coat. "Fewer guns the better, I guess," she said.

"Right." Davy made a shooing motion with his empty hand. "You go first, okay?"

Millie jumped away, but not home. Instead she jumped to the edge of the camp, a kilometer away, where Patel had first shown her the roadblock. She waited, frozen, looking toward the glow of the burning armored car. People were coming out of tents and looking in the same direction, wakened by the explosion. Then, from the hilltop, came a flash and the sharp crack of a grenade exploding.

She looked around and found Patel, struggling into a coat as he came around a tent. She got his attention by grabbing his sleeve.

"What happened?"

She pointed at the glow from the riverbed. "Someone stole their armored car and pushed it into the gully where it blew up."

He frowned.

"No one was hurt," she added, "But I'm betting the convoy can get through now."

When Patel turned back to look toward the roadblock, she stepped behind him and jumped back to the Yukon.

Davy was there, looking for her, anxious.

They both exhaled.

Millie said, "Remember the time you gave Cent so much grief for blowing up all her firecrackers at once?"

Davy blushed. "What's your point?"

"Like father, like daughter."

Millie looked at her watch. "If you want to go car shopping with Cent, she gets out in twenty minutes."

EIGHT

Cent: "Daddy! Look at me!"

In art class, the last period of the day, Mrs. Begay took roll. "Where's Caffeine?"

A girl I didn't know said, "She fell in the shower after PE. They took her over to the ER to X-ray her wrist." She looked over at me as she said it, then away.

I blinked and looked straight ahead.

After class, as I walked to my locker, kids were glancing my way and whispering to each other.

Great. First day of school and already notorious. Oddly enough, even though the halls were just as crowded they'd been in the morning, I had no trouble walking. They didn't clear a huge path, but they also didn't bump and jostle me. I should've been glad, I guess, but it just made me more aware of the watching eyes. My ears were hot and I put my head down and walked faster. It was just above freezing outside and the cold air felt good on my hot face.

I heard feet scuff the ground and a voice said, "Hey."

I jerked my head around, eyes narrowed.

It was Tara. She flinched back when she saw my face and I held my hand up and smiled weakly. "Hey."

She still looked at me warily.

"Sorry," I explained. "Thought you were someone else."

"Someone else like Caffeine Barnett?"

I looked away.

"What happened?"

"What did you hear?" I asked.

"What *didn't* I hear?" Tara held up her fingers and counted them off. "I heard that Caffeine broke her wrist punching you in the head. I heard that *you* broke her wrist using jujitsu. I heard that she broke it punching a wall. Oh, and Linda Romas gave Bobby Marisco a blow job under the gym bleachers."

I let out a deep breath. "I didn't need to hear that last one. Did anyone say Caffeine just slipped and fell?"

"Oh, the *official* line. Sure. But nobody believes that. Everybody heard what she did during PE and how you showed her up. And the girls who left the shower said Caffeine was 'bringing it' when she came in."

"I didn't touch her!"

Tara raised her eyebrows.

"Really, I didn't. She charged me, but I dodged and she ran into the wall and then slipped and fell. I skedaddled."

"You 'skedaddled'?"

"I'm not *stupid*. Would you have stayed?"

"Oh, no. I, too, would have 'skee-daddled,' or perhaps I would have 'va-moosed.' Or 'high-tailed it.'"

I felt my shoulders drop and the corners of my mouth twitched. "You're sassing me, that's what this is. Or should I say 'disrespecting'?"

"Sassing works for me. Some words are just *timeless*. Unlike, say, 'skedaddled.'"

I swung at her arm but she skipped back out of range.

"Nice skedaddling," I said.

There was a buzzing noise and she took a beat-up cellphone out of her hoodie pocket and glanced at it.

"Jade wants to know if it's all clear."

I raised my eyebrows.

"See, for all we knew, you're as psycho as Caffeine. Uh, Jade hates confrontation."

I raised my eyebrows even higher.

"Okay, so maybe you're not psycho. But we just met you. Been burned before."

"What are you going to tell Jade?"

"Java, East of Krakatoa."

"The coffee place?"

"Right. For homework, but we'll have to move. The tables go quick."

"Uh, I'll have to check in."

"You want to use my phone?"

"Sure." I dug into my pocket for the card with the house's new phone number, installed especially for school registration. I punched in the number but Tara had to tell me to push the "call" button.

Mom answered.

"Everything all right?"

I gave her our all-clear phrase, "Good as can be expected." If I was making the call under duress, I was supposed to say, "Great."

"What's up?"

"We're going to the coffee shop to do homework."

"First person plural. Who makes up the plurality?"

"Jade and Tara. Tara is in my biology class. She's a sophomore. Jade is a junior. I will learn how to interact in an informal social environment, gaining valuable insights into the local customs and mores."

Tara rolled her eyes.

Mom chuckled. "Very nice, dear. Find your father, though. He was going to pick you up to go car shopping, so you should let him know what's going on."

I grimaced. Dad would probably want to do a big postmortem on my day. Well, he could wait.

"Got it."

Dad was waiting around the corner, on the side of the school that faced toward our property.

I introduced Tara and told him what was going on.

"Oh." He blinked and started to say something, but then shut his mouth. Finally he said, "Okay. You have any input on the car thing?"

I shook my head. We didn't need a car, of course, but it would look strange if we didn't have one.

Tara blurted, "Green. Not the color, I mean. High gas mileage. Low carbon emissions."

I jerked my thumb at Tara. "What she said."

Dad nodded seriously. "Very good."

I hugged him. "What's that smell?"

Dad shrugged. "Diesel," he said. "And, uh, smoke."

I raised my eyebrows but didn't want to ask for details with Tara there.

Dad said quietly, "Home for supper, right?"

"Right."

"My mom works until 6:30," Tara said. "She's a radiology tech, mostly CAT scans. Anyway, no reason for me to be home until later."

"This is the good time to be here," Jade said. "The sports teams are still at practice, and Pep Squad and Dance Committee is still going. When that crowd moves in you can't hear anything, much less find a seat."

We were on the upper landing, at a table by the railing with a view of the tables below and the front door. Big photos of rain forests and Indonesian temples decorated the brick walls.

"What does your father do?" I asked Tara.

Her face closed down and Jade looked anxious.

"I said something wrong, didn't I?" Damn.

Tara clenched her teeth. I could see the muscle bulge at the corner of her jaw. Then she blurted out, "I don't care what my father does as long as he does it far away from me!"

"Oh," I said. "Sorry."

Tara visibly exhaled. "You didn't know. Far as I'm concerned I don't have a father. And the courts agree. Single-parent families for the win."

"We don't talk about him," said Jade. "Clear?"

I nodded. "Clear."

Jade looked back at Tara with the worried look on her face. Tara stared at the table top.

"So, I'm unsocialized and very likely to say the wrong thing. Just want you to know that I was raised in a box, right? I'm not trying to be mean—I'm just stupid that way."

Tara's mouth twitched and Jade's shoulders dropped lower.

I looked at Jade. "Any other awkward topics? Your parents?"

She shook her head. "Nah. They're all right. But we'll have words if you dis my sense of fashion."

Tara said, "Fashion? Is that what you call it?"

Jade jabbed her elbow into Tara's ribs. "Shut up, you."

We did homework. They drank tall espresso chocolate drinks with whipped cream on top. I stuck with water, but bought cookies to share.

Jade was helping Tara with her algebra and offered to help me, too, until I showed her my worksheet. "Oh. Never mind, genius. You should be helping us both." Tara raised her eyebrows. "She's in precalc," Jade explained.

I finished the worksheet, then wrote a humanities essay. I looked up to see both of them staring at me.

"What? I did something wrong, didn't I?"

Tara blinked. "You just wrote four pages . . . and your print is tiny. In like twenty minutes."

"Sorry? I thought we were doing homework?"

"That's homework? It's not like journaling? That's an assignment?" Tara said.

"Humanities essay."

"Ms. Grey's assignment?" said Jade.

I nodded. "Are you in my humanities class, too?"

"Different section, same level. That's not due for two weeks."

"So? I'm done with my other assignments."

Jade blinked. "You're doing it *wrong*. You never write an essay like that!"

I felt my stomach sink. What had I done now?

"You're supposed to wait," said Tara. "Sometime next week

you should start thinking about it. Then, put it off some more."

"Yeah," said Jade. "You *never* write an essay until the night before."

"At the *earliest*," Tara added.

"The true essay is written the morning it's due, or even the period before," said Jade earnestly.

I stared back and forth at them. "Uh, well, it is just a draft." Were they insane?

They both burst out laughing.

"Oh," I said. "I have read of this phenomenon. You are . . . what do they call it?"

They both giggled some more.

"Kidders?" said Jade.

"Procrastinators?" said Tara.

I shook my head. "I believe the technical term is 'assholes.' "

They tried to look offended but instead we all laughed so hard that the kids at the tables below glared up at us. Which made us laugh even harder.

The place really filled up at five, as more kids finished after-school activities, but we stubbornly held on to our table, despite pointed glares and even inquiries of, "You leaving soon?" from older and bigger kids. To justify our occupation I bought another round of drinks, decaf this time, but the baristas could care less. The place was doing brisk business and the noise level was so high that I barely heard Tara when she said, "Isn't that your dad?"

It *was* Dad, sitting in the far corner on the main floor below, with a coffee. He was facing away, but there was a framed picture on the wall at just the right height. I could see his face reflected in the glass, so I knew he was watching us. He'd taught me that trick—to use reflective surfaces to check behind me without seeming to. I felt a deep stab of resentment. I didn't know how long he'd been there—I'd been having a good time.

Tara added. "Do you think he bought a car?"

Jade started shoving her things into her backpack. "Well,

time for me to get home. Maybe your dad could give us a ride."

Dad had bought a plug-in hybrid, used, the sporty one with the electric motors integrated into each wheel and an auxiliary generator for long-range driving. Tara definitely approved. "This has got, like, a seventy-mile electric range, right? Around here, you'll be able to get along on just plugging it in."

But Jade had doubts. "Don't make a big deal of it, okay?"

Dad was amused. "Pardon?"

"This town is all about the oil and gas industry. One of the teachers at school bought an all-electric. It had 'Electric Vehicle' painted down the side in eight-inch letters. She lost three windshields in a month. When she replaced the last one, she had the words painted over as well, and hasn't had any trouble since."

Dad blinked. "Really?"

"Honest," said Jade.

Dad dropped Jade at her house and Tara at her apartment complex, which made me nervous. Dad doesn't really drive much. Mom's the driver. Dad could jump before he was seventeen and never really *had* to drive.

"You were spying on me," I said, when we were alone.

He shrugged. "Just checking out the local scene."

"Spying on me is not cool, Daddy."

He sighed. "Cent, you don't know these people. You don't know what they're capable of."

I knew he wasn't talking about Tara and Jade. " 'These people' aren't *here*."

"You don't *know* that."

I bit back a scream. He was *impossible*. "See you at home," I said, and jumped.

I didn't tell Mom *everything* about my day.

Things I left out: comments about my breasts in the locker room, being knocked down on the basketball court, almost tripping Caffeine on the basketball court, and the shower incident.

OK, pretty much anything related to PE and Caffeine Barnett.

I did discuss Jade and Tara. I discussed Mrs. Hahn's schizophrenic attitude toward girls in math class. I talked about Mr. Hill and biology and how it was okay with *him* to know more than class requirements. Finally, I returned to Tara and what happened when I asked about her father.

"Ouch," Mom said. "So she covers up a lot?"

"Yeah. Really baggy pants, this enormous hoodie. She *could* be cold. Her arms are really thin."

Mom frowned. "Oh."

"Oh, what?"

Mom shrugged. "Hard to say. I'd like to meet both of them."

I narrowed my eyes. "Why?"

"It's a parent's job to peer and pry into every facet of their child's life. Didn't you know? Meet any boys?"

I stood up, very dignified and said, "None of your beeswax."

"Ah," Mom said. "Maybe you'll meet some tomorrow."

I stamped my foot. I hate that she knows me so well.

Dad came in the front door, which was really weird, you know? He doesn't usually use doors at home.

"I think I scraped the new car on the garage door."

Mom laughed.

Dad looked offended, but I could tell it was put on. "How was school?"

"Okay. But I need a phone."

He looked shocked, as if I'd asked him for crack. "Absolutely not!" Dad said.

"Why not?"

"Location services."

I looked at Mom. She was frowning. She looked back at me. "It's true, honey. Think about it: a cell phone checks in with the network even when you're not using it."

Dad got his haunted look. "You jump to another city, then back, the network will note the different cell towers with no time between. If nothing else, it will probably generate an alert for an illegally cloned phone. If anyone else is looking specifically for us, it's exactly the kind of thing they'd search for."

"Most of the kids have cell phones. They look at me like I'm from Mars when I say I don't have one. And I could check in with you guys after school without having to borrow one."

Dad probably doesn't realize it, but when he's getting stubborn about something, he juts his jaw forward. He was doing it now.

"I'll only carry it at school. When I'm not there, it will be on its charger, here."

Dad shook his head again. "That won't work. It would take just one slip. Just one instance of leaving it in your pocket when you jumped someplace else."

Mom tilted her head. "I wonder if there's a way to limit the phone to one locale? Program it not to connect to nonlocal networks. Maybe limit it based on GPS?"

I looked back at Dad. "Yeah, like that!"

His jaw still projected forward.

Mom said, "It couldn't hurt to investigate. I'd feel better if there was a way for us to get hold of her after school."

Dad looked at Mom as if she'd stabbed him in the back.

She raised her eyebrows. "It's a tradeoff, obviously, but if she jumps home every five minutes to let us know where she is, that also has problems, right? Someone could see her. The same problem exists for us, you know? We can't follow her around."

Dad looked down at the floor. "She should be at home after school. We just said she could go to school. We didn't say she could go anywhere she *wants*."

My mouth dropped open. "Daddy! *Look at me!*"

He reluctantly raised his head.

I stretched both hands out and pointed back at myself.

And jumped.

I was in New York City, on the edge of Washington Square Park. It was dark and cold but I was still wearing my snowboarding jacket, hanging open. I zipped it up and walked, not really paying attention to where I was going. I went down streets that got progressively more narrow and twisty. I was surprised when I found myself staring across traffic at the Hudson River. The wind off the river was hard and damp, numbing my face. I looked at my watch. It had been twenty-five minutes since I'd jumped.

I went back to the house in New Prospect. Mom was there, Dad wasn't.

Mom sighed but didn't say anything.

"Did he get the point?" I said. I was trying for defiant but it came out strident.

"He did."

I looked around.

Mom said, "He's waiting at the cabin. I was waiting here." We'd been calling the Yukon house, 'the cabin' and the house in New Prospect 'the house' to differentiate. "Go tell him supper is ready."

Supper was a little tense. I would have sat silently through the whole thing, but Mom drew me out and I talked about humanities and biology and math and, very briefly, about PE. At the very end of the meal Dad said he'd talk to somebody about the phone thing, and I apologized for jumping away during the earlier argument.

"Where'd you go?" he asked.

I smiled and didn't say anything.

The very first day of school I'd walked the entire way from the house. A path cuts through the wooded rear of two neighboring properties, well away from the road and houses, before it enters the public woods that are part of the park adjacent to the school grounds.

The second day of school, now that I had my bearings, I jumped straight to the last bit of woods, not on the path, but to a ledge above it, halfway up a limestone cliff. You couldn't see this shelf unless you were above looking straight down, or twenty feet up one of the trees growing below. This let me peek over the edge and make sure no one was around before jumping down to the path where it left the woods.

Most of the kids arrived at the front of the school, dropped off by parents or busses or driving themselves, but there was a cluster of smokers at the edge of the athletic field, sheltering from the wind in the lee of the bleachers and stamping their feet in the crusty snow while they got their fix.

I swung wide, keeping the collar of my jacket pulled high. One of the smokers was a taller girl with one of her sleeves hanging empty. When I reached the door, I glanced back and confirmed what I'd thought. It was Caffeine. Her jacket was partway open and I saw the sling, inside. Worse, her head came up sharply when I turned to look back, and I saw her scowl. I went inside trying not to hurry, but my heart was pounding.

I dropped off my coat in my locker and headed for biology. My heartbeat slowed and I did some slow deliberate breaths, a trick Mom taught me, to finish calming. Tara, it turned out, had a seat at the very back of the classroom.

"No wonder I didn't see you, yesterday. You're way back here in Outer Mongolia."

She nodded. "I'm a buffer zone between nations." She pointed at the empty desk to her left. "Daniel-vania gets a little too talky with Becky-stan." She pointed at the desk to her right. "So Mr. Hill put me here, as an intervening neutral power. Noise in this part of the classroom dropped twenty decibels."

"Did you mind?"

"Nah. Mr. Hill asked me to do it, as a favor."

"Do they pay any more attention in class, now?" I gestured left and right.

"Depends if they're in possession of their cell phones. If they are, then they spend the whole time texting each other. Mr. Hill won't take their phones away if he notices, as long as they're quiet, but a lot of the other teachers follow the cell-phone policy to the letter."

I'd been given a copy of the policy when we enrolled but I wasn't even going to read it, since I didn't have a phone. But then, at the end of the process, they wanted my signature on all the student-behavior policies, so I'd skimmed it. No phone use in the classroom, including texting or any audible alerts or ringtones. Phones confiscated and only returned to the student's parent or guardian at the end of school day.

But I'd still seen people using their phones in class. Between classes, they sprouted in kids' hands like blossoms after desert rain.

"When are you going to get a phone?" Tara asked.

"Working on it," I said.

I gave the school cafeteria one more try at lunch but it was no good. When you have to be told that the green beans are, well, green beans, you know they've been cooked too long. The entrée was breaded mystery meat baked so dry and stiff that it defied the plastic cutlery. When I picked it up and tried to bite it instead, it defied my teeth.

"Look on the bright side," said Jade. "Jell-O!"

"Uh oh," said Tara. "Caffeine approaching."

I glanced around.

Caffeine was juggling her tray, her lunch half eaten, and her backpack with her one good arm. It looked like she would drop one or the other at any moment. I wondered why she hadn't just left her backpack and gone back for it after she'd bussed her tray, but then I realized she was walking in the wrong direction to drop off her tray. The dishwashing window was on the other side of the cafeteria.

"Maybe she's changing seats?" I said, half to myself.

Tara said, "She keeps looking at you."

I pivoted off the bench seat and stood, abruptly, while Caffeine was still a few yards away. Her eyes went wide, her tongue went to her lips and she lurched forward, as if she had tripped. But I had my hands on both sides of the tray and, though the food and milk carton slid sideways, I lifted it up and kept it from spilling.

"Oh, you poor thing," I said, loudly. "Let me help you with that."

Caffeine's face twisted, ugly, and I knew I'd guessed right.

She'd planned to "accidentally" spill it on me as she went by. There were three teachers on lunchroom duty so she couldn't attack me overtly.

"Where are you headed? I'll carry it."

She jerked her chin toward the dirty dish drop-off window.

"No need for you to go. I'll get it."

I went wide around her. I wouldn't have been surprised if she'd tried to trip me, but I got her tray and dishes to the window without incident. By the time I'd returned, Caffeine was headed out the door.

Jade and Tara looked unhappy and a little disturbed.

"What?"

Jade said, "She *spit* on your food."

My mouth opened but it took me a moment before I could think of anything to say. "Just when I thought the cafeteria food couldn't get any *worse*."

Tara giggled and Jade's hunched shoulders relaxed. The corners of her mouth twitched slightly.

"I think I'm going to start bringing my lunch," I said, and bussed my tray.

PE improved immensely since Caffeine was now spending that period in the resource study center until her wrist healed. I learned that it was a bad sprain, not a break, so she would probably be back in PE in a matter of weeks, not months.

Too bad.

My basketball skills had improved to the point that I could actually play in the games, but Coach blew the whistle at me so many times the first game that I went home and looked up the rules. My big sin was traveling, apparently, and something called the backcourt violation. Basketball also does something called a "jump" shot but it wasn't my kind of jump. Tempting. I could really show them "traveling."

On Friday it started snowing midmorning and came down so thick and heavy that they dismissed school two hours early. It was chaotic as parents arrived or didn't arrive to pick up kids. I looked for Jade and Tara but I couldn't find either of them, so I started walking home. It seemed like the school vanished before I'd made it halfway across the field, shrouded from my view in the falling flakes. I could just barely make out the bleachers, but the woods and the town were completely invisible, so I just jumped directly to the house.

No one was home, which surprised me for a moment. Someone had been there when I'd called home after school each of the previous three days, letting them know I was going off to Krakatoa for homework. When I'd get home when promised, they'd both be there, eager—perhaps *too* eager—to hear how my day had gone.

But then I realized that they didn't know school had gotten out early. I laughed at myself for thinking they just hung around waiting for my every appearance. That wasn't how they'd behaved before this school thing, after all. They must have been making sure one of them was at the house just before school got out.

I jumped to the cabin. Neither of them was there, either. I wandered up and down the stairs. Buzz was working again, thankfully. I could hear the distant humming from the top of the basement stair, which was reassuring. But it still felt weird that Mom and Dad weren't around. Sure, I'd been left alone before, many times, but this was not the same.

It was snowing in the valley, too, but lightly, nothing like New Prospect's blizzard. I thought about snowboarding, but it was too cold here.

I jumped back to the house in New Prospect. Tara or Jade could call. They might go to the coffee shop. Perhaps I should jump there to find out.

I slapped my forehead. Sure, I'd hardly ever used a phone but that was no excuse. I'd been watching movies all my life. I got Tara's number out of my backpack.

She answered after one ring. "Can you believe this snow?"

Sure, it was heavy—but she hadn't lived in the Yukon in winter.

"Fluffy," I said. "Did you go home?"

"Yeah, Mom said I had to go straight home. She didn't

want me out if it got worse. Jade's Dad pulled the same thing when she called to see if she could go home with me." She sighed. "They're not *that* far away. I don't think her parents approve of me."

"Oh? Why?"

I could hear her breathing but it took her a while before she said, "Did you do the worksheet on protein synthesis yet?"

"Don't want to talk about it, eh? Yes, I did it in class."

"You finished it? He gave it to us at the *end* of class."

"Ten minutes *before* the end of class. I'd already read the chapter."

"Which *wasn't* assigned until he handed out the worksheet."

"You don't read ahead? Why don't you want to talk about Jade's parents?"

She ignored me, saying instead, "What is the bit with the difference between the intron and the extron?"

"That's exon. Not extron."

"Exxon is an oil company."

"Do you want an answer? One 'X' not two. The introns are *not* coded into proteins. The exons are."

"It should be extron. A little robot that makes proteins."

"Well, the introns have something to do with regulating the expression of the genes, if that makes you feel any better. But it's exons that get translated into proteins."

"I don't think they like my skin color."

"Seriously?"

"Well, we're not rich, either. Jade's mom is an orthopedic surgeon. Her dad is an engineer. They have a huge house. Someone comes in to *clean*."

I thought about the house in the Yukon and this one, which wasn't exactly small. On the other hand, Tara wasn't crowded into a refugee camp on the Pakistani border, either. I wondered who was really doing the comparing, Jade's parents or Tara?

"Well, if that's true, it's totally lame."

"It's just—hang on a second. Jade's calling." I thought for a second she'd hung up, but there was no dial tone. Then her voice came back. "Call you later? Jade wants to watch *Tenchi Muyo!* together."

"I didn't know you guys were *otaku.*"

"Hell, yes! You?"

"Yes. But I thought you were stuck at home. Both of you."

"Oh, yeah. We watch it separately, the DVDs, but we stay on the phone."

"Now *that's* just weird. What season?"

"We're watching *Tenchi Muyo! GXP.*"

"Sick," I said. "Seina beats up the Daluma Pirate Guild."

"You *are otaku!*"

"Sure. I even have the manga."

"No way!"

"Well, I do. I'll lend them to you, if you want."

"Where did you get them? I saw an issue, once, at the anime con in Phoenix, but it was the only copy and someone was buying it when I saw it. It was the second season, *Shin Tenchi Muyo!* The manga came after, right?"

"Yeah. They're not really canon so don't get upset when you see stuff that wasn't in the anime."

"What kind of—shit! That's Jade. We'll talk, yeah?"

"Sure."

I jumped back to New York, to Washington Square Park. It was cold, windy, late, even dark, afternoon, and something smelled really bad. The smell was coming from a person wearing so many layers of clothing that I couldn't make out a gender, sitting against one of the two trees that bracketed my jump spot.

"Oh, excuse me," I said.

The person, man?, yelled—a deep, hoarse voice—and scrambled out onto the sidewalk, climbing awkwardly to his feet and hurrying away from me, his face peering fearfully over his shoulder.

Damn. I walked the other way. I really needed to get a different jump site in New York City.

I walked under the arch and up Fifth Avenue. The sidewalks were crowded and people brushed against me, edging around, walking much faster than I was. I worked at it, increasing my pace, avoiding elbows and shoulders, trying to create more of a presence. *Fear me!* I thought fiercely. It didn't seem to help. They didn't even seem to *see* me.

It was just like the school hallways.

Well, it was just like the school halls before they thought I'd broken Caffeine's arm.

I passed what I thought of as the pie-wedge building, the odd-shaped skyscraper between 22nd and 23rd streets, where Broadway crossed Fifth Avenue, then took the crosswalk to Madison Square Park.

It was less crowded over here. I sat down on one of the benches. Hundreds of people passed by but it didn't make me feel any less alone.

Shit. Was that what I'd been trying to do? Feel less lonely?

I walked back down Fifth Avenue to the big Barnes & Noble at 18th street. I spent some time looking through the manga but it only reminded me of Jade and Tara. I moved over to the YA section, checking favorite authors for new books. Though there wasn't anything that grabbed me, I saw several *old* friends on the shelves. But I didn't need to buy any of them, they were waiting for me at home.

I jumped away from the revolving door, half in, half out.

The book I wanted was at the cabin but I took it to the house, to be near the phone in case somebody called.

But nobody did.

NINE

Davy: Phone

"Amerikate" was an expatriate mobile-applications developer living in Bristol with her partner and two daughters. She'd already written an application that mapped cell towers to GPS coordinates and was quite willing to modify it quickly for the kind of money Davy was offering.

"Why restrict it, though?" she asked.

"There's a nondisclosure agreement involved. I'm not at liberty to give you more details," Davy said.

"Suit yourself. If I knew more, I might be able to give you a better solution."

"If you can restrict it as discussed, it will do just fine."

"Get the carrier's best Android phone and then root it."

"Root it?" Davy pictured burying the phone in the back yard until white rootlets sprouted from plastic.

He was in an Internet café in Tornoto and they were talking computer-to-computer, voice over Internet. Both their cameras were turned off but, like he did every time he used a public computer, he'd stuck a Post-it over the computer's camera anyway.

"Get root access. Most carriers lock it off but we'll need access to take control of the phone's radio."

She's not even trying *to speak English.*

"You can give me directions?"

"I'll point you to a website. It's easy. I'll e-mail you the app and you can install it on the phone."

"Three phones."

"All with the same need? Location confirmation before tower connection?"

"Right."

"Okay. Same procedure for all three. The GPS stuff is going to eat battery, but I'll make it turn on and off when it needs to verify a new tower. That should help. I always buy a bigger battery, myself."

"Right. Bigger batteries. Check."

"Half to start?" she suggested.

"The fee? I transferred the whole amount ten minutes ago, to your PayPal account."

He heard keys clicking. "Ah. So you did. Give me three days."

"Yes, ma'am. Uh, if I misplaced one of the phones and needed to locate it, do you make an application that could do that?"

"No need. Several people make those kind of apps."

He winced. "I don't want just *anyone* to be able to locate it!"

"Not a problem. You get to set the security. I use one called 'Where's My Droid.' If I text the correct keyword to my number, it returns the GPS coordinates. A different keyword causes it to scream with a siren sound. You get to choose the keyword and, of course, you have to know the phone number of the handset, right? So, fair security."

Davy showed up with dinner, South Carolina BBQ, in the Yukon kitchen at 6:30 PM Mountain Time and found a note which said, "We're eating at the house."

He jumped to New Prospect and found Millie staring out the window into a snowstorm. He put the food on the counter then did a double take at the snow piling up on the window ledge. "That's pretty heavy. I didn't even notice at first because—"

"Yeah," Millie said. "We're used to it up north. Did you know Cent's school got out at noon because of this?"

"Nope."

"Well, neither did I."

Davy began removing the containers from the bags. "What did she do with herself? Go to the coffee shop with her friends?"

"Her friends were picked up by their parents and taken home. They didn't want them out in this." Millie looked at Davy. "We should have, too."

Davy blinked. "Why?"

"We should've known that school was let out. If we were normal people, we would've heard it on the radio. We would've been here and seen the snow coming down and *checked*."

Davy didn't see what the fuss was. "Even if she *couldn't* jump, it's only fifteen minutes along the road. Less, through the woods."

"On the road she could get hit by someone who didn't see her in the snow. And she could get lost in the woods."

"Millie? She *can* jump. She won't get lost in the woods. She won't get hit by a car." He crossed his arms. "This isn't about Cent, is it?"

Millie looked away.

This is also about Millie *not having a normal life.*

Davy started to get plates out but Millie said, "The table's set. Cent did it."

"Is that why we're eating here? Because Cent wants to?"

Millie nodded. "She keeps checking the answering machine, even though she's been here. She doesn't want to miss a call."

"Ouch."

"New friends, you know?"

Davy shook his head. "Not really my thing."

Millie raised her eyebrows. "Yet you said 'ouch.' "

"An old thing," Davy said.

"A Vineyard thing?"

"Oh, no. Way before that." He stared out at the swirling snow. "Remember when I reconnected with my mom?"

Millie winced. His mother had been killed shortly after that *and* in that same few weeks Millie and Davy had nearly ended their relationship, though not because of his mother's death. "Yes."

"I'd sent a letter through her lawyer?"

"Yeah, I remember," Millie said. Davy would never have sent the letter without Millie's persuasion. "Was it the waiting between the time you sent the letter and the time she called?"

"No. The first call went to my answering machine while I was visiting you, but she didn't leave a number, just said she'd call back in twenty-four hours. *Longest* twenty-four hours of my life. That's what I was thinking about."

Millie put her arms around him from behind. "Ah. Well, I don't think she's quite there, yet, but I'm glad you can sympathize."

Cent came up the stairs, yelling, "Is there food yet? Some of us would like to *eat,* you know?"

Davy turned around and looked into Millie's eyes.

They both sighed.

Davy bought prepaid smartphones at Walmart and a stack of prepaid phone cards to top off the voice and data credits, as needed. He paid cash and though he had to enter names when he activated them, there was no identification requirement.

At the San Jose Fry's Electronics, he bought high-capacity batteries and extended phone back covers.

While rooting the phone wasn't easy, exactly, he finally muddled through the process, and by the time he'd done the other remaining two phones, it was routine.

When Amerikate e-mailed him the program, he was ready. He installed the apps, set the range of locations allowed, and jumped all over the country. As hoped, the phones refused to connect to cell towers anyplace but the vicinity of New Prospect, though they could still connect to wireless Internet hotspots.

He'd avoided cell phones, though Millie had used a prepaid phone once, back when he was a prisoner on the Vineyard. He was both fascinated and repelled by the devices.

This should be interesting.

TEN

Cent: "Was he hitting on you?"

The snow continued all the way through Saturday night, piling up at least three feet. I was worried that they might cancel school on Monday. Mom laughed at me. "Be aware that your peers will probably have a different reaction to a snow day."

I'd moved my anime and manga collection from the cabin to my room at the house and set out the first few volumes of the *Tenchi Muyo!* manga for Jade and Tara. While I was at it, I moved some of my other books, too.

Dad saw me organizing the new shelves and said, "I wouldn't do that. If we have to bug out, do you really want to leave these behind?"

I hadn't thought about it like that, but I shrugged. "That would be bad, all right. But they're just books and movies, right? Replaceable."

He looked horrified. His mouth opened and he blinked several times, but the only sounds he made weren't words.

I went up to him and hugged him. "It's all right, Daddy. I won't let them get my books."

He looked even more alarmed at this. "What? NO! You see any sign of them you jump away. You don't run back into a burning building."

I grinned. "Right."

That night we went swimming on a deserted stretch of the north Queensland coast, though in Australia it was early morning. The sun was barely up but the water was still lovely warm. Dad and I got into an epic splash battle which I won by jumping twenty feet into the air and then cannonballing down into the water beside him while he was staring around to see where I'd gone. He got mad for a moment but Mom was rolling on the beach laughing, and his glare turned into a sheepish grin.

"I'll remember that trick," he said.

I slept well.

In the morning the snow had stopped and the sun was glaring off the transformed landscape. By midday the plows were out in force, clearing the roads but piling the snow shoulder high in front of everybody's driveways. Dad went out to shovel ours, but I'm sure he cheated because when I went outside to see how he was doing, the shovel was back in the garage and the driveway was not only clear, it was bone dry. I walked down the road a bit. Even the people who'd used snowblowers on their driveways had a layer of packed snow and ice left behind.

Tara called the house at lunch time.

"We're sprung. Want to go sledding?"

"Where?"

"Chevron hill," said Tara.

I waited a second before asking, "And that's located? . . ."

"Right. You're new. Behind the Chevron station, the one near school."

I was still drawing a blank. "I'm guessing it's west of the school, since I live east and I haven't seen a gas station around here."

"Right. About a half mile, maybe. On Thunderbird."

Thunderbird was our road, up the hill from the house. It ran east-west past the school.

"Is it a long hill? I could bring my snowboard."

"Sure. Lots of kids do."

Mom drove me, since I'd never been there, parking at the Chevron station and getting out to survey the hill.

It was busy. The hill dropped off behind the gas station in a series of dips and flats, continuing down into the river valley but, unlike behind our house, the creek was on the other side of the valley, leaving a gentle flat to kill velocity after a run. There were lots of kids with sleds, inner tubes, sheets of cardboard, and even one queen-sized inflatable mattress that shot down the hill with five shrieking kids atop it. There was a handful of boarders, too. Older kids, mostly.

It was a long run and while I saw a few kids struggling back up the hill, most of them walked farther east, to where a road cut across the valley, and waited. A pickup came down the road and the driver climbed out, collected something from the kids, and they climbed in the back with their sleds and tubes. The truck turned around and drove back up the road. After a few minutes, it came around the bend on Thunderbird and the kids piled out on the shoulder. There was a paper sign in the window that said only "50¢."

"You bring any money?" Mom asked.

I looked at the sign. "Why would I need a ride?"

Mom glared at me. "You'll get a ride or you'll walk. Not with all these people around!"

"Okay, already. Do I have to walk home, too?"

"No. But be discreet, right?"

"Yes, Mother."

Mom looked at me over her glasses. "Millicent, you promised."

I had. It was the deal. They cooperated about going to school and I promised to be careful. To be discreet. "Sorry. Yes, I'll be discreet." I checked my pockets. "Yeah, I've got a ten. That's twenty runs."

She gave me a twenty and jerked her chin toward the Chevron food store. "You might want hot chocolate or something."

I took my board over to the empty expanse, next to the station. The run was flat at the top, by the road, but the level area was not as deep as the gas station's lot.

Tara and Jade showed up then, dropped off by Jade's father in a dark, sleek Mercedes. Jade had a snowboard. Tara had a tractor tire inner tube that took up the entire trunk of the car.

Jade hefted her board and said, "Tara said you boarded, so I brought mine."

"Cool."

The boarders stuck to the left, on the steeper side of the slope, and the sledders favored the right or the center. "But you gotta be careful," said Jade. "I've seen big guys jump on a tube and barrel down the hill with absolutely no control. Two years ago, one of them took out a kid at the bottom of the hill and he ended up with spinal cord damage. The kid, not the jerk on the tube."

Tara shook her head. "Peter Morales. He's walking again, but with crutches."

"So keep your eyes open, right? My parents didn't let me sled here for a whole winter after that."

"Well, you've scared *me*," I said.

"See you at the bottom," said Tara. She looked around and then dove down the hill, face down on her inner tube.

Jade approached the edge and sat down, ratcheting her bindings. I copied her.

"You lead," I said. "You know the hill."

The snow was good, still powdery. I was shivering a little at the start but warmed up quickly. Jade was a competent, though careful, boarder. I could've zipped past her at any time but I didn't see the point. It wasn't a race, after all.

The boarders had built up a ramp on the second flat, and Jade took it tentatively, killing a lot of her speed before lining up on it. She flew a few feet in the air and dropped down. I kept all my speed and as she cut off to the right, I crouched and, at the end of the ramp, popped up off my tail. Jade yelled as I flew by at head height, traveling so far that the hill dropped away before I touched down, and I landed on the downslope, flat bottomed and whisper smooth.

I used the velocity to travel across the flat at the bottom, passing Tara as she was trudging toward the road.

There were a few other boarders and a lot of sledders standing in a rough line waiting for the pickup. All of the boarders were male, and I recognized a few of them from school.

"Awesome jump," said one of the familiar faces. I think he was in my biology class.

I looked back up the slope. You could just make out the top of the ramp from here. I looked back at the boy. Well, boy-man. He needed a shave. "Thanks."

"You're Cent, right?"

I nodded.

He jerked his thumb at his chest. "Brett."

Tara caught up. "I thought I'd beat you here," she said. "You must've really been booking."

I shrugged, suddenly shy.

Jade coasted halfway across the flat before her momentum failed. She undid her rear binding and push kicked the rest of the way.

"You nearly gave me a heart attack," she said as she took off the other binding.

"Sorry. Didn't think I was that close," I said. "I kept to the left of the ramp."

"Oh, it wasn't that. It was how high you were. I was afraid I'd look down the hill and see pieces. Guess you had good boarding up there in Canada."

I shrugged again.

A pickup came down the hill and turned around on the flat. The road had been plowed and graveled, but it was still some-what slick. The truck had chains.

The driver looked younger than me and I recognized him from school, too. He collected money and made change, work-ing down the line. The truck filled up and the driver stopped the loading right before me.

Brett, already in the truck bed, shoved over, raising a faint protest from the guy next to him. "There's room for one more," he said.

The driver looked in the bed and then back at me, lifting his eyebrows.

"I'll wait," I said, tilting my head toward Tara and Jade. "We're together."

Brett opened his mouth to say something, but then his friend shoved him back into the corner of the truck bed.

I turned back to Tara and Jade, not looking at the truck.

As soon as the truck pulled away, Tara started laughing and not that quietly.

I felt my ears get hot.

Jade blinked. "Oh. My. God. Was he hitting on you?"

Tara laughed again. "Definitely."

"He was just being friendly," I said.

Jade shook her head. "*Really* friendly. He didn't have to move over. You could've ridden in his *lap*."

I stooped and slowly made a snowball, looking pointedly at Jade as my hands patted it firm.

Jade took a step back. "Oh . . . kay. He was *just* being friendly."

Tara laughed some more until the snowball hit her in the forehead.

A brief period of snowy violence ensued.

The line started building up again. A different truck came down the hill and we paid our fare and climbed in. "How many people do this truck thing?"

Tara shrugged. "Depends on the day. It can be tricky if there's only one guy running. Sometimes they jack up the price."

Jade nodded. "But that can backfire. There was a day that Ronnie Arkle tried to charge two bucks when he was the only one here."

"Yeah," said Tara. "Kids have phones. He may have gotten a fare or two, but then there were moms with SUVs running kids up the hill for free. He'd have made a lot more money if he hadn't gotten greedy."

Brett's snowboarding buddies had gone down the hill already, but he was still waiting at the top.

Tara started giggling and I said, "There's just as much snow up *here*."

"Er, right. You going to do that jump again?"

"Sure," I said.

"Let me get down first, so I can see, okay?"

"You just want to get out of range, don't you?"

She started giggling and slid away on her tube, this time sitting, face up.

When Jade and I had fastened our bindings, we slid off to the left and paused. Brett stood up and slid off down the hill in front of us.

"He's showing off," said Jade.

He was doing ollies and aerial to fakies, popping off the ground and switching the ends of his board a hundred and eighty degrees, then back. Then he went to wider, high-speed carved turns, building up velocity as he lined up on the ramp. In the air, he did a 720, two full revolutions, upright—what Dad calls helicoptering when it's on skis—but he caught an edge on landing and went head over heels down the last bit of the slope.

I bit my lip, but he got back up again, beating the snow off, and took off one binding and started kicking across the flat.

"Well," Jade said, "It was spectacular."

"Yeah," I said.

"Can you do that move?"

"I can. Sometimes *just* like he did."

"Well, I'm going to try for some more speed this time, when I take the jump," said Jade.

I nodded vigorously. "Sure. If you clear the lip of the hill, you'll actually have an easier landing than if you land on the flat."

She looked doubtful. "Right. Why don't you go first?"

I headed down the hill, doing wide carving turns to build up speed and line up on the ramp. I did a layout backflip, a nice slow turn, leaning back, head tilted, to spot the landing. I hit the downslope like before, smooth and friendly. Tara whooped as I cut wide across the flat. I reached her at the road just as Brett kicked across the last few yards to where the line formed.

I was intensely aware of Brett, but I turned back to watch Jade, pumping her fist in encouragement. She ollied off the end of the ramp and flew, just reaching the top of the downslope, which really lessened the impact. Though she wobbled there for a moment on landing, she brought it together without falling, and made it most of the way to the road on momentum. Tara and I whooped.

One of Brett's friends said something I couldn't hear and Brett said, "Oh, like you could even *reach* the edge of the hill last year."

I smiled, but not where they could see me.

When the truck came there was room for all of us. I ended up sitting next to Brett, but I talked to Jade. "You nailed it, girl. Nice distance on that jump."

Jade shrugged, trying to look cool, but her mouth kept breaking into a grin.

"You ever board?" I asked Tara.

Tara shook her head. "Nah. Tubing is more my style."

Jade's smile dropped and she went from exhilarated to worried in nothing flat.

"Tubing's fun," I said.

Tara glanced at Jade and smiled. "Tubing's cheap. We can't all afford to spend weekends in Telluride."

Jade looked away, frowning.

"Telluride is awesome," said one of Brett's friends.

Brett shrugged. "So is Durango, though, and easier to get to." He jerked his chin sideways at the hill. "Even this is nothing to sneeze at. I learned to board on this hill. And no lifts, not even trucks. I walked back up the hill."

I found myself nodding. "There's a hill by our house in Canada, too. That's where I learned. There wasn't a lift but at least the stairs were covered."

He turned to me and smiled. "Do you still own that house? Are you a Canadian citizen?"

"It hasn't sold yet," I said, not exactly lying. "I've got dual citizenship. I was born in Canada but my parents are both U.S. citizens." Really, I had *no* citizenship, since neither country knew of my birth. Millicent Ross was a manufactured entity. Fake name with fake papers. *I* was a fake.

I liked his smile, though. I liked how I felt when he smiled at me.

Next jump, Brett did the 720 again, this time nailing it without falling.

I meant to do an upright 360 myself, but gave it just a little too much twist. Fortunately I was able to bring it around and landed fakie with a 540, riding like that all the way to the road.

Jade let her speed increase even more this time, definitely clearing the top of the hill. But her landing wasn't as clean and her board toed in, and she went head over heels. My hand went to my mouth, but when she finally stopped tumbling and slid to a stop, I could hear her laughing.

Tara started to run back across the flat, but Jade was already climbing to her feet so Tara stopped short and waited.

The truck was loading and Brett called. "You coming?"

I smiled at him and said. "No."

He frowned and shrugged and the truck went on up the hill.

Jade asked me about it when they finished walking across the flat. "Why'd you wait?"

"What do you mean?"

"You could have ridden up the hill with Brett."

"Yes, I could have. You all right?"

"Sure. What did I do wrong?"

"You brought your toe down ahead of your tail. Bend and unbend your knees together. Meet the slope even or tail first."

"Yeah, that's what I thought." Jade's fall had put a lot of snow down the neck of her jacket. While we waited for the next truck, she took her jacket off and Tara brushed off the snow she couldn't reach.

"So why didn't you ride up with Brett?" Tara asked it this time.

"Who asked me to go sledding?"

She laughed. "It's not like you're my *date*." She glanced at Jade.

"Of course not," I said. "But *he* certainly isn't. Even if he does have a cute butt."

Back up top Jade said, "I'd better do this again, right now."

Tara shook her head. "You don't have to."

Jade said, "But if I don't . . ."

I nodded. "You want to get back on the horse."

"Well, yeah."

"This isn't macho bullshit, is it?" Tara said.

"No," said Jade. "I just want to get it one more time without falling."

I went first, keeping my speed down, ollied off the ramp, and grabbed the edge of my board Indy, between the bindings toeside. I hit the downslope smoothly, then cut over sharp to the left, to stop out of the way of the run, but near enough to render aid if Jade fell again.

She didn't fall, landing even farther than before, both legs coming down together, and I grinned.

I slid off to follow her and I heard the scrape of a board on snow. Someone yelled, "Oh, CRAP!" I sensed movement and jumped—not far, just a few yards ahead.

Brett passed through the space I'd just been. His board hit the snow tail first and he cartwheeled head over ass for several rotations before actually landing on his board and carving into a drunken turn.

He fell over when he'd killed most of his speed and I slid down and skidded to a halt next to him.

"I'm *so* sorry," I said. "I shouldn't have crossed the hill there."

He was shaking his head. "I don't see how I missed you!"

"I ducked," I said. "How many fingers am I holding up?"

"You're holding up fingers?"

I popped his bindings and turned to wave for some help, but Jade and Tara were already running over through the snow.

When Brett stood on his own I decided it was probably okay to help him walk over to the truck. Jade and I each took an arm and Tara brought the board.

He seemed to know who the president was and what the day and year were and even what the Advanced Biology homework for Monday was. His right shoulder was stiff, though, and he decided to call it a day when we helped him out of the truck, at the top of the hill.

"Do you have a ride?" I asked.

"I drove," he said. He pointed to a beat-up Honda parked on the opposite shoulder of Thunderbird.

One of his friends climbed up the hill, hauling his own board. "I was halfway down. I didn't see the fall but I saw you tumble out below. Wow."

I glanced down the hill. From here you could barely see the downslope. From further down, the crest would've blocked the view. I hoped nobody saw my jump. Nobody else had mentioned seeing anything weird as we drove up. The direction I'd jumped was almost directly toward Jade and Tara so they wouldn't have seen much of a shift even if they were looking.

Brett's friend was a gawky, skinny kid with oversized hands and a nose like a beak. Tara had pointed him out in the cafeteria at one point but I forgot why. He took Brett's keys when Brett started fumbling with the lock. "Easy there, Jocko," he said. "Let me drive, okay? It's just up the hill after all."

"I thought you only had your permit," Brett said.

"Nope. Got the provisional last week. I'm good to go."

Brett frowned. "Uh, but—oh, fuck it. Sure."

They put the boards in the back seat, angled to fit, and drove slowly off.

"What's his friend's name?" I asked.

"That's Joe," said Tara. "He's that skateboarder I told you about, the one who's also a jock, since he's captain of the snowboarding team."

"And he's the reason Brett is on the team, too," said Jade.

"Really? Brett looked okay on a board, I thought."

"Oh, he's okay on the snow. But if Joe didn't help him with his schoolwork, Brett wouldn't qualify academically."

My face dropped.

Tara glanced sideways at me. "He's still got that cute butt."

I remembered helping him over to the truck, tucked into his side, his arm over my shoulder. I wasn't thinking about his academics *then*. "I guess."

Clouds were moving in and it was getting colder.

"Who wants to come to my house and shoot pool?"

"I thought it was luck the first three times, but that's the fifth bank shot you've made." I said.

"Really?" said Tara, deadpan.

We were playing cutthroat and Tara was kicking our butts. She had been kicking our butts for the past five games.

Jade was better than me but she was also losing.

"There should be the table's-owner-automatically-gets-to-win rule," I suggested.

"Good luck with that," said Tara, knocking in another ball. "By the way, you're out."

"Aaaagh!" I shook my fists at the ceiling and made faces for the amusement of all. "Who wants more drinks?"

"I'm good," said Jade, swirling her half-full Diet Coke.

"Me, too," said Tara. "Gonna have to go after this game, anyway."

I watched her hit the ball cleanly, watched it go from stationary to a white streak across the table as if it had accelerated instantly. I knew that wasn't the case, but it reminded me of the way I could go from falling off the deck of our cabin to a dead stop under my bed without a single newton-second of imparted momentum.

At supper I asked Dad, "When I jump, can I increase my relative velocity?"

"You do, all the time," he said. "Remember when we talked about jumping from the cabin to the desert?"

"Well, that's matching the local frame, not coming out with a velocity different from the local frame. What happens if I jump to exactly where I already am, but with a change in velocity?"

His jaw started jutting forward. "Remember what we said about smashing through walls? Or having your limbs ripped off?"

"Yes, but . . ."

"But nothing! Don't even *think* about it, young lady."

Mom took a deep breath and I held up my hand. "I was just wondering, Daddy." Okay, I *was* 'thinking about it.'

It wasn't worth getting Dad strung out, though. *And* I'd also avoided promising I wouldn't try any experiments.

He opened his mouth, as if to add something, but now Mom was giving *him* the eye and he closed his mouth again.

Mom said, "Don't *you* have something to tell Cent?"

"I was going to wait until later, but okay."

He turned and reached behind him, to the sideboard next to the dining room table, and grabbed a small cardboard box that he handed to me.

"Here. Reach out and touch someone."

I squealed, then sat back, my mouth open. "Did I just squeal? Tell me I didn't just squeal." I still felt like squealing.

Mom was no help. "I'm gonna have to come down on the side of 'you just squealed like a teenage girl'."

Dad nodded. "Yep . . . squeal."

I breathed out heavily and closed my eyes. "Okay. Let's just pretend that never happened, all right?" The box was already opened. It was a small but thick smartphone with a touch screen. There was a volume rocker and a power switch but everything else was on the touch screen. It was already on and fully charged. "What's the drill?"

"It's like your mom suggested. I found someone to program these so the cellular radio won't come on unless the phone is within a set radius of a GPS-determined position. I've got it set for downtown and a radius that pretty much takes in the entire county. If it loses connection with a cellular tower for any reason, it shuts down the radio until it's verified the position again. You jump out of the area and obviously it will lose the tower. There's a lot of metal roofs around here so if you've lost the tower for more prosaic reasons, you may have to go outside before the GPS receiver can verify the location."

"And I can text?"

"Prepaid. I'll keep it topped off. It just won't work out of

county. If you go out of town on a school trip, we can modify
your location settings appropriately."

I got up and hugged him. "So I can call you here at the
house?"

Mom nodded. "Yes, but Dad got us phones, too. Same deal.
If we're not in county, calls will go to voice mail, texts won't
be delivered until we come back. Ditto for yours."

Dad showed me how to turn the phone on, where the contacts were stored. He'd already added ones labeled *Mom, Dad*,
and *Home*. I scrambled downstairs and got phone numbers for
Tara, Jade, and Grant's big sister, Naomi, from precalculus.

Dad hovered while I entered the numbers, but I glared at
him and Mom patted the couch beside her and said, "Give her
some room, Davy. She can ask for help if she needs it."

"Right." He pulled the manual out of the box and laid it on
the table, and sat down by Mom.

I sent him a text almost immediately and he jerked, like
he'd been poked. Mom and I both laughed and he fished the
phone out of his pocket. "It's set on 'vibrate'." He read the text
aloud. "*Thx4tehfone*." He spelled it out. "Uh. Thanks for the
phone? You misspelled 'the'. Also 'thanks' and 'phone' and
'for.' I did say we had *unlimited* texting, right? You don't have
to abbreviate everything. Won't cost a penny more."

I rolled my eyes. My phone buzzed in my hand and I jerked,
nearly dropping it.

Dad laughed. "It's set on 'vibrate'."

The text was from him. *UrWlcm*.

ELEVEN

Millie: FERPA

Millie dropped by the school office.

"I understand getting calls on my home number, but why am I getting calls from the PTO on my cell phone?"

The secretary blinked. "You didn't give it to them when you signed the PTO membership during registration?"

"I signed up for the PTA. What is this PTO?"

The secretary said, "We have both. Our Parent Teacher Organization isn't part of a national group so it isn't as limited in what it can fund. I believe they share the phone list with the PTA, though."

"I didn't give it to either of them." Millie leaned forward. "It's a brand new phone. I didn't *have* it at registration. I've given the number to my daughter, my husband, and, who else? Oh, yes, *you*, two days ago, as an emergency contact number."

The secretary looked down the connecting hallway to the vice-principle's office, then leaned forward and whispered. "I'm *so* sorry. Once it's in the system, even as an emergency contact, *any* of the administration and teaching staff can see it. Some of them are deeply involved with the PTO." She glanced down the connecting hallway again. "*Some* of them."

Message received.

"Didn't I receive a FERPA information brochure at registration?"

The secretary turned pale. "And read it, too, I see."

"Yes." Millie held up her hand. "Don't worry, I'll take this up with the PTO."

"Darice Mendez? This is Millicent Ross."

"Oh! Excellent, I can mark you off my list! Will you be attending the mixer?"

The "mixer" was a cocktail party/funding drive to supplement the high school's budget.

"I will."

"Oh, *excellent!* You have the location?"

"I do. The back room at the Resplendent, yes?"

"That's right. We had our Christmas party there. It was *very* nice. So I'll put you down for two?"

Millie had already brought it up with Davy with predictable results. He'd said, "No, and make damn sure they don't get hold of *my* cell phone number, too!"

"Just myself," Millie said into the phone.

"Oh. Is Mr. Ross out of town?"

Millie resisted the urge to snap, *Want the man of the house there for a* real *donation?*

"Let's just say this is not his kind of event."

"Oh. Very good, thanks for call—"

"One more thing," Millie said, before the woman could hang up.

"Yes?"

"Some of your messages came to my cell phone."

"Yes?"

"I'm afraid that some helpful person from the school must've passed that number along, but it was for emergency contacts only."

"Oh, that's all right! We don't share our list with *anyone*."

Millie said, "That's not the point. Whoever gave it to you was in violation of the Federal Family Educational Rights and Privacy Act."

"Yes?" The woman didn't sound overly concerned.

"That means they're endangering the school's federal funding. I believe that would include the Bureau of Indian Affairs funding that makes up half the school's budget."

That got her attention. "Really?"

"Really. I want that number removed from your records and I strongly recommend that you let Ms. McClaren know about this issue before she provides any more emergency contact numbers."

"Yes ma'am, I'll tell her!" She inhaled sharply. "I mean, so she can find out who might be doing it."

Right.

"And the phone number?" Millie asked.

"I've crossed it off my list and I'll tell the PTO's secretary!"

"Thank you. Will I see you at the mixer?"

"Indeed."

"I look forward to it."

Davy almost relented when he saw Millie dressed up for the reception.

"*¡Que linda eres!* Maybe I should go along to fight off your admirers."

She kissed him, then pushed his hands away as they strayed toward her bodice. "If you want. If it's like any PTA meeting I've ever seen, they will be talking about school budgets and pushing for donations and volunteers to run fund-raisers. You want to run a bake sale?"

He shuddered.

"There is an open bar, though, *unlike* any PTA meeting I've ever been to. I will be dulling the pain by drinking heavily, so your chance of getting laid afterward goes way up."

He brightened. "How about I just lie in wait until you stagger home, then take advantage of you?"

"That works."

The Resplendent was a restaurant/bar two blocks off Main

Street. Millie had lunched there after accepting the invitation to the mixer, to acquire a jump site. She was extremely glad she'd done so. Though it had stopped falling, the streets were still under a foot of snow.

Her jump site was inside, behind a large ficus in an alcove near the restrooms. Shrugging off her long coat and hanging it over her arm, she bypassed the restaurant's receptionist and checked in with a diminutive woman wearing a sequined pantsuit and holding a clipboard.

"Ms. Mendez, I presume?"

"Darice, please. Mrs. Ross, right? Had to be you, I know everyone else. That's a *gorgeous* dress. How did you get here without freezing to death?"

"Just Millie." Millie shook the woman's hand. "I just avoided the snow as much as possible. *Striking* pantsuit."

"Thank you." Darice leaned closer and whispered conspiratorially, "Long underwear! My car wouldn't make it out of the driveway. Had to walk six blocks and change my shoes here."

She pulled a preprinted name tag off the clipboard and held it out, looking for an appropriate place to pin it, but the lines of Millie's dress defeated her.

"Here," Millie said, holding up her clutch purse. "Pin it to this."

Darice did.

"Great. Check your coat over there. Bar is *there*, and the chairman will be giving a presentation at *that* end in about a half hour."

Millie didn't have to go to the bar. Three different men offered to fetch her a drink before she reached the crowd surrounding the bar.

She accepted the third offer, from the man standing with his wife who introduced herself after reading Millie's name tag. "I'm Misty Chilton. That was Tom. Your daughter's been hanging out with our girl, Jade."

"Ah! And Tara—the Krakatoa homework club. Is Cent being a bad influence? She's always wanted to be a bad influence."

Misty laughed. "In a way. I understand she does her homework *weeks* in advance. She's badly diminished the procrastination quotient at their homework sessions."

Millie shook her head. "I am sorry to hear it. Whatever happened to waiting until the last minute?"

"Or 'my dog ate my homework?' There are honored traditions in our educational institutions, for goodness sake!"

"Kids these days," agreed Millie.

Misty introduced her to the two men who'd also offered to get Millie a drink. "Stay away from these bums, especially my colleague Dr. George here. He's newly divorced and desperate. Leon, here, is happily married but he'll still try and look down your dress."

Leon looked amiably affronted. "Hey, I don't grab, like *some*." He glanced across the room toward a cluster of men talking at the end of the bar.

Misty looked less amused and sighed. "No, dear, you certainly don't." She changed the subject. "So you moved here from out of the country," she said to Millie. "And that's why you've been homeschooling your daughter?"

That and the people trying to kill or capture us. "Yes. But she wanted to finish high school in an *actual* school. So here we are." She smiled brightly. "Where's my drink?"

Tom Chilton arrived shortly and handed Millie her gin and tonic and his wife a white wine. "I think I deserve a medal. They're about to declare martial law over at the bar. I'm sure I was nearly shot several times."

Misty kissed him on the cheek. "There, there, dear, I'm sure our health plan covers psychiatric care. We'll get you a nice therapist and you can suck your thumb on his couch."

Tom smiled at her and didn't look the least bit traumatized. "Just get me through Bob's pitch and I'll be happy."

"Amen to that," said Leon.

"Bob?" said Millie.

"Bob Chanlee. He's the chairman and the biggest contributor to the PTO," said George.

"And our biggest problem," said Misty with a lowered

voice. "Wants all our support to go to the football team." She smiled fondly at her husband. "Tom's the PTA president this year. We're here to remind people that there are other places their money could go."

Tom sighed. "If we could serve alcohol at our meetings, I bet we'd get more donations for the library and teaching budget."

Millie looked at Misty, doubtfully. "Football? I came out in this snow for a fund-raiser for football?"

Misty nodded.

Millie said, "I'm going to need another drink."

"So, how much money did we donate to that PTO thing?" Davy asked, some time after she had returned home.

"Nothing."

"Really? I could've sworn that wasn't your intention."

Millie settled deeper into the sheets, her thigh across Davy's bare belly. "We did donate to the PTA, though, six thousand. It's going toward teaching assistants in the more crowded classrooms."

"And what would it have gone to at the PTO thing?"

"Football equipment. Maybe an assistant coach."

Davy winced.

Millie said, "I had them take our name off the list."

"Did I ever mention what a good wife you are?"

"Well, you just showed me."

"I could show you *again*."

Millie pretended to study a nonexistent watch.

"I *guess* I can fit you in."

"Good answer."

TWELVE

"Good reflexes!"

I snowshoed to school.

While the county had plowed the roads, the path through the woods was still buried deep. I could've jumped to the edge of the woods, but if someone backtracked me it would look weird, my footsteps appearing out of nowhere. I figured I could establish a trail and then, barring more snow, anyone back-tracking me would see the path.

I left a half hour early. Breaking a fresh trail always takes more time and energy, but even though it was predawn gray, the woods were gorgeous and I enjoyed it.

The smoking crowd was at the bleachers, including Caffeine. It was cold but the air was still so they were more spread out. I moved wide, shuffling along on the top of the snow. Caffeine saw me coming and moved out to intercept me, but the minute she stepped beyond the snow packed down by the smokers, she sank thigh deep.

I heard her swear and grinned involuntarily. I tried to take my face back to neutral, but she'd seen my smile. The expression on her face was poisonous. She climbed back onto the packed snow and headed across toward the door, but I was out of the bindings of my snowshoes and inside the school before she got there.

It was a bit cramped, getting my outerwear and the snowshoes into my locker. I'd made good time so I was the first one into biology class, beating even Mr. Hill out of the teachers lounge. Tara came in five minutes later and spent some time admiring my phone.

Brett didn't show up until almost second bell, nipping in at the last minute. His seat was near the back on the other side of the classroom. I was looking at him as he came in, but he didn't even notice me.

I didn't know whether to be relieved or mad. I was hoping to exchange phone numbers with him. He was late, but when class was over he was out the door before I'd even picked up my backpack.

Tara joined me at the door. "You okay?"

"I guess. Why?"

She shrugged. "You looked a little upset there."

"Really?" I shook my head. "I will wear my heart upon my sleeve for daws to peck at."

"Oh, so you *were* upset? What are daws?"

"Some kind of bird, I think."

"What does that have to do with wearing your heart on your sleeve?"

"It's the entire phrase. Iago says it in *Othello*."

"Daws. Huh. So, did you want to talk to Brett?"

I winced. "I thought I did. Maybe not."

She nodded. "Donna probably wouldn't approve."

My stomach twisted. "Donna?"

"His girlfriend."

"He has a girlfriend?"

"Duh."

"Why didn't you say something about that yesterday? When he was hitting on me?"

"He's a *guy*. Just because he's flirting doesn't mean he isn't taken. Besides—*guys*. Being in a relationship don't keep them from seeing other girls."

I could feel my ears getting hot.

Tara raised her eyebrows.

"Homeschooled, remember?" I looked away. "See you at lunch."

Later, in the cafeteria, Tara and Jade looked at me warily, but I smiled and said, "Sorry I was such a spaz this morning."

Tara said, "I'm sorry. I didn't think about the homeschooling thing. You haven't had much experience with boys?"

I blew out through closed lips. "You don't know the half of it. Raised in isolation, that's me. I'm not very good at people of any gender."

"I looked up daws. It's short for jackdaw, member of the crow family."

They'd both bought the cafeteria lunch but I pulled mine out of my backpack.

"Oh, wow," said Jade. "Where'd you get the bento box?"

Dad had picked up an *ekiben* for me from an all-night bento stall at the Tokyo train station. I'd taken it out of the disposable box it had come in and repacked it in a traditional lacquer lunch box.

"Told you, I was going to bring my own lunch."

Jade said, "You *win* at lunch. Your prize? You get to give me one of those breaded shrimp."

I used the chopsticks to drop it next to her cafeteria mystery meat. "*Lucky* me."

Tara licked her lips. "Can I have a taste of that salmon roe? Where did you even get *ikura* around here?"

I smiled mysteriously and borrowed her spoon to get a generous heap of sushi rice topped with salmon eggs. "Here ya go."

She tasted it and her eyes rolled back in her head. "I had this once in San Diego," she said in a reverent hush.

They both looked at their cafeteria lunch and then back at mine.

"I think I'm going to start bringing my lunch, too," said Jade.

We did drills in basketball, first passing, then guarded jump shots, with the tallest girls in the class doing the blocking. It was frustrating because they casually batted away nearly all the shots. No matter how high I leaped, they were taller. Pogo girls.

I wanted to jump, to teleport up into the air, higher than them. But that would be pretty unmistakable—pretty dumb. But I wished I could leap higher. My thigh muscles weren't flabby. Snowboarding wasn't exactly effortless.

What if I could add some velocity to my leap?

And what if you add enough velocity to smash through the roof?

I did get one ball past the guard, feinting a leap so that she was coming back down while I went up, but I still missed the basket.

To add to the humiliation, Coach had us switch, to guard the basket against the tall girls who constantly scored against us.

"What do you expect?" said Paula, seeing my face twist in frustration. "It's really *their* practice." She tilted her head at the taller girls. "They've got a game tonight."

"Oh," I said. "Didn't realize they were on the basketball team. But why'd they have to be so tall?"

"Pity them," said Paula. "They're last in the division."

I saw Brett's girlfriend, Donna, before art class, leaning against him. She was my height, but older. I'd seen her before, outside, with the smokers, and in the cafeteria where she sat with Caffeine.

Perfect.

Caffeine was still milking her wrist injury for maximum sloth, though I knew she was scheduled to resume PE the following week. In art class she told Mrs. Begay, "I can't really draw left-handed." Her right hand was still in a Velcro-secured wrist brace.

Mrs. Begay looked skeptical but she let Caffeine read instead. Reading for Caffeine consisted of opening her notebook and using it to conceal her cell phone while she texted.

It didn't take a genius to notice the pages never turned, and I could tell Mrs. Begay knew what was going on.

After class, Caffeine lingered by the door, ostensibly looking at her phone, but I saw her glance my way as I put away my sketchbook. The rest of the students filed out and Mrs. Begay went to the supply closet in the back, putting away the still-life models we'd used in class.

Instead of leaving, I went to Mrs. Begay and said, "Do you need any help with that?"

Caffeine shook her head sharply and I heard her mutter "Kissass." She left the room.

Mrs. Begay shook her head. "That's sweet, Cent, but I've got them organized just *so*. It would take me longer to describe my system than it would to just put them away myself."

I said goodbye and halfway to the door, while Mrs. Begay was still turned away, I jumped outside, behind the evergreen bushes at the end of the wing. Three steps took me to the glass doors at the end of the hallway.

Caffeine *was* waiting outside the door of the art classroom. *Let her wait.*

I crunched though packed snow to the west door and ducked in to get my coat and snowshoes.

For the first time (outside our living room) I used the new phone to check in with Mom before walking to Krakatoa with Jade and Tara. This took a lot longer than usual because, even though the streets and sidewalks were mostly plowed, both of them wanted to try the snowshoes. We had to hopscotch around to find snow deep enough, first using the school's front lawn, then moving to a series of empty lots that only vaguely led toward the coffee shop.

I'd already done most of my schoolwork. Half of my teachers put the assignment on the board at the beginning of class and, if you're caught up on the reading, which I usually was, the lecture actually gave you the answers. But I was even more obsessive than usual about it, since it kept me from thinking about Brett.

Which is why I was surprised when he walked up to our table up on the balcony.

"'Sup?" he said.

I stared at him blankly.

He looked uncomfortable.

"Uh . . . hi?" I finally said.

This apparently didn't help much, but then I saw someone standing behind him.

It was Joe, the friend who'd driven Brett home after his fall. He pushed forward. "Hey."

I looked at Tara and Jade, mystified. They were looking at Joe.

"Hey, yourself," said Tara.

Joe turned back to me. "You're Cent, right? I'm Joe Trujeque." His voice was deep for someone so skinny. Resonant.

I nodded. "Hello."

"Saw you boarding on the hill."

I'd seen him, too, but hadn't been looking that closely. Once I'd seen Brett's smile, I'd only had eyes for him. "Yeah," I said. I was still confused. Was *he* coming on to me?

The silence stretched and Brett broke in, saying in a rush, "We need more girls on the snowboarding team."

Joe turned his hands over, indicating both Jade and me. "Because of Title IX, the school won't spring for transportation to practice and events without at least one-third girls on the team, and we're down two members. One messed up her knee and is out for the winter. The other one didn't qualify this semester."

"Didn't qualify? She wasn't a good enough boarder?" I carefully didn't look at Jade when I said that. Jade was okay, but I didn't picture her as a competitive snowboarder. I didn't picture *myself* as a competitive snowboarder.

"Academically. She was on probation but she didn't pull up her grades. Now she's off." He turned to Jade. "I know *your* grades are good enough." Then he nodded at me. "You're new so you're a blank slate. You could make straight F's this semester and you'd still be eligible until spring grades come out, which is after the season is over, see?"

F's? I was speechless. *Who do you think I am? Who do you think* you *are?*

Jade looked surprised. "You guys must really be desperate to ask *me*."

Joe spread his hands. "A little. But you can board. You have your own equipment."

Tara laughed. "Ha. It's more about the transport than anything. You could probably be crippled, blind, and deaf and they'd take you, just so the boys' team can get to the meets."

Joe glared back. "It's not just the boys' team. Lany has a real shot at state in the half-pipe and Carita is doing really good in the slopestyle. Lany has a better chance than any of us *boys* at placing." He looked back at me. "What do you say?"

I was still pissed. *F's?* I took a deep breath and exhaled. "Joe, is it? What I say is: please excuse us for a moment."

He stood there, puzzled.

I rephrased. "Go *away* while I talk to my . . . colleagues."

His eyebrows went up. "Oh. Right." He backed up and, when Brett didn't move, grabbed Brett's arm. "We'll go downstairs and get a drink, then check back, okay?"

He threaded his way back to the stairs, glancing back over his shoulder a couple of times.

Tara laughed when they finally dropped out of sight down the stairs. "Well, you've got them by the short hairs." She looked at Jade. "What do you think? You wanna be a jock?"

"A jock? This isn't being a jock. This is more like chess club. They're not a real team—just a club in the state league." She looked like she was thinking it over. "What do *you* think?" At first I thought she was talking to me but she was looking at Tara.

Tara shrugged. "Up to you. It's six more weeks, right? They practice every Saturday at Durango and I think there's three more general meets. Sundays, I think. Doubt if you have to worry about the state meet but you might have to go along to cheer Lany on."

Jade blinked. "Lany's all right, but isn't Caffeine on the team?"

My stomach clenched. "Caffeine? No thanks!"

Tara shook her head. "Lany and Carita are *still* on the team, so, if I'm not mistaken, Caffeine is the one who got bumped for academics. She certainly doesn't have the bad knee. That was Dulcey Cardenas."

"Oh," I said. "Won't that piss her off, though? For me to go on the team?"

Jade tilted her head to one side. "So what's your point?"

I snorted. "She's already laying for me. Can't see how this can make things worse. Will your parents go for it?"

"Probably. They think I spend too much time lying around watching anime. Yours?"

"Don't know." I looked over the rail down to the main floor. Joe and Brett were still in line at the counter. "I'll call and ask."

I got Mom who, after asking a few questions, said, "Yes, if *you* want to. If it's something you'd really enjoy."

"Yes, please."

"Right."

I'd let *her* sell it to Dad. They tended not to contradict each other so if one of them had already said "yes" it usually meant "yes." If one of them said "no," ditto—which was why I'd asked Mom first.

Jade had touched base with her dad while I was on the phone with Mom.

Brett and Joe came back with espresso drinks and Jade said. "Where's ours?"

Brett blinked. "Yours, uh, yours? I thought you already had some?"

Jade said, "You're trying to get us to say yes to this insanity? And you didn't bring *us* anything?"

Joe held his coffee out and said, deadpan, "You can have my mocha. But I spit in it."

I couldn't help myself. I giggled.

Joe said, "So, did you guys decide?"

I could see Jade was set to give him more trash so I quickly said, "Yeah. We'll do it."

He raised his eyebrows. "Really? And you think your parents will let you?"

I raised my cell phone. "Permission already acquired. Oh brave new world that has such technology in it. You should know, though, that Caffeine, for some reason, hates my guts. Does that matter to you guys?"

Brett shrugged. "Knew it." He shrugged again, spreading his hands.

Joe, though, widened his eyes. "Oh. Are you the girl from PE? I pictured someone bigger. You fight a lot? That could get you kicked off the team, too."

"I don't fight *at all!* Caffeine slipped and fell. Didn't touch her."

He digested this. "Okay—not a problem for *me.* She won't be riding to events with us anyway, but she might show up at practice. She still has her season pass." He dug in his backpack for a binder from which he removed several sheets of paper. "Permission slips for participation and for transportation, liability waiver, supplementary insurance for both the events and the transportation, and the registration form for a student season pass at Durango. It's halfway through the season so it will be reduced."

He was organized, I'll give him that.

"The van leaves from school for practice at 7:30 AM Saturday. We don't have a meet this Sunday but there's one the Sunday after."

"Do I have to ride in the van?"

"You can't drive yourself, but your parents can."

I hadn't been thinking about *driving.*

"So with us, there's four girls on the team now. So, eight boys?"

He looked surprised. "You heard?"

"It's called math. You said you needed at least a third girls and you were down two."

"Right. Eight boys. Four girls with you two."

I almost said, *Maybe I* won't *get all F's.* Instead I said, "Okay. We'll be there."

Dad didn't overturn Mom's permission but it was a close thing.

"You could get killed!"

"I *already* snowboard, Dad. It's not like I'm stopping. They've got a coach—one of the instructors at Durango. It's like *really* intense lessons."

"It's a public venue. People will take pictures."

I stared at him blankly. "Excuse me?"

"Pictures which people put up on their social networks and websites and send to other peoples' phones!"

I looked at Mom. She closed her eyes and sighed.

"Uh, are they going to steal my soul?" I said.

He blinked. "No, but *they* could see the pictures."

There was no pretending I didn't know who *they* were. "So? *They* don't know I exist, remember? Now if it was *your* picture, I could understand. Do I really look that much like you?"

I did, sort of. I've got his nose but Mom's coloring and eyes. And his stubbornness. "I'm a sixteen-year-old girl—not a forty-three-year-old man."

Mom nodded at this and Dad glared at her.

"Dearest," Mom said. "As sports go, she'll be covered up more than most, right? *We* can even watch the meets because we can bundle up all the way to the eyes, covering *everything*. It's an outdoor winter sport. They hold it in *winter*. Where it's *cold*."

Dad's mouth twitched.

"Besides," Mom said. "I already said yes."

He opened his mouth and then closed it, licked his lips, then muttered, "Don't blame me when she comes home in *pieces*."

"*You're* the one who started her snowboarding in the first place."

He showed up two hours later with a new board for me and a bag, one that would hold two boards. That's totally Dad. *No, you absolutely can not! Well, you'll need this then.*

"I checked out the state league website. They do half-pipe, slopestyle, boardercross, and grand slalom. Your board is pretty good for freestyle, but this one is for racing. I didn't buy the bindings yet."

I'd been on the Internet, too. "Right. I'll need new boots." Racing uses a stiff boot, like an alpine ski boot, which require different bindings.

Dad nodded. "Thought we could go try boots and bindings."

I looked at my watch. It was nine at night. "Where?"

He shrugged. "Niseko Village."

"Hokkaido? What is it, one PM, there?"

"Noon."

I jumped up and hugged him—surprising him, I think—then pushed him out of the room so I could change.

Niseko Village, on the northernmost island in Japan, is famous for its powder. Dad took me there when I was learning to ride in deep snow, like we get in the Yukon.

Fortunately, they hadn't had fresh snow lately, since I needed to try out the boots and binding on groomed snow. We got back at midnight, having picked out bindings and boots. Dad took them away with the new board to have them mounted, and I tried to sleep.

My quads and stomach muscles hurt the next morning—not horribly, just the kind of ache a really good workout brings. The thought of snowshoeing, even just the stretch from the woods to the school, was daunting. I jumped all the way to school, to my spot behind the evergreen bushes near art class.

I was early and it was too cold to wait outside, but I spotted Joe Trujeque reading in the library. I plopped the sheaf of filled-out paperwork on the table in front of him.

"Money orders? Can't they write a check?"

"Our account isn't local," I said. "Better you get something that will clear immediately."

He shrugged. "I'll see if I can run down George."

"George?"

"Mr. Hill."

"The biology teacher?"

Joe nodded. "He's our sponsor. Not exactly our coach—

that's Ricardo over at Durango. George likes to board, but he's really more our chaperone."

I held out my hand. "I've got him first period. I can give them to him."

He handed them back. "I thought you were a sophomore?"

"So?"

"Isn't that Biology II?"

"So?" This was as bad as his comment about all F's.

Some of my irritation must've shown on my face because he leaned back and said, "Uh, thanks. If you could take them to him, that would be great."

"Right." I left, rather abruptly. Not as abruptly as I *could* have, though.

Mr. Hill looked mildly surprised when I handed him the paperwork. "Joe said he got somebody, but I didn't realize it was you. You been boarding long?"

"Since I was nine."

"Well at least we won't have to worry about *your* academics," he said thoughtfully as he looked over the paperwork. I smiled at his bent head. I was sure he didn't mean it like Joe had. *He* knew what my work was like.

We were eating lunch when I heard Caffeine's voice over the already loud cafeteria noises—loud, and then louder.

"What? WHAT? *WHAT!*"

I looked back over my shoulder because it was her voice, but most of the cafeteria was staring, it was that loud.

Caffeine was sitting with Brett's girlfriend Donna and staring at her, mouth wide open. Her head swiveled and then she was staring across four tables, right at me, and her face twisted so much that I hardly recognized her. She climbed to her feet and she kept climbing, onto the bench, then right onto the top of the table, shrugging off Donna's arm. Then she leaped, table top to table top, her hands reaching out, her fingers curved like claws.

I pivoted, got my legs over the bench, and stood just as she dove at me.

I jumped a foot to the side and ducked slightly. I felt her clawing hand glance off my shoulder, and she slammed into the table top, skidding across the table, driving like a wedge between Jade and Tara, and knocking them sideways on their bench. Caffeine went arms-first down onto the floor between our table and the next.

Vice Principal McClaren and Coach Taichert, on lunch duty, were there almost immediately, had probably started moving when Caffeine first climbed on the table.

"What's this about?" said McClaren. She was looking accusingly at *me*. Coach Taichert helped Caffeine up and then restrained her from climbing back over the table at me.

"Ma'am?"

"You must've done something to provoke her!"

"I was just sitting here eating lunch," I said.

Coach Taichert said, "Janet? I saw the whole thing. Caffeine just went for her. Cent didn't turn around until Caffeine started shouting."

McClaren frowned at Coach and he blinked, his face going still. He took a half step back.

Caffeine was breathing heavily, her eyes murderous.

Tara said what I'd been thinking—rather she asked it. "Was it because she heard that Cent joined the snowboard team?"

Coach Taichert's mouth made an "O" shape.

McClaren looked confused. "Why should that matter? Caffeine's not *on* the snowboard team anymore."

Caffeine hauled off and kicked the bench in front of her. Trays jumped on the table top.

Ms. McClaren gasped and Coach Taichert pulled Caffeine further back from the table. He frowned at Ms. McClaren and said, "Maybe we should move this down to admin?"

"I should think so!" said Ms. McClaren. "Come along, Camelia."

"It's Caffeine!" Caffeine said, and pulled back as Coach Taichert tugged her toward the door.

"Take it up with your parents, Camelia. You'll be talking to *them* soon enough," Ms. McClaren said. She pointed at the door.

Caffeine ripped her arm out of Coach Taichert's grip and stomped toward the door. Donna met her there with her backpack. Caffeine took it without saying a thing. Donna stood there biting her lower lip.

I started to sit back down but Ms. McClaren, trailing Caffeine and Coach Taichert to the door, said, "You, too, Millicent."

I wanted to snarl at her like Caffeine had. *It's Cent!* Instead I schooled my face to stillness. Tara looked at me and raised her eyebrows, then picked up her book bag and walked along with me. Jade trailed behind her.

Out in the hall Ms. McClaren noticed my friends. "I didn't call you two."

"Why not?" said Tara. "Caffeine actually hit *us*."

"She wasn't after *you*," Ms. McClaren snapped.

"How do you know that?" said Tara. "Jade is also a new member of the snowboarding team."

Ms. McClaren straightened her spine and narrowed her eyes. "It isn't a *team*."

Tara let out her breath in exasperation. "It's not an official *school* team, no, but that's not the point. Jade is also a new member of the snowboarding *club*. Why are you taking Cent to the office and not us?"

I held up my hand in front of my stomach and shook it side to side. "Guys, it's all right. I'm sure Ms. McClaren just wants to know if there is any sort of animosity between me and Caffeine, before she makes any disciplinary decisions."

Ms. McClaren looked at me, surprised. "Well, yes." Her eyes narrowed. "Is there?"

"She doesn't seem to like me," I said. "It's been like that from my first day. However, the only thing I've ever done is like what I did in the cafeteria."

"What's that?" Ms. McClaren asked.

"Move out of her way." There. That was the exact truth.

Ms. McClaren frowned at me, then glanced back over her shoulder. Coach Taichert and Caffeine had reached the door to the front office.

"All right. I may have questions for you later, Millicent." She walked off.

I waited until she was definitely out of earshot before I said, "It's *Cent*."

Jade laughed softly.

"Uh, thanks guys. But you didn't have to."

"Yes we did," said Tara. "Dr. Prady is at the Southwest Principals Conference with Dr. Morgan."

"So?"

"The only time Ms. McClaren handles disciplinary activities is when they're both is out of town."

"I must be dense but—"

Jade said, "That's the only time she's *allowed*. Not after the homecoming dance."

"What happened at the homecoming dance?"

"The lawsuit, uh, right. You weren't here. The short form is that Ms. McClaren just *knows* things."

At my expression, Tara added, "She knows things that have no basis in reality and she dismisses any evidence that happens to disagree with what she *knows*."

"She found papers and a half-empty baggie of pot behind the stage curtains and had Leo Neztsosie hauled off by Deputy Tomez, saying he'd put it there."

"Oh? She saw him?"

Tara shook her head. "Well, she *said* she did. Later she said she just *knew* he put it there."

"Thank god for cell phones," Jade said. "Monica Munez was getting some video of the dancing, and in the background you could clearly see Shelly Clew put the baggie behind the curtain. I mean, clearly."

"Monica didn't even see it. A week later she put the video up on her Facebook page and someone else spotted it." Tara said. "The school district settled out of court. I don't know how much, but Leo says his college is paid for."

"Why did Ms. McClaren think he did it?"

"He was sitting at a table at that end of the room. She also doesn't like him."

"Why does Ms. McClaren still have a job?"

"The school board was split on it," said Tara.

Jade snorted. "Yeah. There was the half that wanted her fired and the half that were members of her church."

"Be fair," said Tara. "One of the board members that wanted her fired was also a member of her church."

Jade said, "Yeah, I guess." She looked sideways at me. "I couldn't believe how *fast* you got out of her way."

Tara laughed. "Good reflexes! I blinked and missed you moving, but Caffeine's expression changed from fierce to *oh shit* as she realized she missed you."

I smiled weakly. "Just lucky, I guess."

I hoped everyone in that room thought they'd blinked.

The bell rang and we went our separate ways.

By the end of the school day I was sick of people.

It was the incident in the cafeteria. In PE they stared. In humanities they stared. In art they stared. They stopped talking in the halls as I walked by and their voices resumed in hushed tones after I passed.

I hoped it was just the bit with Caffeine jumping across the tables. Or that I was a weirdo because of the way I acted, or dressed, or who I hung out with, or even that I must be one tough girlchild because Caffeine had gone for me more than once without effect.

As long as it wasn't because I could jump.

Jade and Tara suggested Krakatoa, but the thought of more eyes watching was too much and I begged off.

"Saturday morning, though," said Jade. "The van to Durango. I swear, you don't show up and I'll quit."

I crossed my heart and then made a straight line across my throat, something I learned from Mom, but they didn't get it, so I had to say, "Cross my heart and hope to die."

Mom looked surprised when I showed up. She was sitting

in the living room and reading some kind of report, her phone sitting beside her on the end table.

"Everything okay?" Then she frowned. "No. It's not, is it?"

Sometimes I don't hate that she knows me so well.

I only left out jumping, that time in the shower, and *how* I got out of Caffeine's path in the cafeteria.

Oddly enough, Mom seemed more concerned about what I told her about Ms. McClaren than about Caffeine.

"Tell you what—you ever get called into that woman's office, say you have to go to the bathroom, then come get me or your dad."

I held up my phone.

She nodded. "Sure, try that first since it would get us anywhere in the county. But if we're at the cabin you might have to come fetch us."

Part of me wanted to protest that I could handle the crazy Ms. McClaren but instead I said, "Thanks, Mom. Glad you got my back."

THIRTEEN

Millie: Old Allies

Millie was listening to an argument about anthropogenic climate change at an international relief conference in Washington DC. The meeting was being held at the Ronald Reagan Building, convenient to the U.S. Agency for International Development. It was one of many different meetings happening there; she'd almost walked into a symposium on computer forensics in law enforcement just down the hall.

She was tired and really annoyed at the two gentlemen who were not arguing about the evidence, but about the nomenclature. Global warming. Climate change. Anthropogenic global warming.

I should have gone with the computer symposium.

The particular session was an emergency meeting added at the last minute to discuss the impact of a particularly nasty storm system headed into the Bay of Bengal. It was five months until the regular monsoon season would start, but there it was nonetheless, carrying a ridiculous amount of moisture and headed right for Bangladesh.

The moderator of the panel finally quashed the argument about names, and the panel started discussing areas of particular sensitivity regarding the impending rain. Of particular interest to Millie were a couple of areas not normally at risk but in peril because of repair projects on flood control embankments and dikes damaged during a nasty cyclone seven months before, at the end of last monsoon season.

Millie took a lot of notes.

As she exited the session she came face to face with a woman with short silver hair who was heading for the door to Woodrow Wilson Plaza. The woman sidestepped Millie, saying, "Excuse me," and the voice confirmed Millie's first impression.

Millie controlled an impulse to jump away. She took a step to the wall and looked around for observers, but there weren't any obvious watchers, just people streaming by in both directions—coming out of the meeting rooms, heading to the restrooms. Millie turned and followed the woman, catching up and falling in step with her in the middle of the plaza.

"Becca."

Millie was wearing a red wig and slightly tinted glasses. Becca Martingale, FBI, looked sideways at her and raised her eyebrows, but clearly didn't recognize Millie.

Well, it had been seventeen years.

"Do you have time for coffee?" Millie gestured at the Starbucks a hundred feet away. "Or we could go to the one at the Metreon."

Becca froze midstep, and Millie, walking past, had to turn back to face her.

"Millie?"

"Yep."

Becca stared at her, mouth half open. "I guess I didn't imagine it all."

"I wish."

"Are you all right? Your husband?"

Millie nodded. "Yes. I wasn't seeking you out. I didn't recognize *you* until I heard your voice."

"I thought you'd heard—" Becca looked around, checking the environment. "We should definitely get a coffee." She pointed at the Starbucks. "*Not* the Metreon, though."

"All right."

FOURTEEN

"Cent, in the desert, with a blunt instrument."

Mom went to a reception at a refugee conference in DC but said, before leaving, "Dad's handling dinner tonight at the cabin, okay?"

I rolled my eyes. "At the cabin?"

"It makes him feel safer. Seven, right?"

"Right."

That gave me three hours.

It was sixty-eight degrees in the desert in West Texas, where I'd had my encounter with the young rattlesnake, and the air was still.

I'd arrived standing still, despite the fact that I was several hundred miles south of where I'd left, so my velocity west to east had probably just increased by a good chunk.

I jumped to the edge of the pit, the sinkhole with the water and the island in the bottom. Without pausing, I stepped off the edge and let myself drop toward the water fifty feet below.

I flinched—that is I jumped away—finding myself in the pillow cave under my bed, when I'd only dropped a few feet.

Scaredy-cat.

I returned to the cliff's top. It was fifty feet to the bottom. It would take just a bit over a second and a half to drop to the surface of the water below. I tested my hypothesis with a rock. *One-one thousand. Two-one—* Splash.

I should at *least* be able to hold off to the one second mark. And shouldn't I be able to return to the pit's edge instead of my bedroom every time?

I made it to "one-one thou—" before I found myself back under the damn bed. The next time I managed to jump back to the lip but didn't even make it to the second "one" in the cadence.

I kept at it.

At the end of the hour I was dropping a full second and a half and jumping away to wherever I chose. Once I waited slightly too long and my boots splashed into the water before I was gone. They were barely wet on the outside, and the water hadn't had time to soak in.

That was pushing it a bit, but even then I managed to jump back to the pit's edge instead of hiding under my bed.

Good enough.

Considering just the local frame, after falling a second and a half, I was moving forty-eight feet per second. I had to go back and use my desktop to translate that: just under thirty-three miles per hour.

Okay. So I was changing my frame of reference, going from thirty-three mph to zero mph, pretty much instantly. I was changing my physical location about fifty feet when I did this. What I wanted to do was stay in the same place but change my *velocity*, instead.

There was a sandy brush- and cactus-free wash farther out in the desert. If I fell down there, I wouldn't get stabbed or hit my head on a rock. I got out in the middle and started by jumping to exactly where I was.

Nothing happened. I didn't really jump. I guess my subconscious knew I was already there.

I jumped a foot to one side, like I had when Caffeine dove at me in the cafeteria. That worked, so I tried a half foot. Jumping a smaller distance was harder, but I *could* stay right where I was and change my orientation, as if I'd spun around really, really fast. One second I was facing the darkening east and the next I was facing the sun, which was nearing the horizon.

I bet *that* looked weird.

Okay. This time I tried to add velocity.

It didn't work.

I was hoping for the same velocity I'd achieved at the end of the one-and-a-half second drop, thirty-three mph, only up. I'd just changed my velocity that much over at the pit, but when I tried it, nothing happened.

"Crap." I kicked at the sand.

It was like my first jumps. Frustrating, totally out of my control. Maybe it wasn't something I *could* do, even though I was obviously doing it every time I jumped from a moving vehicle, or north or south of my position. Certainly I'd been doing it from the drops in the pit.

Breathe, I said to myself. It was weird but when I say that, it's *Mom's* voice I hear. I dropped my shoulders and stretched my neck side to side.

How had I gotten control before? Not those panicked reflexive flinches, but those measured, conscious jumps?

Right, it had been the smell of things.

But how do you *smell* speed?

I thought back to the pit, to how it had felt as my feet neared the water and the air rushed by. The most memorable thing was the noise, the rising pitch of wind that rose to a shriek as the air rushed by faster and faster. Louder and louder.

I closed my eyes and tried to remember that rushing sound, the feel of the wind, only coming from above. I didn't want to appear in the wash with a downward velocity of thirty-three mph. I wanted to—

"Shit!"

The ground dropped away and I tumbled up, losing my balance, flailing my arms, tilting forward, watching the wash drop below me, like I was looking out of a rising glass elevator. The drop slowed almost immediately, and several stories above the sand I stopped rising and began dropping again, watching the sand come up faster and faster like the water in the bottom of the pit.

I did end up back under the bed this time.

Don't even think *about it, young lady.*

Ha.

I kept my eyes open the next time and tried to stay balanced, reaching for that right pitch and volume of shrieking air, of flapping clothes, and I was flying up, like a thrown rock. I still tilted forward when I bent my head to watch the ground, but not as much. I waited for peak altitude and the beginnings of the drop, then jumped back to the sand below.

I laughed out loud.

Happy thoughts. Think happy thoughts.

It was purely ballistic, like basic physics classes. If I was starting with the same velocity reached at the end of a fifty-foot drop, then I was rising fifty feet before gravity killed my upward velocity. I knew the relevant equation. I sang it out loud. "Distance equals one half A T squared."

Wash. Rinse. Repeat. I'd clearly done it enough times when my heart stopped pounding as I shot into the air.

I thought about the girls on the basketball team. I crouched and leaped, doing the velocity jump at the same time. How many people do *you* know who can jump fifty feet into the air?

I let myself drop most of the way to the ground before I killed all velocity by jumping back to the sand.

If I tried the same thing in the gym I'd crash into the ceiling.

Less velocity. Less noise? Certainly less air rushing by.

I worked on that same leap-jump, reducing the amount of velocity until I slowed to a stop with my head about twelve feet in the air.

Bet I could slam dunk a basketball. Tall as the girls on the basketball team were, I didn't think *any* of them could.

If I could reduce the velocity, could I increase it?

What would four times as fast be like?

I tried to imagine what four times as fast would sound like, crouched, and leaped up into the sky.

I wore my nicest kimono to supper with the full *katsura* wig in the *shimada* hairstyle, and the white pancake makeup. The kimono and obi are normally a real pain to put on by myself. This time it was almost impossible. My feet made knocking sounds as I walked across the wooden floor in my willow-block *okobo*.

"Why are your eyes so red?" Dad asked.

"I got face powder in 'em."

"Ouch."

I bowed politely and covered my face with my fan.

So far, so good.

It must have been at least ten times as fast.

I'm guessing—I certainly didn't have an airspeed indicator, but it was like hitting a wall and, in the instant before I flinched away to the pillow cave under the bed, the wind ripped off my clothes, wrenched at all of my joints, and blackened both my eyes.

I hadn't really gotten face powder in my eyes.

I finally found my second boot in a stand of prickly pear. I never did find one of the socks, and my jeans were completely ruined, ripped in two separate pieces, with several additional tears in each leg. My flannel shirt stayed on but was ripped at the shoulders and pocket, and the sports bra never even shifted.

The panties were in the middle of the wash near the first boot.

Don't even think *about it, young lady.*

Well, maybe Dad *did* have a point.

Mom arrived, took a look at me, and bowed formally from the waist, hands on her thighs, *"Konban wa o-genki sou desu ne,* Cent-*san."*

"Arigato, okaasan." I bowed. "Uh, you look nice, too."

"Are we having Japanese?"

"Indian, actually," Dad said. He looked back at me. "You want to go change into a sari?"

I shook my head. It was the makeup that mattered.

I moved very carefully when we sat down.

"Don't fall off your shoes," Dad teased.

"Leave her alone," said Mom. "I think she's doing very well."

In truth, my knees and ankles hurt so much that I was afraid I'd collapse.

Eating was difficult. Managing the sleeves of the kimono put more stress on my shoulders and elbows. I should've dressed as a mime, instead.

I bent over my plate and tried to move as little as possible. I *was* hungry.

Mom said, "I saw Becca Martingale this afternoon."

Dad, using his fork to pile some *dahl* onto a piece of *naan*, froze. "How did *that* happen?"

"She was attending a meeting in the same facility as mine. I said hello."

Dad licked his lips. "That's taking a chance, isn't it?" He remembered the *naan* in his hand and took a bite.

Mom shrugged. "She's not our enemy."

"Is she still with the bureau?"

"She retires next year."

"What did you tell her?"

Mom sighed and shook her head. "Just that we were well, that's all."

Dad's eyes shifted sideways to me and Mom said, "No, I didn't mention Cent."

His shoulders dropped a little. "What did she have to say?"

"Hyacinth Pope was transferred out of her high-security penitentiary to a low-security facility, ostensibly because of prison crowding."

Dad's calm evaporated—his voice raised. "Is she still there?"

"She never arrived."

"Bastards!" Dad whispered, but it sounded more vehement than if he'd shouted it.

"Well, yes," said Mom. She was calm but she didn't look happy. "It probably *was* them, though you can't discount personal initiative."

Dad was staring at across the room, focused on nothing. His mouth twisted. "No. Not with Hyacinth."

"I've heard that name before," I said, tentatively.

Dad bit his lower lip.

"Yeah," Mom said. "She's the one who drugged your father, when—" She did air quotes with her fingers. "—*they* got him. She murdered Brian Cox, your father's NSA contact. She also tried to snatch me, more than once."

Dad said, "I'm not sure we should be—"

Mom laughed but there was *no* humor in it. "You can't have it both ways, Davy! You want Cent to be careful, to watch out for *them*, but you don't want to tell her *about* them? Remember our first fight?"

Dad blinked at the sudden shift in topic. "When you called my New York apartment and got the police?"

Mom nodded. "What did we agree, after that? When we finally got back together?"

Dad said, almost reluctantly, "Never lie to each other."

"What kind of lie caused the fight in the first place?"

"Lying by omission." Dad shrugged. "It's not *that* simple. Cent is our child. I don't lie to her, but she's our *child*; I don't tell her *everything*, either." He looked at me and smiled sadly. "And I *know* she doesn't tell me everything."

I tried to look offended.

Mom said, "Cent is a young woman who can be thousands of miles away in a heartbeat, going places you *cannot* follow. You *can't* control her but you *can* educate her. You can give her the information she needs to be safer."

Dad pushed his food around on the plate without taking a bite. Mom watched him, eyes narrowed, head tilted slightly forward.

Me, I froze in place, looking at the table, trying to become invisible. I wouldn't disturb this conversation for the *world*.

Finally, Dad turned to me. "All right, Cent, I guess it's time you knew."

I turned to him, eyes wide.

He cleared his throat and wiped his mouth with the napkin.

"I may have been less than honest about that Santa person. And the Easter Bunny? Total fabrication."

I hit him with my fan.

After supper, Dad built a fire in the big stone fireplace, the one that's for show, and we gathered around it while he and Mom told the story again, but in a new way. This time they named the characters, they described them, and they even showed me photographs.

Not of the dead, mind you. No point, there. But they showed me a picture of Hyacinth Pope from sixteen years before and from four years before, taken in prison, that Mom pulled off of an online wanted poster after she talked to the FBI agent, Becca Martingale.

They talked a lot about drugs and darts and tracking devices and being handcuffed to immovable objects. Mom talked about the time they'd flooded her apartment with anesthetic gas in hopes of knocking her out before she could jump away. Dad talked a bit about the device they'd implanted in him and the conditioning they'd used to keep him in specific areas.

They'd told me the story before, but this time they talked about about how helpless they'd felt—Dad when he was chained to walls or electronically tethered to one location; and Mom when she was stuck in the Eyrie, before she could jump, and later, when she could jump but had no idea where Dad was.

She looked at me sideways. "I was falling off a cliff the first time I jumped. Your Dad was escaping a beating with the buckle end of a belt."

Dad blinked. "Huh. Wasn't that your first time, Cent? When I made your mother cry?"

I hid my face behind the fan.

Mom laughed softly. "What did you say earlier, Davy? 'I know she doesn't tell me *everything.*'"

Dad's eyes widened. "You mean—"

"Avalanche!" I blurted. "A cornice gave way."

Mom nodded and Dad went white. White as, well, snow.

"An avalanche? The only way you could've gotten caught in an—" Dad's voice started low and steadily rose until Mom held up her hand, palm outward, like a traffic cop halting oncoming cars. Dad actually stopped midword.

"Zip it, dear."

"She was snowboarding, without clearing it with us!"

Mom shook her head. "And you wonder why she *doesn't* tell you everything?" She looked back at me. "I'm guessing Dad's wet ceiling was involved."

I covered my face with the fan.

Mom gently moved it to one side. "You know that pancake keeps us from seeing your cheeks blush but your ears still give you away."

Damn. I gave in. "Yeah. Several cubic yards of snow."

Dad sagged back on the couch, opened his mouth, and then closed it again after Mom tilted her head at him.

"I tried to get it all up, but more of it melted than I'd realized."

"That's why you washed all the cushions," Mom said.

"Them I just dried. Needed the washer for all the clothes on the floor—they were all wet and most of them were dirty, too."

Dad was still frowning, and Mom said, "Look at the bright side, dear. Her room has never been cleaner."

"Yeah," Dad said drily. "Before or since."

Mom snorted.

"Okay. I'll clean up my room."

"Rooms," Dad said.

"Right, rooms." I agreed. My room in New Prospect was slightly cluttered but that wouldn't take long. I licked my lips, and took a deep breath. "Dad?"

"Yeah, bunny?"

I licked my lips. "I didn't get makeup in my eyes."

Dad's mouth closed with a jerk, and he held up his hands. "Breathe, Davy," he said softly. He exhaled slowly, inhaled.

"Breathe." He threaded his fingers together and settled his interlocked hands in his lap. "It wasn't pot," he said. There was no question in his voice.

"Let me take off the makeup," I said, and jumped.

When I came back down stairs, again, jumping, I was wearing pajamas and I'd removed the makeup.

This time it was Mom who went, uh, ballistic.

"Who did that to you?"

Dad was the calm one—he held his hand up—not quite the traffic *halt* that Mom had done before. More of a *listen.*

To answer Mom's question, I raised my hand, like in class, and said, "Present."

Dad's voice was almost mild compared to Mom's. "It looks like you got punched by an airbag. Were you in an auto accident?"

"No," I said. "Air, yes. Bag, no."

He frowned and leaned forward. "How fast were you going?"

"I don't know. Fast enough that it ripped off most of my clothes before I jumped away."

Mom's hands were up in front of her like she wanted to reach out and touch me, to run her fingers over my limbs to make sure I was all right.

I smiled to show I was okay, really. "I was wearing my favorite jeans, Mom. I'm going to need another pair."

"What did you *do*, girl?" asked Mom. "Jump outside a jet aircraft?"

The roof beams in the living room are well over twenty-five feet off the floor. I was sitting on an ottoman, my back to the fire. I pointed at the ceiling and said, "Up, up, and away."

I did the short impulse, the one I'd practice for twelve feet. I didn't bother springing to my feet or even standing. From their perspective I just shot into the air, still seated.

Dad made a small "Ha," noise. Mom gasped and jerked back against the couch cushions as I rose up.

At the apex, I just jumped back down to the ottoman. My

joints still hurt and the thought of physically absorbing the landing was too much.

We're used to seeing each other jump. (At least *I* was used to seeing *them* jump.) But this was different.

Dad mouth was twisted in a strange smile.

"You can fly?" Mom said.

"You just have to have happy thoughts," I said.

Dad laughed. "We mean no harm to your planet." He shook his head. "She's not flying. She jumped." He laughed, again. "Jumped. Ha. I saw her flicker. She jumped right to where she was, don't you see? But with a change in velocity." He pointed his finger toward the ceiling. "Thataway. How fast were you going? You slowed, I thought, before you jumped back down."

I nodded. "About twenty-seven feet per second. Yeah, I was at the top, about to drop."

"Twenty-seven feet per second," Mom said. "Uh, how fast is that in real speed?"

Mom's actually fine at math, but I guess she was a little rattled. "Eighteen, nineteen miles per hour," I said.

"How fast were you going when, uh—" Mom gestured at my face.

"I was *trying* to do two hundred feet per second. Uh, about 130 miles per hour."

"Why that fast?" asked Dad.

"I was doing these jumps where I'd go fifty feet into the air. I calculated the velocity was about fifty-five feet per second. I wanted to quadruple it." I touched the skin below my right eye. "I think it must've been more like ten times, maybe more. Like three hundred miles an hour."

Dad shook his head. "All right. *Where* were you doing this?"

"Near the pit."

And Mom said, "Cent, in the desert, with a blunt instrument. Besides your face, how do you feel?"

My knees, hips, ankles, shoulders, elbows, and wrists all throbbed.

"A bit stiff," I said.

This full disclosure thing took some getting used to. *Better not overdo it.*

Dad couldn't help himself. "I *did* warn you! You're lucky you're not dead or paralyzed!"

Mom ignored him. "I think, perhaps, you should stay home from school tomorrow."

I didn't fight that.

The next morning, Mom showed up with a bowl of chilled cucumbers for my eyes.

"What's the science on this?" I asked. "This isn't some woo like echinacea, is it?"

"Hold still. Lie back."

They *did* feel good.

"Anything cold would help. Chilled, wet tea bags, a cold spoon, a wet cloth, an ice pack. Cucumbers smell better." I heard her bite into one. "And they taste good."

I took the bowl out to the hot tub and soaked in the heat, administering the cucumbers externally and internally until there were none left.

My eyes looked less swollen when I was done, but the bruising was still there when I looked in the mirror. Can you say "raccoon"? I knew you could.

Even if I stayed home on Friday as well, I was supposed to go to Durango with the snowboarding team on Saturday. I didn't think the shiners would be gone by then, though the whites of my eyes were clearing and I had hopes they would be less bloodshot by then.

When I was twelve, when my periods started, I went through this phase where I wanted to try everything girl. Within reason, Mom indulged me, though she drew the line at shaving my legs, since it was all still downy nothing. I did dresses and stockings and high heels and on top of everything, I did makeup.

We would go out to fancy restaurants and once, to an opera, but I twisted an ankle really badly in the heels and went back to jeans and athletic shoes when I could walk again. Sure, occasionally we'd still dress up, but I guess I'd gotten bored with it.

A year later I got acne really bad. I mean, Mount Vesuvius bad. Mom jumped on it right away, and we saw a high-priced dermatologist in San Francisco who put me on antibiotics and prescription creams. Still, for about eight months, I was glad I had some madd makeup skilz.

If I could conceal a cheek-wide volcano eruption of *acne vulgaris*, I should be able to cover up a couple of black eyes.

The eyes themselves improved somewhat the next day, with the redness lessening, and an application of Visine reduced the rest.

The bruises, though, were trickier than I thought. Oh, sure, it was easy enough to cover them up, but I was hoping for something that still looked like me without makeup. It didn't. It made me look older, polished, pompous, idiotic—well, not really.

Lots of the girls at school wore makeup—too much, really. Caffeine did this flaming eye shadow and heavy eyeliner thing that made her look like a refugee from a rock concert. They all overdid it, reminding me of myself when I was thirteen.

Turns out, what worked best was a good powder-based foundation, with a softened brown eyeliner, and wine colored eye shadow that blended into the bruising. It hid the black eyes but it was fancy-formal and I decided I'd have to dress up a bit for school, to match it.

I wore a dark blue suit the next day, white tights, two-inch pumps, and my very long wool coat.

Like two days before, I jumped to the evergreen bushes near the art room. The door at the end of the wing was locked and there were a few people in the hall so I couldn't jump past the locked door. There was still enough snow on the ground that I worried about walking in the heels. I peeked through the window to Mrs. Begay's room—she wasn't there yet, so I jumped inside. The doors to her room were locked but you could open them from inside and I slipped out into the hall and walked to my locker.

Okay, they *were* staring.

I wondered if the black eyes were showing through the makeup or, perhaps, someone had noticed I hadn't just "moved" out of the way when Caffeine had come at me in the cafeteria.

I concentrated on my footwork. They were only two-inch heels but you could still have a nasty spill.

"Hey, Cent!" It was Grant Meriwether, Naomi's little brother. He had two equally gawky boys with him.

I stopped and smiled. "Good morning, Grant." I don't know why, but dressing up changed my word choices, made them more formal.

He blinked and opened his mouth but nothing came out. One of his friends jabbed him in the side. "Oh, right. This is Tony and Dakota." At my blank look he added. "They wanted to meet you."

I blinked. "Uh, okay! Glad to meet you."

Tony took my hand but instead of shaking it, he squeezed it slightly and didn't let go. "En . . . chanted." He said it like that, with a long pause in the middle of the word as he looked meaningfully into my eyes.

I tried very hard not to laugh out loud.

Grant jabbed him in the side. "Let go of the hand, Tony."

Dakota took my hand in his and bowed low, then lower. At the last second I realized he was going to kiss it and I jerked back. It didn't free my hand but it did pull it far enough forward that he ended up kissing his own wrist.

I pried his fingers off. "Whoa there, Bessie. Don't you know it's flu season?"

Dakota blushed. "Uh, sorry. I'm just so *happy* to meet you."

"I can . . . tell. Uh, why are you so happy?"

"You got Caffeine kicked out of school," Dakota said.

My stomach clenched. "What?"

Grant looked at me. "Suspended for two weeks."

"I didn't do that," I said. "Go kiss Ms. McClaren's hand."

Grant and Dakota made faces of revulsion and Tony said, "Gross!"

I smiled. "But really, it was *Caffeine* who got Caffeine suspended. Thank *her.*"

"Shit no!" said Dakota. His affable goofiness had changed abruptly to vehement anger. Grant's and Tony's faces had also lost their smiles.

I raised my eyebrows and Grant said, "Caffeine's little gang has been on us all year."

Tony said, "The enemy of my enemy is my friend. Uh, would you like to go get coffee sometime?"

It was hard, but I managed not to laugh in his face. *The enemy of your enemy is not your girlfriend.*

I looked at his shoes, his pants, his shirt, then his face. He could use some of my madd makeup skilz—pimples on the chin—but he wasn't bad looking.

"Freshman?"

He looked defensive. "Yeah."

"What's your grade point average?"

He looked confused.

I added. "To date *me*, you have to have a solid 3.8."

All three of their faces dropped.

"It was *so* nice to meet you!" I smiled sweetly and walked on.

Behind me I heard Dakota mutter, "A 3.8? What is she, an Ivy League school?"

This time I did laugh.

A hundred feet down the hall, another boy approached. He was older, broad shouldered, with blinding white teeth. I'd seen him before; a junior or senior, I thought. "Hello," he said. "I'm John."

I blinked. Was this another victim of Caffeine's posse? Didn't seem likely. He didn't look like the sort people picked on. Possibly quite the opposite.

"Hello," I said neutrally, not stopping. "I'm Cent."

He fell into step beside me. "Sent where?" he laughed at his own little joke.

"To class, John. To class."

"Hang on. I haven't seen you before."

He slowed, obviously expecting me to slow as well. I didn't, and he lengthened his stride to catch back up.

"I'm new in town, but I was here all last week. I certainly saw *you*."

He grinned, broadly. "I hear that a *lot*."

I turned abruptly at the water fountain and took a quick drink.

The quick change surprised him and he staggered as he pivoted to follow.

"Sorry," I said. "I just threw up in my mouth a little, there."

He looked confused, then irritated. "Something you ate?"

"Something I heard. Good day!"

I turned down the wing toward biology class, but he took a quick step after me, reached out, and grabbed my arm. His hands were big. I'm not skinny and his hand encircled my bicep. "Hold on, darlin'."

I glanced around. The only people visible were a boy and girl talking at the far end of the hall. "Let go of my arm," I said, looking back over my shoulder.

"Wait a minute," he said, *not* letting go. "I wasn't finished talking."

I jumped.

Not away. I did one of the things I learned in the desert, where I jumped in place, but turned 180 degrees, going from facing away from him to facing him instantaneously. My arm ripped out of his grip and my face was suddenly *right there* before his.

He yelled and fell backward.

I walked away. When I turned to go through the biology classroom door, he was still sitting on the floor, one hand scratching his head.

Tara was just sitting down at the back of the room. I waved frantically at her, beckoning her over, and said, "Look down the hall. Who is that?"

She stuck her head out the back door of the classroom.

I joined her as she returned to her desk.

"Why's John Chanlee sitting on the floor?"

I smiled weakly. "I heard that name somewhere."

Tara shook her head and came back inside. "Yeah, I told you about him. Football team. His father owns the quarry. Rich kid."

"Jade said something."

Tara got an angry look on her face. "Yeah. He trapped her in the back of a school dance and groped her. From what we've heard, she wasn't the only one."

"Nobody report him?"

"Rich kid, remember?" She ran a finger over the fabric of my suit jacket. "Why are you dressed so nice?"

Apparently heels and makeup are some sort of indicator. Three more boys introduced themselves as I tried to get to the cafeteria at lunch. One suggested dancing, another coffee, and the third Bible study.

When I finally showed up, Jade was relieved to see me.

"Christ! I thought you were a teacher for a moment, dressed like that."

"Oh, yeah, a *short* teacher," I said.

"It's the heels," said Tara, "plus the suit. Besides, even without the heels, Mrs. Nizhoni is shorter than you."

"Forget that crap," said Jade. "We're still on for tomorrow morning, right?"

"Tomorrow?" I frowned, as if I had no idea.

"The snowboard team?" she said, frowning back.

"Well, I'm still a little stiff. . . ."

Jade's eyes widened and I could hear the air rushing in through her nose. Before her mouth opened I grinned and said, "I'll be there. Promise."

She shook her fist at me. Tara laughed.

I took the lid off my bento box. It held hot food today: Japanese curry with breaded chicken and pickled cabbage. The steam rose up.

"How the hell do you keep it hot?" asked Tara.

Dad had grabbed "takeaway" from a place in London a half hour earlier and I'd collected it from our kitchen five minutes ago, jumping there and back from a stall in the girls bathroom.

"I wrap it," I said. "What's going on with Caffeine?"

"Oh, right. Um, you know that she was suspended for two weeks," said Tara.

"Heard that one."

"Ok, how about the rumor that *you* were suspended, too, yesterday?"

"Huh. That one I didn't hear."

Jade shrugged. "It didn't last long. Mr. Hill explained that you were sick. But people did say you were home quaking in fear, and others said you'd been injured by Caffeine or her peeps and that was why you weren't here."

"Peeps." I blinked. "Am I in danger from Caffeine's peeps?"

Tara held out her hand and waggled it. "Hard to say. She's the one who usually picks the targets for that crowd."

Jade looked worried. "Uh, didn't she already *pick* Cent?"

Tara licked her lips.

"Who *is* in her posse?"

"Can we sit here?"

I twisted my head around, a little surprised. It was Grant, Tony, and Dakota, lunch trays in hand, their heads turned toward us but their body language saying, *just passing through.*

It reminded me of my first encounter with Tara.

Jade glared at them and was about to say something so I said quickly, "Sit. I have questions."

Jade and the three boys stared at me, frozen.

"*Now*, ladies!" I scooted a bit to the right.

Dakota moved first, sitting beside me, and there was a comical moment while Grant and Tony tried to get to the empty spot on my other side. Tony won and Grant sat on the other side of the table, next to Tara.

Tony took advantage of the small footprint of my bento box to push his tray, and himself, closer than was appropriate or comfortable. I used my chopsticks to lift a piece of chicken to my mouth, raising my elbow higher than truly necessary. The suit fabric grazed his face and he jerked back. "Oops. Perhaps you should shift a little," I said. "I would hate for there to be an *accident*."

Grant laughed. Dakota, on my other side, shifted slightly away from me.

"You know these guys?" I asked Jade and Tara.

Tara nodded. Jade sniffed and said, "Freshman . . . I believe."

I saw Grant frown and I said, "Yes, scummy freshman— but they're *my* freshman. Supposedly I delivered them from evil or at least Caffeine. They are grateful."

Jade raised her eyebrows and said, "Oh! I see."

Tara looked interested. "You were the one they taped to the bike rack, weren't you?" she asked Dakota.

I look sideways at Dakota and saw him blush. "Yeah," he muttered.

"Have things really changed for you guys so much?" I asked, "in just two days?"

"In two *minutes*," said Grant. "We decided, the three of us, we were done."

Dakota said, "Fuck, yeah. We're not taking their crap anymore."

"No more losing lunch money to those bastards," added Tony.

"And *definitely* no more running their packages into school."

"Packages?" Jade said. "What kind of packages?"

Tony and Grant exchanged glances and clamped their mouths shut. Dakota cleared his throat and became very interested in the back of his hands.

It was Jade who said, "Pot. Also ecstasy."

"No way," Grant said weakly.

He didn't sound very convincing.

Tara laughed softly. "It's not much of a secret. So they bullied you into carrying them past Tomez?"

"Who's Tomez?" I asked.

Jade said, "Sheriff deputy. He's *our* cop, assigned to the school district. But that means mostly here and a little bit over at the middle school."

"Half narc, half truancy, and half gang activity," added Tony.

Tara raised her eyebrows. "One hundred and fifty percent? How you doing in math there, Tony?"

Jade flipped her palm up. "Tomez *does* work long hours."

I'd seen Tomez after school where he stood around at the main entrance, but hadn't realized he was specifically for the school.

"So you were running *drugs* past the cops?" I said. I kept my voice neutral. They didn't *seem* like criminals.

"*Technically*, we don't know that," said Grant. "We never saw the contents."

Jade snorted.

"Why didn't you just refuse?" I asked.

Grant looked away.

"Threats of violence?" I tried.

"It doesn't matter," said Tony, abruptly. "What matters is we don't do that anymore." He glanced at me, then away.

I turned to Dakota and he tried to meet my eyes but he dropped his gaze almost immediately. I looked over at Tara, mystified, and she shook her head side to side, very slightly.

"Right, then. So, what *do* you guys do—chess club?"

"Of course," said Grant.

I'd been kidding. "Really?"

My surprise must've shown, because Grant sat back.

Tara said, "Nothing wrong with chess." She met my eyes. "You certainly don't see any of Caffeine's crowd in there."

"*Exactly*," said Grant.

I liked to play chess. Dad and I used to play all the time, but not in the last few years. "But not *just* that, right? You aren't in there just to avoid an overdose of Caffeine?"

Dakota snorted. "Ha! Caffeine overdose. *Perfect*."

Tony smiled. "Well, you know what they say. Too much caffeine gives you the jitters."

Grant smiled, but the smile faded as he said, "Just hope we don't get one of those caffeine headaches from quitting. We like chess, all right. Dakota's quite good."

Tony added, "Yeah. Dakota's seeded number three in the club."

I looked back at Dakota and his chin came up, but his eyes looked nervous. "And still a freshman," I said, nodding in what I hoped was an approving way. It must be rough when your accomplishments are the things bullies use to make fun of you.

"Yeah. The first two seeds are seniors." He said it in an offhand manner but his eyes darted at my face to see how I took it.

"Nice." I glanced at the clock. "Oops. Only five minutes until the bell. Eat up, gentleman." Jade and Tara were already finished. They'd started bringing lunches, too, and when you don't have to wait in the lunch line, you have more time.

I lifted the box and began flicking rice into my mouth. The guys stared at me, unused to seeing someone eat with chopsticks, I guessed. I ignored them.

No sweat off my brow if they didn't finish their own lunch.

FIFTEEN

Davy: "Looking for Hyacinth"

While it was possible that Hyacinth Pope had escaped on her own, Davy thought it more likely that her previous employers had helped.

The building formally occupied by Bochstettler and Associates in Alexandria, Virginia, had been purchased by a political consulting firm almost fourteen years ago. At roughly the same time, the Virginia State Corporation Commission had ordered the dissolution of the Bochstettler and Associates corporate entity after it failed to meet its mandatory filing and reporting requirements, *and* no officers could be contacted at the addresses on file.

Davy, though, had managed to locate some of its previous employees, and, oddly enough, at the same *different* firm.

The offices of Stroller and Associates were in an industrial park five minutes from *el Aeropuerto Internacional Juan Santamaría*, outside San Jose, Costa Rica. Like Bochstettler and Associates, their apparent activities were U.S. business development throughout the world. In the months that Davy had been watching them, it was clear that most of their local activities involved going to and from the airport.

Davy's main interest, though, was in finding out the identity of their clients—the people who hired them—and it was for that reason that he focused on William Stroller, the CEO of record.

He jumped to the Melico Salazar Theatre in downtown San Jose, but he didn't have any Costa Rican *colones* for the Multipago pay phones and he didn't want to use a credit card. He walked down the street until he found a closed travel agency. It had a steel grating pulled over the window but he could see through it and the plate glass, so he walked into the next shadowed doorway, jumped into the agency, and used one of their phones.

"Hola Ramón, soy yo."

Ramón was a gardener on the estate neighboring the *muy grande* hacienda of William Stroller. While Stroller discouraged his domestic staff from discussing his affairs, half of them were Ramón's cousins or nieces. He'd sent an e-mail that morning to one of Davy's many accounts.

"¡Saludes, Jefe! El pájaro está volando."

Like most Costa Ricans he didn't trill the "r", pronouncing it more like Americans did.

Davy's eyebrows went up. *The bird is flying?* *"¿A dónde?"*

"A Los Angeles."

"¿Cuándo?"

"Mañana. El amanecer."

Davy didn't know the last word. *"¿A qué hora en el reloj?"* *What time on the clock?*

Ramón said, *"A las seis y quince de salir de la casa."*

At 6:15 they leave the house. But morning or evening? *"¿Con la salida del sol?"* *With the sunrise?*

"¡Eso es lo que he dicho! El amanecer." Davy could almost hear the unvoiced, *Extranjero estúpido!* Ramón continued. *"He escuchado de el chófer."*

So, *el amanecer* must mean 'dawn.' And Ramón had the departure time from Stroller's driver.

"Mi gratitud es profunda."

Davy had started out paying him piecemeal, but this had encouraged Ramón to over report, so now Ramón received a monthly stipend for his news and Davy stopped dashing to

Costa Rica every time Stroller travelled to the local golf
course.

When Davy checked the scheduled flights, there were still
several possibilities, so dawn found him inside security, wearing a dark mustache that itched and a tropical-weight suit that
was woefully inadequate for the cold in the Yukon *and* the
air-conditioning in the terminal. He was betting on TACA,
which operated the only nonstop flight to LA.

William Stroller came through security at 6:40 with his
assistant/bodyguard pulling both their cases. They paused
briefly before the entrance to the airport's only VIP lounge
but, after checking the time, continued to the TACA gate that
Davy had been betting on. Davy waited long enough to see
them stand when the first-class boarding began, and then left
his own way via a nearby restroom.

He went back to bed.

Seven hours later, Davy was waiting when Stroller and his
assistant walked through immigration control in Terminal 2
of LAX.

Instead of a dark mustache Davy wore a blond wig and
goatee. He was in business casual: khaki slacks and a button-
down shirt and, like nearly every other person in the con-
course, he pulled a small rolling suitcase.

Stroller and his assistant were met in the meet-and-greet
lobby by a man with a sign which said *Daarkon Group*. He
was in a suit but not dressed as a chauffeur (or *chófer* as
Ramón would say.) As soon as he saw Stroller he pulled out
a phone and talked into it, then took the luggage from Stroller's assistant.

Davy took a small radio out of his pocket and said, "Five
minutes."

Mr. Leung was in a plain white Toyota Celica and he met
Davy, as arranged, at the last piece of curbside at Terminal 2.
He popped the trunk and jumped briskly out of the driver's
seat. He was a Chinese-American man in his sixties.

"Slow down, please, Mr. Leung." Davy said. "Their car

hasn't arrived yet." He glanced back to where the three men were waiting, a hundred feet away.

Mr. Leung nodded, then grabbed at his back. "Ow. Ow!" He clutched the side of the car, for support.

Davy left the suitcase on the curb and went to his side, solicitous, all concern. "Uh, that is an act, yes?"

Mr. Leung winked at him. "Mostly. I did tweak it a little at the *kwoon* yesterday, doing dragon form."

Davy smiled. "Let me help you back to the driver's seat."

Davy had first met Mr. Leung two years before, by chance, on a short China Southern Airlines flight from Guangzhou across the water to Hong Kong.

At that time, Mr. Leung's great aunt, with no family still living near in her home province of Hubei, was dying of liver cancer. She wanted to travel to her extended family in the U.S. Her relatives had pulled every string they could get a hold of trying to obtain the appropriate visas and permissions. Both the U.S. and Chinese national authorities moved with their customary speed and precision, which meant the family could expect the appropriate paperwork roughly nine months after their aunt died.

One night, Great Aunt Lien went to sleep in a crowded nursing home on the outskirts of Wuhan and woke up in Mr. Leung's spare room in Anaheim. She lived five more months, surrounded by her nieces and nephews and their children.

Davy hadn't had a jump site in Wuhan, but that had given him an excuse to ride the Wuhan–Guangzhou High-Speed Railway from Guangzhou in the south. At 197 miles per hour, the train took him the 601 miles to Wuhan, with one stop, in three hours and fifteen minutes. And he'd had to take a taxi to the nursing home.

Overall, he considered his contribution trivial.

Mr. Leung still thought otherwise.

Voices were raised several cars back as an LAPD officer argued with the driver of a Mercedes waiting at the terminal curb, with no passenger in sight. The argument ended with the car driving away to make the large loop around the terminals. The cop was now eyeing Mr. Leung's Toyota.

Davy took his time retrieving the suitcase from the curb and setting it in the trunk. It took him a couple of tries to properly close the lid. As it finally latched, he saw a limousine cut sharply around an SUV and over to the curb in front of the three men. Davy climbed in the passenger side of the Toyota as the greeter handed Stroller into the limo and the chauffeur put their suitcases into the limo's trunk.

Mr. Leung was making a show of studying an LA map. In the side mirror, Davy saw the police officer walking toward them, and sighed.

"We might leave first, but slowly, so they pass us."

Mr. Leung let the policeman get within ten feet of the rear bumper before he turned on his signal and pulled away. The limousine passed them within two hundred yards.

The limo took the 105 to the 110 and exited on 8th Street in downtown LA. The chauffeur pulled to the curb before a large mirrored-glass, multibusiness tower near Pershing Square. The greeter, who'd met them with the sign, jumped out and held the door, but did not pull their luggage from the trunk. He escorted them inside.

Davy got out around the corner. "If you'd circle the block a few times, Mr. Leung?"

"As *many* times as you like."

The directory in the lobby showed the Daarkon Group on the floors thirty-two through thirty-four of the forty-story Rhiarti building. A glance at the security desk showed that people who made it through to the elevators either swiped an electronic building pass, or went through a complex sign-in process that included being digitally photographed. There were closed-circuit video cameras in every corner and in every elevator.

Davy walked out the lobby's far doors, as if he'd been taking a shortcut through the building, and flagged down Mr. Leung as he swung around the rear of the building.

"Where to?"

Davy dropped Mr. Leung's radio onto the passenger seat. "Done, Mr. Leung. I really appreciate it."

"I guess *you* don't need a ride to the airport," Mr. Leung said. "The debt is not diminished."

Davy shrugged, "I think we're long past even. But thanks very much for driving today."

Davy approached the Daarkon Group cautiously, starting with Internet research from a cybercafe in Leeds.

There was surprisingly little information available. They had a listing with the U.S. Chamber of Commerce and they were mentioned in the Conservative Corporate Donations register. They contributed heavily to the Heritage Foundation and other organizations that called for reduced regulation of large businesses.

The only link he could find to Stroller and Associates was a picture posted on a social networking site, tagging William Stroller at the Daarkon Group Christmas party from two years before. There were five other people in the photo, all men, but only one of the others was named, a James B. Gilead. Stroller was on the fringes of the photo. Gilead was dead center, dominant.

Davy wondered if he had an implant under his right collarbone or if he ordered such devices put in others. It was a long time. Did they even use such devices any more?

Did they have something more effective now?

He shuddered, and moved closer.

The buildings surrounding Rhiarti Tower, where Daarkon's offices were, were not quite as tall, but one had thirty-three floors, so its rooftop was even with Rhiarti Tower's top floor. And while there were some video cameras to evade in the lobby, Davy easily jumped to the second floor using binoculars and waiting for a hallway to clear.

He deliberately entered in the morning rush, as people streamed into work. There were CCTV cameras in this building, too, and he would stand out after hours. He was barely visible riding a packed elevator to the thirty-second floor.

He went to the thirty-second floor because it was shared among multiple firms, unlike the top floor which was occupied by a single architecture and engineering firm, whose receptionist station was in front of the elevators and would know he didn't belong. On thirty-two, people exited the elevator, heading in different directions. He walked slowly and by the time he reached the stairwell, the hallways had cleared.

The entrance to the thirty-third floor required a keycard, and the roof access had an alarmed push bar, but he was able to look out the armored glass at the stretch of gravel-covered tar, so he could jump past it.

He gazed around an air-conditioner stack to look at Rhiarti Tower, but the mirrored glass windows across the street just reflected the hazy LA sky.

Davy recorded a jump site in the nook between the elevator housing and the A/C cluster, and returned, as he thought of it, to winter, in the Yukon.

SIXTEEN

"It's for the yearbook."

Dad drove me to the school parking lot, getting there in time to meet Mr. Hill and Joe, the team captain. They talked while I unloaded my bags. Dad can be charming when he wants to, and I heard him offering to help out at future practices.

I glared at him and he raised his eyebrows back at me. When he hugged me goodbye, I said, "No spying!"

He seemed undaunted. "Sez who?"

Joe and Mr. Hill were loading the van.

"How many bags do you have?" Joe said.

Mr. Hill said, "Got a helmet?"

"Yeah, in my boot bag."

He looked down at my feet. I was wearing my soft freestyle boots.

"Those aren't your boots?"

"Helmet's with my slalom boots."

Joe's head twisted around. "You have a slalom board? Rigid bindings?"

"Uh, yeah. You guys do compete in the slalom, don't you?" I was wondering if I'd screwed up again.

"Yeah. Carl has a slalom board but mostly we're freestylers. In the all-around meets, we're required to do all the events, but most of us just use our freestyle boards. Ricardo will be happy."

During the drive, most of the team slept or listened to MP3 players. Jade and I ended up sitting on a bench seat with Lany, who promptly leaned against the window and closed her eyes. The roads were clear and we made it to the ski area by the time the lifts started running. The rest of the team went up the mountain while Mr. Hill shepherded Jade and me through the process of getting our pictures taken for the season pass.

Mr. Hill suggested I bring both boards up the hill, so I bagged the slalom board and boots and slung them over my back. We met up with the rest of the team at the Paradise Terrain Park.

The coach, Ricardo, *was* pleased when he examined my equipment, but he was also sharp. "That board is brand new. Those bindings have only been on sale for three weeks. Did you replace a board or is this your first rigid boot?"

"First I've *owned*," I admitted. "Tried several rentals when I was choosing."

Ricardo nodded. "Right. We're going to do slalom in the afternoon." He held out his hand. "I'll store them in the lift house."

I wasn't the worst freestyle boarder on the team and what's more, Jade wasn't either. That honor belonged to Carl, who managed the most amazing crashes without dying or even, apparently, breaking anything.

The guys would occasionally pull out their cell phone cameras while waiting for other team members to jump, but they'd almost always take video of Carl. Brett said, "We have our own YouTube channel: Carl's Crazy Crashes. Good thing he's better at slalom."

My first couple of slalom runs were awful as I fouled the gates or missed them entirely, but my third run I finally learned to trust the ability of the new board to hold an edge on quick turns and got into the rhythm. It's a parallel course, with red and blue flags, so you run it against the clock *and* another boarder. This run I'd gone against Lany and I beat her down by a board length.

"That was a *good* run, Cent. You still need to get out of the gate quicker," Ricardo said. He pointed at Carl. "Guys can heave themselves out pretty quick, 'cause they have more upper-body strength, but you keep doing your turns like that last run and you can make up the difference. Still, *heave* yourself out of the gate." He gestured again to Carl. "Show her how you do it. You two make the next run together."

The gate had two pipe-like uprights that you grab to pull yourself out. I wasn't used to it, so I'd used them more as supports, afraid I would lose my balance, if I pulled too hard.

Carl and I rode the lift together and he talked about meeting the gates. It was okay to brush against them with your body, but the board had to stay clear, something I hadn't always managed on my first few runs.

At the top, we went into the gates and he demoed his launch a couple of time. "You try it."

I fell over twice and he laughed at me.

Right.

"Let's do the run," I said.

When the signal flashed, I didn't use the uprights to launch myself. Instead, I jumped in place, adding an instant twenty miles per hour out the gate. I flew twelve feet through the air before my board hit the snow. I was through the first three gates before Carl reached the first one, and maintained that lead all the way down.

"*Nice* heaving," Ricardo said. "You sure you didn't do slalom before?

"Just lucky," I said.

Carl looked mystified.

Ricardo sent us back up and I toned it way down, getting out of the gate under muscle power alone. I didn't mind outcarving Carl, but the jumping thing was *cheating.* Carl beat me down the rest of the day, but on the last run I stayed right on his tail, crossing the line only a half a board behind him.

I was exhausted by the time we got to the van. I dropped my bags in the growing pile and sat in the open sliding door. We were leaving a half hour before the lifts closed to try and beat the traffic, but lots of people streamed down the stairs to the parking lots, apparently with the same idea. I was watching them idly, not really paying attention, when I saw Dad go by. He was looking back at me and when he saw I'd seen him, he raised his eyebrows and jerked his head back up toward the main building, then turned around and walked back up.

I shook my head and followed him.

"Where you going?" asked Jade.

"Bathroom break," I said.

"We just *went*," she said.

"I'll be quick."

Dad was waiting just inside, between day care and one of the ski shops.

"What are you doing here?"

"Just thought I'd give you the chance to avoid another two-hour drive. I can 'show up' and say I'm driving you home."

"And how did you get here? You don't like to drive."

He smiled. "No, of course not. I took the shuttle bus from town."

Ah. We'd driven through Durango on our way from Colorado Springs, where we'd rented the truck. Dad must've secured a jump site then. And now he had one at the ski area, too.

"And what happens if Jade asks to ride with us?"

He shrugged. "The car is full of furniture. I've only got room for one."

It was tempting. My muscles were already stiffening up. I couldn't imagine what they'd be like after two hours in the van. So of course I said, "No. I'm in this with Jade. It wouldn't be fair to her."

Dad looked unhappy.

"I'm sorry you went to all that trouble."

He shook his head. "It's not that. Driving isn't . . . well . . . it isn't *safe*." He shrugged. "I worry."

Now *that* was the understatement of the year.

"I'll see you at the cabin." Jade didn't need my company— she slept the whole trip back and I got a cramp in my thigh.

Jade's dad met the van at the school and they dropped me off on their way home. I didn't even walk down the hill. Once they were out of sight, I jumped directly to the Yukon, stowed my equipment, and took a long soak in the hot tub.

I spent the first part of Sunday in bed. Mom poked her head in a couple of times but left me to it, mostly. When I did stumble down to the kitchen, she was wearing a cotton sari over a short-sleeved blouse.

She said, "I'm going to be in Banaripara for the rest of the day."

I blinked. "Uh, Bangladesh?"

She nodded. "Right. Flooding."

"Do you need help?"

"Don't think so. Just meetings right now. If it changes I'll let you know."

She vanished.

Dad was off someplace, too, though he popped in at eleven. "Have you seen Mom's binoculars?"

"The image stabilized ones?"

"Yes."

"I think they're at the house. Mom was looking at birds. By the kitchen window, I think."

"Ah." He left.

I jumped to the kitchen in time to see him vanish again, binoculars in hand. Oh well. Glad he found them but I felt a little abandoned—even more so when I checked my phone for texts and messages and there weren't any.

I went back to the cabin and threw my clothes in the wash, did the one bit of homework I had, then cleaned both my bedrooms. It surprised me how little time that took. Guess I didn't mess them up as much when I was at school all week.

I thought of taking one of my boards off to Durango or Niseko Village, but my muscles were stiff enough as it was.

Instead, I jumped to an alley near Krakatoa.

It was windy and cold, the sky overcast. The snow piled high from last week's plows hadn't had a chance to melt. Most of the sidewalks were clear but you had to watch out for patches of ice. City maintenance workers were knocking down the dangerously large icicles forming on the edges of roofs. I hurried out of the alley and into the warmth of the coffee shop.

Sure it was colder in the Yukon, but hot springs kept the house above seventy even if it was below zero outside. And we hardly *ever* went outside the cabin this time of year.

I bought a tea but didn't see Jade or Tara. I wandered upstairs, but they weren't on the balcony, either. I took my phone out of my pocket several times, but each time I put it back without calling or texting anyone. I didn't want to come across as "needy." Maybe later in the day.

I was turning to walk back downstairs when I saw two figures outside, through the glass door. It was Dakota and Tony, two-thirds of my fan club, coming into the coffee shop. I thought about going back into the dark corner of the balcony and jumping away before they saw me, but they didn't make it through the door.

Caffeine, also outside, stepped in front of the door, blocking it. I recognized her by her jacket, her dark roots, and her attitude. She wasn't alone—two guys stepped behind Dakota and Tony. Two *big* guys.

Tony stepped back, closing ranks with Dakota, his eyes wide.

I went down the stairs but as my head dropped below the railing, I jumped back outside, to my jump site in the alley. When I peered around the corner, I saw Caffeine, her arms linked with Tony's and Dakota's, walking down the sidewalk, the two bruisers right behind them.

It looked all friendly until you noticed that Tony and Dakota were both leaning *away* from Caffeine.

There were a few cars moving on the street, but no pedestrians. I jumped closer to Caffeine's group, across the street to where a brownstone had an old-fashioned stoop that blocked my position from them, but I needn't have bothered. They didn't look around, so I followed them, careful not to scuff my feet. When they turned right at the next intersection, I ducked into a doorway, in case they looked back up the street.

I peeked down the cross street in time to see them pulling Tony and Dakota into an alley.

That can't be good.

I thought about getting Dad, but he wasn't home—he'd come for the binoculars and left. Mom was in Bangladesh. I could call 911—I had my cell phone—but Dad was pretty clear on that. Keep away from the authorities in general. We had pretty good ID, but you poke and pry enough and the fabric tears, the dyes fade.

Dammit!

I stepped into the alley, trying not to crunch in the crusty snow, and saw exactly the sort of scene I'd been imagining. One of the big guys held Tony from behind, one arm across Tony's throat, while his other arm cranked Tony's wrist up between Tony's shoulder blades. The other guy had Dakota facedown in the dirty snow, straddling him, his knees on Dakota's shoulders.

Caffeine was talking. "You bitches don't quit *me.* You're *my* little butt boys, or do I have to remind you?" She swung her cupped hand up into Tony's crotch, rubbing him through his jeans.

Tony did not look like he was enjoying it.

I held up my phone and said, loudly, "Uh, could you do that again, but this time smile? It's for the yearbook."

All of them, even Dakota, flat on the ground, twisted to look at me.

"Get that picture!" yelled Caffeine.

I waited there until all three of them were in motion. The quickest was the guy who'd been holding Tony, but Caffeine and the guy on top of Dakota were right behind. When they were still ten feet away, I stepped around the corner then jumped half a block to Main Street. They came out of the alley and slowed, not seeing me at first.

I held up my phone with both hands, like I was composing another photograph.

Caffeine said, "There!" and sprinted toward me.

When they were uncomfortably close, I stepped around the corner, intending this time to jump to the alley behind Krakatoa, but a man and woman were walking toward me, ten feet away, with three dalmatians on long leads.

"Excuse me!" I yelled, and dashed around them, barely avoiding the dogs, straining at the full length of their leashes. I concentrated all my effort on running, looking straight ahead, but the eruption of barking and yelling that followed immediately told me that Caffeine and her peeps had not been as successful in avoiding the dogs or their leashes.

I reached the spot where the old stone stoop came down off the brownstone, ducked behind it, and jumped back to the alley behind the coffee shop. It was really the same alley they'd been threatening Dakota and Tony in, only a block over. I started back up it, but froze at the sound of feet crunching through the snow. My view was blocked by a parked delivery truck. I stepped behind a Dumpster and peered over it.

Dakota and Tony came pounding around the truck. I stepped out into the alley proper and struck a pose. "'Sup?"

They stumbled to a stop.

"You're all right!" Tony swiped at his eyes with the sleeve of his coat.

"Sure. Are *you*?"

Dakota rubbed at a scrape on his chin. He looked like he wanted to be nonchalant and cool, but his voice shook. "F-fine."

Tony wasn't even trying to look calm. "Where are they?"

I gestured north, toward Main Street. "They got tangled up with a couple walking their dogs. I lost them."

Dakota looked up and down the alley. "Are you sure?"

I raised my eyebrows. "Reasonably sure."

Tony stepped past me to the other side of the Dumpster, huddling up against the wall. "Did you really take a picture of them?"

I shook my head. "No. Just wanted to get their attention."

"Damn," said Dakota. "We could've used it."

I scratched my head. "Is the yearbook really that hard up for material?"

Dakota looked at me, confused, then shook his head. "Uh, no. We might have been able to trade it."

"Trade it? For what?"

He looked at Tony and they both dropped their eyes.

I heard a familiar voice from the street and pulled Dakota over to join me and Tony behind the Dumpster. We ducked as Caffeine and her two peeps jogged by, looking back over their shoulders toward Main Street but not down the alley.

Softly, I said, "Wonder what happened with the nice doggies?" I straightened. "Anyway, you ladies were about to go into the coffee shop?"

Tony said, "Don't call us *ladies*." It wasn't quite a shout but he was angry. I took a step back.

Dakota put his hand on Tony's arm.

"Calm down. *She's* not Caffeine."

I licked my lips. "Sorry. Let me rephrase it. Would you guys like to join me back at Krakatoa?"

They didn't come out of the alley until they'd both peered around the corner and made sure Caffeine was gone. When we went over to the coffee shop entrance, there *was* a police car pulled over in the next block. I thought about going over there to see what had happened, but the couple with the dogs might recognize me.

"Dakota, go see what happened."

"*You* go see what happened!"

"They'll recognize me. Go on—I'll buy you a drink."

He looked down the cross street again, to see if Caffeine was coming back. "All right, but make it a large."

"A large what?"

"Mocha. Extra whipped cream."

"Right."

Dakota came back about the time the drinks were ready. When we were seated at the back of the balcony, he said, "They knocked the man down and he hit his head. His wife called 911. They asked me if I'd witnessed it."

I felt bad. "Is he okay?"

"Yeah. A little blood. A goose egg. They're going to the ER just in case."

Crap. "Wish I'd run the other way."

"*You* didn't knock him down, did you?" Tony asked

I shook my head.

"How'd you find us?" asked Dakota.

"I saw them intercept you on the sidewalk." I pointed downstairs. "I was up here. You didn't look happy."

They looked at each other, then back at me, without saying anything.

"Was I wrong? Would it have been better if I hadn't stuck my big nose in?"

They spoke at the same time. Dakota said, "Yes." Tony said, "No." They looked away from me *and* each other.

"Really?" I said.

Dakota said, "It's not that we don't appreciate it, but you may have made it worse."

"How much worse?" said Tony. "From my viewpoint, it's about as bad as it can get!"

"Oh, yeah! And when the video is all over school?" said Dakota.

Tony clamped his mouth shut.

"What video?" I asked.

Dakota looked away. "None of your business."

I looked at Tony. He was looking down at the table. He shook his head without saying anything. I took a napkin and tore it in half. I wrote my phone number on each piece, set them on the table, and walked away.

I wasn't very happy with Tony and Dakota. They were being stupid and I wondered what kind of stupidity they'd been involved in earlier. I didn't have a lot of personal experience with them, but everything I'd read and everything I'd seen, showed me that teenage boys didn't always make wise decisions.

And, apparently, they'd managed to get the results of one decision recorded on video.

I walked back around to the alley. I didn't know what Tony and Dakota would do. It wasn't really my business, even if Caffeine was involved. It was cold outside, too.

Dammit.

I'd need some warmer clothes.

I returned to the alley thirty seconds later, the extra clothes clutched under one arm. I'd left my usual snowboarding coat behind and was shivering, but I hadn't wanted the boys to leave before I got back.

There were no windows opening on the alley where I stood but you couldn't see the front door of Krakatoa and somebody could walk or drive up the alley at any time and see me.

I jumped in place, adding enough velocity to rise fifty feet up. When I could clearly see the roof behind the balustrade, I jumped to the center, near the A/C unit.

I kneeled on the gravel-covered tar and looked around. Most of this roof was clear of snow, probably melted by the building's heat, though snow still drifted against the west and south balustrades. One building in the immediate vicinity rose to six stories, higher than the coffee shop, but that was the Wells Fargo Bank and it was Sunday, so I doubted anyone was in there. Even if they were, they would've had to be looking at this building at exactly the right time to see anything odd.

I shivered. The wind was brisker up here. I pulled on a fleece and then my sheepskin-lined gray hoodie. Before I pulled the hood up, I put on my helmet liner, a black balaclava that came down over my forehead and up over my nose. Good as a ninja mask, any day.

Now I was warm enough and I could do stuff without necessarily being recognized.

The boys left a few minutes later—slowly, tentatively. I had no idea where they lived or even if they were going home. After deciding the immediate vicinity was clear, they headed east up Main. I thought about jumping down to the sidewalk and following them but I just watched instead. When they got to the next block, I jumped to the roof of the building on that corner. This building either had better insulation or they hadn't been running the heat as much 'cause I found myself standing in two feet of snow.

On the sidewalk below, Tony and Dakota peered around the corner, then went south on Fourth Street.

A few more blocks later, the commercial downtown changed to residential, and I couldn't jump from pitched roof to pitched roof in broad daylight without attracting attention. I jumped home and got my binoculars. They weren't image stabilized like Mom's, but they were good enough to stay well behind Tony and Dakota while keeping an eye on them. Walking was better, anyway. The wind wasn't quite as sharp at ground level and I'd been getting cold sitting motionless on the roofs.

They stopped, finally, in front of a split-level ranch, its front yard dominated by a huge blue spruce. Tony, his back to the house, gestured over his shoulder with his thumb. Dakota looked down at the crusted snow for a moment, then shook his head. Tony shrugged and went to the house, unlocking the door with a key.

Dakota continued on down the sidewalk, his head swiveling to check the street. I was a full block away, watching him through binoculars across the hood of an SUV. When he reached the corner, he cut left on Maple.

I jumped to the blue spruce first. Its limbs reached all the way to the ground, shielding me from most of the houses. Next I jumped to the corner, between a beat-up panel van and a four-wheel-drive pickup with oversized wheels.

Dakota had crossed to the far sidewalk. He was still looking over his shoulder. I waited until he was farther down the block before I crossed, too.

He looked back while I was in the middle of the street and began walking faster.

Think I'm one of them, do you?

I turned away from him when I reached the far sidewalk and headed in the opposite direction. When I reached Third Street, I glanced back. He was standing at the intersection at the other end of the block, looking toward me. I turned the corner and when I was out of his line of sight, jumped back to the panel van and off-road pickup.

Dakota had walked on, but he was still looking over his shoulder.

I used the binoculars and jumped ahead of him, and then a block further, past Sixth Street, so I was well in front of *him*, behind a pile of plowed snow made higher by the snow cleared from someone's driveway.

I was glad I'd changed to the hoodie. It was practically the local school uniform. Tony and Dakota had each been wearing one, though Tony's had been white. Dakota's was gray, like mine.

I kept my eyes open for Caffeine, too. Anybody walking got a scan with the binoculars, but I almost missed Caffeine and her buddy because they were in a car. I saw her by chance. I was checking out a figure a block behind Dakota when a tricked-out Honda Accord turned the corner toward me. The side windows were tinted so it was hard to see into the interior but as I scanned past the car through the binoculars, the driver turned her head and I saw a flash of blonde with black roots. I flicked the binoculars back and confirmed it: Caffeine driving with one of her guys in the front passenger seat.

Dakota, from half a block away and without binoculars, took one glance over his shoulder and ran, so I guess he recognized the car.

He was pounding up the sidewalk toward me. I heard the engine on the Honda rev up as they spotted him. I ducked down. When Dakota shot past my snowbank, I snagged his arm and pulled. He crashed into the snowbank on the other side of the driveway opening. Before he could get up, I grabbed his shoulders and jumped away, back to the gap between the SUV and the panel van, two blocks back.

He was thrashing, trying to get up, to turn, but I jumped away before he ever saw me, going back to the driveway where I'd snagged him.

I arrived just before Caffeine's Honda passed the gap and they saw me, or at least the gray hoodie, and rubber on asphalt shrieked. I ran back down the sidewalk, in the other direction. Caffeine didn't bother to turn the Honda, but threw it into reverse.

I cut left at the intersection, not wanting to lead them back to Dakota. Sixth Street had been plowed, but obviously before all the snow had finished falling, because the asphalt was still covered with packed and rutted snow dappled with sand spread for traction. Caffeine backed past the intersection and then turned in. She gunned it, but the tires slipped and the front end walked sideways for a second, so she had to cut back and accelerate more carefully.

I waited until they were almost up to me, then ran out into the road, in front of them.

Caffeine hit the brakes, but the crusted snow didn't have enough sand on it and the car slid. I could hear the "tuk, tuk, tuk" of the antilock brake, but the car wasn't slowing noticeably. I waited until the Honda was about ten feet away and then "tripped" falling forward, still in the street. I jumped away before the car reached me, but later than I'd intended.

I'd felt the bumper brush my leg.

There was the sound of breaking glass and cracking plastic and a car alarm went off. I was back in the cleared driveway just around the corner, on Maple. I ran back and peered down the street.

Caffeine must've jerked the steering wheel in an attempt to miss me, 'cause her car was jammed into the side of a parked Nissan, the source of the car alarm. There was steam around the front end of the Honda from a ruptured radiator. The driver-side door was open and Caffeine was in the road, on her hands and knees, looking under the Honda.

House doors were opening and a woman, coming out of the house in front of the Nissan, was talking on a cellphone. With her other hand she pointed something toward the Nissan and the siren cut off.

Caffeine's friend got out of the passenger side of the Honda slowly, unable to open his door fully because the car was jammed up against the Nissan. He had one hand pressed to his forehead and blood seeped down into his eyebrow.

They hadn't been going *that* fast.

Somebody wasn't wearing his seatbelt.

I looked back down Maple but there wasn't any sign of Dakota.

Good.

SEVENTEEN

Millie: Hilltop

Millie got to the site by hiring a boat taxi in Bhangura and traveling down the Baral River fifteen kilometers, using her own GPS to verify her location. When she'd gotten as close as she could, she paid and dismissed the boatman and walked west on a raised path between rice paddies and jute fields.

Her destination was in sight almost immediately. The ridge rose only a bit around the surrounding farms, but it looked taller because of a stand of trees.

The Bangladeshi army had set up a mobile clinic at the north end of the trees.

Akash, an aid official with Pabna District who was coordinating with the local Bhangura *Upazila*, told Millie, "There are higher sites north of here, but the ground is steeper and prone to mud slides."

He was greatly relieved when Millie told him she was bringing in two tons of rations.

"Bloody marvelous! I was counting on Hunger Free World, but most of their supplies went south. This just isn't the season. Four more months and we'd be ready for it."

Davy brought in a U.S. Army surplus tent, fourteen by fifteen feet, double-walled, which broke down into two luggable bags. They could've set it up themselves, but enlisted men from the army medical unit next door, already set up and waiting, came over and with much confusion and laughter got the thing set up and thoroughly anchored. The forecast called for winds up to ninety kilometers per hour, and Davy had brought extra stakes and straps to reinforce the structure.

"When do your rations arrive? We will be glad to unload the trucks," the medical unit's lieutenant said.

"Tomorrow," Millie said.

"Before the rain, I hope!"

"Early," Millie said. *Very early.*

The next morning, as the winds picked up and the rain began, Akash came to Millie, worried. "Where are your trucks coming from? The road to Bhangura is going to be a swamp, soon."

Millie led him into the tent.

Though the tent had an integrated floor, they'd stacked the rations on doubled pallets, in the event there were any local drainage issues. The cases were piled nearly to the roof of the tent. Davy had also brought all the water filters from the warehouse, but this was only a few cases.

Akash blinked. "Oh. Didn't see them come and go. I guess that was while we were setting up tarps." The aid workers had been stringing tarps through the stand of mixed trees, both overhead and horizontally, attempting to turn the woods into a giant rain shelter.

Millie made a noncommittal "um" sound. "Hope to have more water filters, later."

Akash nodded. "Well, I'm glad they got through. Roads are mostly mud."

"Good timing, then. Is there anything else you need?"

He sighed. "We're short on rope. Someone sent half as much as we were supposed to get." He looked around, then said quietly, "Someone took a bribe, I think, to sign the manifest as 'received in full.'" He gestured at the cases of rations. "Your shipment *was* intact, right?"

Millie nodded. "Oh, yes. Our people supervised it the whole way."

Akash went back to the tarp-lashing project. Millie walked to the edge of the grove and looked at the rope they were using to tie down the tarps. It was eight-millimeter jute, the same fiber that grew in many of the fields between the ridge and the river.

It was midnight in Michigan and the only rope she found in the warehouse were scraps or in use, but she was able to jump to a still-open Home Depot on Oahu, in Pearl City.

They didn't have raw jute, or even hemp, but she bought ten packets of quarter-inch nylon-and-polypropylene braided rope, one hundred feet each. She transferred it from the store bags to a battered cardboard box and found Akash back in the trees.

"Can you use this? We had extra in our supplies," she said. He looked in the box. "Bloody marvelous!"

EIGHTEEN

"Tag, you're it."

I was at school a half hour early and intercepted Grant as he arrived. "Let's talk," I said.

"What about?"

He started backing away and I reached out and snagged his backpack strap and pulled him forward again. He didn't resist but he looked worried.

I said, "Have you spoken to Tony and Dakota about yesterday afternoon?"

His mouth opened like he wanted to say something but nothing came out.

"So you have." I threaded my arm through his in a way I thought of as friendly, but then I remembered Caffeine walking down the sidewalk with Tony and Dakota in much the same way.

Too bad.

I kept my arm linked and led him to the library. Mrs. Bancroft, the librarian, was in the morning staff meeting in the teacher's lounge, but in this cold weather, the library opened early, staffed by student aides. It wasn't a likely place for Caffeine's crew. They would either be in the cafeteria or out by the bleachers, smoking.

I took Grant back to one of the study tables out of sight of the main door. There was one of those antishoplifting mirrors in the ceiling corner, but it was angled to let the guys at the information desk see this area, not anyone passing in the hall.

"Have a seat," I said, pulling out a chair. He stood there, so I put my hand on his shoulder and pushed down.

He resisted, then gave way suddenly, dropping heavily into the chair. He exhaled, loudly. "What do you want?"

I took the chair across from him. "I want to know about Caffeine. I want to know what she has on Tony and Dakota."

The blood drained from Grant's face.

I raised my eyebrows. "You, too?"

He shook his head vehemently.

I pretended to believe him. "Right. Just Dakota and Tony."

"Why?" His voice was a whisper. He looked around but there was no one at this end of the library.

"She's got to be stopped, right?"

He looked away from me. "Not necessarily."

My eyebrows went up. "Really?"

He still wouldn't meet my eyes. "I mean, it would depend on the cost, wouldn't it?"

I sat back and waited. He glanced at me, then away again.

Finally I said, "The cost to *who*? Caffeine? Her peeps?"

He shook his head. "Oh, no. I don't care what happens to *them*."

"So the video is that damaging? What did she catch them doing?"

If I thought he looked upset before it was nothing to his expression now. "You know about the video?"

"Of course. I mean, who doesn't?"

He stuck his hand in his mouth and I relented.

"*Nobody knows. I* only know that there *is* a video. From Dakota."

"*Dakota* told you about the video?"

I shook my head. "He mentioned the video when he was talking to Tony. He didn't say what was on it. He just said, 'And when the video is all over school?' That's when Tony shut up."

Grant exhaled and looked slightly less miserable. After a moment, he said. "Oh."

I tried to do that thing Mom does, aiming for stillness yet engaged and nonjudgmental.

He tried to meet my eyes but couldn't. Finally he said, "I can't talk about it."

"Can't or won't?"

"Both." He looked like he was trying to say it firmly, but the underlying desperation was obvious.

I shook my head, got up, and walked away.

We were playing volleyball during PE, and the class neatly broke down into four teams and a few extra. I'd just rotated off to the sidelines when I saw Donna duck into the girl's locker room.

I was sensitized to her because she was Brett's girlfriend, but the thing that made me think twice was that she was also Caffeine's friend. She didn't have PE this period and there was something odd about the way she'd looked around before pushing through the door.

It was egotistical of me to think I had anything to do with her visit, but even if it did, I wasn't particularly worried. My backpack was on top of my PE locker but the only things in it were my art supplies and a few pens. Everything else was either locked in my PE locker or in my hall locker.

I didn't see her leave but there was no sign of her when we went to change before last period. However my backpack was not as I'd left it. Nothing was missing, it was just turned ninety degrees to the left and the zipper on the back pocket was partially open when I remembered zipping it completely closed.

I wondered what she'd been looking for, then laughed.

I'd pretended to take that picture of Caffeine and her guys roughing up Dakota and Tony the day before. I actually hadn't but *Caffeine* didn't know that.

I kept my phone in my front jeans pocket most days. We're not supposed to use them in class or even have them on, but most kids did, texting throughout the day. Dad said as long as I was going to have a phone he wanted me reachable in emergencies, so it stayed in my pocket, switched to vibrate.

So the phone had been in my jeans, in the locker, where she couldn't get at it. Normally I would've left my locker open while I showered, but this time I didn't. I'd started out amused by the situation, but the more I thought about it, the more irritated I got. When I finished dressing, I was surprised that I was the last one in the locker room.

Shit. I'm gonna be late for art.

I heard the door and I thought it was just the girls coming in for last period, but then I remembered they didn't have any PE sections for last period. I leaned over to look past a row of lockers to the door.

It was Caffeine and she wasn't alone. Her two large friends from the day before were with her, including the guy who'd hit his head on the windshield. He wore a white dressing taped across his forehead.

I snagged my backpack and she stepped around the lockers into view.

"I'll take that phone, now," she said.

Her friends hadn't come around the corner yet but I could hear slight movements which made me think they were working their way around the lockers to come up behind me. I wasn't feeling kind and I definitely wasn't feeling *friendly*.

"I know you can't take it from me by yourself." I slung my backpack over my left shoulder, raised my right hand, and pointed behind her. "Can they?"

She frowned and looked behind her. The instant her head was turned, I jumped the distance between us so that when she looked back, I was *right there*.

She screamed and recoiled away. I heard movement behind me, but it was well behind me, where the two guys had just rounded the row of lockers. I darted past Caffeine and pushed through the door to the gym.

At the far corner of the gym Coach Taichert was leaning out of his office, frowning. "Who screamed? Was that you, Cent?"

I ran toward him and called, "There are men in the girls' locker room, Coach, and I don't think they're students."

Caffeine's two friends came through the door. I saw Caffeine right behind them, but she ducked back as she saw Coach.

Coach Taichert said, "Cent, go see if Deputy Tomez is in the office or out front. If he's not, ask the secretary to call the police." He raised his voice. "You two. Come here!"

I headed for the hallway door but heard feet running away as I did. I glanced back and at the far end of the gym, one of the outside fire exits banged open, spilling snow-reflected light across the floor.

I didn't go to art class.

Dr. Prady, the principle, was out, but Dr. Morgan wasn't. We used Ms. McClaren's office and she was in the room, along with Dr. Morgan, Coach Taichert, and Deputy Tomez. Deputy Tomez asked most of the questions.

I decided not to mention Caffeine, not yet.

"I had just finished dressing when I heard the door open. I went up one aisle of lockers and they came down a different one. When I saw them behind me, I ran out and got Coach."

"That's when you screamed?"

I shrugged. "I don't *remember* screaming, but I wouldn't be surprised."

Well, actually, I would. Not that I wasn't ever scared, but the first thing I'd probably do was jump, not scream.

They had me look through the previous year's yearbook, especially the juniors and sophomores who were seniors and juniors this year, 'cause "You've only been here a month, right? You might not know all the students."

It was possible, but I'd thought I'd checked out all the boys. I was wrong. One of them was in last year's junior photos, but I let my finger slide past him without pausing. My friend with the bandage on his head was named Hector Guzman. He was a senior this year.

Ms. McClaren said, "Are you *sure* you didn't know them?"

"She already said, no, Janet," said Dr. Morgan.

Ms. McClaren wouldn't leave it alone. "It wouldn't be the first time that a student was *meeting* with a nonstudent on campus." She used those words but the emphasis she used on "meeting" made it all too clear what she meant.

My jaw dropped open.

Deputy Tomez took one look at me and said, "Thanks, Ms. Ross. I don't have any other questions. Do you want a ride home?"

I shook my head. "No, thank you."

The bell rang. Dr. Morgan said, "Are you sure you're all right? I could call your parents for you."

"If you want," I said. "But I'll definitely be talking to them." I glanced at Ms. McClaren as I said that and she narrowed her eyes in response.

"Very good. I will touch base with them, myself." Dr. Morgan held the door for me.

I went through to the passageway to the main admin office, but as soon as I was out of sight, I stepped to the wall where I could hear through the partially opened door.

Coach Teichert said, "Really, Janet, she's only been in town three weeks and you think she's meeting men on campus? Fast work for a sixteen-year-old."

"I *don't* trust her," said Ms. McClaren. "There's something about her—"

Dr. Morgan said, "Let's calm down, why don't we? The last thing the district needs is *another* lawsuit."

I heard an intake of breath from Ms. McClaren, but before I heard what she said, footsteps approached the passage from the reception area and I jumped away.

I told Mom about the two men in the dressing room and she was upset, but not for me. She spent twenty minutes talking to Dr. Morgan on the phone.

After the call she took a moment to calm herself. "What if someone had been there who couldn't get away as easily? Dr. Morgan says Deputy Tomez will be hanging near the gym and they're going to make sure only the main doors open from outside, where the ladies in admin can see who comes in."

I hadn't told her the men had been there for me or that Caffeine had been with them.

"That'll put a dreadful strain on the bleachers crowd," I said.

"What's the bleachers crowd?"

"The smokers. They come and go by one of the gym doors."

And so it did.

Almost immediately they'd propped the door open with a block of wood, so they could come and go rather than tramping all the way around the building to the main door. But Coach Taichert put an end to that, coming by between classes and collecting whatever object had been used to keep the door from closing.

Several people were late to class.

Next, someone figured out that if you taped the catch shut with duct tape, the door looked like it was completely closed but you could still get in. It only took Coach seeing one person pulling the "locked" door open to figure that one out. He took to sitting near the door during the passing periods and routinely checked the door for tape.

People caught messing with the doors got detention.

I thought, *It won't stop one of their peeps opening the door and letting someone in.* Still, Coach Taichert was around and I doubted they'd try to come in that way, or at all.

After all, I wasn't at the school all the time.

The next morning, they were waiting for me in the woods.

I'd decided to take it easy on jumping near the school. I thought I had a good place, behind the evergreen bushes at Mrs. Begay's end of the building, but in the past few days, I'd noticed footprints there that weren't mine. My first thought was that they were Dad's, but they weren't. I checked the size against a pair of his shoes.

But I wouldn't put it past him.

Then I noticed the footprints came in pairs and they were facing each other and standing, uh, really close.

Anyway, I decided I really didn't want to appear on top of two kids making out in the bushes. That kind of thing could really put you off your breakfast.

This morning, I jumped to the cliff ledge at the edge of the woods, above the path from my house. I was about to jump down to the path itself, without even looking, when I caught a whiff of cigarette smoke.

I stepped closer to the edge, but the snow up here had melted and refrozen into a hard crust and my foot *crunched* though it loudly.

Someone moved below, two short steps through crusty snow.

Maybe someone was also using the path to go to school? There were other houses back this way. And they took a moment to smoke a cigarette?

Then someone spoke. "Just melting snow falling off a tree, I bet."

And someone else said, "I guess."

Caffeine.

I stepped sideways to where the snow had melted off of a higher ridge of rock and walked along it until I could peer over the edge.

They all wore hoodies, but Caffeine's blonde-on-dark-roots hair stuck out just enough to identify her. She and one of her big friends stood behind a cedar near the base of the cliff, and two more figures were just visible on the other side of the trail, hiding behind two tree trunks as they peered up the trail, away from school.

Despite the risk of running into people snogging, I jumped to the spot behind the evergreen bushes. No one was there and I jumped into Mrs. Begay's classroom after checking through the window that no one was inside.

I hope they froze out in the woods.

After school, when Jade, Tara, and I headed over to Krakatoa, I spotted a tail, a reflection in a storefront window.

Dad?

I bent down and tied my boot, to check. Then laughed to myself.

It was Caffeine. She was wearing a leather jacket over a gray hoodie, the hood pulled forward, but face on I could just make out the black roots and blonde hair. Besides, she hadn't changed her *walk*.

I wondered if any of her friends were around. Looking back up, I saw Tara and Jade, talking anime while they waited patiently for me, and it suddenly didn't seem so funny. I knew *I'd* be all right, but they could get hurt.

"What's wrong?" asked Tara.

"Caffeine's following us," I said. *"Don't look!"* They had both started to turn their heads. I kept walking and they fell into step with me.

"Are you sure?" Jade said.

I sighed heavily.

"Why is she doing it? Still pissed about getting suspended?" Tara asked.

I opened my mouth, but then closed it without speaking.

"Give!" said Tara. "What did you do to piss her off *this* time?"

I looked down at the sidewalk. "All right, I interrupted one of her little strong-arm sessions. She and two of her peeps pulled Tony and Dakota into an alley. I pretended to take a cell phone picture and they chased me, and I led them away from the kids.

"Unfortunately, now she thinks I have an incriminating picture of them and she wants my phone. Wish I *did* have the picture. I could just post it online and be done with it."

Tara and Jade exchanged glances, then Jade said, "For a newbie, you really have a gift for getting into trouble. Usually it takes people a couple of months at a new school."

I laughed. "Thanks." I meant it. I'd been feeling pretty grim until she said that.

"How *did* you know she was following?" asked Jade.

For the rest of the walk, I gave them the quick course in

using reflective surfaces—car windows, store windows, even chromed automobile trim. They each spotted Caffeine for themselves. "And if you want a good look, Jade, you'll touch up your mascara."

She touched her face. "What? Oh! The mirror, right?"

I nodded.

Jade started to swing her backpack around, but Tara pulled her onward and said, "*Next* time. What I want to know is how a girl like you knows about this surveillance stuff."

"I watch a lot of spy movies?"

From our usual table up in the balcony, I could see Caffeine's feet where she waited in a shadowed doorway across the street, watching the entrance to the coffee shop. When I bent down to put stuff in my backpack, I could see her talking on her phone.

"I'll be gone for a few minutes. Watch my stuff, will ya?"

Jade glanced at the window. "Caffeine? Sure you don't need witnesses?"

I smiled. "I *do* need witnesses. I need you guys to witness that I went to the bathroom and that you didn't see me go outside."

Tara frowned and I said, "Don't worry. You *won't* see me go outside, I promise. No lying required."

I jumped home from the bathroom stall. At my computer, I composed and printed out a single page of text, then smeared white glue over the blank side.

The doorway in which Caffeine was lurking was deep—there was ample room between her and the door, so she didn't see me jump in behind her. The page was balanced in my gloved hand, glue side up, and I shoved it onto her jacket, right between her shoulder blades, sending her staggering away across the sidewalk. By the time she'd gained her balance and turned around, I was walking out of the coffee shop's downstairs bathroom.

I was able to watch through the window as she charged back into the doorway and tried the locked door, then came back onto the sidewalk and looked left and right.

The paper must've rustled because she twisted, looking over her shoulder, turning her body like a dog trying to reach its tail. Finally she reached behind her and caught an edge of the paper, and pulled it off.

The page said:

Overuse of caffeine may lead to
irritability, anxiety, restlessness,
confusion, insomnia, headache, and
DELIRIUM.
This paper may not be real.
This message may not be real.
The glue?
You decide.
YIF
(Your Imaginary Friend)

Caffeine stared at the words, then back at the doorway. She turned the page over and felt the wet glue, reached over her shoulder and tried to touch the back of her jacket. She crumpled the paper and threw it into the gutter, between two cars, then took her jacket off to examine its back. Still holding it, she started across the street toward the coffee shop.

I hurried back upstairs so I was back at our table when she came in, but she didn't even look around. Instead she grabbed several napkins from the counter and headed for the bathroom. I heard the door slam from up on the balcony.

Tara and Jade were both looking at me, frowning, and I wiped the smile from my face and tried to look innocent.

"She looks pissed," said Tara.

Jade added, "Even more than usual."

And Tara said, "And . . . worried."

I felt the corners of my mouth twitch up and used my hand to pull them back down.

Tara said, "What did you *do*?"

"I walked downstairs and went to the bathroom, then came

back up. Why?" I gave them a stern look. "Did you see anything that would indicate otherwise?"

Jade said, "No, Mother."

"Good. Lend me your compact."

She fished it out of her backpack. It was a small case with
the makeup side divided between two shades of eye shadow.
I opened it and set on the edge of the table where the mirror
reflected a view of the front door and the cashier between the
railing balusters.

Caffeine came back into view, this time looking around.

"Don't look at her," I said, picking up my notebook. "Say
nothing—"

"—act casual," finished Tara.

Caffeine went to the counter and ordered a quad-shot
espresso. While she waited for her drink, she looked up at us,
but we were working studiously, eyes on our books.

The barista called to her, putting her drink on the counter.
When she stepped over to claim it, Caffeine leaned closer and
said something to him, quietly.

He shook his head and said, "No. Nobody's come in or left
in the last twenty minutes—except you."

Caffeine looked back up at us one more time, then left.

Later, after Tara and Jade had been picked up by Jade's
dad, I went back across the street. At first I thought she'd come
back for the crumpled paper, but I found it where the wind
had pushed it under a parked car. The glue had dried, sticking
parts of the paper together, but you could open it enough to
read some of the message.

I put it in my backpack.

We had a practice and a meet that weekend.

The meet on Sunday was not an all-around one, so Ricardo
and Mr. Hill wanted us to enter in our best events. For me,
this meant slalom. Sure, I was better than a lot of the team in
freestyle, but I was the best women's slalom racer on the team
so they asked me to concentrate on that.

I was getting better at it. I even managed to heave myself out of the gate without falling over.

Jade was gaining confidence in freestyle and besides a large number of board grabs, she'd started doing a layout back flip without falling over or, as she put it, "Without dying."

There was no doubt that she wasn't in the same class as Lany, but Lany started giving her tips and encouraging her, so if nothing else, Jade was having a good time.

Me, I concentrated on clearing the start without cheating and making carved turns. The highlight of the afternoon was beating Carl down by several yards, without cheating, just by dint of a clean start and a clean run. But, to be fair, it was not at all his best form.

Still I felt good and the rest of team happened to be at the bottom of the slalom course when I did it, so I got cheers from them (slightly louder from the girls), and Carl got grief from the boys.

Ricardo said, "I wish we'd had you at the start of the season. If you're doing so well after two practices, think how good you'd be doing after ten."

I smiled and didn't tell him that two evenings a week I was jumping to Hokkaido to practice on my own. I usually did just an hour, but *I* didn't have to wait for the lifts, so an hour of boarding for me was like half a day's regular practice.

Brett made a space for me when we ate lunch at the midmountain lodge. I exchanged glances with Jade and she pushed me forward. I had butterflies but Brett just talked with everyone as usual. But I totally noticed when his leg or elbow brushed against mine.

At the end of the day, he was there, suddenly, when it was time to carry stuff down to the van. He grabbed my boot bag before I reached it.

I didn't want to ask about Donna, but I thought about it. When Jade and I slid into our usual bench, he took the third seat, beside me, instead of sitting where he usually did, in the very back seat with Joe.

About fifteen minutes into the ride, Brett pulled out his

phone and said, "Damn. No signal." He looked at me and smiled that smile and I felt tingly. "How about your phone?"

I knew mine didn't. Even if there was a compatible network nearby, we weren't anywhere near New Prospect, so the phone's programming wouldn't even *try* to find a cell tower. Still, I fished it out and showed him that the top of the screen said "no service."

He plucked it out of my hand, saying, "Neat phone! We should take a picture." He tried to work the screen but the locked phone dialog appeared, asking for a four-digit pin to unlock it. "How do you get to the camera?" Brett asked.

I held out my hand. I was going to unlock it for him, but he said, "I can do it. Just tell me how."

Oh, shit.

I felt like crying. He wasn't being friendly because he liked me. He was trying to get at my phone, just like Donna had in the locker room.

Like Caffeine.

I said quietly, "Give me my phone."

He held it away still smiling.

Jade, who'd been ignoring us, said, "Don't be a dick, Brett." Brett said, "Just tell me."

I said, "Give it back. Or else."

He raised his eyebrows.

"Or else what?"

I raised my voice. "Mr. Hill?"

Two rows forward, in the front passenger seat, Mr. Hill turned his head around. "Yes, Cent?"

Brett flipped the phone into my lap and I closed my hand over it.

"What time will we get back to the school?" I said.

Mr. Hill glanced at his watch and told me, "Usual time. About 5:30."

"Thanks," I said. I tucked the phone back into my inside jacket pocket and, though it was warmish in the van, zipped my jacket all the way up.

Brett looked at me like he couldn't believe I'd done that.

Did he think his charm was enough to let him get away with stuff like that?

I was somewhere between hitting him and crying. Instead I said, "Did you do it for Caffeine or for Donna?"

His expression said one thing, his voice said another. "Don't know what you mean."

"Why don't you go back and sit with Joe," I said.

He got a stony expression on his face. "I'm fine here."

The van reached the long line of cars at the traffic light where we joined the interstate. While we waited for it to change, I unbuckled my seatbelt and climbed past Brett. His hands started to rise as I moved in front of him and I jerked my elbow up until it was right in front of his nose and I glared at him. He dropped his hands flat in his lap and leaned away from me. I went back to the rear bench seat, where Brett usually sat, and buckled in.

Joe, in the far corner, was dozing, but he jerked his head up when I sat. He blinked and looked up to where Brett was sitting. He opened his mouth to say or ask something, and I leaned back into the opposite corner and shut my eyes.

When we got back to the school parking lot I pulled my feet up and let Joe worm his way out with the rest of them. While they all climbed out, I reached over the seat back and fished my bags out of the cargo area. When the rear hatch began to rise, I jumped all the way to the Yukon with my stuff.

Mom wasn't there but Dad was, reading a book on the living room couch. "Hey. How was practice?"

I shrugged. I was afraid if I said anything I'd cry.

"Hmmm." He said. His eyes were narrowed and he was studying me carefully.

I jumped to the back hallway and stored my boards and boots. When I returned, Dad was slicing sharp cheddar cheese in the kitchen.

"You want soup with your grilled cheese?"

I nearly lost it. Grilled cheese and canned tomato soup was my comfort food. Mom's, too, which is why she used to make it for me when I had a skinned knee or a bad cold or an argument with Dad. But if I said yes, it meant I was in *need* of comforting and I guess I wasn't ready to admit that.

"Just the sandwich, please."

Maybe I said it funny. Dad took a can of soup down anyway. "Well, I'm going to make some for me."

He used sourdough bread and butter, letting the cheese melt out from between the slices and sizzle on the iron skillet, where it formed a hard cheesy crust along the edge of the sandwiches.

That's the best part—the crusty cheese. He put mine down on a paper towel and added a cup of the soup.

"Where's Mom?"

He shrugged. "Bangladesh. The water hasn't receded and they've got another tropical depression approaching. They're trying to pre-stage supplies this time."

"Is she trying to bring them in herself? Does she need help?"

He shrugged. "Planning stages right now. I'm scheduled to move a shitload of water filters later."

"Do *you* need help?" I didn't say *my* help. I wanted to leave that open. Not that I didn't want to help. It was just that Dad didn't see me that way much. Sure, I might be hauled along to *learn* something, but as a resource?

He shook his head. "Not for the water filters." He paused and then said, "However, depending on how bad the storm is, we might need you later."

I blinked. *That* was a first.

"Besides, you have a meet tomorrow, right?"

I nodded.

"Well, then. You'll need some rest. We'll see what you can do after, right?" He gave me a one-armed side hug.

I drank my soup and was, well, comforted.

There were two voice mails waiting when I popped back to New Prospect to let my phone connect.

The first one was from Jade and the time stamp was right after I'd jumped to the cabin from home.

"Hey, where'd you go? My Dad's here. Do you need a ride home?"

There was a similar text from her as well.

The next voice message was from Joe. "Cent, you left before we talked about tomorrow, but the van leaves at the usual time."

The league meets were at Cedar Mountain ski area, which was pretty central to all the participating high schools. We'd have to drive farther, but the meet wouldn't start until midday, so we didn't have to leave earlier than usual.

Joe paused and then said, "If Brett is being a jerk, let me know. I *will* take care of it."

I stared at the phone. *Oh, really? You'll make him like me for my own sake?*

I texted his phone: *CU@Van 7:30 a.m.*

I texted Jade: *Sorry phone was off. Thnx for ride offer but I was ok. CU a.m.*

I left the phone on the charger in my room at the house and went back to the cabin. I showered and when I'd changed into pajamas and was sitting in front of the fire downstairs, brushing my hair, Dad brought me a dish of Rocky Road ice cream—my favorite.

"We didn't have this in the freezer," I said.

He raised his eyebrows. "What's your point?"

He'd gone and got it, as Iago said in *Othello*, "especial." I ate it too fast and got brain freeze. But I gave him a good hug before I went up to bed.

I tried to sleep, but kept coming around to Brett's face and his smile and his hair.

And his behavior.

I couldn't help it. The first sobs were soft, and I was burying my face in the pillow to muffle them, but they grew stronger, louder.

Earlier I'd heard Dad come up to bed, but he was probably still reading just across the hall.

I jumped to my bedroom in New Prospect and cried myself to sleep.

NINETEEN

Millie: Floods

There were heavy winds and torrential rain the first four hours, but then the rain slowed to a steady drizzle for the next two days. Millie thought they'd dodged this bullet. Up-country the soil had soaked up more water than expected, unlike during the monsoon season. The river did rise, but it was still within its banks.

"We might have to move the rations back to warehouse."

"Really?" Davy put his hand on his lower back. "I guess that's good, right? No one flooded out of their homes."

"You hurt your back?"

"It was the tent. I shouldn't have tried to move both bags at once."

Millie put her arms around him and rubbed his lower back.

"Mmmm." Davy said. "We should continue this in the tent. Or, better yet, at home."

Millie kissed him. "Whatever your feelings about Cent going to school, you've got to admit it's been nice to have the cabin to ourselves in the afternoon."

Davy's response to this was nonverbal. Millie returned to the tent two hours later. Though rain still fell lightly, there were breaks in the clouds, and sunlight shone through in glorious glowing columns.

"Well, do you think we're okay for this storm?" she asked Akash as he walked by.

Akash shook his head. "You haven't heard the forecast, I take it? That depression near Sri Lanka is now a tropical storm and it's coming straight up the Bay of Bengal. This—" He gestured at the clouds and light rain. "—is just a prelude.

"We're in for it."

TWENTY

"Chukri."

Dad was gone when I got up, but Mom appeared shortly thereafter and made me waffles and eggs. "After all, it's your first athletic event. You need the fuel."

She looked tired.

"Have you been up all night?" I asked.

"It wasn't *night* where *I* was. I slept yesterday, but I'm definitely upside down in my sleep cycle." She gestured toward me. "Dad said you weren't your usual self last night."

For a moment I thought he'd heard the crying, but decided it was just how I'd looked when I got home. I shrugged. "Teen angst. I had a crush on someone but it is not to be."

She studied me silently. When I didn't say anything else, she said, "Had? Crushes don't just evaporate, usually."

I looked away.

"You want to talk about it?"

I shook my head.

"Maybe after the meet," she said.

The meet, by its nature, included Brett. I changed the subject. "Dad said you might need some help with the flood supplies."

She raised her eyebrows and looked at me, considering. "It's possible. I've been locating high ground near places likely to flood. Especially those places that will be cut off." She ran her fingers through her hair. "We've done a pretty good job of getting supplies to the NGOs but their warehouses aren't very evenly distributed. Also, we've had some trouble with local authorities appropriating the supplies, even if their people aren't the ones with the most need."

"So you might need to move the supplies?"

"Yes. So, we'll see. The flooding from the last storm is just starting to fall, but the new system was just upgraded to a tropical storm." She shook her head almost angrily. "This is supposed to be the *dry* season."

I winced. It made my troubles seem petty.

"I'd like to help," I said.

"Forty-eight hours will tell. If I need you, it will be then. Good?"

"Good."

I jumped myself and equipment to my cliff ledge near the edge of the wood and determined that today, at least, no one was lying in wait for me. I hiked across to the bleachers and around the school to the parking lot, hauling my bags.

I'd made sure I was on time, but with very little to spare. I didn't want to stand around waiting with Brett. I didn't want to *ride* with Brett, either, but I didn't have much choice.

Most of the team were there standing next to the van, but Joe saw me first. He said something to Brett and Brett turned, a pained expression on his face. I was wondering what that was about, when Brett started jogging across the parking lot toward me.

I froze, but Brett slowed to a stop about ten feet away.

"Go away," I said.

He held out his hands palm out. "Please. I'm to apologize."

I stared at him.

"I'm sorry. It was wrong of me to look at your phone without permission. Yes, Donna asked me to look for a picture you took of Caffeine. She said it was embarrassing and I should delete it if I could. But I was doing it for Donna, not Caffeine."

"Embarrassing? She said it was embarrassing? Not, say, felony assault?"

Brett blinked. "She said it was horsing around."

I wondered if he'd ever been kicked by a horse. "Caffeine and her peeps were beating up freshmen in an alley. It wasn't 'horsing around.' Donna went through my backpack in the locker room."

"I didn't know that," he said.

"Which?"

"Both."

I was getting tired of holding my equipment. "Who told you to apologize?"

He looked at the ground.

I looked back at the team. Joe was watching us intently.

"Ah. Joe did, didn't he?"

Brett twisted awkwardly. "Maybe."

"Cause if I quit the team, the transportation dries up, right?"

He waggled his hand. "He said *he'd* quit the team if I made things unpleasant. He said he had enough of that shit when Caffeine was on the team."

I raised my eyebrows. "And you care because? . . ."

"He's my friend. I wouldn't be *on* the team without his help. I would've flunked geometry and physics."

I started walking again.

"I can help carry your stuff," he said.

I shook my head and tried to ignore the small voice in the back of my head that said, *Let him.*

He turned and walked back, ahead of me, not *with* me.

Joe said something to Brett when Brett neared the van, but Brett shrugged. I went to put my bags in the back and Joe was there, taking them from me. "Did he apologize? I meant it. I'll kick his butt if he's still being a jerk."

"He said the words. Just keep him away from me and we'll be all right." Joe still looked worried so I patted his arm. "S'cool, Joe."

Joe and Brett sat in the very back, Jade and I had our usual middle bench.

I was not expecting Donna *and* Caffeine to be at Cedar Mountain.

I don't know which was worse. Caffeine in *any* form or watching Brett tongue wrestle with Donna on the lift chair ahead of me.

Lany placed first in women's freestyle, Joe came in fourth in the slopestyle, and I came in third in women's slalom. The girl who took first had shoulders as wide as Carl's and could really heave herself out of the gate. It would've been trivial to win with just a little bit of added velocity at the start—my time was only four tenths of a second behind.

But I doubted if Brett would like me any better if I'd taken first.

At the end of the meet, we all took a few runs for fun. Jade and I were doing a nice broad intermediate slope when she yelled, "Look out!"

I jumped in place, killing all of my forward velocity, and Caffeine shot across the slope in front of me, stupidly fast. She would've run right into me if I hadn't stopped so suddenly. She wiped out, trying to turn at the edge the slope.

I slid down the hill slowly, taking my cell phone out, and, when I passed her, upside down on the snowbank, I took a picture.

"For the yearbook."

Dad met me at the base.

"I didn't know you had a jump site here," I said fiercely. "I would not have minded missing that van ride this morning!"

He shrugged. "Didn't have it until right before the meet started." This meant he'd gotten as close as possible, then taken public transportation. He pulled a video camera out of his pocket. "Had to record your races for your mother. She's knackered—catching up on her sleep."

"I didn't see you."

"Goggles, scarf, hood. Too many other people taking video and pictures. You want a 'ride' home?"

"Hell yes."

He pretended to be shocked at my language, then jerked his

thumb back toward the van. "I'll just clear it with George, then."

Jade was cool. She didn't see any difference between riding four hours in the van and four hours in my imaginary car, even if her parents had given the necessary permissions ahead of time. "And I know you'd just as soon be away from Brett boy."

I rolled my eyes. "That obvious?"

"Duh."

I wished I could tell her the truth—give *her* a ride home in seconds. Dad carried my board bag and I took the other and we walked down to the lower parking lot. When we were screened from sight by two SUVs, Dad met my eyes and we jumped to the cabin.

Mom wandered downstairs in a bathrobe almost as soon as we got home and Dad cued up the video. I'd never seen myself boarding before. I saw my arms were not as still as they should be, something Ricardo had mentioned once, but that they were better than they'd been during my first practice.

Mom cheered loudly for recorded-me and after said, "You beat the other person each run. Why didn't you win?"

I smiled. "I didn't race against everyone, Mom. Some of them were faster. I had the third best time."

She gave me a one-arm side hug. "I'll definitely have to be there next meet."

I looked down, pleased. "How's the flooding?"

Mom sighed. "I'll know more tomorrow. Maybe you could come home after school instead of going to the coffee place, this once?"

Dad looked at her, his eyebrows raised.

She patted his leg. "Just in case."

I said, "Definitely."

Mom said, "Good."

I hadn't been keeping track of the days, so it was a surprise when I saw Caffeine's blonde hair and black roots again in the school hallway. I shook my head. I wondered how long it would take her to get home if I jumped her to Washington

Square Park in Greenwich Village. I could do it in such a way that she'd never see me.

I cheered up. She didn't know it, but *she* was the one who should be worried.

When she spotted me I was still smiling.

She pushed away from the wall and took a step toward me.

Someone cleared his throat loudly. I looked up the hall and saw Coach Teichert. He was looking at Caffeine. She looked at him and then turned abruptly and went down the hall in the opposite direction.

I nodded as I went by and Coach said mildly, "Don't provoke her, Cent."

I bobbed my head again and didn't say anything.

My three freshmen—Dakota, Tony, and Grant—had been avoiding me ever since I started pressing them about the video. Now, lunchtime on the first day of Caffeine's return, they appeared, clustered together, and asked if they could sit at our table.

I didn't think it was a coincidence.

Jade and Tara looked at me, but I just looked at my big bowl of udon and kept fishing up thick noodles with my chopsticks. Jade shrugged and Tara, still watching me, said, "It's a free country."

Grant sighed and said under his breath, "I *wish*."

I winked across at Tara and Jade, but kept my attention on the noodles.

I wondered if they were there to talk to me but decided, pretty quickly, that they weren't. They were there to keep Caffeine from talking to *them*. When I got up to go to PE, I said, "Wouldn't it be better if you didn't have to worry about her?"

I didn't wait for a response but as I turned away I saw them exchanging glances, thinking about it.

Good.

We ran relay races in gym that day, teams of four, each team member running one circuit and transferring the baton in a standard twenty-meter hand-off zone. Teams were decided by pulling colored sashes from a bag.

Caffeine pulled out an orange one.

So did I. I looked at Coach and he shrugged his shoulders.

For the first race, I ran the first leg and Caffeine finished, so I didn't have to deal with her at all. We won our heat, running against two other teams. But for the second race, Coach had everyone rotate forward, which put me in fourth position and Caffeine in third.

I'd have to take a hand-off from her.

When our second teammate handed off to her, we were slightly ahead of the other two teams. Caffeine gained on them but I saw something in her face as she neared the handoff zone. I started running and she pushed the baton toward my hand, but as I closed my fingers she jerked it back slightly and let go.

If it hit the ground, we were disqualified.

I jumped in place, killing my speed, and it dropped into my hand. Then I ran, flat out, trying to catch up, but I'd killed too much of my forward velocity.

For a moment, I considered regaining the lost velocity by jumping in place and adding it back, but instead I just ran my best.

We came in last.

My two teammates had been watching, so I didn't think they were mad at *me*, but they were mad.

Coach had us switch the order. I was now first and I would be handing off to Caffeine. While we waited for our team's turn to race again, I considered doing the same thing to her, fumbling the pass and letting her drop it, but that wouldn't be fair.

When the time came, I ran fast, hard. Ten meters from the handoff zone, well before Caffeine began running, I added five meters a second velocity and closed in on her like a missile.

She flinched, flinging up hands to stave me off, and I slapped the baton into her hand and killed my velocity at the same time. She staggered away, but then ran, fast—not quite racing as much as running away from me.

I made sure I was sitting up on the bleachers by the time she came around to hand off to our third runner.

We came in first, but only because the team in the lead fumbled a hand-off, dropping the baton, disqualifying themselves.

That was it for class. In the locker room, Caffeine shrank away from me while we changed, though I kept my eye on her.

She kept her distance and, though she also eyed me occasionally in art class, she left me alone.

Good.

I'd already told Tara and Jade I couldn't do the coffeehouse after school because I was helping my mom with a project, so I walked into the bathroom once I had my things, and, finding it empty, jumped to the house.

Neither Mom nor Dad were there, so I put my backpack in my room and jumped to the cabin. Dad *was* there, standing in the kitchen with rain gear on. He was dripping.

"Still raining, eh?"

"After landfall the system stalled. Worst possible combination." He pointed to a pile on one of the kitchen chairs. "Rain gear."

It was offshore foul-weather gear. The pants were like overalls, coming all the way up to my arm pits with straps over the shoulders. The hooded jacket came down to midthigh and there were knee-high rubber boots in my size.

"You might want to hit the bathroom, first. And don't bring anything that can't get wet."

I left the cell phone on its charger back in the house, used the bathroom, and changed to lighter clothes before donning the rain gear.

"Ready," I said.

He held open his arms and I walked into them.

Dad was braced, but I wasn't, and I staggered sideways when he let me go. The weather may have been downgraded to a mere tropical depression, but the rain was not so much falling as flying sideways, driven by a heavy wind. The fat drops felt like projectiles even through the jacket.

It was dark and Dad switched on a strong flashlight. We were in a small stand of trees at the edge of fast-moving water. I could barely see the other side of the waterway.

"What river is this?" I had to shout over the rain.

Dad shook his head. "*That's* the road to Bhangura. It normally has a tiny stream beside it. Got this site?"

I took a deep breath and smelled something like burlap, torn vegetation, tropical flowers, and earth. "Got it."

"Just in case. Mostly we can jump from the tent, but sometimes—" He shrugged.

Dad led me through brush, up a small rise, and pointed the flashlight down as the ground dropped away again. Several yards in front of us boats were pulled up onto the grass. Beyond them, the water stretched out until it vanished in the rain. "*That's* the Baral River. You normally walk twenty minutes from here to get to its closest bank." He started walking up the slight slope, parallel to both bodies of water. "The water is *still* rising."

At first I thought we were coming to a building with trees close around, but it *was* the trees. Plastic was stretched between the trunks and stretched overhead and it was noisy, even above the storm, flapping and magnifying the sound of the rain drops. A few lights cast shadows on the plastic sheeting, trees and the outlines of people sitting close together. I had the impression there were hundreds.

"Don't drink any water here," Dad said, leaning close. "You had the oral vaccine for cholera but it's only eighty-five percent effective." He was talking about the Dukoral we took last year before spending some time in Nepal. "You can go home to drink. Leave the potable water for *them*."

We continued to skirt the trees and tarps to where the trees thinned out again on higher ground. Seven jungle-camouflaged large tents stood in the open. Beyond the tents the ground dropped away again.

"Is that more water?"

"Yeah. This hillock is temporarily cut off, but it will be okay as long it doesn't rise another two meters." He looked back at the water and pointed the flashlight, blocking the rain from his eyes with his other hand. "Shit. Or if we get swamped with more refugees."

I followed the flashlight beam. Figures in the rain were wading toward us, chest deep in the water, carrying belongings on top of their head or children on their shoulders.

Dad led the way into one of the military tents where I found Mom, eyes shadowed, counting boxes by the light of several battery-powered fluorescent lanterns.

"More refugees," Dad said. "Wading in from the north."

Mom smiled at me briefly before saying, "From the north? Why are they heading *our* way? The high ground would lead them to Bhangura!"

"Yeah."

Mom tapped one of the boxes. "We're good on water filters but the temperature is lower than we expected. Do we still have those bundles of blankets in the warehouse?"

"The synthetics? Yeah."

She pointed at the back corner of the tent, where a panel of canvas hung down, making a private nook. "Do you think you could fetch them, Cent? I need Dad to watch the tent while I find out what's with the new arrivals."

"Sure," I said.

Like me, she was wearing foul-weather gear, but she'd taken off the jacket. She fished it out from behind a row of emergency rations and pulled it on. "I thought the road took to the hills north of here, but if it's cut off, we could see a lot more refugees." She left.

I went to the nook and inhaled. Besides the moist jungle smells I got a whiff of musty cloth overlaid with mold. It would do. I jumped to the warehouse, but after five minutes of looking, I had to jump back.

"Uh, I'm not seeing the blankets, Dad."

He sucked on his lip. "Oh, yeah. They're wrapped in black plastic—big bundles almost as tall as you. In the corner near the door. I could barely jump them. You'll have to open them and bring the contents in smaller batches."

" 'kay," I said, and jumped.

Once I knew what they looked like, I found the blankets easily enough. They reminded me of giant cotton bales but there was a small label that said *Blanket, Emergency Relief, Material Post Consumer Polyester, Color Green.*

I jumped home to grab shears, then cut through the heavy black plastic wrapping. The blankets came in shrink-wrapped packs of twenty-five, weighing fifty pounds per.

I began jumping these smaller bundles, one at a time, to the tent, stacking them opposite the shielded nook. It only took a few minutes to stack twenty bundles.

I had the twenty-first package in my arms and was about to ask Dad if I should go for more when I heard Mom's voice, loud, I thought, even over the rain. I dropped the package of blankets to the floor and sat on it.

Mom came through the door with a Bangladeshi man in a poncho. "Akash says the road to Bhangura is blocked by mud slides. The military is working to clear it and they're trying to get some boats to go around, but the water is still running dangerously fast."

The man nodded and in lightly accented English said, "We'll be okay on food but shelter will be an issue. Are those blankets?" He looked at me, a puzzled look on his face. "Did another boat arrive?"

Mom shook her head.

"We could really use more blankets in the clinic tent."

"Sure," said Dad. "Fifty to start?"

"Yes. That would be excellent."

Dad gave one of the bundles to Akash and took another himself. "I think we can come up with more tarps," Dad said as they left the tent.

"Should I take blankets over to the people in the trees?" I said to Mom.

She shook her head. "In a bit." She was counting the ones I'd stacked. "Are there this many more?"

I nodded. "Easily."

"Okay. Grab twenty more packs. Always jump from behind

the screen. If you hear me talking loudly, it means someone besides your father is in the tent, right?"

I nodded. "Thought so."

Back in the warehouse I had to open another of the large, black-plastic bundles, but I had twenty more packs (five hundred blankets) stacked along the back of the tent within ten minutes.

"Done."

Mom nodded. "Let's take some blankets over and see if we get any takers."

It was less like a car wash and more like a shower when we went outside. The rain was as heavy, but the wind had lessened so the fat drops weren't moving sideways. The ground was covered with thick grass, but I felt like I was wading because the ground was mostly level and the rainwater was draining away slowly. I was grateful for the rain gear but it felt like I was a walking tent.

Mom ducked under into a large communal area under the tarps and I followed. It was wetter under the shelter than I expected. Water poured down from the edges of tarps and it was pooling. Some of the thin plastic tarps had ripped, either from the wind or where water had collected instead of running off, until the weight had torn the material.

The refugees sat or huddled, trying to avoid the places the rain splashed through, women in saris and men in *lungi*, a tube-like sarong. Kids wore a mix of traditional and modern clothing, including saris, *lungi*, and soccer shorts. There were raincoats and ponchos and umbrellas and it was a riot of color—a bit overwhelming.

Raised tree roots were prime real estate, letting people rest out of the mud and water. A few people had folding chairs and there were a few portable cots and some air mattresses, but many people squatted or sat in the water, some of them holding kids in their lap, to keep them above it.

"That can't be good," I said to Mom, tilting my head to where five girls were standing in knee-deep water at the far edge of the shelter. I didn't understand it at all, since there were other places under the tarps where the water wasn't as deep.

They stood in a cluster, holding onto each other for warmth. None of them had rain gear and their saris, though colorful, were soaking wet.

Mom saw them, too, and moved through the crowd saying, *"Dekhi. Dekhi."* She went up to one of the aid workers, a young man in a red poncho. *"Apni Ingreji bolte paren?"*

He rolled his eyes. "I went to MIT, lady."

Mom smiled. "What's with them?" She indicated the young women with a tilt of her head.

The man sighed. *"Chukri.* They got away from their *shordani* when the floodwaters came into their, uh, house and floated down from Bhangura on wreckage."

"Um. Different English they must speak at MIT. *Chukri?"*

The man looked at me and then stepped closer to Mom and said something I didn't hear. Mom frowned and then said, "And what's *shordani?"*

"Uh, landlady, sort of. She holds their contracts."

"Got it, so why are they in the deep end?"

The man sighed, heavily. *"They* know." He tilted his head toward a group of men sitting in one of the drier sections. "They chased them there. They tried to chase them outside entirely, but we were able to stop that."

Mom looked like she could spit.

"What's your name?"

The aid worker said, "My *bhalo nam* is Ramachandra. At MIT they called me Rama."

"Rather presumptuous," Mom said.

"What do I care? I'm Muslim."

"Fair enough." She shoved the package of blankets into the lap of a man sitting nearby and ripped open the top. She gestured at the people immediately around him and mimed passing them out, then looked back at Rama. "Will you translate for me?"

"Sure," he said.

"This way," said Mom heading toward the girls.

"What about *these* blankets?" I asked, hefting the bundle I carried.

"Bring them."

Mom just waded into the water, walking directly up to the girls. I thought they were all younger than me, but now that I was closer, I wasn't sure. Their eyes were old and wary and they looked at Mom with distrust.

"Cent, start giving them blankets," Mom said quietly. I ripped open the bundle and snaked out a blanket and tried to hand it to a girl whose skin tone and bony thinness reminded me of Tara. She shrank back from me and put her arms behind her and said something.

"She thinks you're a man," said Rama. "She doesn't want to take something from a man where *they* can see. They've said quite enough."

"Oh," I said. "It's the trousers, isn't it?"

"Probably," said Rama. "Also—" he touched the left side of his nose. All the girls standing in front of me wore ornamental piercings in their left nostrils.

I reached up and pulled the hood of my rain jacket back and shook my head. My hair wasn't anywhere near as long as theirs, but it was longer than I usual wore it, well over my collar. And I wore earrings, little garnets that I'd started wearing when I first noticed Brett.

I didn't have my nostril pierced but I didn't *think* I looked like a guy, despite the trousers.

The girl's mouth opened and she let her arms come out from behind her, but she still didn't reach for the blanket.

I handed the bundle to Rama and unfolded the blanket until it was doubled, then I stepped up beside her and draped it over her shoulders like a shawl.

She said in a small voice, "*Bhalo achi.*"

I glanced at Rama.

"Thanks," he translated.

"How do I say, 'you're welcome'?"

Rama wrinkled his forehead. "How long have you been in-country?"

Mom broke in, "She was diverted here because of the floods. She didn't train for this destination." All sort of true. To me, she said, "It's '*kichhu mone koro na*'."

"*Kichhu mone koro na,*" I repeated gravely to the girl. She smiled and stepped back.

After that, they were a little more trusting. As I handed out the blankets, Mom had Rama translate as she told the girls, "We have a place for you to rest, where you don't have to stand in the water. And there's food."

She and Rama led the way and I brought up the rear.

Mom followed the empty stretches where the rain came through between the tarps or the mud was particularly bad, but some of the refugees, nowhere near the girls, twitched their clothes or belongings away, as if they'd be touched. Others ignored them, and some men smiled and called out. At first I thought they were being friendly but I saw the girls look away, their faces becoming even stonier than before.

We were almost to the door when a large man wearing a formal tunic, a *sherwani*, stood up and stepped forward, shouting. We'd just passed him, so I was closest, but he reached past me, to the last girl and grabbed her blanket away. He shook it in the air and was talking loudly, not to the girls, but to all the people around him.

I grabbed the edge of the blanket, angry, and tried to pull it back, but he was twice as big as me—not only tall, but heavy. He laughed at me and some of the men sitting nearby laughed also.

I clenched the blanket with both hands and jumped in place, adding an instant twenty feet per second, toward the door. I flew away from him and he tilted forward, the look of contempt abruptly replaced by one of shock and surprise. He let go of the blanket, but it was too late. He fell forward, hands waving, and belly flopped into the mud.

While some of the men had laughed before, now all the women and men laughed loudly, easily heard over the rain on the plastic.

Shifting his mass forward had absorbed my velocity and I barely stumbled before turning to follow the girls, now scurrying, outside.

The girls dashed through the rain to our tent, holding their blankets over their heads for protection. I flipped my jacket hood back up, trailing them, but my eye was on the place where we'd left the shelter of the tarps. Nobody followed us out into the rain, but I couldn't tell if they watched.

Dad was back from taking blankets to the clinic tent and he watched the influx of young girls with a bemused expression on his face. Rama was doing some more translating for Mom. The girls were toweling themselves off with their blankets. Mom gestured to me.

"You all right?" she said quietly. "I didn't see what was happening until I turned, going out the door, when he fell down."

"I'm fine," I said. "Do you know what it was about?"

She grabbed another bundle of blankets and ripped it open, offering dry ones to the girls. "Rama? Who was that man? The one who was shouting."

Rama grinned. "He's a teacher, the headmaster, at a madrasa in the valley. A very traditional, and just now wet, madrasa. He's been giving everybody a lot of trouble, shouting at women for being immodest because of the way their wet clothing clings. The local Imam shouted him down and quoted several Koran verses on compassion.

"When the *chukri* showed up, he wanted them driven into the flood. When you gave them blankets before his 'chaste' students received any, he became angry again and started preaching to the crowd."

I stepped closer to Mom. "*Chukri?*"

Mom pursed her lips for a moment, then said quietly, "All right, they're indentured sex workers."

"Prostitutes?" I said, shocked. They were younger than I was!

"Their families sold them. Sometimes a new wife will sell her stepdaughters. They have to work for a year to pay off their 'debt,' but their *shordani*, the landlady who holds their contracts, charges them for all sorts of expenses, and the debt increases instead of decreases. It can go on for years."

She opened a case of bottled water. "Some of them were probably born in the brothels, of other *chukri* or of nonindentured prostitutes, who sell them back into the system."

My jaw dropped. I tried to think of something to say but I was speechless. Finally I said, "Why can't they just run away?"

"*They* did." The corner of Mom's mouth turned down. "But usually they can't. They can't even go out to shop. They buy overpriced food in the brothel and go further into debt. It's like a prison." She shook her head and said, "Enough. Let's feed them."

While I handed out water, Mom gave them each a twelve-hundred-calorie emergency rations bar. They aren't bad—like lemon-flavored shortbread in taste and texture but with tons of protein and vitamins. You can drop packages of them out of a low-altitude airplanes without damaging them, though I'd hate to be the impact zone.

Rama assured the girls that they were okay to eat for Muslims or Hindus and demonstrated by biting into one himself.

Later, Rama got some refugees to come over from the trees to collect more blankets, and followed them back to supervise their distribution.

We shifted some rations and water filters to where the blankets had been, clearing part of the integrated floor. The tent was on higher ground than the tarps in the trees, so for the girls, the expanse of dry tent floor was like heaven after their time in the water.

Fed, warm, and mostly dry, they were asleep in minutes, and I found myself yawning, suddenly, surprised at how weary I was.

Dad looked at his watch and then at me. "Bedtime for you, too, bunny."

The sky had brightened outside and now you could see the rain, not just feel it. I checked my watch. It said 9:30 which was U.S. Mountain Time at night. Local time was also 9:30, but morning. I didn't normally go to sleep this early, but I hadn't slept that well the last two nights.

Huh. I looked at the girls sleeping at the side of the tent, like a litter of puppies. I hadn't thought about Brett in hours.

Good.

TWENTY-ONE

Davy: "Janitorial"

At night, when the Daarkon Group's offices were fully lit so the janitorial staff could clean, the mirrored glass of Rhiarti Tower was no longer opaque. Davy used a telephoto lens from the opposite rooftop, both securing jump sites and getting shots of the custodial uniform the janitors were wearing.

The next day Davy bought the uniform from a uniform supply store on Foulkrod Street in Philadelphia. "Oh, yeah. Want us to embroider the logo?" The clerk pointed at the emblem over the breast pocket in the photo. "Don't recognize the company. Youse here in the city?"

"West of town." This was true since it covered everything from the suburbs to the Pacific ocean. "They have patches for the company logo."

The clerk snorted. "Patches. Cheapskates. Youse all right with shoes?"

Davy waited until the janitor vacuuming the corner office moved out into the hallway before he jumped. This was clearly the executive level, judging both by the furnishings and the number of offices. The two levels below had fifteen offices on this side of the building. This floor had six.

He was wearing the custodial uniform and his dark goatee. The beard itched. The uniform didn't. He'd run it twice through the wash to get rid of the "just manufactured" creases.

He shook out the large plastic bag he was carrying and pulled the trash can out from under the credenza. It was heavier than he expected and he saw that it had a crosscut shredder built into the top.

This must be the place.

Certainly normal businesses had perfectly legitimate reasons to shred documents, but it warmed his heart nonetheless. He dumped the bin into his bag.

There were no obvious motion detectors or cameras in the room, so he secured a jump site. The name on the door was Mark Liebowitz. Moving cautiously out into the hall, he saw the man with the vacuum moving down the hall away from him. Beyond the man, a woman with rags and a spray bottle walked into another office. Davy walked the other direction, down the hallway around the corner. As he had thought, there *were* cameras in the corners of the building, covering the hallways. He kept his head down and turned into the next office, which was labeled *Todd Hostetler*. He bent over to pull out Todd's shredder and an alarm went off.

He hadn't touched the bin yet, so he doubted it was wired. He didn't see any motion detectors.

Bet it was the cameras in the hall.

Davy walked back to the first office and saw all four custodians exiting into the stairwell at the end of the hall. A secondary alarm, on the door itself, was shrieking. He heard footsteps from behind and looked back around the corner. Two men in identical monogramed blazers were coming up the hallway, checking each office in turn, right hands inside their jackets in a way that made Davy want to jump immediately away. The one in the lead saw Davy but instead of pulling a gun from his jacket, he called out, "Fire alarm. Exit the building!"

Davy blinked, then waved his hand in acknowledgement and walked away, toward the shrieking door.

If it was the camera, they would know it was a guy in a janitor's uniform.

Once in the stairway the door alarm was painfully loud. There weren't any cameras evident, so Davy jumped away.

How did they know?

TWENTY-TWO

"Mastaans"

I woke up two hours before my alarm was set to go off—4:30 in the morning. I looked at the clock and tried to close my eyes, but they popped right open again.

The cabin was silent. I hadn't shut my door last night and the light in Mom and Dad's room was still on.

I swung down from my bed and padded across the hall.

Mom and Dad's bed was empty. I jumped downstairs but they weren't there, so I checked the house in New Prospect—also empty. I jumped back to the cabin and put on my school clothes, then the rain boots and gear.

It had stopped raining in the little stand of trees south of the refugee shelter but the water had risen. I arrived standing in a foot and a half of water, and the temperature was warmer. The air felt heavy, warm and very humid. The sun was near the western horizon, shining through broken clouds. I jumped back to the mud room at the cabin and hung up the rain gear, but kept the boots.

Good thing there was a drain in the floor. Several quarts of floodwater had splashed through when I'd jumped.

When I returned and exited the trees, people were all over the hillock, including just outside the stand of trees. If it wasn't for the high water, they'd probably have been in there, too. I wonder what they made of my splashing.

Many stared at me, strange western girl in what they probably considered to be boy's clothes, threading my way through the crowd. I nodded and smiled, weaving my way between people, repeating what Mom had said when moving through the crowd the night before, *"Dekhi. Dekhi."*

I hoped I was saying "excuse me."

There were more boats pulled up on the shore. Traditional short and narrow oar and pole boats, a few long, fat-waisted boats with woven rounded covers over their midships, a rigid hulled inflatable with army markings, and a forty-foot, flat-roofed passenger ferry with an inboard diesel.

As I passed the trees with the tarps stretched among them I saw that there hadn't been a huge increase in refugees. Most of them had just moved out onto the grass, trying to get out of the mud, I guess.

I saw last night's angry teacher from the flooded madrasa. He'd rinsed the worst of the mud out of his tunic, though it was still stained. He was sitting on a box surrounded by his students. I averted my eyes as I went by but I heard someone say something and several heads turned. I walked on, trying not to show any anxiety, but I could feel my head dropping down between my shoulders and my footsteps speeding up.

The door side of my parents' tent had been rolled up, and a row of boxes with a blanket thrown over them formed a counter across most of the open side.

The *chukri* girls were still there, only now they seemed to be working the counter. I looked toward the back of the tent and saw Mom, cross-legged on the floor, leaning back against a pile of unopened blankets. Her eyes were shut.

Seven refugees were standing in front of the counter while my friend from last night, the girl who reminded me of Tara, demonstrated how to use a water filter, pumping dirty river water from a pail, though the filter, and into a clear plastic bottle. When she finished the demonstration, she apparently asked if they had any questions. Then two of the other girls handed out packaged water filters, blankets, and ration bars to the audience.

There was a chorus of *"Bhalo achi!"* and the girls answered, *"Kichhu mone koro na!"*

I went around the end of the counter, nodding to the girls. They smiled back and bobbed their heads.

Mom opened her eyes as I walked near, scuffing my feet deliberately. "I wasn't sleeping, really."

"Sure, Mom."

"Was I snoring? I'll bet I was snoring."

"Where's Dad?"

"He's got some errands," she said, vaguely.

I gestured at the girls at the front desk. "I see you've got help."

Mom smiled. "Oh, yes."

"What will happen to them?"

"Rama is working on it. He's contacted a local Imam whose part of an antitrafficking network. Most of their activities are educational—prevention—but there are a few communities that help rescued trafficking victims. One of them is just downstream, but it's on the other side of the floodwaters."

"So they'll be okay?"

Mom rocked her hand back and forth. "No promises. But a better chance than they had before they floated away from the brothel." She shook her head. "They don't swim, you know. Rama has been translating for me. They grabbed onto floating wreckage and pushed out into the storm. Pretty brave."

I thought, *Or maybe drowning wasn't as scary as what they had to face every day.*

"I've got a couple of hours before I have to be at school. Why don't you go home and get some sleep?"

Mom blinked and her shoulders sagged. I could tell she'd been keeping herself going by willpower alone.

"Well, okay. Your father should be back soon, anyway. *They* know what to do," she jerked her chin toward the girls at the counter. "Be discreet, but don't be stupid. If there's any danger, jump away."

She stood up slowly, tilting and twisting her neck. She stepped up to the counter and looked around. "Not that there should be any danger."

"Right."

"If you need a translator there are several *Ingreji* speakers in the medical-clinic tent." She gave me a sideways one-armed hug and left, ostensibly by the rear door, but really from the screened corner at the back of the tent.

I smiled at the girls at the counter and pointed to myself, careful to do it with my right hand. "Cent." I tapped my sternum. Then tilted my hand out toward them.

The girl who reminded me of Tara was called Anika. And there was Rupa, Megh, Kanta, and Sathia. We amused ourselves for several minutes by testing my retention of each name. All of them had black hair and amazingly beautiful brown eyes, but fortunately their saris were of different colors and their nose ornaments differed.

More refugees came for water filters and rations and I stepped outside, watching the river, while the girls did their spiel and demonstration.

There was commerce happening. Several boats were selling vegetables and fruit to those refugees with money. And some boats were taking money to ferry refugees away, possibly to family in unflooded areas, since most of *these* people's homes were still inundated.

I heard the whine of a powerboat and saw a white-and-green fiberglass police launch come in from upriver, planing, way out in the regular channel. It turned toward us and slowed, coasting on its own bow wave for a moment, then came in slowly, occasionally detouring around flooded structures and trees.

As it got closer I saw one uniformed policeman driving with an older women in elaborate dress standing beside him. Four other men wearing tube sarongs—the *lungi*—and starched white shirts, sat in the bow.

I wondered if they were more aid workers, when one of the girls behind me gasped.

I looked back at them, but the front of the tent was empty. I went to the counter and looked over. They were on the floor, huddled into the corner where the tent wall met the counter.

They looked terrified.

I looked back at the police boat as it gunned its engines to push the bow up onto the grass at the shoreline. The men in the white shirts were helping the woman over the bow. She shrugged their arms off and jumped down, looking around, then waved her hand at them, flapping it toward the crowd. They moved off while the policeman tied the boat's bowline to a stunted shrub.

I reached up and began releasing the ties that held the rolled-up tent wall. The girls saw what I was doing and leaped, up to the other ties, quickly freeing the panel. It dropped down onto the counter and I tugged it outward, letting it fall all the way to the ground, then ducked into the tent at the corner. There was still a battery-powered fluorescent light on at the back of the tent. I held my finger to my lips, stepped back to the light, and turned it off.

I went out the back door and tied the flap shut, then went looking for Rama.

"Anyone speak English?" I asked at the clinic tent next door.

A man wearing a Bangladeshi army uniform, with a stethoscope slung over his neck said, "Yes?"

"I'm looking for Ramachandra, one of the aid workers."

He nodded. "Rama, yes. I saw him this morning, but not lately. Have you looked at their supply tent?"

"Sorry. Don't know where that is."

He pointed out the door toward the trees and tarps. "In the middle."

"Thanks. Uh, *bhalo achi*."

He grinned, a flash of white, and said, "I wish you luck." But it came out like one word. "Iwishyouluck."

It was a lot easier to walk through the trees than it had been eight hours earlier, but the mud was still bad and I was grateful for the boots.

I found Rama outside another army tent set up in the middle of the trees. I hadn't noticed it the night before. The rain had made everything dark and the tent's dark green fabric had faded into the murk. Rama was lying in a string hammock, reading.

"Rama," I called.

He turned his head and his eyebrows went up.

"Where did you go all day, little one?"

I shrugged. "Slept. Not adjusted to this time zone. Can you translate for me?"

"The *chukri* girls?"

"Yes."

He groaned. "I've been talking to Shahjahan off and on all day. I thought he was going to leave them alone?"

"I don't know who you mean."

"The teacher from the madrasa. The one who fell in the mud?"

"Oh. No. It's not him. A police boat just pulled up with a policeman, a woman, and several other men. When the girls saw them, they hid. They looked terrified. I need to ask them what's going on."

Rama swung out of the hammock. "No idea. Let's go see."

He led me out of the trees on the river side, near the madrasa students and teachers. The policeman was there, talking with Shahjahan, the headmaster. Rama threaded his way to the outer ring of seated students and asked one of them something in Bengali. I moved closer as the student answered. Rama turned to me and said, "They're looking for the girls. The policeman says they're thieves—that they stole valuable property under cover of the flooding."

I frowned. "What? Did you see them bring anything?"

Rama shook his head. "Only themselves."

The madrasa headmaster apparently had the same point. He said something back to the policeman and Rama translated. "What property did they steal? They arrived here with only their clothes."

I winced. I guess we'd gotten beyond the point of claiming they'd never arrived here.

Rama exhaled. "You said he came with a woman? A police woman?"

"No uniform. She wore a fancy sari." I swiveled my head around. "There she is."

The woman was up at the north end of the crowd, walking through the refugees, peering at faces, occasionally asking questions.

"I bet she's their *shordani*. And they brought *mastaans*." Rama said. At my blank look he translated. "Musclemen. Gangsters."

"Why the policeman, then?"

"Oh, he's *their* cop, probably. The local police on the take. The brothels have to pay off the police to operate."

The policeman was shouting at Shahjahan now, but his students didn't like it, apparently, for several of them stood up abruptly. The policeman's voice dropped in volume, suddenly, and he stepped back.

I heard a scream and then another from the north, from the tents. I said, "They've found the girls!"

Rama yelled something in Bengali and ran toward the tent. I ran back into the trees and jumped to the screened back corner of the tent.

It wasn't as dark as it was before. The front flap at the corner had been pulled up onto the counter and there was a gap. I heard a man yelling and saw movement between me and the light.

I moved forward and saw a silhouetted man struggling with two of the girls, pulling them along by their upper arms. I jumped in place and added thirty feet per second toward him. My left shoulder hit his back. He flew into the counter and flipped over it, ripping the wall of the tent away and tumbling out into the sunlight, wrapped in the heavy fabric. I fell to the floor of the tent, my shoulder numb, the wind knocked out of me.

With the light flooding in I saw that the girls he'd been manhandling were Rupa and Kanta, now staring at me and rubbing their arms where the man's grip had torn free. The other girls were not in sight. Gasping, I struggled to my feet and leaned over the counter. Two men were pulling Megh and Sathia toward the boat. The woman, the *shordani*, was already stepping up onto the bow, pulling Anika after her by the hair.

The students from the madrasa were following Rama up the shoreline, hampered by the other refugees scattered across the grass. The refugees had jumped to their feet and were looking around, trying to figure what danger the crowd of students was running *from*.

Rama was shouting, the students were shouting, the policeman, trying to catch up with the students from behind, was shouting. I wished I understood Bengali.

The policeman went straight to the boat, pushing though the crowd until he reached the water's edge and then splashing up the shallows.

The students stopped, forming a barrier between the two men with Megh and Sathia, and the boat.

The *mastaans* tried to push forward, pulling the girls behind, and the students shoved the men back, some of them also pulling at the girls, trying to get them away from the *mastaans*.

The *mastaans* yanked the girls back and one of them reached under his shirt to the waistline of his *lungi*, coming out with a blocky automatic. He fired a single shot into the air and the crowd shrank back.

Oh, no.

I was breathing again but the numbness in my shoulder was changing to a sharp ache. I thought about jumping to the man with the gun, but I saw him duck suddenly, as a rock flew overhead. He pointed his gun toward the thrower, and three more rocks hit him from different directions. He clutched at his head and dropped to the ground. Sathia, released, turned to Megh and pulled her away from the remaining *mastaan*, who dropped his hands to his sides and eyed the crowd.

The motor on the police launch roared to life, and it backed away from the shore even as the crowd lunged toward it. I could see the *shordani*, one hand still gripping Anika's hair, yelling at the policeman as she gestured back toward the shore with her free hand. The policeman gestured at the crowd and yelled back.

The fourth *mastaan*, who'd been at the south end of the camp and not part of the struggle, came running up the shoreline before plunging into the water, to swim out to the boat. The *mastaan* who'd released Megh shoved his way through the crowd and followed, leaving the man who'd been struck with stones and the man I'd shoulder-checked back at the tent.

I would've just let them go except for Anika.

I jumped to the boat.

The policeman tried to twist around when I hooked his belt from behind, but I added thirty feet a second velocity *up* and we both rose off the deck.

I jumped back to the control station almost immediately. The policeman, yelling, rose to fifteen feet before he fell back down. The current had moved the boat sideways enough that he splashed into the water, just missing the gunwale.

I turned my head to the *shordani* and grinned. She let go of Anika and leaped off the side of the boat, shrieking.

Anika looked at me with wide eyes, but she stayed where she was. There were lifejackets under a bench locker and I threw four out, two toward the *shordani* and the policeman, and two toward the *mastaans* who'd were swimming toward the boat. The controls were straightforward, a throttle and a wheel, and I gunned the engine, pulling well out of range of the *mastaans*, then turned the boat back into the shore. The crowd shrank back as the bow skidded up onto the grass but Rama came forward, slowly, followed by Megh, Sathia, Rupa, and Kanta.

Rama was looking stunned. "How did you sneak onto the boat? You were behind me!"

I like *your version*, I thought.

"And how did you throw the cop into the air?"

I smiled weakly. "Adrenaline?"

He opened his mouth to say something else but I cut in. "I'm thinking you might use this boat to take the girls over to that village you found, the one with the Imam from the antitrafficking network? I mean, if you're okay in a boat."

He looked offended. "I'm Bangladeshi. I can *handle* a boat."

"Then, after, maybe you could leave the boat someplace *different*? Someplace away from here?"

He looked out into the water. The life-jacketed *shordani*, policeman, and *mastaans* had drifted past the end of the refugee camp, well into the current.

"I'll take it back upstream to Bhangura. That's where it belongs." He gestured at the distant orange dots. "But when that policeman gets to a phone, you probably want to be gone from here, you know?"

I nodded. "How do you say goodbye in Bangla?"

"*Abar dakha hobe.*"

I smiled at the girls, put my hands together, and said "*Abar dakha hobe.*" I thought about jumping away, right there, but there was always the chance that the people really thought I'd stowed away on the boat.

A chance.

Anika looked upset and said something quickly, in Bengali, her eyes shifting back and forth between me and Rama.

Rama translated, "She hopes you aren't leaving because of helping them, that you won't get in trouble with the police."

I shrugged. "I have to get back to school. I could only be here a short time, anyway. Good luck in your new lives."

Rama translated.

Almost in unison, the girls said, "*Bhalo achi!*"

I nodded gravely. "*Kichhu mone koro na.*"

Back at the tent, the man I'd turned into a tent burrito was stirring. I wondered if he had spinal damage, but he suddenly sat up, twisting back and forth, trying to get clear of the tightly wrapped fabric.

Can't be too bad.

An army corpsman from the clinic tent came over and helped the man worm his way out of the tent fabric. I thought about hiding but was pretty sure he'd never seen what—or who—hit him.

Behind me, I heard the motor of the police boat rev up again. I looked out to see it pull away from shore with Rama at the controls. The girls saw me looking and waved.

The man shook off the corpsman and staggered toward the boat, but it was well out from the shore by the time he'd managed ten steps.

I waved back until the girls were too small to see.

The man walked toward the shore and found his bleeding compatriot sitting on the grass where he'd been felled by the rocks. The corpsman hadn't discovered him yet. There was no sign of his gun. I hoped *he* didn't have it.

I went back to the tent and checked inside, looking for anything personal that Mom or Dad may have left. But there were only the supplies: rations, tarps, water filters.

I stepped back into the screened corner and jumped away.

Dad was at the warehouse.

He took one look at me and dropped the box of rations he was holding onto the concrete floor. "Are you all right?"

I nodded.

"Something happened," he said. It *wasn't* a question. I wondered what my face looked like.

"Don't go back to Bangladesh before I talk to you, okay? Want to catch Mom at home."

His eyes widened and he jumped before I did. I arrived in my room and stepped across the hall to their bedroom doorway. Dad was standing by the bed looking down at Mom, who was asleep, her mouth open. I stood still, frozen by the naked tenderness on his face.

He exhaled, then glanced over at me. "She's fine," he said.

I looked down at my watch. Unbelievably, I still had another half hour before I had to be at school.

Mom stirred, opened her eyes blearily, looking first at Dad, then at me. She mumbled. "—ing okay?"

Dad nodded. "Shhh. Everything's fine. But don't go back to Bangladesh without talking to me, all right?"

She sat bolt upright.

"What happened!"

Well, at least I didn't have to tell the story to each of them separately. It still took a few moments for Mom to become fully awake. We ended up downstairs at the kitchen table with tea all around.

"You should've come for one of us!" Mom said sharply when I'd barely started.

I blinked. It was *Dad* I'd expected to freak out. "By the time I knew I needed you it was too late. The boat was out in the river with Anika."

Dad held up his hand to Mom. "Let her finish."

I said, "Yeah. I'm going to be late for school otherwise."

I finished the story.

Dad was staring at me, open mouthed.

"What?" I said. "He was moving when I left, honest."

"You can add velocity horizontally?"

"Any direction, really."

He shook his head. "That's fascinating. I always wondered wh—"

"It means she could break her neck!" Mom said.

It took a lot of effort not to reach up and rub my aching shoulder. "Well, *I* think you should be more upset about my jumping in public and messing up the relief work."

Mom bit her lip and Dad smiled slightly.

"We were done," Mom said. "We were only hanging around to make sure the *chukri* girls were taken care of."

Dad nodded. "We don't like to linger in any one country. There's too much chance that someone will snap a picture that gets to the wrong people. I didn't used to worry, but the facial recognition software is getting better every year, combing every social network and photo-display site on the planet."

Mom tried to look stern, but she couldn't hold it. "Nobody died and the girls got away. The rations and water filters won't go to waste." She smiled tiredly. "I can live with that."

Dad shook his head. "But maybe we need to rethink this involving you in the relief projects."

My mouth dropped open. "What? I kept those girls safe!"

"Not *you*, though," Dad said.

Mom said, "That's not fair, Davy. Especially given *your* history."

"We're not talking about *me*," Dad said.

I took a deep breath. "You're right," I said.

Dad said, "Besides you—what?"

"You're right. It's dangerous for me to be involved in your projects."

Mom and Dad looked at each other, eyebrows raised.

"So, I'll just go do my own projects, instead."

I jumped.

I walked to school from the edge of the woods. I was hoping that Caffeine's posse was hanging around. I wanted to show them some tricks with momentum.

They weren't.

I was calmer by the time I crunched through the last bit of old snow next to the school building, but still angry.

I'd been helping Mom and Dad with relief efforts all over the world *before* I could jump. And now that I could jump it was *less* safe? I slammed my locker shut a little harder than necessary. Kids flinched and stared at me.

"Sorry," I muttered. My face went hot and I barely kept myself from jumping away. I walked to Mr. Hill's class with my head hunched between my shoulders and my bag clutched across my chest.

The bell rang as I went through the door. Tara and I exchanged glances before I sat, and I saw her sit up straight, frowning.

That won't do. I took deep breaths and worked on dropping my shoulders. By the time Mr. Hill started talking I think I at least *looked* normal and by the end of class I even *felt* normal.

Tara touched base with me in the hall as we left. "You all right? You looked kinda *mad* when you came in."

I surprised myself by laughing. "A fight with my dad. Stupid fight, actually. One of those he can't win, but that doesn't mean we won't still have the fight."

"Boys?" asked Tara.

I stared at her blankly.

"Dating? Girls?"

I shook my head. "No. Not *that*. Though now that I think about it, maybe I should bring up the possibility." I grinned. "Does your Mom ever tell you you're too young to do things that you are quite capable of?"

Tara laughed. "When does she not? The only thing she thinks I'm old enough to do is homework and housework. Everything else? Not so much."

We went our separate ways.

The abstract focus of math was a welcome distraction and, since I was caught up with assignments in humanities, I was able to read ahead.

But sometime after I sat down for lunch Tony staggered into the cafeteria, his nose a bloody ruin.

Coach Teichert was on duty and he stuck his head out into the hallway before scooping up a handful of paper napkins from the lunch line. He pressed them up against the red flow. "Who did it?"

Tony yelled at the pressure. I think his nose was broken.

"Who hit you?" Coach asked again.

Tony mumbled something.

"What?"

"I fe' down," Tony said louder.

Right. He fell down.

I don't think *anybody* believed that.

I looked over at Caffeine. She'd been in the cafeteria the whole time, sitting with Donna at her usual table. She was smiling slightly and she certainly didn't look *surprised*.

Coach Teichert escorted Tony out, destined for the school nurse.

A few minutes later, Hector Guzman came in the cafeteria and sat at the other end of Caffeine's table.

Jade said, "Hector *was* wearing a hoodie right before lunch."

I looked over. He was wearing a black T-shirt.

"It's not like it's warm in here," Tara said, eyebrows knitted together. It wasn't. The school district was pinching pennies on the heat.

"Maybe he's all warm from punching out Tony," I said.

Jade nodded. "And maybe he has Tony's *blood* splashed across his hoodie."

I thought about the *chukri* girls and the *mastaans*. "Where is Hector's locker?"

Jade shrugged but Tara said, "Down by the physics lab."

"That's not close at all. He couldn't have put his hoodie there."

"Yeah, but he could've given it to someone else."

"Maybe, but he could've put it in a trash can, too. Watch my bag, okay?"

The hoodie was in the third can I looked in. Not one of the two big cans by the cafeteria doors, but the one near the girl's restroom across the hall.

Coach Teichert was standing outside the nurse's office, talking to Dr. Prady, the principal, when I walked up and showed them the bloody front of the hoodie, part of it still wet.

Dr. Prady's eyes widened. "Where did you get that?"

I told him.

He took it by the edges and looked at the collar. Hector's last name was written below the size tag in faded marker.

Coach Teichert nodded when he saw the name.

Dr. Prady asked, "Did you see anything?"

I shook my head. "I was in the cafeteria when Tony came in with the bloody nose."

Coach Teichert exchanged glances with Dr. Prady and said, "Let's see what Tony says *now*." He looked at me. "Thanks, Cent. Uh, keep this to yourself, all right?"

"Yes, Coach."

I got back to the cafeteria before the bell rang.

We did high jumps in PE. I was sorely tempted to add velocity on my vaults. My shoulder still ached and I didn't do as well as many of the other girls.

I kept my eye on Caffeine, but she left me alone, even walking wide around me on more than one occasion.

I didn't know whether to be glad or disappointed.

TWENTY-THREE

Davy: Old Data, New Application

Two weeks after his last trip into the Rhiarti Tower, Davy tried again during the early morning rush hour. The alarm had gone off last time when he'd been in the second office. He jumped into the first office he'd entered on his last visit wearing his most business-formal suit, an aquiline false nose, and horn-rimmed glasses.

The office was empty.

Davy glanced out into the hallway and saw a woman carrying a stack of files, walking away from him. He stepped into the hallway and walked in the opposite direction.

His goal was to find the fanciest office in the company and read the name on the doorplate.

The alarm went off, again.

Dammit!

He made the first left, a hallway into the interior of the tower, away from the coveted outside offices. He passed the bathrooms, a coffee station with an espresso machine, and smaller offices, mostly empty. Then a far door opened abruptly and two men in identical blue blazers came out.

This time they did *not* think he belonged there.

They already had weapons in their hands but they weren't guns. They were bright yellow plastic pistol shapes, blocky and wide. Doubled laser spots danced across the carpet, then raced toward him as they lifted their hands.

Tasers!

Davy jumped past them and, before they could turn, stepped quietly into their office.

From the hallway, someone said emphatically "Fuck! It's him!"

The door was unmarked but it clearly was the security office. Two desks before a bank of flat video monitors that showed the hallways and the elevators.

Davy slid between the door and the wall, holding his breath.

He heard the guards move in the hall, one set of footsteps receding, the other coming closer. Through the gap between the door and the frame, he saw a slice of blue blazer frozen in the doorway.

Then the man in the doorway turned away and called down the hall. "He's not on any of the cameras! Check the south and west offices. I'll check the restrooms, and then north and east."

"He could jump in behind us."

"Right. I'll reset the alarm first. So we'll know."

Davy sucked back into the corner as the guard stepped into the room, but the guard didn't go toward the monitors, where he might have seen Davy. Davy heard keyboarding from the far side of the room, and the alarm in the background stopped. Then the man left, swinging the door shut behind him and rattling it, to make sure it was fully closed and locked.

What kind of alarm will discriminate between all the people coming into the office and me?

For a horrible moment he wondered if every one on the premises had an implant, and that anyone who didn't set off an alarm. It wouldn't have to be an implant. It could just be a key card every one carried.

No. They said "jump."

He looked over at the end of the room where he'd "reset" the alarm.

There was a rack of equipment, around waist high, with a

monitor and keyboard pulled out of the top rack position. There were various modules below, the most prominent of which was labeled, *Power Module* and *Micro g LaCoste*. He folded the monitor over the keyboard and slid the unit back into the rack. This revealed a manual on the top of the machine: *TAGS Air III Gravity Meter, Turnkey Airborne Gravity System with Aerograv Data Processing Software.*

Ah.

He remembered a test done when he was held captive so long ago. They'd used a gravitational survey aircraft to monitor some controlled jumps. What had their pet physicist said? Oh, yeah: *The gravitational signature actually overlapped for two hundred milliseconds.* He'd also said, seventeen years ago, that the device was sensitive enough to measure the gravity of a three-year-old child at one meter. How much more sensitive was *this* device, almost two decades later? Apparently sensitive enough to measure that doubled gravitational signal on this floor at least. Probably the adjoining floors, too.

They'd set this up just for jumpers.

This must definitely *be the place.*

Part of him really wanted more information. Part of him wanted to leave and *never* return.

He wondered what would happen if he just turned it off. He did so, listening for the distant alarm, but nothing happened.

They probably jury-rigged it into their existing system, so it didn't fail-safe to an alarmed state.

Good.

He left the keyboard/monitor and it slid into the unit.

He looked up. The ceiling was concrete with a small ventilation duct distributing A/C, and square and round conduits running across it and down the walls to the equipment. The lines for the computers, monitors, and phones all ran into the next room through a square opening high on the wall.

There was a connecting door in the same wall, and he opened it. Cold air and white noise pushed out, at least fifteen degrees cooler than the security room. The ceiling light was off but hundreds of LEDs blinked at him. He hit the light switch. It was the firm's wiring and server closet, with Ethernet switches, patch boards, phone equipment, and wiring patch boards, as well as a head-high stack of rack-mounted servers. It also had a suspended ceiling, though a third of the panels had been removed so wires could run up into that space. A small stepladder leaned against the wall, and he climbed it to peer into one of openings. There was two feet of clearance, but the framework was light aluminum supported by wire, and the lightweight panels were clearly fragile, as the broken pieces of one were leaning against a wall.

There was, however, a three-inch water pipe running through the space, just above the panels, feeding the sprinkler heads. It was suspended from heavy metal straps anchored in the concrete above. He climbed back down the stepladder and put it back against the wall.

Using a wall bracket he carefully climbed atop the server rack, then lifted the panel above and shifted it to the side. The pipe ran down the middle of the space and it was very dusty.

I'm going to ruin this suit.

He pulled himself up onto the pipe and perched there, one hand bracing against the concrete above. He lifted his feet up and pulled the panel back into place, then gingerly set his feet wide apart on the aluminum frame, each near a support wire.

The opening into the security room was three feet away. He shifted his butt along the pipe and his feet along the frame until he was near it.

And without putting my foot through a panel.

And now I wait.

It seemed like an eternity but his watch told him it was only twelve minutes before the guards returned and made a phone call. He could only hear one side, but it sounded like one of them was calling and the other was operating the monitor console.

"This is Larson, Mr. Gilead."

Pause.

"No, sir. We definitely had an alpha-class event. Both Mc-Ginnis and I saw him teleport away."

Pause.

"We reset the alarm and checked the premises. We didn't find him anywhere, and the alarm hasn't gone off again."

Pause.

"Like last time, the cameras show he came out of Liebow-itz's office, but then he cut back through the central hallway right toward our office and we saw him almost immediately. That's it."

Pause.

"No sir. Not a janitor this time. Still male. Business suit. Glasses. No beard. I'll compare the video with the file."

Pause.

"Are you sure that's necessary, sir?"

Davy heard a raised voice from the phone, but couldn't make out the words.

"Yes, sir! Sorry, sir."

Larson hung up the phone.

"The executive committee is going to the Retreat. They won't come back to the offices until we've caught or killed the bastard. Probably not even then."

The other guard—McGinnis?—said, "The Retreat? I thought that was just a rumor. Where is it?"

"No idea."

"Oh, shit. I just bought a condo. Are they going to move operations again? Any chance it will still be the city?"

"I have no fucking idea. Pull up the Rice file and compare today's images. See if it's him."

"Well, it sure as hell wasn't his wife."

Davy had been amused up to this point. Now he had a sudden urge to jump into the security office and take both men far, far away.

At least they didn't know about Cent.

He wondered how long it would take them to figure out the gravity unit was off.

He jumped away.

TWENTY-FOUR

"Going ballistic"

After school, at the coffee shop, Tara and Jade filled me in on the gossip. "Tony's still not talking. They had Hector in to confront him about the hoodie but he says he left it in the hall and Tony must've bled on it after his 'accident.' "

These were confidential interviews, so of course the whole school knew about it by the end of the day. I thought about talking to Tony myself, but I decided to let it go for now.

At supper Dad chewed me out for *agreeing* with him about not working on their relief projects anymore, then said the only relief projects I *could* work on were theirs.

Mom, behind him, bit her lip and looked at the ceiling.

I was sorely tempted to just jump away again, but instead I said "Yes, Daddy."

Then he apologized for his statements that morning and I was so surprised I hugged him.

"Did you check on Anika and the other girls?"

He and Mom exchanged glances.

Mom said, "They made it to the village. I think they're going to be all right." She frowned, though.

"What?" I said.

Dad said, "We can't find Ramachandra. He saw the girls to

the village Imam and when last seen, he headed upstream in the police boat."

I said, "I told you he was going to get rid of it back in Bhangura. That's where it was from. Do you think the *mastaans* got him? Or the police?"

Mom and Dad exchanged glances.

I looked at Dad. "You think it's *them*."

He looked away.

Mom raised her shoulders, spread her hands. "We don't *know*. But we also don't know it's *not*."

"If it *is* them, Rama could have a pretty bad time of it," Dad said. "Remember what I said about witnesses?"

He opened his mouth to say it, but I beat him to it. "When the lemon gets squeezed, it's hard on the lemon?"

Dad nodded. "That."

Mom exhaled. "He has nothing to hide. If it's them, they'll interrogate and release, really."

I shook my head to clear it. *Interrogate and release.* Like wildlife biologists? *Tag and release.*

"Hopefully," Dad said. "If it's them, then this is their first indication that there are three of us."

"I've been other places with you before this," I protested. "All over the world."

"But you didn't jump, then," Dad said. "This is their first indication that there are now three of us that can *jump*."

The next day, Dakota fell down and broke his left forefinger.

There were no witnesses. Not even himself, apparently. "Don't know what happened," he'd said.

Right.

When I saw Hector and Caffeine leave the cafeteria ten minutes before the bell, Jade, seated across from me, flinched.

"What did I do?" she said.

I blinked at her, surprised. "Huh?"

"You looked *furious*."

"Oh. Sorry. I was watching Hector and Caffeine pop out for their after-lunch cigarette." I rolled my neck, trying to get the tension out of my shoulders. "It certainly wasn't anything *you* did."

Tara said, "Word is *Caffeine* broke Dakota's finger."

"Not Hector?" I said.

"No. He was getting in trouble for smoking in the bathroom when it happened."

Jade said, "Wonder if getting caught smoking was deliberate—an alibi."

"If there were no witnesses, how do people know Caffeine did it? Dakota certainly wasn't saying anything."

Tara smiled grimly. "Doesn't mean Caffeine didn't. I mean, if she's sending a message it is probably to more than just Dakota."

"Or Tony," added Jade, touching her nose.

"Or Grant," I said.

"What happened to Grant?" asked Jade.

I said, "His sister said he threw up this morning, in the front yard, on his way out to the car. She was glad it happened before he got *in* the car." It was Naomi's car. She normally drove her brother to school.

"Stomach bug?" said Tara.

"That's what Naomi thought. She was worried she might catch it."

Jade said, "Grant was awfully pale yesterday."

I said, "Was that before or after Dakota 'accidentally' broke his finger?"

"Uh. I didn't see him before," Jade said.

Tara said, "I did. He wasn't *cheerful* before, but after Dakota's broken finger, he was shaking."

Dryly I said, "Something he ate, no doubt."

For the hundredth time, I wished I knew what Caffeine had on the three boys.

I wonder where she keeps that video?

Mom was in the kitchen, brewing a cup of tea and staring out the window at the icicles flowing from the roof right down to the bank of snow that blocked the lower two thirds of the window. We got them every year and they were beautiful, but I never realized how much they looked like bars.

"I need to go shopping," I said to Mom.

She reached for her purse and opened it. "For what?" she asked as she fished for her billfold.

"Armor."

"Armor?"

"Yeah."

"For bullets?"

"Bullets? Jeeze, no. For impacts. I was thinking off-road motorcycle armor."

"Motorcycle? You're not—"

"Riding a motorcycle?" I shook my head. "No way. But I'm still experimenting with adding velocity when I jump and I thought it would be better to be safe than sorry." I rubbed my left shoulder. "Certainly don't want to hit *anything,* but motorcycle armor is also designed to stay on when the wind is tearing at you and that's gotta be a good thing." I was serious about that part. Losing my panties in the wash was *not* a treasured memory.

And while it was true I didn't want to hit any stationary objects, the same wasn't necessarily true in regards to certain *people*.

Mom thought it over.

"You're not immortal, you know."

I blinked. "What?"

"You can die. You can be severely injured. You can break bones."

I thought about Dakota's broken finger. "I *know.* Why do you think I want armor?"

"Armor won't keep your brain from bouncing off the inside of your skull if you impact something and decelerate to a complete stop. I'm going to tell you something and I promise it isn't personal. It's about *all* teenagers."

"Is this going to take long?"

She tapped her purse. "Who was it that wanted something?"

I dropped down onto a kitchen chair, crossed my legs and sat up straight, all attention.

She snorted, then said, "Teenagers tend to think they're immortal. It's probably evolutionary. When the hunter gatherers were attacked by predators, it probably helped that the young men and women distracted the attackers long enough for the older folks to get the children out of harm's way. If these young hotheads didn't survive it, at least the adults, with the tribes' store of experience, and the children, with their genes, survived further."

Mom leaned over and looked in my eyes. "Don't be the one who gets eaten by the saber-tooth, all right? It's no longer an evolutionary advantage."

"I will *definitely* avoid any saber-tooths I see."

Mom stared at me steadily.

"And I'll be careful."

She shook her head and sighed.

Mom jumped us to San Antonio International Airport, to a cul-de-sac near one of the bathrooms outside security. She made both of us wear hats.

"Video cameras."

Our destination was up U.S. 281, almost close enough to the airport to walk, but we took a cab.

"Moto Liberty?" I asked, once the cab had dropped us at the store.

"They got good online reviews."

I ended up with an Alpinestars Stella Bionic 2 Protection Jacket. It had a fully armored spine, shoulder, chest, and elbow protection, and it looked cool: black with thin purple trim around each of the plates. Matching pants, thin, went under a pair of articulated knee/shin armor that cost more than the jacket did. When I added boots, I felt like the Terminator. We finished the outfit with armored gloves designed to save your fingers when you drive a motorcycle too close to a tree; goggles; and an open-faced helmet.

"Wouldn't you be safer with a fully enclosed helmet?"

"I don't want people sneaking up on me," I said, touching my ear.

"What kind of motorcycle does she ride?" the salesman asked Mom.

"A Kawasaki KX-65," Mom said. "She's just sixteen, after all."

He looked me over and nodded judiciously.

Outside, lugging our bags of gear, I asked, "Is that an appropriate motorbike for me?"

"Of course not! But the same forum that recommended this store talked about that model for lightweight, experienced teens. And by experienced, I mean experienced at racing motocross—which means, I guess, teens whose parents want them to *die*."

"Don't sugarcoat it, Mom. Say what you *really* feel."

We walked around the corner and jumped home.

I wondered how fast I could go in my new outfit.

Turns out there was an app for that.

My smartphone's GPS default interface could display velocity but it wrongly assumed that I'd just want to measure speeds parallel to the surface of the planet. So, sitting in a car, you could tell how fast you were going along the road, but in an elevator, it would show you as stationary, even if you were rising upward at twenty feet a second.

But there are pilots and hang-gliders who *do* want that vertical velocity, so there was a variometer app that would measure your velocity in three dimensions: sideways, up, or on a thirty-degree glide path. It also displayed altitude.

I bought a phone case, designed for runners, that strapped firmly around my forearm. Last thing I wanted was to drop my phone while moving at a 180 miles an hour.

It took me fifty jumps in the desert, near the pit, to determine that 180 mph was the edge of my comfort zone, the equivalent of a skydiver assuming a head-down, streamlined posture while plummeting.

The air rushing by at this speed sounded like a hurricane and my clothing snapped and tugged, but it didn't rip and it didn't come loose.

The goggles were a must.

Standing in the same sandy wash where I'd first experimented with velocity, I added 180 miles an hour vertical speed and shot into the air, my eyes glued to the speedometer on the smartphone display. As my velocity diminished, the sound went from the roaring shriek to a howl, to a whistling rush, to a gentle breeze. When the gauge read zero, I glanced away from the screen and, shocked at how high I was, I flinched all the way back to the reading nook under my bed.

I hadn't done the math ahead of time.

I did it now, in my head, then checked it on my computer. Fudging for air drag, I'd risen for over eight seconds and reached a thousand feet above the ground.

I did this several times, flying straight up. Usually, as soon as I began dropping again, I'd jump back down to the sandy wash. The next time, when I coasted to a stop near the apex, I added another 180 miles per hour upward and shot another thousand feet into the air.

The ground looked scary-far and the horizon was opening up around me. I did it again and this time, I didn't look at the altimeter. I just waited until the air stopped whistling past my helmet, then did it again, and again, my ears popping almost continuously. When I finally looked at the altimeter it read eight thousand feet, a full mile above the ground below.

If I keep this up, I'm going to need an oxygen set.

I stopped adding velocity and let myself drop, tilting forward into the skydiver's spread-eagle. In fifteen seconds I'd stabilized at 119 miles per hour, about two miles a minute, but I'd dropped several hundred feet in the interval. The ground was still far away, but the altimeter scared me. Not because of the altitude it was reading but because how fast the numbers were changing.

I jumped back to the ground, shivering.

It wasn't that cold here—in fact the sand was pleasantly warm. But a mile higher, with the wind tearing by at over a hundred miles per hour, it was *not* warm.

I stretched out on the sand, face up, and thought about Mom's homily about throwing myself before a saber-tooth.

No, I thought. *The objective is to let someone else do it.*

Grant missed one day and returned to school the next morning.

"Let's talk."

Grant whipped his head around, flinching. But when he saw it was just me, the panicked look faded.

But not completely.

"I can help you, you know," I said.

We were in the hallway, near the library. Grant had just come in from the parking lot, where his sister had parked.

He kept moving, still looking around nervously. I matched his step, waiting for him to say something, but he didn't. His destination was the oak bench directly across from admin, in plain sight of the receptionist.

Ah. Sanctuary, or at least witnesses. A place where Caffeine's gang was unlikely to jump him.

I sat down beside him.

"So, bloody nose for Tony. Broken finger for Dakota. What do you think they've got in mind for you?"

He squirmed on the bench. "Leave me alone."

I shook my head. "The thing is, if you ask me, I will. But try asking Caffeine to let you alone—I don't think that will work. Didn't you already try that?"

"We can't—" He shut his mouth and looked down at his lap. It was Caffeine, walking in from outside. She'd already spotted Grant and turned in our direction. She had a pencil in her hand, rolling it between her fingertips and thumb. She didn't look at Grant but as she passed in front of him, she took the pencil between both hands and broke it in two.

Grant jerked back against the bench and it rocked underneath me.

Caffeine turned abruptly and walked over to the trash can at the end of the bench, tossed the pencil pieces in, then looked at Grant. He leaned away from her, bumping into me. Caffeine smiled, showing her teeth, then turned and walked away.

I got up, swinging my backpack onto my shoulders, then looked back down at Grant. I raised my eyebrows.

"Okay," he said in a whisper. "It's a date."

"A date?" I said.

"Tonight. At The Brass."

I'd never been. The Brass was a music venue for teens, or at least for nondrinkers. They did food and dance, and weekend and Wednesday nights they had live music. Today was Wednesday.

"What do you mean, a date?"

"Dinner. You have to dance with me at least twice."

My eyes went wide. "Oh, really? And you'll answer my questions?"

He looked shocked, and I wasn't sure if he was shocked at himself for asking or shocked that I hadn't refused him out of hand.

"Uh, yeah?" he said, far more of a question than a statement.

I thumped my finger into his chest. "Is that an actual answer? Come on. Yes or no?"

He exhaled then licked his lip. "Yes."

"You don't drive, right?"

"Right." He sucked on his lower lips then said, "But I'll still pick you up. Get my mom or sister to drive us."

"When?"

"Seven?"

I nodded. "At seven."

He looked totally taken aback. "Aren't I too young for you? I mean, girls dig older guys, right?"

"Some do. Some like all kinds." I laughed. "*My* mom is three years older than my dad." His eyes went wider and I said, "It's *just* a date."

"Yeah!" he said suddenly. "A *date*!"

Oh. I guess it all depends on where your set point is.
I sighed. "I'm going to regret this."

I begged off our usual Krakatoa homework session after school.

"I know," said Tara. "You've got a hot date."

"Hot? Who said it was hot? Forget that—who said I had a *date*?"

"Who didn't? Why, is it a secret? Cause Grant sure isn't acting like it's a secret. More like the best thing that ever happened to him."

I pinched the bridge of my nose. I thought back to a couple of strange looks I'd gotten earlier in the day and was enlightened. I'd been right—the date was three hours away and I already regretted it.

"Ah," said Jade. "Young love. *Really* young love. I mean. . . ."

"I agreed to go out if he'd answer my *questions*," I said. "About Caffeine."

"Is there kissing involved?" Tara asked mildly. "You could always use him for *practice*." She pursed her lips and blew a kiss out into the general world.

I felt my face get hot. "That would just be mean."

"Oh, thought about it, eh?" said Jade. "What else were you thinking of practicing?"

"There's never a snowball around when you need one. Why are you giving me such a hard time?" I said. "You two don't even like guys."

Jade looked a little surprised, exchanging a glance with Tara. Tara shrugged. Jade said, "What do you mean?"

I rolled my eyes and said, "Is it really such a big deal?"

Tara took Jade's hand. "Around here, yeah it's a big deal. Mom knows. Jade's parents know but they're, like, in denial."

"Homophobic?"

Jade shook her head. "They're worried for me. They want it to be 'just a phase' because they know how hard it can be for lesbians."

"A phase?" I said.

Jade amended it. "Well, that I might be bi. Get a nice boyfriend later."

Tara snorted.

"We're *discreet*," said Jade.

"Sure," I said.

"Who told you, then?"

"Your eyes, your voices, your faces. You can touch someone with more than just your hands."

Jade frowned and Tara laughed. They looked at each other.

I said, "See?"

"I've got a date tonight," I said to Mom. "I won't be eating at home."

Dad, reading at the other end of the couch, looked up from his book. "A date? A *date* date?"

I nodded.

"Who with?"

Mom looked at him and laughed.

Dad looked offended. "You don't think I should ask that?"

She shook her head. "It's not that. It's the edge of panic in your voice and the extra white showing around your irises."

He frowned. "I didn't start dating until I was *eighteen*."

"Technically you were still *seventeen*," Mom said, "It was forty-five minutes before you turned eighteen. I was there, remember?" She turned back to me. "My first date was when I was *fifteen*."

Dad winced.

"It's Grant Meriwether. He's taking me to The Brass."

Dad raised his eyebrows and Mom said, "The music club down on Main."

Dad said, "Isn't he a little young for you?"

I doubled over laughing and Mom joined in.

Dad turned bright red.

Grant showed up at the door five minutes early. He was wearing a suit.

Little jerk.

I was wearing jeans and a nice shirt.

"Oops. Sorry, time got away from me—haven't changed yet. Have a seat and I'll be right back."

Mom followed me around the corner and, when I jumped to my room back in the Yukon, she followed. "He *really* dressed up," she said.

I bit my lip. "Yeah."

"You could've just gone as you are, so I guess you want to dress up a bit, too?"

"I don't want to *embarrass* him. Even if this is sort of a practice date."

She gave me a look. "You aren't leading him on, are you?"

"He knows the score. I was very clear."

"That may be, but young men are still capable of not getting the message. In fact, they specialize in that." She lowered her head looking at me to make sure I understood that.

I nodded, my face serious.

"Okay. You could wear your suit, the one you wore to school . . . or you could make him the envy of all he surveys. Which is it?"

There'd be lots of Beckwourth students at The Brass. Maybe even that jerk Brett.

"Let's knock their socks off."

Mom took me to *her* closet.

When we returned to the living room in New Prospect, jumping first to my room, then coming up the stairs, Naomi had come in from the car, apparently to see what was taking so long. Dad had served them ginger ale and was drawing Naomi out about her college plans.

Grant looked nervous, like he was going to throw up.

I smiled and said, "Sorry to keep you waiting."

I was wearing my full-length wool coat, buttoned, with a scarf tucked in at the neck. Normally he was taller than I, but I'd changed to heels so my eyes were slightly above his.

"No problem!" I'm sure he meant to sound cool, but he blurted it out.

I nodded and said hello to Naomi.

She looked at my heels and then up at the small diamonds Mom had hung in my ears. "So this is a real date?"

I raised my eyebrows. "Didn't Grant tell you?"

She swallowed the rest of her ginger ale and said, "Oh, yeah. But . . . it's *Grant.*"

Grant looked offended but, as Naomi was the transportation, he wisely didn't say anything.

Naomi dropped us at the curb and said, "Nine-thirty sharp, right?"

Grant mumbled, "Yeah."

Then, as Grant was sliding out of the car, Naomi locked eyes with me and said, "Unless you want to leave earlier, then just call my cell."

Grant, holding the door, hadn't noticed the look, but he said, "Right."

I smiled at Naomi. "Don't worry." I followed Grant out of the car and strode across the sidewalk to The Brass's entrance. Grant slammed the car door and scrambled to get there ahead of me, lest I open it myself.

There was a beverage/snack bar at the far end of the room, across the dance floor. The stage was a two-foot riser on the left, and on the right, a slightly raised mezzanine filled with mostly occupied tables. The band wouldn't start for another hour, though their gear was set up. Before the drum set, a woman with a ukulele doing the Amanda Palmer thing: solo covers of rocks songs in a torchy way.

Grant paid the cover charge and told the greeter, "table for two." She nodded and said they were cleaning a table now and it would just be a few minutes.

Most of the people, especially the younger ones, were wearing jeans and I *really* felt overdressed. I considered excusing myself, heading for the bathroom and, from a stall, jumping back home and changing back into something more casual. I'd gotten as far as visually locating the restrooms (back by the beverage bar) when the greeter said something I didn't catch and I looked back at her and Grant.

"Coat check?" Grant said, indicating a closet near the door.

I took a deep breath. Right. It was like wearing a costume, I thought. It wasn't about blending in. It was about *not* blending in. "Sure." He helped me off with the coat and I heard his sharp intake of breath.

It was a black, strapless Herve Leger dress that Mom bought to celebrate losing some weight a couple of years before. It wasn't very low cut—it fell just under the shoulder blades in back and ended a handspan above the knees—but it was snug, with just enough spandex to follow *every* curve.

I turned and he stood there, frozen, holding the coat up in front of him like a towel, as if he'd been caught naked in the bathroom. I took off my scarf and shoved it into the coat sleeve. "Give it to the nice lady, Grant."

He managed to trade the coat for a numbered plastic tab, and by the time we returned to the greeter's station, our table was ready.

Grant stumbled on the three steps up into the dining area but I caught his arm and steadied him. I kept my arm tucked in his until we were at the table. There was an inadvertent competition as the waiter pulled out a chair at the same time Grant did. I sat in the one Grant offered, but thanked the waiter.

As we were studying the menus, I said, "Don't stare, Grant, it's rude. Besides, you need to chill, right? Like you do this every day. Think of our audience."

Grant glanced around. We *were* being watched—five sophomore girls at a table near the dance floor kept turning their heads our way and whispering.

Grant blushed. Then I blushed, too, and there was more skin exposed to show my blush. I didn't do this every day, either. Fortunately the lighting back in the dining area was dim enough that it wasn't obvious. I *hoped* it wasn't as obvious as it felt, anyway.

"Why do you care about the audience?" Grant asked.

I leaned over the table and straightened his tie. "*They* don't know that I'm only going out with you so you'll answer my questions. If you play this right, they'll wonder about the

freshman who takes out older women." I ran my fingers down
the tie and leaned back. "But you've got to play it right. Running around the school bragging about getting a date makes
you look *needy*."

He blushed again. "You heard about that?"

"Of *course* I did." I shifted my eyes toward the other table.
"You think any of them are going to want to go out with you
if their names are dragged all over school? You've got to treat
it more matter-of-fact. Your cred would've risen a lot more at
school tomorrow if *they* were the ones who first spread word
about your date."

The waiter came back with our drinks and took our meal
order.

Grant looked back at me. The blush had faded while he
ordered, but he still looked confused. "I just wanted to go out
with *you*."

"Sweet. And you are. But only because I want information
about Caffeine. Is that really the way to get a woman to go out
with you?"

"Woman? Uh, you're just sixteen, right?"

I smiled broadly and kicked him sharply on the shin with
the edge of my pumps.

He jerked and hissed, "Jesus! Why'd you do that?"

"Think about it, *boy*." I reached over and patted the back of
his hand. "Do *you* want to be treated like an adult or a child?
More importantly, do you want *them* to treat you like a child?"

He shut his mouth and looked thoughtful.

The woman on stage started singing a slow version of Green
Day's "Good Riddance." I said, "I *love* this song. Let's dance."

He rubbed his shin. "No one else is dancing. I thought we'd
dance when the band started."

I tilted my head and didn't say anything.

"Uh, I mean, I'd *love* to dance."

I laughed and smiled at him as if he'd said something bril-
liant. People turned their heads.

"That's better." I took his arm as we threaded through the
tables.

There were people on the edge of dance floor but they weren't dancing. I steered him out into the middle.

Grant could dance.

I'd learned how to dance from Mom and Dad—more Mom, actually—so I wasn't hopeless, though the heels were a challenge. Grant, though, actually knew how to swing dance, and when the singer picked up the tempo, he was there, moving into faster steps, dips, and crossovers.

The singer slowed the beat back down and drew out the last phrase, *hope you had the time of your life*, and we ended up close and swaying as she ended with a flourish. I leaned a little close and he backed up suddenly, twisting awkwardly to the side. If our roles had been reversed, I'd say he'd fallen off his high heels, but he was wearing sensible shoes.

He pointed back at the dining area. "The salads are here."

I hung on his arm on the way back.

"Where'd you learn to dance?" I asked, over the salad.

His smile was smug. "Naomi was taking a class, but she needed a partner and she'd just broken up with her boyfriend. It was Mom's idea and both of us fought it, but the lessons had been paid for and Mom insisted."

"You ever dance in public before?"

He shrugged. "Once at a school dance. It's the living room, mostly."

I nodded to myself. Boy who could dance. Dressed up okay. Maybe I should just keep him? I looked at him over my salad fork. He didn't always close his mouth when he chewed and the acne was a definite issue and, mostly, my heart didn't go pitter-pat.

Ah, well.

I tilted my head slightly to the side, toward the table of giggling girls. "*They* saw you dance. Hope I didn't mess you up too much—you're a better dancer than I am."

"I don't care. I don't like any of *them*," Grant said.

I shook my head. "That's not the point. They'll talk around school." I ate another bite of salad. "And how do you know you don't like them?"

He winced. "Experience. Five heads with a single thought. They're like bees or ants or termites."

"Hive intelligence?" I said.

"No, that would indicate cooperation. Queen bee makes the decisions, especially about who goes out with who. The eligible pool consists of seniors and juniors and maybe a few sophomores, but freshmen *without cars* are right out."

I pushed my salad plate aside. "What if they changed their mind?"

He looked uncertain but said, "I don't want to go out with someone who has to get their dates okayed by their friends."

"Good on you, Joanie," I said.

He looked pleased.

A shrill beeping sound, uncomfortably loud, came from the back of the club, but it shut off almost immediately with the slamming of a door.

The waiter, arriving with the entrées, looked annoyed. I asked him about the noise.

"Kids trying to let in their friends, to avoid the cover charge. The door has a giant sign, 'Alarm Will Sound,' but someone tries it most band nights."

I'd ordered the fish. Grant had the chicken. I waited until he had eaten most of it before I said, "What's on the video, Grant?"

He choked on a mouthful of potato. "You might let a guy finish eating!" He no longer looked pleased. He looked nauseated.

I held up my hand. "All right. As long as you don't renege on the deal."

He tried some to eat some more, but he finally pushed his plate to the side. I felt guilty, but didn't relent.

The ukulele torch singer sang the last song of her set, but the applause was substantial and she came back for an encore.

Grant leaned forward, his elbows on the table, and whispered. "Sex"

I nodded, "I wondered." I couldn't really think what else it had been. "All three of you?"

He nodded, miserable.

"At the same time?"

"What? No! Three different videos."

"So also, not with each other." I didn't think any of them were gay. I was pretty sure Grant's discomfort at the end of our dance had been an erection.

"No!"

I nodded again.

"And you didn't know about the camera, right?"

"Of course not."

"So what was so bad about it?"

He looked away.

I tried a different tack. "Okay. Unless you were just masturbating, someone *else* is in the video."

He looked down and said something, but I couldn't hear it over a burst of applause as the singer left the stage.

I briefly joined the applause, then said, "Didn't hear that."

"Caffeine."

I suspected, but I was disappointed, too.

He saw my face and winced. I took a deep breath and tried to go back to a less negative expression. I thought about Mom's therapist face and tried for that. Nonjudging, neutral, receptive.

"That's embarrassing, but you know they'd be the ones in trouble if they showed it. Child porn and all that."

He looked away and shook his head. "I'm not a child."

Another thought passed through my mind, an ugly one. "Uh, you guys didn't force her, did you? I mean it was consensual, right?" I couldn't possibly imagine a circumstance where any of them, or even all three of them together, could force Caffeine to do something against her will.

"What? We didn't force her to do anything!" He shut his mouth abruptly and looked away, blushing furiously. I waited, but when he finally looked back he said, "There. I did my part. That's as much as I'm going to say."

The band started up then and more people arrived. Neither of us felt like dessert so Grant paid the bill and we moved down to the floor. As promised, I danced one more time with him but halfway through, he grabbed my arm and pulled me off the floor, going toward the bathrooms.

"What is it?" I had to shout near his ear to be heard.

"Hector and Calvin came in!"

I swiveled around, but I couldn't see them through the dancers. "Calvin? Was he with Hector and Caffeine, when they grabbed Dakota and Tony in front of the coffee shop?"

Grant jerked his head in a nod and pulled me around the edge of the raised dining area to the narrow path back to the emergency exit, which did indeed have a sign in foot-high letters, *Alarm Will Sound If Opened.*

We could go out that way, but it would be conspicuous. I could leave *my* way, but I didn't want to leave Grant in the lurch. I considered jumping Grant away but that was right out. Dad would move us out of town in a "New York minute."

"Did they see you?"

He nodded. "They pointed at us."

"Shit!" I was angry at Grant suddenly. "There were other reasons you shouldn't have bragged about our date all over school!"

I saw them now. I pulled Grant further around toward the door, in the shadow of the railing around the dining area, but they saw the movement.

"Grant, I need you to trust me, okay?"

He looked at me, his eyes wide, lots of white showing. "What?"

"When they get close, I'm going to shove you from behind. When I do it, I want your protect your head with your arms and curl up into a ball."

"We're fucked. What are you talking about?"

"Let's just say that Caffeine's little accident in the showers was no accident."

Hector and Calvin were clear of the dancers now, glancing around to assess the witnesses. Then they grinned at us.

"Go ahead," Hector shouted over the band. "Caffeine and Marius are on the other side of that door!"

Delightful.

I stepped behind Grant, like I was hiding behind him, and put my hands on his shoulders my forearms down both sides of his spine, my hips right up against his.

"Protect your head, all right?" I said in his ear.

He nodded and I felt him raise his hands in front, in preparation.

Calvin and Hector grinned at each other and stepped closer, Hector first, Calvin right behind.

I jumped in place, adding twenty-five feet per second toward Hector, about the speed you'd get after dropping ten feet. Grant flew forward, his forearms jerking up and together in front of his face, his knees pulling up.

Hector tried to punch him, but his strike went past Grant's head as Grant's elbows slammed into Hector's solar plexus and Grant's knees slammed into Hector's thighs. Hector flew back into Calvin, the back of Hector's head striking Calvin's nose, and all three of them spilled down the passageway, Hector and Calvin on their backs, Grant falling forward onto his hands and knees.

Grant was up at once, cradling one of his elbows. Hector and Calvin were not unconscious, but they were having trouble breathing, much less standing up.

The nearest dancers had seen the boys fall back, but hardly anyone heard it over the band. The majority of people were still dancing. I took Grant's good arm and led him along the edge of the dining area at the back of the dance floor.

"You okay?"

His eyes were wide and he was staring at me.

I raised my voice "Are. You. Okay?"

"Yeah. Banged my funny bone." He looked over his shoulder. Both Calvin and Hector were still down, but some of the dancers were leaning over them and a club employee with "Security" on his T-shirt was walking back that way.

"Stop holding your elbow and let's go."

I texted Naomi while Grant found the coat-check tab and recovered my coat. I walked out the door still shrugging it on while Grant scrambled to keep up.

"Naomi's not here yet!"

"Neither is Caffeine. I told Naomi to pick us up at Krakatoa." In a minute Hector or Calvin might recover enough to call Caffeine's cell and I'd just as soon not have another incident. "Come on. My treat."

"How did you do that?"

"Do what?"

"You pushed me so hard I *flew* into Hector."

I shrugged. "I shoved and you leaped. It was both of us." I curled my right arm up in a body builder's pose and tapped my biceps with my left hand. "Though I'm stronger that I look."

He blinked and looked uncertain, but by the time we reached Krakatoa I could tell the memory of what had happened was shifting around to something more acceptable.

While we waited, I bought three hot chocolates with whipped cream. When Grant walked me from Naomi's car to my front door we were scraping out the last of it with our straws.

"You have some whipped cream on your face," I said.

"Where?"

"There." I kissed him on the whipped cream and licked it away.

Yes, it was on his mouth. So what.

Practice.

TWENTY-FIVE

Davy: "Looking for Rama"

"No, you may *not* go follow Cent on her date!"

"But—"

"No 'buts,'" Millie said. "Leave her alone! You want to go 'protect' someone, see if you can get a lead on Ramachandra!"

Davy still stuck his head into The Brass before going on to Bangladesh. He walked in behind a group of six teens wreathed in a cloud of hormones and laughter, and as they dealt with the woman collecting the band cover charge, he jumped past them all into the shadows near the cloakroom.

He spotted Cent immediately, the only bare shoulders in the restaurant section. He hadn't realized that Millie had loaned her *that* dress.

Christ, she looks so grown up!

Grant was dressed nicely, too, but his posture, the way he held his head, showed how ill at ease he was. Cent, poised, looked years older.

It took him back. She looked so much like her mother, and Davy winced at Grant's awkwardness. *Too much like me at that age.*

Davy found the tension dropping out of his shoulders. He'd told himself he was here to look for the enemy, for those who hunted them, but his reaction told him differently—he'd wanted to check on Cent.

She's not really involved.

He realized it almost immediately. Her first date ever and she was relaxed—at ease. He felt the tension going out of his neck. This wasn't the real thing.

He checked the environment, looking for any of them, but all he saw were teens. Sure, they were looking around and quite a few kept looking over at Cent and Grant's table, but obviously, nothing covert about it.

He realized that if he jumped over near the restrooms, he could get close enough to hear what they were talking about. He remembered Millie's injunction.

You're one of those *fathers, aren't you?*

He walked back out the front door and jumped away.

Fortunately, Davy had been to Pabna several times before, so he didn't have to duplicate the seven-hour bus trip from the nearest airport that had marked his first visit. He took one of the three-wheeled taxis from his riverfront jump site.

Akash didn't recognize him out of context. The skies were clear, neither of them was wearing rain gear, and the setting was a small cubicle in a rundown administrative complex in the district capital.

"We worked together on the hilltop south of Bhangura."

Akash blinked rapidly. "Ah, yes. How is your oh-so-charming wife?"

"Fine, thanks."

"And your daughter? I presume it was your daughter. She was the spitting image of your wife."

Davy lied. "A cousin. But the resemblance is remarkable."

"Indeed. What may I do for you today? Your tent and supplies ended up in our compound in Bhangura. Is that what you're inquiring about?"

Davy shook his head. "No. I was checking on Ramachandra. Is there any word?"

"Oh. No word. You just missed his supervisor from World

Without Hunger, Ostad Aniketa. He, too, was checking, but he is driving back that way this afternoon."

"Back to the hilltop?"

"Mr. Aniketa is going to Bhangura. To talk with the police."

Davy's eyebrows went up.

Akash shrugged. "I know, but the police really seem to be stirring themselves."

"Well, I'm glad someone is looking."

"What should we do with the tent, and the leftover rations and water filters?"

Davy smiled. "For the next flood."

He'd never been to Bhangura township itself, so he had to go back to Millie.

"Can you hop me to Bhangura? I want to check in with Ramachandra's supervisor. He'll be talking to the police there."

"Isn't that a bit dangerous? We know they're working the area. What if they brought in one of those gravity thingies?"

Davy shrugged. "I doubt that they haul those around the globe. Wouldn't think they'd do any good, unless maybe there was a facility they needed to protect. Besides, it's not magic. They'd still have to locate and catch me. And once bitten, twice shy. You know how *careful* I am."

"Paranoid," she corrected.

He tilted his head forward and glared at her from beneath his brows.

She amended her statement. "Not that that's a *bad* thing in this case." She gave up. "All right. I can jump you to the old jute mill by the bridge and you can get a water taxi down on the river. Or you can catch a bicycle rickshaw van or one of those *noshimon* bus-thingies up on the road."

"*Noshimon*? Are those the ones powered by converted irrigation pumps? Double row of bench seats in the back, facing each other?"

Millie nodded. "And painted like a carnival, yeah."

"Let's go."

It felt odd when Millie jumped him someplace. It was rare that she had the jump site and he didn't, but it was happening more and more with her relief work.

Odd or not, he liked her arms around him.

She let go and started to step back when they appeared in Bhangura, but he didn't, pulling her back and kissing her. She smiled midkiss, he could feel it.

"You want me to stay?" she asked.

He shook his head. "Not if *they're* around. But it would be nice to just wander someplace, to be a tourist again."

She nodded. "Maybe tomorrow. It's the dry season in Goa."

He smiled. "It's a date."

She vanished.

There was a market near the police station and he shopped, buying a silver *baju bandh* (armlet), a sari, and a bag woven of dyed and undyed jute. He saw Ostad Aniketa arrive, only recognizing him because his Toyota Land Cruiser had the name of the NGO on the sides in both English alphabet and *Bangla lipi*. When Ostad left the station and neared his vehicle, Davy walked up to him.

"Mr. Aniketa?"

The man raised his eyebrows. "Yes?"

"My name is David. I worked with Ramachandra during the recent flood south of here."

"Yes? Have you seen him?"

Davy shook his head. "Ah, no. I was wondering if you had any word. Akash told me you were making inquiries so I thought I'd check in with you. Were the police helpful?"

The man deflated. "No. The officer working for the *shordani* has actually been discharged, but I really couldn't tell you if it was because they're cracking down on corruption, or because he lost the boat, or because he couldn't make his payments up the chain since that brothel was flooded. Even if they arrest Ramachandra for 'stealing' their boat, we'll at least know where he *is*. They were able to tell me where they found the boat, but the man who left it there was *not* Ramachandra."

"How far downstream did they find the boat?" Davy asked.

"Oh, only a mile."

"A mile south of the hilltop? The camp?"

"Oh, no. A mile south of *here*. It was tied up at the sugar mill dock. The man who left it told the guard that he would return shortly. The guard thought he must be a plain clothes policeman since he was driving the boat. When the boat was still there the next morning, they talked to their constable and he made inquiries. Alas, the person who left the boat was much older than Rama and balding."

"Did anyone see the boat anywhere else?"

"No one has reported seeing it, but the flood was still at its height. Many boats were out in it. The last time anyone saw Ramachandra was when he pulled away from the camp with some, ah, passengers."

"Yes. The *chukri* girls."

"I can't imagine what he was thinking!" said Mr. Aniketa, suddenly angry. "Leaving with those, those—"

Mr. Aniketa, Davy decided, was a prude with a dirty mind.

"I have been informed of the circumstances. Surely you don't think Ramachandra was doing anything but helping those girls escape from the *mastaans* and the *shordani*?"

"Then where did he take them?"

Davy knew the name of the village and the girls' madrasa but he wasn't so sure he wanted to tell Mr. Aniketa. The information was all too likely to go from his lips to the police to the brothel, and he didn't want the *mastaans* showing up there.

"He took them to an Imam who belongs to COMPIAT—the antitrafficking network, you know? Then he headed back upstream. He said he was going to return the boat to Bhangura."

"When was this?"

"That same afternoon."

"*Eesh!* That's hardly any more than we already knew." Mr. Aniketa gave Davy his card. "This has my cell number. Please let me know if you hear anything." He sighed. "I went to school with Ramachandra's father. I've known him since he was a baby."

Davy gave Mr. Aniketa a card with one of his many e-mail addresses. "And please let me know if *you* hear anything, too."

TWENTY-SIX

"Escalation"

Hector was limping in the cafeteria the next day, a fact that cheered me immensely.

"So there's Hector Guzman and Calvin. And then there's someone named Marius. Is that it?"

Jade blinked and Tara said, "What do you mean?"

"The guys in Caffeine's little gang."

Jade said, "Caffeine's gang? It isn't Caffeine's gang."

I blinked. "Oh. Whose is it?"

Tara spoke, "I don't know, but Caffeine and friends are just the high school minions. Like comparing the paper boy to the newspaper or the newspaper's publisher."

Jade said, "Yeah. I've seen that black Hummer cruise by and stop, and whatever she's doing, whoever she's talking to, she drops what she's doing and runs across the street, fast, and gets in the back."

Shit.

I sat back in my chair, suddenly overwhelmed. I thought I was just dealing with Caffeine, Hector, and a few sociopathic high school dropouts. Now it felt like I was facing a vast organized crime syndicate.

I wonder if she shared the video with the gang at large?

I hoped not.

After lunch, Grant asked me out again.

I guess I shouldn't have kissed him.

"No. But I'll pretend I like you when we're here at school."

He looked devastated. "Pretend? You'll *pretend*?"

I took his arm and tucked it through mine. "It's okay, Grant. I'm not pretending, but no more dates. We both need to branch out." We were walking through the crowded hall. "I'll even kiss you on the cheek when we're done talking if you answer one question."

He looked wary. "What question?"

"*Where* was the video made?"

He looked down at the floor. "It's because of Caffeine, isn't it? That's why you won't go out with me again."

"Look on the bright side. If it weren't for Caffeine, I wouldn't have gone out with you at *all*." I patted his arm. "We're all entitled to mistakes. I had a good time last night and I'd certainly dance with you again, but we are *not* dating. Sorry, that's just a fact. Answer my question."

He looked like he was going to cry which made *me* sad and then angry. I jabbed him in the ribs. "Have you noticed how *many* girls are checking you out as you walk through the hall?"

His head swiveled back and forth and he looked slightly less upset.

"Come on," I said. "I have PE—where was it?"

He told me and I kissed him on the cheek.

If there is a wrong side of the tracks in New Prospect, it is over by the oil field service companies, a patchy mix of run-down houses interspersed with fenced lots stacked with drill casing, mud tanks, and disassembled drilling rigs.

I moved through the neighborhood wearing the anonymous gray hoodie with a balaclava pulled up over my lower face and the hood well forward. On the first pass, I walked down the sidewalk on the street-side of the lot. Their "clubhouse" was a detached two-door garage, once adjacent to a large house, but the house was now a wreck, the victim of a fire, roof gone, some walls half standing. The garage, by contrast, was in good repair, its stucco sides mottled where not-quite-matching shades of paint had covered up graffiti. The ruin was bordered by a warehouse, a fenced lot stacked with mud pumps, and a construction equipment dealership.

There was no movement and I couldn't see any lights or activity, but access to the garage was from the rear of the lot, not the street. I went down to the next block and came back up the alley.

Judging by the weeds and litter accumulating across the garage doors, they weren't used much. The side door, though, was clear, and it was apparent from the ruts in the crusted snow and mud that cars usually parked on this side of the garage.

There were no cars parked there now, though.

I circled the building. There were no windows for me to get a look through, so I couldn't jump inside. I thought about breaking in, using a cinder block and accelerating it to 180 mph toward the door—jumping away before the impact, of course.

And that wouldn't exactly keep your visit secret, would it?

I wanted one of those cameras with the flexible fiber optic pickup that I could shove under the door. Something that would let me see inside.

I walked back to the ruins of the old house and looked for a nice hidden corner to use as a jump site. While I scrambled over the remains of one of the walls I glanced back at the garage and saw the gray sky reflected in something on its roof.

Ah. I stood up on the wall. There was a skylight.

I picked a jump site where two of the ruined walls came together out of sight from the adjoining lots and the garage. Most of the debris from the fire had been cleared out, but enough dirt had blown into this corner that a tumbleweed was growing.

When I returned to the rear of the garage, I couldn't see anybody. I experimented a bit, adding enough upward velocity to clear the parapet of the garage's stucco wall but with a slight forward component, not just straight up. I landed lightly on the roof without having to jump a second time.

It was an old-school skylight with frosted glass panes, but one of the panes had been replaced with transparent glass. I could see down into the garage and though there weren't any lights, the skylight provided enough illumination for me to make out carpeted floor and a couch.

I made sure my hood was well forward and the balaclava pulled up as far as my nose, and jumped into the garage.

No one leaped out of the shadows, which I saw, as my eyes adjusted, were not very deep. The floor was covered with irregular swaths of carpet, unmatched in color, texture, and thickness. Three couches formed an open square, facing away from the vehicle doors. An avocado-colored refrigerator flanked the side door and I heard its compressor kick in. Inside the refrigerator were several six-packs of soft drinks, two cases of beer, and some leftover fast food.

The room smelled musty, slightly mildewed, with overtones of sweat and, I thought, marijuana, which I'd smelled in Amsterdam. It was cool in the room, but not as cold as outside. Two electric radiators were plugged in at opposite sides of the space.

The rear of the garage had rough closets walled with warped and torn paneling, and in the far rear corner was what used to be a laundry room. The utility sink was still there, but the dryer and washer were long gone and a toilet had been mounted in the middle of the little room atop an old floor drain. A hose ran across the floor from the old washer fittings to the flush tank's inlet valve. I peered into the toilet and backed away. It looked and smelled like something you'd find in the restroom of a badly maintained gas station.

I went through the closets. There was bedding, some men's and women's clothing, and a cluster of baseball bats, one of which had brownish-red stains on it.

In the last closet, opposite the three couches, I found the hidden video camera.

A camera mount, clamped to one of the closet's interior studs, held the video camera lens directly against the paneling. I walked back around and found the small hole at the back of a shelf, framed on one side by a tool box and some packaged oil filters on the other.

I went back and examined the camera. It was plugged into a power adaptor, so it didn't have to depend on batteries. It used solid-state media, a little postage stamp-sized SD card, which I popped out and examined. It was a sixteen gigabyte card. I pushed it back into the slot and powered up the camera. The directory in the little fold-out LCD monitor showed one file only, dated the previous week, too recent to be one of the freshman blackmail videos.

I hit play.

The camera was zoomed on the center couch and there was a guy sitting there, lounging back. He was old—in his late twenties or early thirties, I would say. He was looking slightly to the right of the camera, where the closet door would be, then I heard the door close and Caffeine entered the scene and went to the couch and kissed him.

Not like you'd kiss your dad, either.

When she moved down his body, unfastened his pants and pulled his zipper down, I pulled my hands away from the camera and banged against the back of the closet. By the time I turned the camera off she was going down on him.

I jumped away, all the way to my reading nook, in the Yukon, blushing furiously.

It's not like I'd never seen porn before. Internet access and all that. I was embarrassed enough the first time I'd seen video of two humans having different kinds of sex, just as I was embarrassed when I heard kids talk about who was "doing it" at school. But I'd never put the two together—*seen* a person I knew in real life do *that*.

I shuddered.

Did I really want to find the blackmail videos? Wouldn't I have to look at them? Was I really ready to see Grant, Tony, and Dakota "doing it?"

A blond woman wearing surgical scrubs was sitting in our kitchen in the Yukon, crying. I nearly jumped away before I realized it was Mom, wearing one of her wigs.

My next thought sent my heart thudding. "Is Dad all right?"

"He's fine." She shook her head. "It's *my* mom."

"What's wrong with Grandmother?"

"She fell and broke her hip last week. While she was in recovery, she threw a blood clot into her lungs and had to go on a respirator. She's back off of it, now, but she's going to need to move over to the fully assisted side of her retirement community. I don't know if she'll ever be able to go back to her apartment."

My heart slowed a bit. I'd only met Grandmother three times.

Some of the retirement community employees were watching for us—well, for Mom or Dad since they didn't know *I* existed. Dad didn't know if it was for *them* or the NSA.

Mom and Dad had jumped Grandmother away from there a few times to spend weekends with us, but the increase in surveillance after these mysterious absences had been intense. Mom and Dad decided it was too dangerous for Grandmother if they'd kept up the visits, though they'd asked her if she'd like to live with us full time.

Grandmother was torn, but in the end, refused. She had her other daughter and many friends. She wasn't ready to walk away from that life.

I fetched a box of tissues from the living room and hugged Mom. It was all I could think of to do.

"Did you see her?"

She nodded against my shoulder, then sat back. "Yeah. Talked to her after she got off the respirator." Mom waved her hand at the wig and the scrubs.

I saw that she was also wearing her green contacts.

Mom bit her lip. "She asked to see you."

It was my turn to bite my lip. "What does Dad say?"

"Dad doesn't know she asked." She blinked and added,

"Yet." She was frowning. "Dad is in Bangladesh, seeing if there is any word of Rama. He hasn't heard about any of this. I just found out this morning, when I checked the e-mail drop."

"Aunt Sue?"

Mom nodded.

Sue was Mom's sister. I'd met *her* exactly once.

"Yeah. There were six e-mails in the box. We should check it more often."

"Should I visit her? I could do the Girl Scout thing."

Mom blinked. Once she'd jumped me close by and I'd visited Grandmother posing as a Girl Scout selling cookies. We'd sat on a bench outside her apartment and talked for an hour, but we kept getting interrupted as other retirees came up to buy cookies.

Mom smiled and blew her nose. "Think you're too big for that, now."

"Some other disguise, then."

"We'll see."

In the middle of the night I went into the school administration office and looked up Caffeine's home address. I figured it would be in a file cabinet, but the file room was locked and windowless, blocking me effectively.

However, I found her address and basic info in the school computer system. The database client was browser based and the secretary's computer was in sleep mode, still logged in. It didn't even require a password on wake up.

Besides Caffeine's address I also learned that she had three half sisters from her mother's current marriage and four half brothers from her father's previous and subsequent marriages, as well as two stepbrothers, children of her mother's current husband from a previous marriage. There was a reference to ongoing behavioral issues but that info was apparently in the physical file.

Hector Guzman had three older brothers and a younger sister. There was no mention of his father in the record, just his mother.

Both of them lived near Tara: Hector in the same apartment complex and Caffeine across the street in a housing development. She lived with her mother and stepfather. There was an address in Colorado for her father, but for emergency contact. His home was not designated as one of Caffiene's residences.

I'd worn gloves for this investigation, and left everything as I found it.

I saw the black Hummer the next day as Tara and Jade and I walked to Krakatoa for our usual after-school study session. The windows were deeply tinted and I couldn't tell how many people were in it or who they were. It had chrome wheels and a vanity license plate which said, *2KOOL4U.*

"Is that the one?" I said, as it cruised slowly past.

Tara nodded.

When we turned onto Main, it was pulled over near Krakatoa, but still blocking most of its lane. The passenger door opened and a man got out, young, but older than high school. It was tricky to tell because his scalp was shaved smooth and he wore a hipster soul patch. He was big like Calvin, bigger than Brett.

He walked around to the driver's side. The window slid down for a moment and it looked like words were exchanged, then he turned and went into the coffee shop. Just before he passed through the doorway, he glanced toward us.

"Who was that?" I asked the girls.

Jade shook her head and Tara said, "Don't know. Seen him around."

"Not Marius?"

"*Yo no se.* Could be." She said and added in a British posh accent, "Never been *properly* introduced."

The man was accepting an iced coffee from the barista when we came in. He went upstairs to the landing. I thought for a moment he'd take our table, but he took a smaller two-top near the head of the stairs.

I handed Tara some cash, as usual, and headed up the stairs

to secure our table before the rest of the after-school kids flooded in.

The bald man stood up as I came up the stairs, which surprised me. He'd just got there, after all. His coffee was still on the table, so maybe he was just going to the bathroom. The staircase was narrow, against the wall, with a railed balustrade on one side, and plain paneling with no rail on the other. He shifted to the rail side, to make room for me to pass and I twisted against the paneling, holding my pack in front to eel past him.

I wasn't expecting anything, really, but I was watching him just so I'd know him later. Just before I passed him, he rammed his shoulder across the space, right at my face.

I jumped, well, *flinched*, past him, just up two steps. I heard him yell as his unchecked momentum took him forward. His arm flailed, trying to catch himself on the smooth paneling, but he fell forward, down the stairs. He cushioned the immediate impact with his arms, but bumped down the remaining stairs headfirst, on his stomach, knees, and elbows, then crunching up into a ball when his arms reached the no-skid mat at the bottom of the stairway while his torso and legs kept moving.

I watched this from up above, moving up the stairs and stepping quickly over to our table. He finished in a heap, butt up in the air. The barista and the manager were there almost immediately.

"Whoa there. Stay down. I'll call 911," said the manager.

The man ignored her, unfolding and pushing up onto his knees. He'd avoided hitting his head, but he was holding his arms across his torso, like they needed to be supported. "I'm all right!" he snapped when the manager tried to help him.

Jade and Tara, still waiting for our drinks, stepped around the corner of the counter, away from him.

The man reached down and gingerly touched his right leg, just above the knee, then winced.

The manager had stepped back after he snapped at her, but

she was still watching him carefully. "Are you sure? That was a nasty spill. I can still call an ambulance."

"No!" He surged all the way to his feet and looked back up the stairway, then sideways, until he located me, seated at our table. I ignored him and opened my math book.

He looked furious, though, and I thought, *Good.*

He walked out of the shop without coming back upstairs for his coffee. I saw the Hummer pull up, again on the wrong side of the street. The window came down and my eyes went wide.

The driver was the older man I'd seen in the video clip with Caffeine. I saw him say something to my stairway friend, his head tilted in inquiry, then he looked surprised when baldy jerked his arm and said something.

The bald man moved around the car to the passenger side and climbed in. He had to shut the door twice to get it properly closed.

Arms not working so good?

I saw the manager come up the stairway, looking carefully at the stair step treads, tugging at the edges to see if anything was loose. "Did you see what happened?"

I shrugged. "He'd just passed me on the stairs. He seemed to be going pretty fast. I think he missed a step."

She nodded and went back down the stairs.

I exhaled.

Escalation. Was it retaliation for last night's encounter at The Brass?

At least they were coming after me instead of the boys. Tara and Jade started up the steps with the drinks, and I went cold. What if they came after Jade or Tara?

Tara said, "Why'd you throw him down the steps?"

Jade started to laugh then caught a look at my face. "What? *Did you* throw him down the stairs?"

I shook my head. "No. But he tried to do that to *me.*"

They both stared at me.

"He missed."

Tara nodded. "I wondered what was up, especially when I saw him get in the Hummer."

Jade looked angry, staring down at the window. "What kind of asshole pushes a teenage girl down the stairs? If you'd gone down those stairs backward, you could've gotten a concussion. Or even broken your neck!"

The Hummer pulled away, chrome wheels flashing in the sun.

Tara nodded slowly. "We don't like them."

Jade nodded. "No, we don't."

They were waiting for me in the woods the next morning. Four figures, two smoking. I watched from the ledge above as they shifted around until I had identified Caffeine; Calvin, his nose still swollen from our encounter at The Brass; and Hector. The last one was the shaved head of the guy from Krakatoa.

Obviously I could bypass them.

I didn't want to.

I jumped back to the cabin and armored up—boots, gloves, armored jacket, and knee and shin guards. In the back of Dad's closet I found *the* jacket.

It was black leather once, but it had faded to an irregular charcoal gray. The zipper still worked but only because it had been replaced about six times. I've never seen Dad wear it, but Mom puts it on occasionally, especially if Dad is away from home.

Of course, it's way oversized on me, but it was just comfortably loose over the armor. A pair of Dad's sweatpants covered the knee and shin guards, though the knees bulged slightly.

I checked myself in the mirror. The jacket fell past my hips. What curves I had were erased, covered. The boots and the helmet added to my height, and the jacket over the armor bulked me up, widened my shoulders. When I pulled the balaclava up over my nose and lowered the goggles, all signs of gender were obscured.

Remember the lentils from Australia? We had hundreds of the empty burlap bags left and I knew about a shaded gully a hundred yards directly down the hill that had been accumulating snow all winter.

First I took Hector, who screamed when the bag went over his head and who was still screaming when I pushed him over the edge into the snow-filled gully.

I jumped back to the cliff top and watched.

Caffeine flinched and took three quick steps backward, toward the cliff face, but the other two took a couple of steps down the hill, toward where they could hear the distant Hector, now swearing loudly as he struggled in the deep snow.

The scream must've sounded odd, right beside them, and then, without a break, off in the distance.

After a moment, Caffeine stepped cautiously forward, moving out in front of the other two, and I hooded Calvin from behind with another lentil bag.

Hector had made it most of the way out of the gully, but had to jump back down, out of the way, as I pushed Calvin over the edge above him.

Back on the ledge I saw Caffeine backing up the path, toward the school, her head swiveling frantically.

The guy from the coffee shop said. "Don't separa—"

I took him like the others. But he didn't react the same. Instead of moving both hands up to clear the scratchy bag from his head, he lashed back with his arm, clipping my helmet, and, as I shoved him into the gully he kicked back at my knee, but his shoe glanced off the armor and he fell forward into the snow, flailing his arms, still hooded.

In the distance, I heard Caffeine yell, "Marius!"

I jumped back to the ledge.

Caffeine was running, already clear of the woods, and headed for the bleachers.

I smiled and let her go.

When I jumped back down the hill, I chose a site well back from the gully, where they couldn't see me appear.

They were helping each other out of the gully. Marius standing at the bottom bracing Calvin, who in turn braced Hector as he reached for the lip above.

My head came into view and Hector flinched back, twisting, causing them all to slide down. They stood there, expressions ranging from defiant (Calvin), impassive (Marius), to scared (Hector) as I walked up to the edge of the gully.

"Who the fuck are you?" Calvin said.

I pointed at them, and then, in as deep and raspy a voice as I could manage, said, "Don't. Mess. With. My. Friends."

Then I leaped off the edge of the gully at them, head first, arms spread, fingers curled like claws.

Hector yelled "Fuck!" They all dove away, back or to the side. By the time they'd recovered their footing and turned back around, I was twenty-five hundred miles away, in the Yukon.

I scrambled into a blouse and skirt back in my room, wool tights, flats, my nice wool coat. The armor was scattered across the bedroom floor, but I was able to pass Caffeine in the hall several minutes before second bell rang, walking demurely and looking *nothing* like the figure in the woods.

I ignored her but she stared hard at me as I went by. She was pale and her eyes were wide, but she had that expression even before she saw me.

Hector was late, coming in after first period. I saw him getting a tardy slip in admin and made a point of walking past him as he came out. He, too, was pretty pale and he stumbled when he saw me, but I ignored him and kept going.

"What's going on with Hector and Caffeine?" Jade asked at lunch. "Did someone die? Or get arrested?"

Tara's eyes got big. "What did you do?" She was looking at me.

I batted my eyes. "What are you talking about?"

Jade eyes narrowed. "Smugness. That's the expression I was trying to figure out. You're smug. Did you get their buddies arrested or something?"

"Me? How on earth could I do something like that?"

Jade looked disgusted and turned to Tara. "See? Smug."

I stuck my tongue out at them.

Okay, maybe I was a little smug. But mostly I was afraid of what those assholes would do next.

I jumped home briefly after lunch and put away the armor properly. I started to return Dad's jacket and sweatpants, but put them in *my* closet instead. I thought I might need them again.

"You've got a meet tomorrow, right?" Dad said while he was fixing supper.

"I do? Oh, right, I do." It was the second-to-last meet for the snowboard club. I'd almost forgotten.

So sue me. I'd been dealing with a lot of things lately, all right?

"Would you like to pretend to drive me, so I don't have to wake up so early?"

Dad nodded. "We're going to come watch, after all."

I phoned Joe to tell him I wouldn't be in the van.

He hesitated a moment before saying, "Okay. Don't be late, all right? You're our best women's slalom boarder."

"I'm your *only* woman slalom boarder. But I think I can manage." I was planning on jumping to Cedar Mountain early and getting in a few runs before the team arrived.

I expected Joe to say goodnight, then, but he blurted out, "Are you all right?"

"Huh? Sure. Why do you ask?"

"It's just I heard that Caffeine and her crowd were, uh, messing with you." He sounded genuinely worried.

"In their incompetent way. Don't worry, I won't mess up the club's Title IX status."

"That's not it!" He sounded offended. "Give me a little credit, here. I know what they did to Dakota and Tony. Everybody knows. . . ."

I didn't know whether to be irritated or gratified at his concern. "I didn't know you cared."

He paused. "Uh, doesn't matter. You're dating Grant Meriwether."

I blinked. "No."

"You're not?"

"I went out with him once for . . . well, not for romantic reasons."

"Interesting." His voice was suddenly more cheerful.

Okay, I decided. *Gratified*. I decided to feel gratified by his concern.

I thought about Joe for a moment, trying to separate him from his role of team captain, and Brett's friend, and even the guy who'd unintentionally put down my academic skills. He was taller than I, not as tall as Brett, but much taller than Grant. He dressed like he didn't care what other people thought, but nothing embarrassing. His complexion was *mostly* clear. I pictured his face, his beaky nose, his angular torso.

My heart went pitter-pat.

Tongue-tied, suddenly, I let the silence grow.

He cleared his throat. "So, if you're not dating Grant, are you dating anyone else?"

My mouth was suddenly dry. "I am *not*."

"Sure you don't want to ride with us in the van tomorrow?"

"Positive, why?"

"Thought we could sit together."

"What about Lany? I thought there was something going on with you two?" They touched a lot, horseplay and hugs.

He laughed. "She's my first cousin. And she's going out with a college boy. How about the van?"

"A four-hour drive is your idea of a good time?"

"Depends on the *company*."

There was that, but the last thing I wanted to do was sit with Joe while Brett was in the same vehicle.

"Not interested."

"Oh." The cheer in his voice vanished.

"In the van ride. But I'm free tonight."

There was a clatter as he dropped his phone. I heard him

saying, "Shit! Shit!" as he scrambled to pick it up again. "Are you still there?"

I didn't say anything.

"Cent?"

"Yes."

He exhaled. "Want to go out tonight?" He said it in a rush.

"Trying to get that in before you drop the phone again?"

He laughed, a breathless kind of laugh. "Yeah. Kinda. You surprised me, there."

I'd surprised *me*.

"Can't stay out too late. I've got this, uh, snowboard thing tomorrow, but you can pick me up at seven." I hesitated. "Oh. You don't have a car, do you?"

"Not to worry—I can borrow wheels! Uh, I already know your address."

You do?

"All right. Seven, then," I said.

TWENTY-SEVEN

Millie: "Letting Go"

Davy rose from the table as soon as Joe and Cent left.

"Where are you going?" Millie asked.

He turned his head quickly, touched his lips with his tongue.

Millie laughed. "No! Don't even think about it."

Davy slowly sat back down.

Millie said, "When you lived in New York, when we met, how would you have liked it if your father had followed you around watching everyone you talked with?"

Davy looked away, saying, "I am not an alcoholic!"

"No. So? What does that have to do with her right to privacy? To her right to make her own mistakes?"

"Making her own mistakes could get her *killed*!"

"If you're not careful, you're going to do just what your father did to you: drive her away."

He looked shocked and angry. "My father was *physically* abusive!"

"Yes, he was. And emotionally abusive, too. But don't compare your behavior to his. We can always find someone who is behaving worse than we are. Doesn't excuse our *own* behavior."

"What is the objective standard, then?"

"You could do worse than the golden rule. If you were in

her shoes, would you like to be followed around by even a benevolent parent?"

"What if she *needs* my help? *Our* help?"

Millie held up her cell phone. "Wait until she asks."

Millie did go out herself, later, to download her e-mail. On reading one, she jumped to the DC Metro and found a public phone.

"Martingale." Millie could hear silverware on china and the clinking of ice cubes in the background.

"It's Millie. Is this a bad time?"

"One second." Away from the phone Martingale said, "Work call. Won't be a moment." The sound of the cutlery faded and Becca said, "Okay. I'm back near the restrooms. You got my e-mail." It wasn't a question.

"Yes. Who saw her?"

"Sheer coincidence. An agent out of the LA office was reviewing some security camera footage related to a bank robbery, checking the previous day's video to see if the suspects had cased the lobby, and she showed up though the window. Nothing to do with the robbery, but the agent had seen a recent circular on her prison escape."

"When was this?"

"Last Thursday—the robbery was Friday."

"And where, exactly?"

"Venice Beach."

"It's not much. Checking the area?"

"Of course. Police and agents. But Hyacinth wasn't alone in the picture. We don't have an ID of the man yet, but we're working it."

"Could you e-mail me that image?"

"Sure. First thing tomorrow, okay?"

"Thanks."

TWENTY-EIGHT

"Potential"

Dad took it well. Okay, he took it better than the previous time.

"Got a date tonight," I said at supper.

Dad didn't say anything, mainly because he'd inhaled some iced tea.

While he was coughing, I added, "I won't be out late, though, because of the meet tomorrow"

Mom whacked Dad on the back, between his shoulder blades, and said, "But you're jumping there. Why should it matter if you stayed out late?"

Dad, still coughing, glared at Mom.

Mom ignored him and kept whacking. "You can sleep in tomorrow morning."

"Sure, but *he* can't. He's on the snowboard team, too, and he'll have to get up early to catch the van."

Dad got his coughing under control. "*Not* Grant?"

"Right. Not Grant."

Dad looked at with raised eyebrows, waiting.

"It's Joe Trujeque, the team captain. You met him when you dropped me off at the van, that first day of practice."

"Isn't he a senior?"

"Junior."

Dad said, "A little old for you?"

Mom and I burst out laughing.

Dad grinned, too, and winked.

Oh. *This time* he was being funny.

Mom followed me back to my Yukon bedroom. "Dressing up?"

I shook my head. I changed to an oversized sweatshirt and added my Yomiuri Giants baseball cap. I only had to use one bit of cover-up for a healing zit. Then I flossed and brushed my teeth really well.

Mom watched all of this, especially the oral hygiene. "This *isn't* another practice date, is it?"

I tried to play it cool, but then grinned. "This one has *potential.*"

"He's not the crush?"

I made a face. "God, no! I'm well away from that jock. Joe hasn't got that disease."

"Joe *isn't* a jock?" Mom said.

I shook my head. "Not like Brett. Joe's a skateboarder and an A student. And he's got the most adorable big honking nose."

Mom looked alarmed. "I see." She licked her lips and then crossed over to the ceramic box on my dresser and tapped it.

I felt my face go bright red and shook my head vigorously. "*Way* too soon." She frowned and I said, "But I know where they are! And *I* can get to them in a millisecond."

She blushed and hugged me, then jumped away.

She'd given me the box the day we "moved" into New Prospect.

I'm not saying go ahead and do this. But don't be stupid. Be safe. Make your own decisions.

I opened it, looked at the condoms inside, and then shut it again, quickly.

Way too soon.

"It's my brother's," Joe explained.

It was an old-school Volkswagen bug, air cooled, older than both of us combined. The starter barely turned the engine over, and Joe looked worried, but then the motor caught and ran smoothly enough.

"Where do you want to go? A movie? Dancing?"

The heater in the car was pathetic. "Pie," I said. "Hot pie."

He took me to Luncheon Junction, a restaurant in a converted train station. It had been decades since there was passenger service in town, but freight trains still rolled through the adjoining rail yard several times a day.

"Pie is kind of their thing," Joe said.

He had the blueberry-apple. I had the cherry pie à la mode. We shared bites with each other.

Pie was *definitely* their thing.

Joe had two sisters in middle school and an older brother who went to college in the East—it was his VW Joe was driving. His dad was a welder and his mom taught composition at the community college. His most serious relationship had ended the year before when his ex, Emily, dropped him for a senior with a car.

He was a reluctant reader.

By this I don't mean he read reluctantly. He read *voraciously.* What he was reluctant about was admitting it.

"Really? I thought you didn't care what other people thought?"

He squirmed a bit and shrugged. "Skateboarders."

"You're pathetic," I said.

It took some more work to find out *what* he liked to read. I had to swear not to reveal his dark secret.

I could've kissed him on the spot.

"She only wrote the six books," I said.

"There are her letters," he said, "and the juvenilia are really very funny and the novella *Lady Susan*—wait, you knew she only wrote six books?"

"Sure. But I've only read *Northanger Abbey* once. Catherine is an idiot, even more so than Emma. But *Emma,* the book that is, has so many other things going for it, and Emma learns better in a more convincing way."

He frowned. "So you've only read *Northanger Abbey* and *Emma*?"

"Don't be silly! I've read the rest of them several times. *Northanger Abbey* only once."

He smiled warmly and I felt the nape of my neck tingle.

"Well," he said. "It's not my favorite, but really, I don't think you're being fair to Catherine. She did eventually get over the gothic novel thing."

"Ha! *Persuasion* blows it out of the water. I'll take Anne Elliot over Catherine Morland *any* day."

He nodded judiciously. "Not really fair. She wrote *Northanger Abbey* before any of the others, even if it wasn't published until after her death. She wrote *Persuasion* last, at the height of her powers."

"I'm not talking about *fair*," I said. "I'm talking about *best*."

He held up his hands. "Okay. Completely agree. *Persuasion* happens to be my favorite, too."

I thought about taking him home to pore over my bookshelves, but the stuff I'd moved to the New Prospect bedroom was anime and manga and my nonfiction reference books. Everything else was still in the Yukon. How would I explain that?

"How late is the library open?"

The Volkswagen starter tried to turn over once and failed.

"Can you drive a shift?" he asked.

I shook my head. "I don't drive at *all*."

"We can push start it. I just thought I'd push while you popped the clutch."

I laughed at him. "Get in the car."

We were on flat ground and it rolled easily. He pushed with the door open, ready to jump in. I pushed from the rear bumper. As soon as he jumped in, I hopped on the rear bumper and jumped in place, adding velocity to the car. I nearly sprained my wrists but the car sped up abruptly. I stepped off and jumped again, just before I touched the pavement, to kill my forward velocity.

The car started easily when he put the clutch in, but he

was now far enough away that he had to U-turn and come back for me.

When I climbed in, he said, "Huh. I guess this stretch is more downhill than I thought." Despite funding cutbacks, the county library was open until ten on Fridays. We browsed the adult and YA shelves, pointing out favorites to each other. Sometimes it was "yes," a shared favorite, sometimes it was a shrug, having never read it. Several times we were reminded of other books that weren't at the library. Rarely it was a "no," we *had* read it, but it wasn't that high on our list.

Made me nervous, though, when I put my finger on the spine of a book by Garth Nix, the one about the Second Assistant Librarian and the Disreputable Dog.

Joe leaned closer, to read the title, and then he kissed me.

So I guess that was a "yes."

I was out of breath by the time I got inside the house. Mom raised her eyebrows.

I held my thumb up. I wanted to throw the door back open and chase the boy down as he climbed back into the VW. We'd kissed in the library, on the library steps, in the car, and on the porch.

My lips were puffy.

"How was *your* evening?" I asked.

I had trouble sleeping but let me tell you, this was *so much better* than the night I'd spent crying about Brett.

The next morning I called Joe's cell phone fifteen minutes before the van was supposed to leave.

"Did you change your mind? Do you want me to tell them to wait?"

Four hours in the van next to Joe *was* looking better but I said, "No."

"Darn."

"Look, I know Brett is a good friend, but can you *not* tell him about us?"

"What? Why not? You said you weren't dating anybody else!"

"Shut up. Drink more coffee. It's not about dating. Until this Caffeine thing is resolved, it's about her guys hassling me. I'd rather they didn't have one more target."

"Oh," he said. "Donna. Brett to Donna. Donna to Caffeine, right?"

"That's it."

"I'm not scared of them. I've got my peeps, too."

"I believe you. But I really don't want to be scared *for you*. Do it for me, okay?"

"Those guys are assholes. It may never be resolved."

Not if I have anything to say about it. "Well, then, two more weeks. Until the snowboard season is over. Whatever happens, even if it's all-out war, then you can tell anybody. If we're still dating."

He sounded alarmed. "Are you having doubts? Was I pushing things?"

I laughed. "Are *you* having doubts?"

His voice got husky. "No. I hardly slept last night."

"Me, too. Good thing I'm *not* in the van. You can sleep."

"I can't tell *anybody*? It's just that it's nice—I want to share that. I can't even tell Lany?"

"You do and I'll tell everyone you think *Northanger Abbey* is the best book Austen *ever* wrote."

"Ohhhhhhh. That's *low*."

"See you on the mountain."

I gave my jacket to Joe at the very last minute and came in second in the women's slalom. The reduced drag put me across the line chilled, but two tenths of a second ahead of the third-place finisher. Also, I got to rub against Joe as he held the coat for me at the bottom of the run.

"Stop *that*," he said, "unless you're ready for a *very* public display of affection."

Mom videotaped the runs and cheered me on, her scarf pulled up high even though it wasn't cold. I only glimpsed Dad once, buried in the crowd.

Jade finished out of the running in slope style, but she

didn't fall once and felt really good about her performance, especially since Lany came in first. Lany was also third in the half-pipe.

I got to kiss Joe once, in the woods, between the slalom course and the half-pipe, but Donna and Brett almost caught us, so we cooled it for the rest of the day.

Caffeine, to my relief, was not at the meet.

As soon as my events were done, Mom said, "I'm going to go check on Grandmother." She gave me a hug and said, "Joe *does* have potential."

I hung out with the rest of the team until it was time for the van to leave.

"Tonight?" Joe said. "We're back in town about 7:30." We were standing close together, watching as the others loaded their gear.

I scratched my nose and, while my mouth was covered, said, "Come to my house. We'll shoot pool."

I waved goodbye to the team at large, including Joe, and then, out of sight, jumped to the Yukon for a good soak in the hot tub.

This beat the crap out of four hours in the van, but I got to thinking about spending some of that time with Joe in the hot tub.

I had to get out of the tub, flushed and overheated. Joe wouldn't be back in New Prospect for three more hours. I moved another bookshelf from the cabin to the house, and started stocking it with some of my favorites. When I was finished, it was *still* two hours until the team van would get back.

What the hell.

I looked over the broken walls and saw three cars parked alongside the garage/clubhouse. One of them was Caffeine's tricked-out Honda with the crumpled right fender. Another was a Toyota with a lowered suspension. I didn't recognize the make of the last one. It was an old Datsun, whatever *that* is.

I jumped to the alley side of the garage roof and crouched, scanning for more cars, but it was just the three. I'd expected the black Hummer. I returned to the skylight. The sky was dark enough that I didn't think I'd be silhouetted.

None of the figures below looked happy. They were hunched in on themselves and Caffeine was gesturing sharply. I wished I could hear what they were saying.

Why not?

It was all too easy to recall the closet with the camera. I could hardly think about it without shuddering.

I appeared standing next to the camera mount in the dark closet. Light came into the closet from around the camera and the edges around the badly hung door. I could hear their muffled voices though the wall.

I moved down toward the door and heard, "—gonna tell Jason?" That was Caffeine talking. "'Cause I don't think you'll like the results. Part of the deal is that we get our share because *we're* taking care of the problems. Jason has to step in, then our percentage goes down."

Hector's voice was so strident that I had trouble recognizing it. "Yeah? I'm not seeing a way to *take care* of this particular problem! What do you suggest? Silver bullets? Garlic?"

I'd been nervous up to then, ready to jump away at the slightest sound, but now my lips tugged up at the corners. *Garlic?* Maybe they'd pull out the crucifixes, too. That gave me ideas for the next time I wanted to make an impression.

Caffeine said, "Shut your mouth. Someone is playing tricks, that's all. I thought it was that new girl, but she was in a skirt when I saw her at school."

Calvin agreed. "She's too small. The thing in the woods was bigger. It tossed us around like we were toys"

Caffeine sighed. "Maybe it's the *Sureños*."

"No way!" That was my friend from the coffee shop stairway—Marius. "They don't give a shit as long as we stick to ecstasy, pot, and 'ludes."

"Well, maybe then it's the *Norteños* moving in?" Caffeine said.

Marius laughed, but not in an amused way. "Was it bullets? Or machetes? Then it isn't the *Norteños* or the *Sureños*."

Calvin cleared his throat. "You just don't want to tell Jason 'cause he won't believe it. He'll say we've been using our own product. I say we need to let him know what we're up against."

And Hector said, "And *what is that? What* are *we up against? Do you know? DO YOU KNOW? WHAT IF—*"

I heard a slap and a gasp.

Caffeine's voice said mildly, "Don't do that. We don't need to be fighting each other."

Hector, almost as strident as before, said, "Jesus! Marius, *you asshole!*"

Caffeine's voice raised. "Hector, shut the fuck up. Grow a pair, already!"

Hector mumbled something, but I couldn't make it out.

"Pussy," said Marius.

Caffeine went on. "We need to increase the pressure on my three little boyfriends. And they need to do more than just carry the stuff in. We need them to start selling."

"They're refusing to carry it in," Calvin said. "What makes you think they'll go for selling?"

"We'll up the pressure," said Caffeine.

"More than a broken finger? A busted nose?"

"Time to bring them back together," Caffeine said. I heard her pat the couch. "Right here, where it all began."

"And how are you going to do that?" Marius said. "Between the broken finger and the broken nose, you think they're going to come anywhere near you?"

Caffeine said, "Sure. 'Cause I'm going to offer them what they want—the video."

The team van got back into cell coverage about an hour short of New Prospect. Joe began texting me: U *sure u want to hang at ur place?*

Why?

Privacy.

I remembered some of my thoughts in the hot tub and blushed. But it was too soon. *And we would need privacy for?*

It was five minutes before his next text. *Ur house ok.*
No witnesses? Your pool skilz that bad?
Are we playing for money?
For kisses, I texted.
How does that work?
Loser has to kiss the winner.
He responded immediately. *How humiliating. Not.*
I grinned. *Winner has to kiss the loser?*
Ur doin it wrong.
No kisses?
Let's not be hasty. Am willing to experiment with oscula-tory scoring system.
For science!
For science.

So, you know that bit where one person is showing another person how to shoot pool so they put their arms around them from behind to guide their hands on the pool cue and talk right next to their ear?

We did that.

We also changed the scoring system. Every time one of us missed a shot, they had to kiss the other.

Turns out we're *terrible* pool shots.

Later, we got serious about the pool. He was better than I was and he *did* show me how to improve my aim.

During a snack break, upstairs, we had a nice discussion with Dad about *The Three Musketeers*, the actual book, and all the different movies made from it. Joe had seen the 1921 Douglas Fairbanks silent version but both of them agreed that the best was the pair of Richard Lester movies made in the seventies.

Then we went back to the pool table. I did pull him into my bedroom, briefly, for a review of some of my favorite titles. And no, that's not a euphemism.

We were both blinking and yawning by eleven and he said, reluctantly, "If I don't go home soon, I'm going to drive off the road on my way."

I walked him up the hill to the car. It was snowing lightly and I loved the way snowflakes caught in his hair.

"Tomorrow?" he asked between kisses.

"I don't know," I said. I felt his muscles tense and added, "I've got this Caffeine thing."

"What?"

"You know my three freshman?"

"Yeah. Grant and his two buddies. Uh, Tony and . . ."

"Dakota. Yeah, those guys. Caffeine is after them. They used to run packages for her, but they refused to do any more."

Joe nodded. "Heard that. That was what the bloody nose was about. And the broken finger, right?"

"Right. And there's other stuff, too. Anyway, I need to work on that tomorrow."

"What do you mean by 'work on that'?" He sounded worried. "You're not going near Caffeine and her peeps, are you?"

I didn't want to lie to him. "I'm just keeping an eye on the kids. If I need help, I'll phone you, okay?"

"So it's like a stakeout? I could help."

"Help distract me. Remember our deal?" I pointed back and forth between us. " 'We' are a secret for the next few weeks."

"What is the other stuff? Between Caffeine and the boys?"

I said, "It's not my secret to tell."

"Ah. Did she do the sex-video thing, again?"

My mouth dropped open. "So, not the first time, eh?" A horrible thought hit me. "Not you?"

He took a step away, "Heard that's how they got Hector into the gang last year. Not that he wasn't willing. But me? Puh-lease. Give me some credit for taste, if nothing else."

"I thought guys liked big boobs."

He reached toward my chest, "I like *yours*."

I knocked his hand aside. "We're saying goodnight, remember?"

"Don't do anything stupid, okay?"

We kissed again and he finally opened the door of the VW. The engine barely turned over, but then started. He rolled down the window and I kissed him once more.

"I'll try not to do anything stupid," I said. "But you know how it is when you start a relationship." I bit his lip gently. "*Anything* might happen."

He groaned and drove off, snowflakes swirling in the car's wake.

Grant spilled the beans without much prodding when I called him.

"She said two PM. At the garage."

"You going?" I was trying for neutral, like Mom's therapist, nonjudging voice.

"She said if we didn't, she was posting it to a public website and broadcasting the URL all over town. But that if we did come, she'd give us the only copies."

"Do you believe that?"

He let out a long sigh. "No. But Dakota wants to believe it. Tony is freaking out big time."

I tried one more time. "What's on the tape that they're so afraid of?"

He disconnected.

Little shit.

At least I wouldn't have to watch the boys. I could confine myself to watching the garage.

It was still snowing when I jumped to the clubhouse roof at one. Caffeine's dented Honda was parked by the side door. I didn't want to risk looking through the skylight. It was all white above. It would be all too easy for someone to notice my head against the snow, helmet and all.

I was considering jumping down into the closet when my cell phone buzzed in my pocket.

I jumped back to the middle of the lot, in the ruined house, and fumbled the phone out of my pocket. It was Grant. I hooked the balaclava down from over my mouth and hit the answer button with my nose since my gloved fingers had no effect on the touchscreen.

"Hello, Grant."

"Uh—" he said and stuck there, making sounds that aspired to be words but failed.

"Deep breath, Grant. What's wrong?"

"Tony. He just hung up on me."

"Ironic, that. Like you hung up on me earlier?"

"Not exactly. I think he's taken something."

"Stolen?"

"No! I think he's swallowed something. I think he's trying to kill himself!"

My stomach lurched. "Did you call his parents?"

"No answer. His family are evangelicals, though. They spend most of Sunday at church. Tony didn't go today. Told them he was sick."

"What makes you think he took something?"

"I called him to talk about what we were going to do, with Caffeine and all, and he was, like, calm—well, no longer freaking out. When I talked to him earlier, he was practically sobbing." Grant exhaled sharply. "And then he said it didn't matter what anybody did. Not anymore." And then Grant said in a rush, "And he hung up on me and he's not answering his cell and not answering the landline!"

"When did you last talk to him?"

"Uh, I've been trying the phones over and over. I guess twenty minutes?"

"Why didn't you call 911?"

I could hear his mouth working but he didn't manage words. "I'll check on him," I said.

Tony's house was in the residential section of Fourth Street, south of downtown. I'd followed him and Dakota there after the incident in the alley. I jumped to the corner and, despite the snow, spotted the huge blue spruce that marked the house.

I rang the doorbell and banged on the door, but no one answered.

Right.

I tried the doorknob but the door was locked. The drapes were drawn over the front windows, but a side window gave me a glimpse of the kitchen, and I jumped inside.

"Tony!" I yelled.

I tore through the house. I found his parents' room and two other bedrooms that clearly belonged to sisters, then came to what should've been another bedroom door.

It was locked.

I went outside and located the room's windows. They were blocked by drawn blinds. I jumped back to the hallway and tried to kick the door open. Nearly sprained my ankle.

Fine.

I stood across the hall from the door, tucked my chin, and jumped in place, adding ten miles an hour toward the door.

The door splintered at the lock and I tumbled into the room, the breath leaving my lungs in a huge gasp, but the armor I wore did its job, spreading the force. I scrambled back to my feet.

Tony was across the bed, face up, mouth open. I shook him. He didn't respond. He was breathing shallowly. I slapped him across the face and his head flopped over. His eyelids fluttered but he was still out. I ground my knuckle across his sternum through his T-shirt. His eyes opened very briefly and then closed again.

His pupils were tiny dots.

I looked around. *What did he take?*

There wasn't anything on the bed or the floor, but a half-open door led to a bathroom. In the sink was a prescription bottle, empty, lid lying on the floor. I snatched it up: *Vicodin ES, 60 tablets 7.5 mg of hydrocodone bitartrate, 750 mg of acetaminophen.* It was his mom's prescription, apparently, for back pain.

I stuffed the bottle in my jacket pocket and, back in the

bedroom, pulled Tony into a sitting position, then over my shoulders in a fireman's carry. He was no lightweight. It took everything I had to struggle upright.

I'd seen the hospital a few times. It was on 87, between downtown and the municipal administration complex, but I really couldn't recall it well enough, so I jumped to the alley behind Main, where it crossed 87. I jumped down the sidewalk to the hospital in fifty-yard chunks, about as far as I could see through the falling snow. Hopefully the snow would confuse anybody who glimpsed my progress. I staggered up the last ten yards of the ER driveway and through the automatic doors.

A man's voice said, "We need a gurney!" and then two figures in scrubs were beside me, taking Tony's weight off my shoulders and lowering him to the ground.

One of them, a woman, said, "What happened?"

I kept my head down as I pulled the bottle out of my jacket. I used my deep, hoarse voice. "Suicide attempt. This is what he took. I don't know how many were still in the bottle. He was talking on the phone twenty minutes ago, so it was recent."

There were security cameras. I kept my face averted. My hair was completely under the balaclava and the helmet, and while I didn't have the goggles over my eyes, they were up on the edge of the helmet, obscuring my face from above like a visor. The balaclava wasn't over my mouth, but it was up over my chin. The weather justified it.

The woman read the label and then yelled toward the back of the room. "Drug overdose. Get the gastric kit!" She checked Tony's eyes. To the man beside her, she said, "Better get the Narcan and the Acetadote out, too."

Two more people arrived with a gurney, which they collapsed to floor level. Three of them picked Tony up and eased him onto it, then raised it. They began rolling it back toward the treatment room even before it locked in the upright position. The woman turned to me and said, "Anything else? He didn't fall or anything?"

"Found him on his bed. The bottle was in his bathroom sink."

She looked out through the doors, then gestured at my helmet. "You bring him on a motorcycle?"

"Of course not."

She looked down at the bottle again. "Well, I'm guessing his name isn't Gladys."

"It's Tony. I think those are his mother's. The address is right."

"Not your brother then?"

"No. A friend of his called and asked me to check on him, worried. Because I was close. He was the one who talked to him in the last half hour."

"Where are his parents?"

"Church. I don't know which one."

"Okay." She pointed toward a double set of glass doors. "Go in there and tell the reception clerk as much as you know." She walked back to treatment.

I passed through the first set of doors, and jumped away.

TWENTY-NINE

Davy: Grainy Image

The image on the computer screen was grainy. Millie had
shown it to him without context or preamble.

He studied it. There was a palm tree visible on the corner
and California plates on the Mercedes and BMWs parked
against the sidewalk. The stores across the way looked like
ritzy boutiques. There was a time/date stamp which put it at
the previous Thursday afternoon.

He focused on the two figures walking on the sidewalk,
then swore.

Millie nodded. "Yeah. This is from a bank lobby in LA—
the Venice Beach area. Last Friday."

"Get this from Becca?"

Millie nodded. "Right." She tapped the screen with her
finger. "Recognize him?"

Davy shook his head. "Who is he?"

She shook hers in response. "Don't know. The FBI hasn't
ID'd him, either. Not yet. Just wondered if you'd seen him at
that building in LA"

"The Rhiarti building? No." The image, taken by a camera
pointed diagonally across the sidewalk, showed both Hyacinth
and the man in three-quarter profile. The man had wide shoulders and a narrow waist and his posture was balanced. "Looks

like one of the guys I'd be more likely to see at Stroller and Associates, down in Costa Rica."

"Hyacinth hasn't changed much," said Millie. "She certainly kept her figure."

Davy shuddered and looked away from the screen. "I'm going to have that dream again, I bet."

Millie shut the laptop. "Should I let Becca know about the Rhiarti building? Or Costa Rica?"

Davy frowned. "Well, I'm already blown in LA. Might as well let the feds know about the Daarkon Group. It could lead to something. Maybe *they* can find out where this Retreat is. Let's reserve Costa Rica for now."

Millie nodded.

"I'll send her an e-mail."

THIRTY

"Serious"

I called Grant from my house.

Mom and Dad were off doing something, which was a relief. If Mom had appeared right then, I would've spilled the entire story.

"You were right," I told Grant. "He took a bunch of his Mom's Vicodin."

"Is he all right?"

"He's in the ER. They're going to pump his stomach."

"You got him to the hospital? Oh, thank you!"

"Next time, *call 911.*"

"I didn't even know you drove!"

"I don't. As far as you're concerned, you don't know anything about how he got to the hospital, okay? You want to talk to people about the video, about the drugs, about Caffeine and the rest of those assholes? Feel free. Or not. *Just leave me out of it!*

"I made sure he got there and made sure they had the information they needed to treat him. They don't have my name and you're not going to give it to them. You owe me that."

He sounded cowed. "Uh, okay. If that's what you want."

"It is." I thought about threatening him if he did, violence or spilling everything I knew, but that was too much like Caffeine. Besides, I *wanted* him to rat out Caffeine. What would it take? For Tony to die?

"Okay. I do owe you. Tony definitely owes you. We *all* owe you."

And then he told me what was on the videos.

Grant sat with Tony's family at the hospital and heard the family briefings. He gave me regular phone reports.

An overdose of Vicodin can kill you two ways. The opiate part, the hydrocodone, can stop your breathing. The other part, the acetaminophen, can kill you through liver failure.

So, the first thing the ER staff did was try to get rid of it.

If Tony had been conscious they would have induced vomiting, since the drug wasn't corrosive. Instead they did gastric lavage—pumped his stomach—but they got both. When the nasogastric tube hit the back of his throat during insertion, he *did* throw up, and they had a nasty stretch where they were using suction to make sure he didn't inhale any of the vomit.

They went ahead and completed the gastric lavage and gave him a dose of Acetadote, to protect his liver from the acetaminophen. His respiration improved after emptying his stomach, so they held off on using Narcan, to counteract the opiate effects of hydrocodone. Narcan has nasty side effects of its own.

By late afternoon they were confident, barring other suicide attempts, that he would recover completely, with no liver damage.

When Grant told me this, my eyes teared up and I had to sit down suddenly.

The family wanted to know who had brought their son to the ER.

The ER staff reported "he" was a stocky young man who was clearly very strong, wearing a motorcycle helmet, bundled up for the weather. The security camera confirmed that much, but there wasn't a good shot of the person's face.

The family was distraught, irritated, and grateful, especially when their son woke up and confirmed that, yes, he'd taken the pills. Some mysterious stranger hadn't forced them down his throat. And he was as mystified as anybody about who had brought him to the ER.

When asked why he had taken the pills, he was less forthcoming.

"Don't know why they confused you for a guy," Grant said.

"What makes you think it was me?"

"Uh, you said you did . . . didn't you?"

"Did I? How? I don't drive. Have I ever been to Tony's house? That you know of?"

"You got someone else to do it? I thought—well, who was it?"

"You don't know."

"I know I don't know! Who—"

"You don't know."

He was silent for a moment. "Oh. You don't *want* me to know."

"I want you to be able to answer truthfully. If asked."

"I don't know who brought him into the hospital."

"Right."

"And leave you out of it, too."

"Double right."

I felt like curling up in my reading nook, buried in the cushions. I wanted to jump to Australia and throw myself into the surf. I wanted to do both of these things *with* Joe.

I did *not* want to deal with Caffeine's bullshit anymore.

Before, I'd found her irritating. I'd expected something like her at school. Everything I'd ever read, both fiction and non, led me to expect queen bees and bullying and other stupid behavior in high school.

Tony's suicide attempt put it way over the edge, though.

I waited two days to see if Tony or Dakota or Grant would go to the police. One cure for blackmail, after all, is making the subject public, to remove the threat of exposure by doing it yourself. But Tony hadn't said anything by Tuesday after school. His family had him admitted to the psych ward for "observation." Which meant suicide watch.

His attempt was the talk of the school and, at first, it even seemed to shock Caffeine—she was pale on Monday. By Tuesday, though, she was back to her old nasty self. I guess she figured he wasn't going to talk.

After all, he was willing to kill himself rather than deal with exposure. Why should he talk now?

I found myself shaking as I watched her laughing with her peeps, after school.

Ah well, if you're going to get mad, use it.

Start with a quart of corn syrup, add one-and-a-third cups of water, then start dripping the red food coloring in, stirring briskly. Don't overdo it. Once it approaches blood in color, add a tiny bit of green or blue food coloring. Then thicken with chocolate syrup to taste, uh, I mean texture.

It doesn't smell or taste like blood, but it sure looks like it.

Three cars were parked beside the garage clubhouse, including Caffeine's Honda.

I set the plastic bucket of fake blood on the roof and went to the edge. I perched on the balustrade for a second, like a gargoyle, before leaping off and dropping seven feet onto the roof of Caffeine's car. The roof crumpled a good half foot under the motorcycle boots, and I absorbed the shock by bending my knees. I was hoping for noise. I got it, too. The car alarm had a vibration sensor.

I was back on the roof before the first of them came out the door—Calvin, followed by Caffeine. I guess she recognized the sound of her alarm. From above, I poured a cup of "blood" onto the snow behind Calvin. He didn't hear it over the blaring of the alarm.

Caffeine finally fumbled her keys out of her jacket pocket, but I dropped a lentil bag over Calvin's head and jumped him away before the car alarm chirped and stopped.

We appeared in the pit in West Texas, about twenty-feet above the water.

I guess it's a family tradition.

There wasn't cell phone reception there, even from the surrounding desert above. Down in the pit, there wasn't any chance of a signal. And once you soaked the cell phone in water you didn't have to worry about the GPS, either.

I watched Calvin splash his way to the shore of the little island before I checked back on Caffeine and company.

When I peeked over the broken wall of the ruin, Caffeine was staring down at the "blood" at the foot of the garage wall while Hector and Marius faced the surrounding lot.

Hector had a gun.

The gun was shaking.

The blood *looked* great, but if they used their noses, it wouldn't hold up. *Better do something before they examine it closer.*

I picked up a half a cinder block, jumped to the roof, and threw it.

Hector's Toyota also had an alarm but, alas, not an unbreakable windshield. All three of them jerked and turned toward the car, spreading out.

I poured another cup of the "blood" behind Hector. I didn't have time to use the hood, but he still never saw me. He appeared in midair over the water and fired his gun reflexively. The noise echoing off of the pit's walls made me flinch away to my reading nook with my head buried in the cushions.

I checked back on him, cautiously, from the rim of the pit.

He'd made it to the island, but Calvin had taken his gun away from him. I wonder if a ricochet had come uncomfortably close.

All the cars were still at the clubhouse when I returned, but the door was shut. I jumped onto the roof, stomped around the skylight, and was rewarded with a muffled shriek from below.

I got another cup of blood from the bucket and jumped to the garage closet with the camera. The closet door was slightly ajar.

Marius and Caffeine were standing across the garage, opposite the outside door, halfway between the wall and the
skylight. They didn't see me—they were looking up at the
skylight and the ceiling. I jumped behind them both and threw
the cup of blood at the wall, then took Marius.

Marius was fast, lashing out with one elbow and then the
other. One of them hit the side of the helmet and the other
glanced painfully off my goggles. When I let him go, I con-
fess he may have been higher above the water than the others.

Like twenty feet higher.

"Oh SHIT!"

I watched him hit the water, from the rim.

Try and push me *down a stairway!*

Caffeine was trying to get her car door open but the distortion
of the roof, from when I'd landed on it, had warped the door
and bound the lock.

I dropped a lentil bag over her head from behind and
jumped her to the sandy wash in West Texas. She flailed, but I
just shoved her forward. She went down on her hands and
knees in the sand, gasping, then pulled the bag off of her head.

As she scrambled to her feet, I backed off a few yards and
crouched, one knee in the sand. I was wearing the entire en-
semble: helmet, tinted goggles, balaclava, armor. Bulky. Face-
less.

When she finally turned enough to see me, she flinched,
took a step back, and dove her hand into her pocket.

Oops. Guess Hector wasn't the only one packing.

It was a small semiautomatic but new to her, I think, 'cause
she was fumbling it. Before she turned it dangerous side out, I
sprang upward and jumped in place, adding a hundred miles
per hour straight up.

Her head tilted up, her mouth wide. The gun hung limply at
her side.

When I was several hundred feet in the air and slowing, I
jumped back down to the ground, but behind her. She twisted
her head back and forth, scanning the sky. I raked the gun

from her hand and shoved her, sending her stumbling forward.

When she turned around, I was crouched again, watching her, the gun on the ground before me.

She ran.

Caffeine's keys were still in the Honda's door lock. I pulled them out and used them to pop the trunk. Her backpack was there, with her laptop in it—the latest Apple product, probably bought with her drug money.

The computer was in sleep mode and woke immediately when I opened it, but it was password protected.

Hmph.

I left the keys sticking out of the trunk lock.

I couldn't see Caffeine when I returned to the wash, but when I shot high into the air and scanned, I spotted her a half mile down the wash, where it deepened to an arroyo. She was still moving briskly when she came around a bend and found me crouching in the middle of the gully, holding her computer.

I used my raspy voice.

"I warned you."

She stepped back, but I guess she'd realized there was no point in running.

I took a crumpled piece of paper from my pocket and threw it toward her.

She picked it up and unfolded it enough to identify it. It was the sign I'd glued to her jacket when she'd been lurking in the doorway opposite the coffee shop, the one that started with, *Overuse of caffeine may lead to . . .* and finished with, *(Your Imaginary Friend)*.

"Who *are* you?"

"Your imaginary friend. Well, maybe not 'friend.' "

"Where are we?" Her gesture took in the gully and the sky and the surrounding desert.

I ignored her and opened the computer, holding it so she

could see the streaks of fake blood from my glove. "What's your password?"

She shook her head.

I set the computer in the sand and stood up.

"Do you really want to make me *more* angry?" I said. And I really was, which made the raspy, hoarse voice sound even scarier. "What is the password?"

She took a step back, still shaking her head.

This time, when I grabbed her from behind, I jumped in place, throwing us up into the sky at a modest seventy miles an hour.

She screamed.

I let go of her and she screamed louder. We drifted apart. Our upward velocity slowed to a stop 160 feet in the air and it felt like we hung there for an instant before the drop. The screaming intensified as we fell again. I jumped to close the gap, grabbing her around the waist, and jumped us back to the arroyo, spilling her into the sand.

I returned to the computer while she shuddered on the ground.

"Password?"

She spelled it out. I had to make her repeat it twice before it was coherent enough for me to type it in.

The account unlocked.

The files were named Grant, Tony, and Dakota. I briefly scanned the beginning of the videos, confirming they were the right ones before I had to watch too much of them. I checked the file dates. "Where else are the videos?"

She shook her head.

I looked at her backup settings. There was a backup volume, and the last backup had been the previous evening. She also had a couple of network cloud storage accounts. I shot into the air again, with the computer, and, fifty feet up, jumped to New Prospect, by the library.

When I connected to the library's WiFi, I found the files there, too, in the cloud accounts. I deleted them and, to be sure, killed the accounts, which was only possible because she'd used the same password for the net accounts as she did for the computer.

I returned to the wash. She was gone again.

I sighed and checked from above. She'd left the wash and headed east across much rougher terrain.

I put the computer in the cabin, in a desk drawer, then returned to the garage rooftop for the plastic bucket.

It was child's play to get in front of her, but this time I didn't hang around and wait for her to arrive. Instead, she'd climb over a ridge or around a stand of lechuguilla, and find "blood" splashed across her path.

She changed course and I did it again. And again. And again, until the bucket was empty.

By then, she couldn't even walk. She'd collapsed on a stretch of gravel, her torso held up by her elbows, her jacket tied around her waist. She was gasping.

I walked loudly across the gravel, scuffing my boots, and Caffeine jerked her head around and stared at me, whites showing, like a deer in the headlights.

"Where is the backup drive?"

She looked at me like the words hadn't made sense.

I pointed up at the sky. "Do you want another ride?"

"Uh, what did you ask?"

"Where is the backup drive for your laptop?"

"My bedroom desk."

"Which is your bedroom?"

"The one at the back of the house. On the ground floor."

I shot up into the air and, from on high, jumped back to New Prospect. I knew where her house was from the school records, but I had to walk three blocks to reach it. Her drapes were open enough to determine the room was empty. I took the backup drive and two thumb drives from the desk drawer, putting them with the computer at the cabin.

This time when I got back, she hadn't moved.

"Give me your phone."

"There's no signal," she said.

I jumped the interval between us and she fell back onto the gravel. I held out my hand.

She couldn't give it to me fast enough. The videos were not on it, not that I could find, but I did a full factory data reset, wiping everything off the phone.

"Why are you *doing* this?" She sounded like she was going to cry.

I flipped the phone back to her once the wipe was done.

"Feel a little *nervous*?" I asked.

"What did I do to *you?*"

"What did *Tony* do to you?"

She winced, but then said bitterly, "He did everything he wanted."

I shook my head. "And then he did everything *you* wanted. And you recorded it. *That* part I'm pretty sure he *didn't* want. Did Dakota and Grant?"

She sneered. "That was nothing! You wanted them jumped in, instead?"

I blinked. *Jumped?* "Jumped in?"

"Beat in. Initiated. Beat to a pulp to prove themselves."

Ah. "Are you saying they *wanted* into your gang?"

She looked away. "They wanted *me*. Same thing. And it was nothing like *I* had to put up with."

"Were you *beat* in?"

She spit on the ground. "They don't do that to girls. At least the little boys only had to do it with me. Not eight guys."

I felt like throwing up. I didn't want to feel any sympathy for her.

Eight guys?

She'd seduced Tony, Grant, and Dakota individually, an attractive older girl, taking them back to the clubhouse and giving them the run of her body. Sure, embarrassing if recorded, even a bit humiliating. Boys were supposed to be like that, right? She'd let them, even encouraged them, to do everything to her, and secretly recorded it.

Including the part at the end when she strapped on the dildo and did them in turn.

Don't get me wrong. It was consensual. Grant had been clear on that. She'd talked them into it. Experimentation with a sexy older woman. Yes, alcohol *was* involved. There was even a degree of enjoyment.

But she'd *recorded* it.

Boys think boys are supposed to *do* girls, not be *done* by them.

The blackmail videos had all been edited down to this last act, with Caffeine's face digitally obscured.

Tony's family was well to the right of religiously conservative. This was too much like gay sex. The threat of his family seeing it had been too much for Tony.

Eight guys?

I shuddered.

Caffeine licked her lips. "Are you going to kill me, too?"

For a second I'd forgotten about the blood. How hard I'd labored to make the earlier snatches resemble scenes from a slasher movie. Then I realized she thought I'd killed the rest.

"Why shouldn't I?"

She pulled the neck of her shirt down and lowered her eyes toward my crotch. "I'll do anything. I've *done* anything."

Eight guys.

I lifted my hand, jumped the gap between us, and slapped her.

She burst into sobs and I jumped all the way back to my room in the Yukon.

I looked down at my hand, then stumbled into the bathroom, clawing at the balaclava covering my mouth. I barely got it down before I vomited into the toilet.

THIRTY-ONE

Millie: Seen Cent?

"Have you seen Cent?"

They were both sweating and underdressed for the cabin in winter. Millie had been in Haiti talking with NGOs and Davy had been watching the Stroller and Associates compound in Costa Rica.

Davy shook his head. "I stuck my head in her room this morning before I left and she was still asleep, but when I came back for a snack midmorning she wasn't here or at the house. Did you check the house?"

"Just came from there. No messages on my phone, either." She paused and licked her lips. "I tried to call her. It went straight to voice mail."

"So she's out of range."

"Or her phone is off. Is she with Joe?"

"No idea. Could you jump your phone back to the house and check your voice mail?"

He vanished and returned after a few moments.

"No messages." He said, his voice *too* neutral. "Should I leave a message on her voice mail asking her to check in?"

"Angry?" Millie asked.

He exhaled hard. "I just think she might let us know where she went or when she would be back."

Millie nodded. "It's okay, Davy. Those are reasonable expectations. You can be irritated."

"Ah." He smiled briefly. "Good."

"Let me talk to her about it, all right?"

He glared. "Afraid I'll lose my temper?"

She laughed at him. "Not impossible."

He mimed choking someone and she laughed some more.

"No word on Rama," he said, which wiped the smile off of Millie's face.

"Ah. Well, she promised not to go back *there* so you don't have to worry about that. It's not like she's facing those kinds of threats *here*."

Davy nodded. "I'm kind of getting desperate. Was thinking of hanging around the docks in Bhangura and letting them come after me."

"No! They tried to control you *once* and it was a disaster for them and they know you've been poking around again. Too much chance they'll just *shoot* you."

He protested. "I'm *careful*."

"They could put a sniper a half mile away. The sound of the shot would arrive seconds after the bullet."

"*I* told you that."

"Yes. You told me that so *I* would be *careful!* Tell you what, why don't you have Cent go hang out on the docks until they make a try for her?"

He looked away. "You're saying, I guess, that I shouldn't take risks that I wouldn't want you or her to take."

She touched her own nose with her forefinger.

He sighed. "So where *is* she?"

THIRTY-TWO

"Spitting Image"

I hate vomiting. The taste is the worst thing, but after that, it's the burning irritation that persists in the throat long after you've managed to rinse the taste away.

I can't imagine how awful it was for Dad during his months of captivity, when they'd triggered his implant and he'd vomited out his guts over and over again.

Gargling helps but I could only do it for so long.

Caffeine was still where I'd left her, but now she'd put her coat back on. Her mascara made dark streaks down her cheeks. It was nowhere near as cold as New Prospect, but the temperature was dropping with the sun.

I didn't appear in front of her. I crunched across the gravel and she snapped her head around, eyes wide. I didn't really want to talk to her anymore, but I had one more thing to say.

"I can just leave you here. You *might* make it out alive."

She clenched her teeth. I could see her jaw muscles bulge.

"Or we could just end it, now."

Her eyes widened even further, whites showing.

I walked closer, increasing my pace as she scrambled back, trying to get up, to get away. I grabbed her coat near her throat and jumped back to the garage clubhouse. She screamed at the transition, and I let her go. She fell back onto the carpet in front of the couches.

"Stop with the drugs at the high school. No more blackmail. You run across any more copies of *those* videos, you delete them." I took an abrupt step closer to her. "Do that and you won't see me again. Be good—"

I jumped behind her and whispered in her ear, "—or else."

She screamed and recoiled, but this time I was really gone.

I returned Marius, Hector, and Calvin to the clubhouse an hour later. Grab and release. Hector and Calvin I left staggering away across the carpet, inside. Marius I dropped off the edge of the roof into a small drift of snow on the alley side of the garage.

I was still holding a grudge, I guess.

Caffeine was long gone and so was her Honda, so maybe she got the driver door open. Or, more likely, she used the passenger-side door and slid across.

Back at the cabin, I did a 7-pass secure erase of the partitions on Caffeine's external backup drive, of her USB drives, and finally the laptop's drive. If it's good enough for the Department of Defense, it's good enough for me.

Caffeine was asleep when I put the stack of equipment back on her bedroom desk in the predawn morning. She was snoring.

For a second I thought about making some noise before I jumped away, but I decided it would be creepier if she just found the computer there when she awoke.

"Missed you yesterday," Mom said Monday morning.

We'd eaten breakfast and I was finally approaching a state of wakefulness. Dad had gone off someplace, but Mom was lingering over her coffee.

I felt my face getting red.

Mom noticed, too, but she ignored it, staring out the window at the heavy icicles. She said, "I don't mean to pry. It's not like I have to drive you around or anything. From what I hear, most teenagers' parents are constantly on the go, either providing transportation or having to buy their kids cars so *they* can drive themselves around."

I nodded. "True. Jade gets it both ways. Complaints that they have to drive too much, but if she tries to walk, say over to Tara's, they complain about that, too, 'cause someone will, you know, molest her."

Mom raised her eyebrows.

"Uh, so you don't have to worry about *either* of those problems, right? Because of my jumping. Don't have to drive me. Don't have to worry about me crashing a car. Don't have to worry about me getting into a situation I can't jump away from."

Mom shook her head. "All I wanted to tell you was that we'd appreciate it if you keep us appraised of your whereabouts. You know, leave a voice mail if you go out. Let us know when you expect to be back. Call us if you're going to be late. But you bring up a more serious issue."

Crap. I never know when to leave well enough alone.

Mom said, "I really wish the only things I had to worry about were acting as your chauffeur and the ordinary dangers of a young woman growing up in America. We both know that's not the issue.

"I'm *glad* you can jump away from danger. But it's a danger in and of itself. You like Joe, right?"

I didn't think I could blush more. I nodded.

"When you jumped in Bangladesh, to help those girls, it was for the best of reasons. I'm *glad* you helped them."

"This is about Rama. He didn't do anything wrong and they took him because of me."

Mom nodded. "Now put Joe in Rama's place."

Ouch.

"Be careful. Also, let us know when you're out and about, right?"

I thought about the last forty-eight hours and winced. Not so careful. The thought of having to move away had been bad before, but with Joe, now, it was sharply painful.

"Right."

Fifteen minutes before first bell Grant was in his usual "safe" place, sitting on the bench opposite administration. I dropped down beside him.

"How's Tony?"

Grant licked his lips. "So-so. His parents kept after him to tell them why until the psychiatrist did a family session with the three of them. Then she asked Tony's parents to stay away for a week."

"Ah."

"Yeah. Tony's thinking about talking to her about, uh, the video. Well, about it and about his parents in general."

"He's not afraid she'll tell them?"

"Patient confidentiality."

"He *is* a minor."

"Yeah, well, she's obliged to act in the patient's best interest, right? It was the threat of his parents finding out that drove him to take the pills in the first place, right?"

I nodded, but I couldn't help thinking that the therapist would also be justified in going to the police if she knew the whole story. After all, Dakota and Grant were at risk, as far as Tony knew.

"Uh, Grant. You might want to tell Tony that Caffeine had a computer accident. Someone wiped her laptop, and her backup drives, and her net storage accounts, and her phone."

Grant's mouth dropped open. "You're not bullshitting me, are you?"

"I have it from a very reliable source."

"*All* the copies of that video?"

"*That* I don't know. How did you see it, originally?"

"She showed it to each of us on her phone."

"Maybe all the copies, then. On those devices for sure. My source was kind of hard on Caffeine, too. They don't think she'll be bothering you again."

Grant bit his lip and looked like he might cry.

"What's wrong?"

"I wasn't going to give in to her!" He said it in a rush, a fierce whisper. "But I'd given up. I just knew the video would come out." He looked down at his feet. "It's almost worse thinking there's a chance it won't!"

I sighed. Damned if you do, damned if you don't.

"Hope is like that, sometimes."

On my way to biology, between first and second bell, I saw Joe outside the library. I walked up and put my arms around him, burying my face in his chest.

I needed that.

His voice rumbled. "Not a secret any more?"

I tilted my head up and kissed him. "Not."

He grinned. "Okay, then."

"And when were you going to tell *us* about this?"

Tara was giving me grief at lunch.

Joe was sitting with us . . . well, sitting with me. We were shoulder to shoulder, hip to hip, and his left arm was around my shoulders.

Jade smirked. "Didn't have to tell *me*."

I raised my eyebrows. "Did you see something at the meet? We were very careful. Kept ourselves *to* ourselves."

Jade glanced sideways at Tara. "You were actually pretty chill. But not Joe's eyes, his voice, his face. You can touch someone with *more* than just your hands." She grinned. "See what I did there?"

I put my hand to my heart. *"Touché."*

She stuck her tongue out at me.

When I looked back at Joe he was blushing furiously, staring down at his lunch.

I leaned into him and put my hand on his leg.

"Haven't seen Caffeine, today," Tara noted.

I studied my free hand's fingernails.

Tara narrowed her eyes and leaned forward, studying my face. *"Or* Hector."

Jade was looking at me now, too.

I turned my attention to my lunch. I'd gone traditional, today: sandwich and an apple.

Joe was less red, now. He glanced down at my face, too, and raised his eyebrows.

I looked back. I liked to look at his face, his brown eyes.

He asked, "Did you do something to Caffeine and Hector?"

"I refuse to answer because the response could provide self-incriminating evidence of an illegal act punishable by fines, penalties, or forfeiture." Then I fluttered my eye lashes.

"Jesus," said Jade. "She killed them."

"No." I gave them a small smile. "Not *yet*."

Joe straightened up and let his arm drop from around my shoulders.

I pouted. " 'And they *all* moved away from me on the Group W bench.' "

He laughed and put his arm back around me.

I kissed his cheek and said, "Until I added, '—and creating a nuisance.' And they all moved back."

Joe had to explain it to Jade and Tara but he stopped me when I started singing the chorus.

Spoilsport.

After school, Joe came with us to Krakatoa. He'd suggested something more intimate and I'd been sorely tempted. But I had schoolwork to catch up on. Between this dating thing, *and* terrorizing the neighborhood, I was falling behind.

By the time Jade and Tara decided they needed to go, I was more comfortable with my homework situation. I had the final draft of next week's humanities paper done, as well as the first draft of a report due the following week. I was up to date on the math worksheets and had a start on the design for my science fair project: drag coefficients and posture in downhill snowboarding.

"You coming?" Jade asked.

Joe and I were discussing the theoretical top speed a snow-

boarder could hit using a thirty-eight-degree slope. He actually knew the world record, 125 mph "and a smidge" set by an
Australian thirteen years before. We were messing with the
values for a board's snow friction and the coefficient of drag
for the upright boarder. Both of us had the calculator apps
pulled up on our phones and several scribbled pages of equa-
tions and graphs.

"You kids better go." I waved Jade and Tara on. "This could
get ugly."

Tara swung her backpack on and said, "Too late."

I was punching in the sine of thirty-nine degrees when the
phone rang in my hands. It was Tara's number. As I hit the
answer button I checked under the table.

"Forget something, Tara?"

"Come downstairs and get in the Hummer."

It was not Tara's voice. I froze, still bent over. It was Marius.
I looked past the railing, out the front windows. I could just
see the black Hummer's custom wheels across the street.

"*Both* of you."

I heard a slapping sound and I heard Tara cry out and Jade
yell. "Leave her alone!"

"You have two minutes."

He disconnected. I swiveled my head sharply, right and
left. Joe and I were the only ones on the balcony.

I stood up and put the phone in my pocket. Joe raised his
eyebrows and I hooked his backpack and pulled him by the
arm toward the back wall, away from the railing.

"Trust me?" I asked.

"Uh, yes?"

"This is going to be weird, okay. You're not going crazy. I
just want you to remember that."

He frowned. "What are—"

I jumped him to Mrs. Begay's art classroom, then steadied
him when he staggered.

"—you—*what the fuck!*"

He sat down suddenly, at one of the classroom desks, and I
dropped his backpack on the desktop. "*Not* crazy."

"*What* was that?"

"Explain later, but if I can't—" The words stuck in my throat for a moment before I blurted them out. "I love you!"

I jumped away before he could react.

Back in the coffee shop, his phone and our combined papers still lay on the table. I dropped his phone into the breast pocket of my snowboarding jacket, but left the papers and my backpack. I used *my* phone to call Dad. It went straight to voice mail so he wasn't in town. Likewise Mom, though I'd talked to her briefly before walking to Krakatoa.

I left the same message on both numbers. I didn't bother telling them the time; the voice mail system would do that.

I stuffed *my* phone inside my jacket sleeve, and went down the stairs, quickly, before I could think about it too much. The traffic was brisk and I had to wait for the light.

Marius rolled down the back passenger-side window as I walked up. "Where's Joe?"

He was alone in the back seat. I could see Jason in the driver's seat, the older man I'd seen once before in this car and the one time on *that* video from the garage. He was wearing dark sunglasses and looked straight ahead, as if he was ignoring us. I tilted my head to look behind Marius and saw Calvin in the luggage compartment, squashed to one side.

Marius got louder. "Where. Is. Joe?"

"He went home," I said. "He left before you called. Where's Jade and Tara?"

In the back, Calvin lifted his arm. His fingers were threaded through Tara's hair and he held a blocky automatic pistol in his free hand, next to her face.

I inhaled sharply.

Marius said to me, "I don't believe you."

"See for yourself!" I said.

I doubted they'd snatched the girls right here on Main. It was too busy, so they probably weren't here long enough to know that Joe hadn't left by the front door.

Marius looked at Jason. Jason, without turning his head, said, "Put her in the car, then go look."

Marius climbed out of the car and held the door for me. I hesitated. Inside the car Tara cried out as Calvin did something.

Right. I climbed in.

"All the way across," Marius said.

I slid over until I was behind Jason, directly in front of Calvin.

"Put on the seatbelt," said Jason. He'd twisted his head slightly and I could see the sunglasses in the rearview mirror.

I felt Calvin's gun press against the back of my head and I nearly jumped away.

I took a deep breath and put the seatbelt on.

Marius shut the door and I saw him move briskly across the front of the car, then dash through a gap in the traffic, over to the coffee shop.

"Phone," said Jason reaching his hand back.

"Give it," Calvin said. He tapped my head suggestively with the business end of the gun.

I took Joe's phone out of the chest pocket and dropped it in Jason's hand. He glanced at it, then tossed it in the front passenger seat.

Marius was back in a minute, climbing into the backseat across from me. "Not upstairs or downstairs, and not in the restroom."

Jason grunted, then pulled out into a gap in the traffic.

"What do you want?"

Jason hung a left almost immediately, heading back through the oil field service companies.

I asked again and he said, "Shut up." He reached over into the passenger seat and flipped a plastic bag back to Marius. "Her hands." The bag held foot-long nylon cable ties.

Marius grabbed my nearest wrist and snaked a tie around it, pulling it snug. "Give me your other hand."

"Around the shoulder belt, or under?" I said. "You want me locked to the vehicle?" Hostages or not, I was going to jump away if they attempted to secure me to the entire car.

Marius looked at Jason. "Don't lock her to the seatbelt," he said.

I tried not to sigh with relief and snaked my left hand under the shoulder belt.

Marius threaded a second tie through the one around my right wrist and snugged my left wrist into my right. He let me settle back but then reached into his jacket and pulled out another blocky automatic, twin to Calvin's.

I wriggled my fingers, checking the circulation.

For a moment I thought Jason was headed for the garage/clubhouse, but he turned away from that side of town and went south, winding down through the lower foothills below town. Was he taking us out to the desert?

Instead, he turned in at the county airport, a small general-aviation facility for private planes. It had a single runway, some T-hangars, and larger maintenance hangars by the fixed-base operator's fueling station.

Flying us someplace?

He paralleled the runway, moving away from the hangars, and pulled the Hummer up to a warehouse outside the airstrip's security fence. He clicked a box clipped to his visor and a garage-style door slid up. He drove the Hummer inside.

There were no other vehicles. There were overhead skylights but the sun was low and, when the door closed behind, it was significantly darker within.

"Wait," Jason said, taking off his sunglasses. He got out and walked through a door in the far wall.

I considered moving then but the numbers still weren't right. I couldn't jump both Jade and Tara out at once, not with my hands bound. I couldn't get Calvin *and* Marius. I wanted to call Dad again. Even if he was still out of range, at least I could update our location, but Marius was watching me, the gun resting in his lap.

Jason came back through the far door, and opened my car door. He reached across and undid my seatbelt. "You give me *any* trouble, and I'm gonna come back in here and have a little party with your friends. And after a while, when they wish they was dead, we'll take care of that, too."

In the back, Tara began crying softly.

Jason looked at me to see if I'd heard him. With his sunglasses off I could see four teardrops tattooed below his right eye. He had a scar running through his left eyebrow, across his upper eyelid, and then continuing on his left cheekbone.

"It goes without sayin' that I will also mess you up."

I kept my face still and avoided his eyes.

He pulled me out of the car, his hand gripping my upper arm. "Come on." He walked me to the far door, pushed it open, and pulled me through.

There were no skylights or lights in the far room. A bit of reddish sunlight outlined a window mostly blocked by closed blinds, but my eyes weren't adjusted. I never saw the loop of wire that dropped over my head and cinched tight around my neck.

Oh, shit.

I froze. Someone had one hand against my spine, right below the wire, holding me away. I raised my bound hands toward my throat and a man's voice said, "Don't." The loop tightened enough to bite into my neck. He pulled me back and to the side, so his back was against the wall to the right of the door, I guess so nobody could come up behind him.

I dropped my hands.

Someone adjusted the blinds, letting the setting sun shine into the room and I winced and narrowed my eyes.

A woman, silhouetted against the window, said, "That's better, we can—" She stopped and took several steps closer, moving to one side to avoid blocking the light.

As my eyes adjusted I could see that she was an older woman wearing a business suit and a long red wool coat. Her graying hair was pulled back so tightly that I thought it was altering the shape of her eyebrows. She was staring at me intently.

"Oh, my," the woman said, "aren't you *just* the spitting image of your mother?"

Oh.

I'd seen her picture. Mom had shown it to me in our living room. This was the woman who'd held Dad captive for months, who had killed his NSA handler, who had escaped from prison.

Hyacinth Pope.

THIRTY-THREE

Millie: "Mayday"

Millie got the message first. She'd been dealing with some
e-mail correspondence and working at her desk in the Yukon
cabin when she wasn't downloading (Ontario) or uploading
(Lisbon). But she'd popped into the house to see what was in
that freezer before deciding what to make for supper.

Her phone made its alert chirp. She glanced at it and saw
that there was a voice mail. She wondered if Joe had asked
Cent out to dinner, but her stomach clenched when she heard
the tension in Cent's voice.

"Mayday. It's local trouble. Gang related. They've got Tara
and Jade. We're at Krakatoa, but not for long. They're driving
a black H3 Hummer with chrome spinner wheels and a custom plate: numeral 2, K, O, O, L, numeral 4, U. Too cool for
you. I'm about to be in a 'great' situation. I'm cooperating
until I can get Tara and Jade away. Could *really* use a hand.
I'll try to update my location when it changes."

She jumped to the coffee shop immediately, downstairs, in
plain site of everyone.

A woman fell away from her, gasping. "Jesus! Where did
you come from?" A man turned around and helped the woman
up off her knees. Other people looked up from their tables but
at the noise, not her arrival.

"Sorry. My fault."

Millie scanned the downstairs, then went to the window and looked outside for the Hummer. There was a large black SUV parked across the street, but it wasn't a Hummer and it didn't have chrome wheels.

She ran up the narrow flight of stairs to the balcony. There was nobody up there, but the table by the railing had cups, a backpack, and sheet of paper on it. She stepped closer and recognized the handwriting. The backpack was Cent's.

She jumped back to the Yukon, took a framed photo of Cent off her desk, jumped back to the balcony, and ran down the stairs to the baristas.

"Have you seen this girl today?"

"We see her *every* day. She ran out about ten minutes ago. I went upstairs to bus the tables and saw that she left her backpack, so she's probably coming back in a minute."

"I'm her mom. If she shows back up, tell her I took her backpack, okay?"

"Thought so. You guys really look alike."

Millie nodded and ran back up the stairs. She scooped up the papers, grabbed the backpack, and went toward the back of the balcony where the head of the stairway was. When the balcony blocked her from the view of the people below, she jumped back to the house.

"Davy!" she yelled, on the odd chance he was there, but there was no answer. She set her phone on the counter so it would it stay in the network, and jumped back to the cabin.

Davy wasn't there, either. He'd told her he was going to do some more surveillance of the Stroller and Associates compound in Costa Rica. Though Millie had a jump site for the beach town of Santa Teresa on Costa Rica's Pacific coast, she had nothing for San José in general, or the area where the compound was, northwest of the city.

There was a whiteboard in the kitchen where they wrote grocery lists and left messages to each other. She grabbed a handful of paper towels, wiped the central section clear, and wrote, *Mayday @ New Prospect House!!!*

She jumped back to the house in time to see Davy calmly lift his cell phone to his ear. "Got a voice mail."

On the chance it was more information—hopefully an updated location—she didn't say anything. She watched his face go from relaxed to tense and wide-eyed. He opened his mouth to speak and she held up her hand sharply, then ticked the info off on her fingers, staccato like.

"Hummer. Chrome wheels. Too cool for you. Krakatoa. They've got Jade and Tara. I've already been to the coffee shop. She left about twelve minutes ago. Anything else? Did she call with a new location?"

He shook his head, but was doing something with his phone.

"If you call her they'll take her phone. Going to call the police?"

"I'm getting her location."

"How?"

"I put an app on her phone. If I text a code word to the phone, it texts back a map link and coordinates. If the phone is moving, it shows the direction and speed as well." He exhaled. "It will take a minute." Then he muttered, "If her phone is still in the county."

It was on the tip of her tongue to talk about spying on his daughter, but considering the circumstances, she was really just grateful. She considered his clothes. He was dressed in tropicals, for Costa Rica. "I'll get your coat," she said.

She jumped to the cabin and grabbed their medium-weight coats—not the heavy parkas they used in the Yukon, but something good for winter in New Prospect.

He was still staring at the phone.

"Let's go to the car," she said. "Unless they just happen to be at one of our jump sites. . . ."

He nodded and vanished. She jumped to the garage and found him opening the passenger-side door. His phone chirped and he said, "Good. Got the map link. It'll take a minute to load."

The car was out on the road when he said, "South, but still moving."

"To the interstate?"

He shook his head. "I don't think so. They're not moving fast enough to be on the state road. More one of these little guys west of the state road." He tilted the phone to show her.

She stepped on the accelerator and headed down Thunderbird Road at twice the posted speed limit, keeping her eye open for pedestrians, cars, and patches of ice.

Davy kept his eye glued to the phone, texting the code word again. In a carefully mild voice he said, "If you crash the car, we won't be able to get to her, even if we jump out of the car before impact."

Millie snarled, "Find her! Leave the driving to me."

She took the next right, a commercial road running in the right direction, and ran two yellow lights in succession.

"The airport. Looks like they're headed for the airport."

"We have an airport?"

"Private, I guess, but they could still fly her out."

She ran a red light fifty feet in front of a cross bound semi. The driver honked angrily, but the truck was already far behind.

Davy didn't say anything.

THIRTY-FOUR

"What were you thinking?"

With the loop of wire securely around my neck, Jason let go of my arm. "So, this is the one? The boys said it was someone bigger."

Hyacinth glanced at him and then back at me. "Probably her father, though the flying stuff is new. I have my doubts about that."

Jason snorted. "Yeah. Crazy stuff. But I can tell Dmitri you got what you wanted?"

Hyacinth nodded. "So far. The finder's fee will be paid. But don't go away. She's only the start."

Jason frowned. "Dmitri didn't say anything about *more*."

Hyacinth smiled. "Call him. Tell him to talk to Mr. Fowler. There will be compensation."

"Huh." Jason took out his phone and stepped out the door, closing it behind him.

There was a moan from the corner and I tried to turn my head.

"Don't!" the man behind me said, tightening the wire.

Hyacinth pulled something from her coat pocket, but I couldn't even see it until she tilted it and it caught the light.

"Steel guitar strings. Very strong. Very thin. Available *everywhere*. These are D strings. A great compromise between strength and cutting." She smiled. "I don't know if you can do what your father can, but try it and you've got a good chance of leaving your head behind. Okay, so it may not be *complete* decapitation, but it will, at the very least, crush your larynx and cut your carotid arteries."

She walked closer. "Let's say you *can't* jump. If your dad or mom grabs you and tries to jump away, the result is going to be the same." She flipped a switch by the door and overhead fluorescents came on. "You wanted to see who was moaning?"

Caffeine was in the corner, though it took me a moment to recognize her. It was her voice, whimpering when the light went on, that let me identify her. I couldn't tell from my usual clue, her black roots, 'cause there was enough blood in her hair that I had trouble even seeing the blonde part. She was duct taped to a metal folding chair. Where her face wasn't bloody, it was purple.

"Why'd you do that?" I blurted out.

"You think *we* did that?" Hyacinth shook her head. "No, no. This was Jason's work. Apparently he has a very strict no-termination policy. Caffeine wanted to quit her employment. She was in this condition when Jenkins and I arrived."

The man behind me sighed and said, "No names."

Hyacinth shrugged. "Right. Sorry." She walked over to Caffeine. "Now, the young lady was *very* responsive to *our* questions. She doesn't know if you can jump or not, but she did talk about some specific encounters that make me suspicious." She narrowed her eyes. "But you aren't the big man they said took them to the pit."

She walked back to me. "It wasn't the reports of teleporting that got me here so fast. My, umm, *employers* have offered that reward for info for years. They've gotten reports from everywhere, from all sorts of gangs and syndicates and cartels. It's the drugs, I think. People sell drugs, they do drugs. They see things. We kept following leads and they came to nothing."

She leaned closer, studying my face some more. "It's really uncanny. You're almost like a clone of her. Except the nose."

I've got my father's nose.

"We scrambled the jet when we heard the description of the *pit*. No one has ever described *that* before. *That* got my attention." She gestured toward the other room. "When the boys talked about being dropped into the water," she shuddered, "that struck a chord. Your dad is very fond of that one."

It runs in the family.

"So, can you jump?"

I didn't say anything.

She raised her hand like she was going to hit me.

I ignored her hand and looked at her eyes.

Her raised hand visibly shook, like she was restraining herself. She shook her head, and lowered the hand, then reached into her coat and pulled a zippered nylon case from an inside pocket. When she opened it, I saw capped hypodermic needles and drug vials.

Oh, shit.

"We'll find out, soon enough. We learned a lot from your father, but he pulled that trick at the end, with the water. They didn't see *that* coming."

She took the cap off one of the hypodermics, inverted a vial, and stabbed up through the membrane in the cap. "Can *you* do anything special like that?"

You will not use me to control my parents, I thought. *Even if it kills me.*

I said, "Just watch, Miss Minchin."

She froze, her mouth open, her eyes slightly wider.

I jumped in place, adding twenty miles an hour velocity, straight back into Jenkins, the man holding the wire. Sheetrock exploded around us as we slammed through the wall, then tumbled across the floor of the main warehouse.

My back screamed where his hand had been pushing against my spine, but I could move. When I rolled over and pushed up onto my hands and knees, the wire was not tight across my neck.

I clawed at it with my still-bound hands and the loop loosened enough that I could pull it over my head. I flung it away from me and its wooden handle clattered across the floor.

Jenkins was sprawled in scraps of Sheetrock, unmoving. His left forearm bent unnaturally, like he had an extra elbow.

Hyacinth was staring through the gap in the wall, then she charged forward, ducking through it, the hypodermic held in her hand like a dagger, thumb poised on the plunger.

You're too late, Miss Minchin.

I dropped forward onto my elbows and, as she approached, jumped in place, adding a modest ten miles per hour toward her. My hip slammed into her shins and she flipped over onto the concrete floor, arms first, followed by her head. Almost like an afterthought, I heard the hypodermic syringe smash against one of the loading-bay doors at the far end of the room.

I stared back at her, looking for any movement, but she was as still as Jenkins. I considered the possibility that she'd broken her neck.

Then I tried to get up and considered the possibility that I'd broken *my* neck.

I hurt. My back hurt. When I lifted both hands to touch my neck it stung, and when I looked at my fingertips, they were bloody. The wire had cut me, but obviously not fatally. There was a lump on the back of my head where it had connected with Jenkins jaw.

"I *warned* you!"

It was Jason. He was standing beside the Hummer with a gun held toward me sideways, gangsta style. Marius and Calvin pulled Jade and Tara out of the rear hatch and down to their knees. Like me, the girls still had their hands secured with cable ties. Marius and Calvin were holding them by the hair, guns pressed against the girls' temples.

Dammit.

I wondered what Marius or Calvin would do if I jumped Jason away. The trouble was, they could flinch and shoot either girl. I could move one or the other gun away from the girls' heads, but not both, not at the same time.

In my sleeve, my phone vibrated, a single pulse. I shook both arms until the unit slipped down, out of the sleeve, and dropped onto the floor by my knee, face up. It showed a text message from Mom, upside down but I could read it.

INCOMING.

Mom and Dad must have started swinging before they even jumped.

The first Marius or Calvin knew of their presence was when the bones in their gun hands broke as the baseball bats knocked the hands and guns away from the girls' heads. To me it looked like the guns smashed into the floor and *then* Mom and Dad were standing there, Mom with a shiny red-anodized aluminum bat, Dad with a beat-up thirty-three-inch Louisville Slugger. In maple.

I knew that bat.

Calvin fell back, releasing Tara, clutching his hand and screaming.

Though Marius's gun was now a good ten feet away, he didn't let go of Jade's hair with his good hand.

Mom pivoted, raising the aluminum bat, but before she swung, Jade twisted and brought both fists up into Marius's crotch.

He doubled over, gagging. Tara staggered up from her kneeling position and kneed him in the butt, knocking him forward. Marius tried to catch himself with his good hand, curling the injured hand close to his chest, but he ended up smashing down onto his shoulder and rolling over onto his side, knees curled up, good hand cradling the injured.

Jason, eyes wide, started to swing his gun around, toward the girls, toward Mom.

Dad appeared beside him.

On the way down, Dad's bat did to Jason's forearm, what I'd done to Jenkins's. On the way back up I suspect it broke Jason's jaw.

Saw that coming.

Don't threaten Mom when Dad is around.

Dad's eyes were wide and his head was swiveling back and forth, looking for something else to hit.

I almost jumped back to Jade and Tara, but controlled the impulse and limped over instead. They were both standing by the time I got there. Like me, they were still bound at the wrists.

Mom was gathering up the guns, ejecting the clips, then working the slide to eject the round in the barrel. She put them on the hood of the Hummer, then turned to us, but angled so she could also watch Marius and Calvin. I noticed she and Dad were wearing blue nitrile rubber gloves.

I held up my cable-tied wrists. "Little help?" Mom nodded and stepped behind the Hummer. When she came back she had a pair of kitchen shears. Snip, snip, snip, and then all three of us were rubbing our wrists.

Tara threw her arms around Jade. "Oh, God."

I stepped closer to Mom. "We need an ambulance." She looked at me, Jade, then Tara. I shook my head then pointed at the hole in the wall. "In there. Jason beat Caffeine half to death."

Mom leaned closer and pulled my jacket open, her eyes widening as she looked at my neck. "What happened to your neck?"

"It's okay. Guitar string garrote. To keep me from ju—" I stopped, licked my lips. "To keep me in one place."

Mom's eyes hardened and her grip tightened on the bat. She pointed at Jason and said, "Was it him?"

I shook my head and pointed at Jenkins's still form between us and the hole in the wall. "It was him and that woman over there—"

From across the room Dad's voice said, "Son of a bitch, it's—"

And we both said, "—Hyacinth Pope."

"You are the spitting image of your mother!"

I was *really* getting tired of hearing that.

Rebecca Martingale looked more like someone's grandmother than an FBI agent. Mom fetched her from DC, though not in front of the girls. As far as Jade and Tara were concerned, Mom had walked outside and returned ten minutes later with the older woman.

It was Agent Martingale who did a quick physical assessment on the suspects (breathing with regular pulse) and then called 911.

Tara asked Dad the question I'd been holding in my head.

"How did you find us, Mr. Ross?"

Dad looked a *little* calmer. He'd frisked Jenkins and Hyacinth Pope for weapons, adding multiple handguns to the pile on the hood of the Hummer. Agent Martingale had used her one set of handcuffs to secure Marius and Calvin, the only two conscious suspects, to each other at the ankle, staying away from their swelling hands. Dad still stood where he could watch Jenkins and Hyacinth Pope and Jason, his bat resting on his shoulder.

"I texted the phone locator app on Cent's phone. If you send the right code word, it returns GPS coordinates. I had to do it several times because you were still moving."

"You spying bastard!" I said, and hugged him.

He squeezed back hard, kissing my hair.

The first siren sounded in the distance.

Dad let go. "Time, Cent."

Mom was standing to the side lightly swinging her aluminum bat. She handed it to Agent Martingale. "In case you need to persuade anyone. Without shooting them, that is."

I ran across to the passenger side of the Hummer. Besides Joe's phone, I found Tara's and Jade's there, too. I scooped them all up and ran back. I passed them their phones, then held up Joe's. "Give this to Joe?"

Tara took it. "Why can't you?"

"We have to go."

"What? Why?" said Tara.

I pointed at Hyacinth Pope. "The people who sent them have been after my parents for years. And they won't stop coming. And they threaten anyone close to them, just like Jason did, to try and get to them."

And now me.

Jade blinked. "Uh, should we say you weren't here?"

Agent Martingale cleared her throat. "I didn't hear that."

Mom shook her head. "Tell the truth to the police. And in court, if you have to testify."

"I'm sorry," I said.

"For leaving?" Tara asked.

"For getting you involved in this." The sirens were getting louder and I saw that Dad was getting more and more antsy. I hugged Tara and then Jade.

"Won't the police see you leave?" Jade asked.

Mom shook her head. "Hope not."

We went through the hole in the wall to the office, stepped off to the side, and jumped away.

Dad helped me clear the books out of the New Prospect bedroom while Mom kept an eye out upstairs, jumping from window to window, looking for any sign of *them*.

We finished the books and shelves, then started on our clothes and some of Dad's specialty cookware.

I took a moment to empty my school locker. It was dark outside and only a few lights were on in the school as the custodial staff moved from classroom to classroom, cleaning. I thought how much trouble it had been just walking through the crowded hallways and teared up.

I dragged my shirt sleeve across my eyes and jumped the last of my school supplies back to the cabin before returning to the house.

Dad and I were looking at some of the downstairs furniture, wondering if it was worth moving to the warehouse, when Mom called down the stairs, "Police unit in the driveway!"

Dad jumped away, probably upstairs to where Mom was looking out the window.

I took the ceramic box off the top of my dresser and tucked it under my arm.

Were they looking for us as material witnesses or as felons? Victim of kidnap or assault with a deadly baseball bat?

Didn't matter. We left before they knocked on the door.

I sat on one of the couches before the cabin's fireplace and waited for the inquisition.

Dad, standing with his back to the flames, began with, "What were you *thinking*?"

"Objection," I said. "Counsel's question is vague and ambiguous."

Dad's eyebrows drew down but before he exploded, Mom said, "Why don't we find out what actually happened before we start getting into cognitive philosophy?" She was sitting on the other couch.

Dad opened his mouth and then shut it with a click. He turned his hand over, palm up, toward her, then interlaced his fingers.

Mom pointed to the couch beside her. "Sit. You're looming."

Dad rolled his eyes and slumped down onto the cushions, his hands shoved into his pockets.

Mom looked at me and raised her eyebrows.

"Where should I start?"

Mom said, "How about the first time you jumped in front of somebody who isn't in this room?"

"Ah."

It had really started with Caffeine, in PE, that first day of school, and, since everything else had really followed from that, I started there.

Dad muttered, "*First* day of school."

Mom elbowed him. "What should she have done? Taken a beating?"

Dad said, "She could have *told* us about it!"

I shook my head. "No, I couldn't. You would have pulled us out of town in a New York minute. And then I would have to go off and find another school on my own. Without you."

Mom intervened. "I want to know *what* happened. Not what *could* have happened. Shush." She gestured for me to continue.

I told them about shifting a foot to the right when Caffeine had attacked me in the cafeteria after I joined the snowboard club. Dad wasn't actually upset about that. "Good call," he said. "They just saw you move really fast. Their minds filled in the interval."

Then I told them about being adopted by the three freshmen, when Caffeine was suspended, and the incident in the alley, where I'd pretended to take the picture of them assaulting Dakota and Tony. "I did jump to keep ahead of them, but never where they could see."

"But you made an enemy," said Dad.

Mom corrected, "She was *already* Cent's enemy." She looked over her glasses at me. "This didn't help, though."

"I asked the boys why they didn't go the cops. Dakota let slip about a video, but they clammed up and wouldn't say anything more, so I left. But when *they* left I was watching. I followed them." In for a penny, in for a pound. I told them about decoying Caffeine away from Dakota and Caffeine's resulting fender bender.

"They didn't know that was *me*, though," I said, trying to justify it.

Dad's expression made it clear he wasn't buying.

"Next time was when they came after me in the girl's locker room. They were after my phone. They thought I'd really taken that picture."

Mom raised her eyebrows. "Oh, *that* was part of all this?" She'd talked to Dr. Morgan about the incident.

"Yeah. Caffeine led them. I didn't know their names, then. While the boys tried to flank me around some lockers, I pointed behind Caffeine. When she turned, I jumped closer. When she turned back, I was *right* there," I held up my hand an inch away from my nose, "and it scared the crap out of her. I ran past her, then Coach Teichert took over. But nobody *saw* me jump."

Dad muttered, "A distinction without meaning."

Mom elbowed him again.

"Caffeine upped the pressure on the freshmen, then. Tony ended up with a broken nose. Dakota ended up with a broken finger. No witnesses. They said they *fell down*. That's when I talked to Grant, trying to find out why the boys wouldn't testify, and he'd said he'd talk to me *if* I went out with him."

"So that's why you went on that date," Mom said. "No wonder you were sure it was just *practice*."

"While we were still at The Brass, Hector and Calvin came after Grant and me. I jumped in place, adding speed, and shoved Grant into them, like bowling. Didn't jump away, though. We walked out of The Brass while they were still picking themselves up. I convinced Grant that he'd done most of the leaping and I had just pushed a bit."

Mom asked, "Did you find out what was on the video?"

"Videos. Yeah. I found out most of it. Didn't find the last little bit, until later."

"So what was it?" Dad asked.

I looked at Mom, then back to Dad. I was already blushing, I could feel it in my ears. I took a deep breath, then said, "Sex, Dad. Caffeine seduced each of them and recorded it."

Mom nodded, like she'd figured this out already.

"Oh." Dad frowned. "Just sex, though?"

I looked down at the carpet. "Some of it was, uh, outside the normative range."

Dad's eyebrows went up.

"Do you really want your *sixteen-year-old daughter* to be more explicit?" I pointed at myself.

Dad blushed. "S'okay."

I moved on. "Uh, right. Next time was when Marius came after me at the coffee shop. I was walking up the stairs and he was walking down. He tried to knock me backward, with his shoulder. That time I jumped past him, a few steps up. He fell down the stairs. Nobody saw me jump."

"*Marius* saw," said Dad.

I shrugged. "Maybe. As you said, the mind fills in gaps. Maybe he thought I dodged him. Well, I *did* dodge him, but maybe he thought I just twisted around him."

Mom looked as angry as Jade had. "He was going to push you down the stairs? Backward?" Her hands clenched.

"He went down the stairs pretty hard." I smiled. "Also, you

hit him with a *baseball bat*, Mom. Broke his hand, I'm pretty sure."

She looked over to where Dad's bat leaned in the corner. "He has *other* bones."

"I got revenge on him. The whole gang was waiting for me the next morning at the edge of the woods, on that path that leads from the house to the school grounds. I armored up, covered my face, and then threw Marius, Calvin, and Hector into a snow-filled gully down the hill. I covered their heads with lentil bags first. Caffeine ran away, freaked. I was wearing a coat over the armor and they thought I was bigger—a guy. Then I did a quick change into a skirt and got back to school within minutes. Almost as fast as Caffeine. That confused 'em.

"They may have had their suspicions of me, but now they thought there was someone else." I looked at Dad. "Hyacinth Pope thought the someone else was you."

Dad said, "Huh. So, when did they go after you again?"

I licked my lips. "Next time, I went after them."

"Why?" It was Mom this time. "What were you *thinking*?" She blinked and covered her mouth with her hand.

Dad laughed. "Uh, gotta agree with that. Why?"

I told them about Tony's suicide attempt and the smile dropped off Dad's face.

"I didn't jump into the ER, though. Carried him. Left before they got my name or a good video. Grant told me they were still trying to figure that out."

"Perhaps it was time for an anonymous call to the police?" said Mom. "About Caffeine and her activities?"

"And have the video come out? Tony already tried to kill himself once, thinking it would."

"So you went after the video." Dad didn't ask, he stated.

"Indirectly. First I scared the shit out of Caffeine."

"Even more than you had?" said Mom.

"Yeah." I described dropping the boys into the water in the pit, leaving the splashes of fake blood behind. "But the pit was a mistake," I said.

"Why?" Dad asked. "Someone didn't drown, did they?"

"No. It was their description of the pit that let Hyacinth know that *this* report was on target. Apparently *they* have a standing reward for information, and various organizations and gangs know about it. Fortunately, they report a lot of false positives."

Mom and Dad exchanged glances.

"I wiped Caffeine's computer and backup drive and her thumb drives and I deleted her net storage accounts. I *think* I got all the copies of the videos. I *know* I put the fear of God into her, telling her to leave them alone, delete any other copies she had, and stop selling drugs. Then I let them all go."

Mom nodded. "Certainly."

The corners of my mouth wrenched down. *"I didn't know Jason would do that to her!"*

Mom moved over beside me on the couch and put her arm around me. "Shhhhhhh. Of course you couldn't know that."

"Dad would've known!" I said.

Dad looked away. "Not necessarily."

Mom pulled me closer. "You already saved Tony's life *once*. Maybe twice, by going after the video. Also, you didn't beat Caffeine bloody, did you? That was Jason."

"You're not responsible for the evil others do," Dad said. "I never killed anyone, but people have died because of some of my actions. Not by my hand directly, but . . . people have died."

Mom looked over at him. "And hundreds have lived who would not. Thousands perhaps, if you count relief efforts." Mom let me sit back up but stayed close, her arm still around my shoulders.

I got my breathing back under control, "When it went down, today, I jumped Joe from the coffee shop to the school."

Dad sighed. "Of course." He no longer sounded angry, just resigned.

"They called me using Tara's phone. Joe and I were still at Krakatoa, but they'd grabbed Jade and Tara as they were walking home. Marius wanted *both* Joe and me to come down and get in the Hummer but I wasn't going to hand them *another* hostage. That's when I called you guys.

"You know everything else."

Dad shook his head. "Not everything." He touched his own neck. "Mom told me about the garrote. How'd they get that on you?"

"It was dark. Jason was taking me into another room. I thought it would be a great opportunity to remove him from the equation, then go after Calvin and Marius. I didn't even see the wire until I felt it tighten around my neck. It was that guy who came with Hyacinth Pope. Jenkins."

Mom shook her head. "That's a new technique. We'll have to watch out for it. How did you get out of it?"

"I did the jump in place thing. Added velocity right into him—the same direction he'd pull from. Broke his forearm and knocked him through the wall."

Dad's eyes went wide. "*That's* what that hole was?"

I nodded. "I was getting desperate. Hyacinth was loading up a hypodermic, probably to knock me out." I reached up and touched the scab on my neck. "Jenkins never got a chance to pull on the wire, but it twisted around a bit as we went though the wall. More abrasion than compression."

Mom said, "We heard you go through the wall. We'd already peeked in through the skylights by then. What did you do to Hyacinth?"

I told them about accelerating through her legs when she ran after me with the hypo. "I was worried about her neck. Do you think I broke it?"

Dad shrugged. "Don't know." From the look on his face, he could have easily added, "Don't care."

Mom saw the look on my face and said, "We'll talk to Agent Martingale and find out."

I exhaled. "So, *now* you know everything."

Two day later, Mom got Agent Martingale's status report.

They couldn't hold the pilot they found in the charter jet parked over at the airport. He worked for the charter company. They made a note of the company that had leased it, though.

They held Mr. Sidney Jenkins on weapons charges. He did not have a local permit and his prints were all over both the handguns Dad removed from his person.

Hyacinth was also good for weapons charges, compounded by her status as a fugitive convicted felon. There was no question about holding her.

Jason, Calvin, and Marius were held for kidnapping with Tara and Jade as initial witnesses, but the most damning witness ended up being Caffeine. Additional charges resulted from the over fifty pounds of marijuana and the several thousand caps of ecstasy found in the office where Caffeine had been tortured. Oh yeah, kidnapping and grievous bodily harm and conspiracy to commit murder.

There was no way Jason was going to release Caffeine in the end.

As I suspected, Jason's jaw was broken as well as his radius and ulna. Marius had breaks in one carpal and two metacarpals. Calvin had two phalanges and one metacarpal broken.

Mr. Jenkins regained consciousness shortly after we left. Like Jason, both bones in Jenkins's forearm were broken. He also had a bump on the back of his head where he'd clipped a stud going through the wall, as well as various related bruises.

Hyacinth had a hairline fracture of her third cervical vertebra, and a concussion. They had considered opening her skull to relieve pressure but her CT scans showed very minor swelling and she regained consciousness after six hours.

Caffeine, whose injuries looked the worst, had no broken bones. She had trouble sleeping, though, waking with screaming nightmares. This got worse when she found out Jason was in the same hospital, though under guard.

They moved her into the secure unit of psychiatric where she felt safer, being locked in.

Mom reported that, in Agent Martingale's opinion, "The tranquilizers probably helped, too. And she met someone she knew there in the ward, who was helping her adjust."

"Really?" I asked, absently. Then I sat up abruptly and said, "Oh my God. Tony?"

"Yes. Tony."

I climbed into bed and stayed there.

It was easy. It was dark inside and dark outside with heavy spring snows. And I *was* sore, but that went away pretty quickly. Mom would bring me a tray, kiss me on the cheek, and, thankfully, leave me alone.

On the third day Dad stuck his head in and I covered my face with the pillow.

He didn't take the hint, pulling the pillow away.

"Really, you want to hear this."

I opened one eye. "What?" I opened the other eye and pushed up on my elbows.

"I got an e-mail from Mr. Aniketa at HFW."

"Who? What's HFW?"

"Hunger Free World. They're the Japanese NGO that Ramachander works for. Mr. Aniketa is his boss."

I sat up, eyebrows raised. "Is? As in? . . .

"He showed up in Bhangura this morning."

"Squeezed?" I said.

"Yes, initially. But mostly they just held him, probably to see if we'd come looking, so he got to sleep a lot and, uh, heal. Finally they put him on a passenger ferry and faded."

"Heal? What do you mean, heal? What did they do to him?"

Dad didn't say anything.

"Was it like Caffeine? Did they beat him half to death?"

Dad looked away. "He'll be okay. Stay away from him, though. Just like your friends from school, they are probably still watching him. I mean it—it's as much for his sake as yours."

I covered my face with the pillow. "Understood."

Dad's muffled voice said, "Good."

After he left I tried to regain the advanced level of lumpitude I'd managed for the last three days, but it wasn't working.

I kept seeing Ramachandra's face, bloody and bruised, like

Caffeine's. I kept doing math problems in my head or revising the thesis statement for my midterm humanities essay. I was wondering if Jade and Tara were back in school and what had happened to Hector.

And I wondered what Joe was thinking.

Then I was picturing Joe, beaten and bruised, like Caffeine.

I got up, took a shower, and under the hot running water, cried.

THIRTY-FIVE

Davy: "Tea and Sympathy"

Millie was in the kitchen, pouring water from the electric kettle into a tea pot. "Still keeps to her room?"

Davy kicked the counter baseboard. "Yes. I chided her for it and she said, 'It gives such an elegance to misfortune!'" He smiled briefly. "I thought she was doing better, quoting Austen like that, but it just sets her off again. Apparently Joe likes Austen, too."

Millie sighed. "Tea?"

"No." He glared at the icicles visible through the window. More gently he said, "No, thank you."

Millie smiled briefly, and got down a mug for herself. "You told her about Rama?"

"Not everything."

"Really? I thought you were going to use it? You said you were."

Davy kicked the baseboard again. "Yeah. I couldn't. She guessed he was messed up already. She thought it was on the lines of what Jason did to Caffeine." He sat down at the table, but couldn't settle, rising again. "Telling her won't bring his eye back."

Millie winced. "No, I guess not."

"I wish she'd go do something!"

Millie nodded. "Physical activity would be good for her. Snowboarding, maybe?"

"I made that mistake. She started crying."

"Oh. Joe. The team."

"Yeah."

"I can't *make* her do anything."

"No. Even if she couldn't jump away from you, you shouldn't."

"It almost makes me wish for the days when she'd yell at me because I *wouldn't* let her go to school."

Millie shook her head.

Davy said, "You know, if I'd let her go to school before she discovered she could jump, she might never have been in this mess."

Millie snorted. "I was waiting for that. It's clearly all *your* fault. I especially like how you arranged for Caffeine to seduce the three freshmen. That was *particularly* clever. *I* would never know how to accomplish that."

"Don't be ridiculous," he said, half amused, half annoyed.

"También, mi amor."

He deflated, sitting back down at the table.

"I feel so *helpless.*"

She sighed and took another mug from the cabinet.

"Have some tea."

THIRTY-SIX

Cent: "Imaginary Girlfriend"

Mom and Dad didn't play fair.

If they'd forbidden me from ever seeing Joe again, told me never to visit Jade and Tara, I would have gone to them immediately. Mom and Dad didn't even mention the people who'd been injured, or the potential for injury to others.

It would have been redundant. I couldn't even think about the guys without seeing Caffeine's face, bloody and bruised.

I guess you could say *life* didn't play fair.

I walked a great deal, mostly in the desert in West Texas. It was meaningless that this was closer to New Prospect than the Yukon. After all, for me, New Prospect was milliseconds away no matter where I was. I wasn't separated by space and time.

The separation was an act of will harder to overcome than mere distance.

I remembered that Dad had walked here after he'd lost his mother. This was where he'd done his grieving but I didn't know whether this thought helped *me* or not.

Would it be any less painful if my friends, if Joe, were dead? It was almost *more* painful that I *could* be with them, at our regular table at Krakatoa, in a heartbeat.

By agreement, whenever I left the cabin, I scribbled my

destination on the whiteboard in the kitchen. It would've made me furious if they'd insisted, but it hadn't been like that. Mom and Dad had started doing it anytime they left the cabin, along with when they expected to return, and they *asked* me to do it, too.

Not told.

So of course I had to.

That's how Dad knew where to find me, walking along a mostly-fallen, rusted barbed wire fence that had stopped being an effective barrier sometime in the middle of the previous century.

"Hey."

"Hey."

He handed me a water bottle, still cold from the refrigerator in the Yukon, and walked along beside me.

I was irritated and I made up my mind to jump away if he said anything, but he didn't. He was just there, not even looking at me, but at the desert around us, seemingly lost in thought. My irritation gradually faded and I realized I was glad he was there.

I finally broke the silence. "Are you thinking about Grandmother?"

Dad looked back at me, almost surprised, as if he'd forgotten I was there. He raised his eyebrows. "No. About *your* mother, actually. Not mine."

"Oh. I thought . . ." I waved my hand vaguely at the ocotillo, gravel, and creosote bush.

"I was thinking about *that* same time, yeah. Did you know your mother had broken up with me right before I found out my mother had died?"

I blinked. "No."

"Your mother didn't know about my jumping, yet. I hadn't *lied*, exactly, but because I hadn't told her everything, I'd certainly misled her. When she found out she was furious."

Dad glanced sideways at me and away. He looked *embarrassed*.

"I'd done this thing—helped a New York neighbor get away from her abusive husband—but he was a cop and it brought me to their attention." He laughed humorlessly. "Do you see the irony?"

I thought about it. "Like me helping Grant, Tony, and Dakota. Or the *chukri* girls. Unintended consequences."

"Yeah. Anyway, when I was out here back then, I wasn't just thinking about my mom's death. I was thinking about your mom, too. Thinking I would never see her again.

"Hard to say which hurt more or even where one hurt stopped and the other began."

The desert blurred and I blinked moisture away from my eyes.

It's not like I can say he doesn't understand.

"I miss Joe," I said. The feeling in my chest, of incipient sobs, waited, just below the surface.

Tentatively he said, "You only went out a few times."

That nearly made me jump away. I stopped and turned my back to him and took a deep breath. When I turned, I could tell he regretted saying it, but I went on. "Are you trying to tell me what I feel doesn't matter? I know what *Mom* would say about that."

"True." He shook his head ruefully. "I'm afraid I come by it honestly. Back when I made the mistake of sharing my feelings with my father, he would do much the same thing—though, I suspect, without as good a motive. He did get better, at the end, though. Maybe there's hope for me."

I glared at him.

"No excuses, ma'am," he added.

I don't know why that should've made me laugh, but it did, and the threat of tears died down. "You're an evil man."

He nodded, and we resumed walking.

I kept expecting him to talk about the danger of trying to see Joe or Jade and Tara, but he didn't. Instead he showed me some coyote tracks in an arroyo and pointed out a long-limbed black-tailed jackrabbit stretching up to eat leaves from a sagebrush.

"What were you going to do, when you thought you'd never see Mom again?"

Dad frowned. "I'm not exactly sure. I wasn't that in touch with my feelings back then. Mostly I was numb." He gestured at a ledge in the side of the arroyo, like a bench eight feet off the ground, then jumped there to sit on it. He patted the stone beside him.

I joined him. The stone had been in the sun all afternoon and was much warmer than the air. It felt good against my legs as I leaned against Dad.

"I had started work on the Eyrie, and the physical labor helped a bit. But it was hard. I was solitary before I met your mother and it seemed probable that I would go back to that when I was done."

"Done with the Eyrie?"

"No. I thought I'd go back *to* the Eyrie when I was done finding my mother's killers. I was thinking of it as my hermitage—going back to being solitary. But your mother reached out to me and we got back together."

I blurted, "Joe can hardly reach out to me. We didn't break up! I don't think he's angry about my keeping my secret, 'cause I don't *know*!"

Dad put his arm around me and I glanced at his face. The corners of his mouth were hooked sharply down and there were tears in his eyes.

I'd been able to hold it together against my own sadness, but his proved too much. The sobs broke free, and I curled in on myself and cried and cried.

And Dad cried with me.

Dad jumped me to the cabin hallway, held my arm while I stumbled into my room and sat on the edge of the bed. He helped me off with my boots, and I fell back onto the pillows. He kissed me and pulled a comforter over me.

The sobs had stopped, but not the tears, and I lay there, angry with myself, with my helplessness, but unable or unwilling to move.

I heard Mom and him talking in their room but I couldn't make it out. At one point Mom's voice raised almost to a shout and then they moved the conversation downstairs.

They rarely raised their voices with each other and, even if they did, it was more likely to be Dad than Mom. Mom was the calm, reasonable one.

At some point I really did fall asleep because I awoke to find the lights out. I was hungry. I was miserable, but still hungry, so I went downstairs.

Mom was on the couch before a crackling fire of piñon logs. She stood when I came down the stairs. "There's food."

"What kind?"

"Oxtail."

"Mmmm."

She pointed at the couch. "I'll bring you a bowl."

She cooks it all day long so the meat is tender and the broth rich, then makes fresh gnocchi before serving. I don't know how long it had been waiting for me but it was as good as ever.

I was not quite as miserable after I'd eaten.

"Where's Dad?" I felt guilty for breaking down like I had, for causing him to cry.

Mom said, "He had to go talk to someone."

I picked up my bowl and got up. Mom made an abortive grab for it, but I was already standing. "Need some water. Do you want some water?"

Mom looked undecided, her mouth open without speaking, but then she shrugged. "Put on the kettle, please."

I went into the kitchen and did that, and got spring water for myself, from the tap. I took a gulp and my eyes strayed to the whiteboard.

My last destination, *Desert near the pit*, and ETA, *back by dinner*, had been wiped through, though you could make out the faint lettering of the dry-erase marker still. Mom's *Warehouse* and *back by three* PM were also imperfectly erased. Dad's line, by contrast, was dark and fresh. *New Prospect, back by 9.*

I blinked. *New Prospect*?

"Mom! What the hell is Dad doing in New Prospect?"

I sloshed water out of my glass and it fell, soaking cold, onto my sock.

Mom sighed and I realized she hadn't been thinking about what she wanted to drink. She'd known that I'd see the whiteboard if I went into the kitchen and she'd been trying to decide if she should keep me from seeing it.

I went back to the living room.

"Now, Cent—"

"If you don't tell me, I'm going to go find out for myself!"

"I'm going to tell you!" she said quickly.

I came back down off my toes.

More slowly, Mom said, "Sit down."

I sat down at the end of the couch, took off my wet sock, and threw it down onto the hot hearth where it steamed and sputtered.

"Don't blame me," Mom said, "if that catches fire."

"Stop trying to put me off." I stretched out my foot and raked the sock away from the fire. *What is Dad doing there?*

Mom took a deep breath. "He's talking to Joe."

My jaw dropped open. After a moment I said, "Why?" Then, "Doesn't that put Joe in danger?"

She nodded. "Yes. Your father and I quarreled about that. But he said you deserved as much of a chance as we did. Your father and I, that is."

"A chance for what?"

Mom looked away. In a barely audible voice she said, "Happiness."

Something flickered in the corner of the room and we both turned our head. Dad was there.

He was not alone.

I thought I was all cried out.

I probably terrified him, first by jumping across the living room to right in front of him, then by sobbing into his shoulder. But, except for flinching as I appeared in front of him, he took it well.

"Shhhh," Joe said, squeezing back, stroking my hair with his hand.

"We'll be upstairs," Dad said. I didn't hear them leave, but when I finally looked up from Joe's shoulder, we were alone before the fire.

"What did he tell you?" I asked.

"That you were an irritation of the spirit and—"

I filled in the rest, "—a great deal of trouble."

He nodded and pulled me back and kissed me. When we separated for air, he said, "But for all that, he said you were probably worth knowing—if I was willing to put up with the danger of being killed or tortured."

"That part was no joke!" I said.

Joe said, "I agree. You're worth knowing."

"Not *that* part!"

"Your dad did not joke about the danger. He gave several examples, in fact." Joe shuddered and tapped his own chest below the collarbone.

"He showed you the scars?"

Joe nodded.

"I'm sorry."

"I'll get therapy," he said.

"You heard about Caffeine?"

Again he nodded.

"People have *died*. They've been after my dad for over twenty-five years, after Mom and Dad since before I was born, and now they're after *me*."

"Your dad told me, Cent. He was *really* discouraging. It was like a gangster movie. 'Nice little relationship you have there. Shame if anything *happened* to it.'"

"I don't want you to get hurt!"

He put his arms back around me. "Shhh. I don't want to *be* hurt. Though it sure hurt when you disappeared like that. Thought I was batshit crazy."

"I *told* you up front you weren't!"

"Well that's what did it, of course. You put it in my head in the *first* place," he said. "I spent the last week wondering if you were *ever* there or if you were a figment of my imagination." He kissed me. "At least your house was still there, though there's police tape across the doors." He shook his head. "Police tape! I was really angry, you know, when I found out where you went."

"After I jumped you to school?"

"Yeah."

"Tara and Jade tell you?"

"They told me as much as they saw."

"Why were you angry? 'Cause of the last thing I said?"

"*That* I liked. No, it was because Tara heard Marius tell you that he wanted *both of us* down in the car. I would've helped, you know. I'm not *useless*."

I nodded. "I know."

"But? . . ."

"You already know the answer," I said.

He shrugged. "Maybe. Tell me anyway."

"It's the *same* thing. Why I didn't take you with me then. Why I *should* say goodbye now. I know you're not stupid. That's one of the things I love about you."

He sighed. "*He that hath wife and children hath given hostages to fortune . . .*"

"Or 'she.' It was scary enough, with Tara and Jade in their hands. I did not want them to have my *heart* as well."

He breathed out, "Your heart."

I looked away.

He stood up and put his back to the fire.

"Do I have a say in this?"

I shrugged.

"It's my risk, too, right?"

"It's nearly *all* your risk. *I* can jump away."

"Then let me have some of the decision."

I frowned.

"They already took away your childhood. Are you going to let them take this—" He reached out and put his hand against my cheek. "—too?"

"We would have to be *extraordinarily* careful."

He nodded.

"You couldn't even tell Lany."

He nodded again.

"It would be as if I were your imaginary girlfriend, just as you said. A figment of your imagination."

He smiled slightly. "Should I have a cover girlfriend in New Prospect? So nobody suspects?"

I jumped, closing the distance between us so I was right in his face. I had to grab him to keep him from flinching back into the fireplace.

"Your imaginary girlfriend would *not* like that."

He let out a breathy laugh. "Understood."

I shook my head. "This is such a bad idea."

I walked into his arms.

THIRTY-SEVEN

Millie: Signs

It was more of a lodge than a cabin but "cabin" is what they called it. The walls were made of heavy, thick logs, after all. The main living area was a broad space flowing from kitchen to dining area to a two-story-high lounge arranged around a tall fieldstone fireplace.

Millie sat on one of the couches, staring out the windows, and smiled. The sun was bright outside and the snow was melting off the trees, off the ground, and off the roof, drip, drip, drip.

She was alone in the room and then she wasn't.

Davy leaned over the back of the couch and kissed her. He was wearing a wetsuit, and though he'd rinsed off his boots, he smelled slightly of river bottom.

"How'd it go?"

"Fine. Did four hours and topped off the lake."

Davy had shifted water from the Nile's flood stage into a lake near a refugee camp at the edge of the Sahara. "They'll be good until the seasonal rains."

Millie nodded.

"Where's Cent?"

"Queensland, surfing."

Davy took two steps back toward the kitchen until he could see the whiteboard.

Burleigh Heads, with Joe, back for supper.

"What time is that, midmorning, there?"

"Yes." She giggled.

"What's so funny?"

"Take a look at her door."

"What? She took down the sign?"

"Come look."

The old butcher paper sign was gone. The new one was in poster board.

HELLO!
ROOM OCCUPIED BY TELEPORTING ALIENS!
HAVE EXTRAORDINARY LIFE.
AND FRIENDS.
(STILL ACCEPTING ICE CREAM.)

Davy laughed and Millie poked him in the ribs from behind. He jumped. "Hey!"

"She's funny," she said.

"Yes. She gets that from—"

Millie poked him again.

SCIENCE
FICTION

$25.99

DATE			